TO THE RHYTHM OF THE MOON

By Chess Capino

To Diana ~
with love & gratitude,

19·11·09

First Edition
2009

Copyright © Francesca Pinoni

This is a work of fiction. Any resemblance to persons living
or dead is purely coincidental.

No part of this book may be used or reproduced in any
manner whatsoever without written permission from the
author except in the case of brief quotations embodied
in critical articles or reviews.

Featherlight Press
PO Box 51958
3509 Limassol, Cyprus

featherlight@cyprusspirit.com

ISBN 978-9963-9651-0-6

Printed in Cyprus by CyPrint Plc

For Alex and the generations to come.

Introduction

Many years ago, obscured by the twisting road of history, there lived in Central Europe a band of gypsies like none other who have lived before or since. Legend has it that they were not of this world at all, but children of the stars. They were known for their beauty and for their talents in singing, dancing and the healing arts. They migrated across the countryside from village to village. Their arrival was greeted with joy and celebration.

If, on their travels, they met children whose parents had died or were too poor to care for them they would adopt that child as a member of their Gypsy band. The child would live with them, travel with them and learn a skill that would enable them to live a fruitful and happy life. These children became members of the band in every way - except that they were not initiated into the secrets that only a blood member of the band was allowed to know.

This is the story of one of the Gypsy Children.

PART 1

THE NEW MOON

Chapter 1

The Gypsies Come

I don't remember my father or my mother. My Grandpa told me that when my mother died on the day that I was born my father left our village in his grief, vowing never to return. Maybe, if I had been a boy-child he would have taken me with him, to travel the world, far and wide. He could have made a deerskin sling and carried me on his back as he rode through the forests and the meadows. I'd grow up wild and free, the birds and creatures of the forest as my playmates. Instead, he left me there with the old man and his wife. She's dead, too, now, but she took good care of me then; always giving me warm milk and bread and singing me a song every night before I settled to sleep under my goatskin blanket.

The old man and his wife lived in a village not far from the river Danube. Their house was on the village square. We always knew what was going on! My Grandpa had been a tailor. But, by the time I came along, his eyes could not see well enough to thread a needle, let alone to do the fine work that had earned him respect in the village and the means to afford a house on the square.

We lived simply, though we always had enough good food to eat. Grandpa would trade fresh milk and cheese from our cow for vegetables and fruit. Sometimes we would go into the countryside together and gather the fat blackberries that grew wild near the stream. Grandpa was always afraid that I'd loose my balance and slip into the rushing water. I used to beg him to let me come with him when he went to the fields. I loved to go into the woods. I loved the smell of the damp soil and of the different plants and fragrant herbs and bright red poppies that grew wild along the edges of the ploughed fields.

Sometimes I wandered out of the village and sat on the old stone wall and watched the farmer who, with his big horse, ploughed the field in preparation for sowing the wheat that would later be ground into flour for the fresh bread that I loved so much. Back and forth, back and forth they would go, horse and man; sometimes pausing to remove a stone that blocked the path of the wooden plough. Always more stones! I wondered where they all came from - each season the field would be ploughed and each season more stones would be unearthed. Our houses were made of these stones, and the walls that divided the fields and marked the boundary between one village's land and the next.

How many times Grandpa found me sitting on that wall - watching the sheep and goats, watching the clouds making patterns in the sky! And he would be angry with me for wandering away, for not staying within the safety of the house, for not helping Grandma with the many chores that she had to do, day after day, year after year, to make sure Grandpa and I had a clean home and good food on the table.

When I was just about tall enough to see out the front window of our house the gypsies came. Not the gypsies that everyone was scared of. When those gypsies came to the village my Grandma and Grandpa made me stay in the house. They made sure that I didn't wander off into the woods on my own. At night, in the distance, we could hear their laughing voices over the sound of a crackling bonfire. After a few days they'd be gone - and somebody would be shouting that his strongest plough horse was gone, too! Or one of the village girls would be missing, deciding that a life on the road with the gypsies was more fun than the hard life she would live in the village. But Grandpa and Grandma whispered in low voices that they thought I couldn't hear, using words they thought I wouldn't understand, "That foolish girl, she has no idea what life will be like with those people!"

That is why I was so surprised on the day my gypsies came. Instead of closing the windows and barring the doors, Grandma and Grandpa became very excited! They smiled and called me to the window to look and see the colourful group of people entering the village square. From all around, the villagers were gathering. Some followed the gypsies into the square, leaving their tools in the fields hastening to join the excited crowd. Ladies put on their bright Sunday kerchiefs and there was a festival mood in the air.

"Who are these people?" I asked Grandma.

"They are known as the star children, my child. They bring joy and happiness wherever they go."

I stood on my tiptoes and looked out the window at the 'Star Children'. At first glance they did not look different from any other people I had seen. But, as I watched them moving around the square, greeting the villagers and settling their horses, I noticed the graceful way they moved. Their faces were very beautiful. There was a glow around them, the glow of happiness. There weren't any old people in the group. Maybe they stayed at home. But where was their home? Before I had a chance to ask, Grandma, in her prettiest embroidered apron, called me over to her. She tied a bright red ribbon in my hair, took me by the hand, and with Grandpa, led me out into the square to join the others in this spontaneous movement of happiness.

Chapter 2

Dancing by the Fire

At first I was overwhelmed by the bustle and activity. Through the noise of laughter and people talking all at the same time I could hear the sound of a viol tuning up. It sounded like a strange bird! But I knew it was a viol. Once before a lone gypsy had come to the village. He looked poor. He didn't have a horse or even a mule. He had to carry all his belongings on his back as if he were a mule himself! I was afraid when I saw him. He was old and dirty and he didn't smell very nice when we passed near him on our way home from the bakers. But Grandma stopped close to him and gave him a loaf of warm bread that she had bought for our supper. He reached out his filthy hand and took it, with a great smile that cracked through the grime on his face.

It was then that I noticed that he couldn't see! How did he know we were standing there? I wanted to ask by Grandma, but before I could I stopped, transfixed, as the old man slowly opened one of his grubby bags and gently unwrapped a viol. Placing it beneath his chin he started to play for us. Such a song! I cannot say that it was a happy song, nor was it sad. It had a sweetness, a longing, like a memory of a sunny summer morning on a grey winter's day.

After he finished Grandma thanked him and we went inside to prepare our meal. I had a hundred questions!

"Who is that old man? Why is he travelling alone? Why is he so dirty? Why doesn't he have a horse? Why did I feel like crying when he played the pretty song? Why can't he see?" I asked.

Grandma laughed and said, "Enough, enough! I don't know all the answers to your questions! I do know that he learned to play the viol from the Star Children. He lived with them for a while when he was a child. Now he travels the countryside playing for bread and wine and a corner to sleep in. He is a good man, but very sad. I don't know why so don't ask me any more questions!"

Grandma wasn't angry with me for asking questions. She just got tired sometimes because I asked so many.

I pulled Grandma in the direction of the music, wondering if it was the same old man returned to our village. I couldn't see where we were going in the tangle of the village women's bright blue skirts. Finally, we came to the edge of the square. The stairs of the church formed a makeshift stage. What a sight! Not only was there a man getting ready to play the viol but there were three other men holding strange things - I guessed that they were musical instruments, too, but I had never seen or heard anything like them.

Then I saw the most beautiful woman I had ever seen. Her long black hair reached below her narrow waist, cascading down her back like the mane of a wild horse. Her lips were full and red and smiling. Her eyes were the most beautiful part of her. They smiled, too, as if with a secret delight it all that was going on around her. She wore a pretty white blouse and a full crimson skirt that swished happily as she moved about the improvised stage. In her hand she held a round thing, like a drum but smaller. Around the edges were disks of shiny metal. When the music started she shook and tapped the instrument keeping time with the merry jingling of bright metal circles.

Others joined in the singing. Meanwhile, the villagers prepared a feast to welcome their guests. Long tables were set out in the village square as if a wedding were about to take place. Women were busy bringing food from their storerooms and larders. They crossed the square carrying heavy dishes to roast in the baker's oven. I heard an awful sound and knew that one of the villagers had slaughtered a pig to be the main course in this feast. What an occasion!

We were offered a seat on a bench near the music. Grandpa found us and joined us on the bench, his foot tapping in time with the happy rhythm of the music. I found my feet starting to move too, all by themselves. I got up and began to dance around. Some other children were dancing, too. I twirled and jumped, carried away by the joyful sound of the viol and drums. I was having so much fun! I didn't want to stop when Grandpa took me by the hand and told me that it was time to join the others for supper. I just wanted to keep on dancing forever.

We took our places at one of the long tables. It was an unexpected treat to have so much good food at one time. On the table were hunks of bread fresh out of the oven, onions, pungent pickles, curly heads of bright green fennel and a huge platter with the meat of the roasted pig. All my favourite things, but I wasn't hungry at all. I wanted to go back to the music and dance some more.

When Grandma and Grandpa finally finished I jumped up and ran off to where the musicians continued their cheerful tunes and the beautiful lady still smiled and danced. But Grandma caught up with me, all out of breath. She told me it was time to go to bed. How could she expect me to sleep! I tried to talk her into letting me stay up and dance.

"You can dance in your dreams," she told me as she led me away from the sparkling crowd.

Chapter 3

Grandma's Journey, and Mine, Begin

We walked slowly to our house, hand in hand. I was glad that at least we lived on the square and could still hear the music. I climbed into my bed, closed my eyes and pretended to be back with the musicians. As I listened to the music and the noise of the many people out in the square it was easy for me to imagine being out there with them.

In my mind, I stood at the front of the crowd watching the beautiful lady. She approached me and smiled, squatting down on her haunches so we were eye to eye, she said, "Hello Milada. Would you like to dance with me?"

My face broke into a smile and I said, "Yes, oh yes!"

My Grandpa and Grandma always called me "Anna" but when the lady called me "Milada" I knew that was my name. In my dream I danced with the gypsies until the faint light of dawn returned the colours to the square.

"I have to go home now," I told the lovely lady. "My Grandma will wake up and wonder where I am."

I ran across the square toward my house. As I neared the door I saw old Dr. Maslev coming out of the house, slowly shaking his head.

"Good morning!" I called to him. Usually when he saw little children in the square he'd reach into his pocket and produce some nuts or an apple or some other treat. This day, though, he did not wave back or even look up and smile when I called out to him. It was as if he didn't even see me.

I ran into the house. Something was strange. Grandpa sat by my Grandma's bed. Usually she was the first one up. I ran over to see what the matter was, a cold feeling in my stomach. In my haste, my foot caught the edge of the hearthrug and I felt myself falling to the ground.

I opened my eyes and realized that I was back in my bed by the fireplace! I looked toward my Grandma's bed to reassure myself that I'd only been dreaming and that this morning was like all the others. In the dim light I saw Grandpa sitting, his head in his hands, beside Grandma's bed, just like in my dream. I quietly got out of bed and went over to Grandpa. Grandma looked strange. Her skin was pale. Something wasn't right.

"What's wrong with Grandma?" I asked. Grandpa said nothing. I repeated the question, "Grandpa, what's wrong with Grandma? When can I have breakfast? I'm hungry!"

Grandpa said nothing. Tears came to my eyes. What was going on? Last night had been so much fun and now something awful was happening.

I heard the door to the house open. It was our neighbour Mrs. Patca and one of the gypsies. The gypsy woman walked silently over to the bed. She smiled at me and put her hand on Grandpa's shoulder. His shoulders relaxed and he let out a soft sigh. The gypsy took Grandma's hand in hers. She looked at Grandpa and softly said, "Her soul has flown away".

Grandpa buried his face in the palms of his hands. I'd never seen him cry before, but from the way his body rocked on the stool I could tell that he was crying now.

I ran over to the gypsy woman.

"What's happening?" I demanded, "Why is Grandpa crying? Why is Grandma still in bed instead of making our breakfast?".

The gypsy lady knelt on the floor beside me.

"Your grandmother has taken the first step of a long journey," she said. "One that will take her to wonderful lands far from here".

I looked at the gypsy lady and then at my Grandma and back at the gypsy lady.

"If Grandma is going on a journey then why is she still here?" I asked, "And why can't Grandpa and I go, too?"

"Ah, little one, you ask many questions! That is good. But the answers to your questions are not so easy to tell, and now is not the time to explain this journey that we all will take one day," the gypsy lady replied.

She stood up and kindled the fire in the hearth. She quietly prepared a simple breakfast for me.

"Come," she said, "Here is your breakfast." In spite of the strangeness of the morning my breakfast tasted delicious.

While I ate I watched as the gypsy lady went back to Grandma's bed. She stood near the old woman's head with the palms of her hands facing downwards and said strange words that I didn't understand. Keeping one hand near Grandma's head she slowly slid the other down over her heart then her stomach and legs. She faced her palms together and intoned a low chant. I couldn't make out the words but the sound of her voice was like the sound of the forest, a soft breeze rustling the autumn leaves. As her song went on Grandpa stopped rocking back and forth. His hands fell to his lap and he was able to look at Grandma's body as it lay on the bed.

The gypsy lady finished her song and silence filled the room with its peace. Grandpa looked up at the gypsy lady and said, "I knew this day would come, but I didn't think it would be so soon. What's to become of Anna? She needs a woman to care for her."

The gypsy lady smiled and gently touched his shoulder, "Don't worry about the child". She looked over at me and smiled and then she was gone.

I approached Grandpa, not knowing what to say.

"Ah, my child," he said, taking me in his arms, "what will life bring to my little one?"

Chapter 4

Layla and Her Firefly

What a day that was. My Grandma lay, lifeless on her bed and the life seemed to drain from Grandpa, too. The happy sparkle in his eyes was gone. We sat together by the fire while the women of the village prepared Grandma.

I watched as they washed her body and dressed it in her best clothes, as if readying her for a festival. Outside in the square people went about the business of daily life. The sound of laughter and the occasional strains of a song came through the window along with the late morning sunshine. The star children were still here.

Maybe Grandma had decided to journey with them. Maybe that was the mysterious journey the gypsy lady told me about! Maybe this is the preparation for that journey. Several times I had watched a bride be prepared for her wedding. Other people dressed her in her best clothes. Then there was a big party. After that she would ride off with her new husband to live in his village. That's it! Grandma was going with the gypsies!

I felt better now that I thought I understood what was happening.

"Don't worry," I said to my Grandpa, "Grandma will have fun with the gypsies!"

He didn't seem to hear me. Not wanting to miss anything that was going on in the square I kissed Grandpa's forehead and ran out the door and right into the arms of the lovely lady I danced with in my dreams! She looked at me and laughed.
"Where are you off to in such a hurry?" she asked.

I couldn't say a word. I was lost in her dark eyes.

"Did you like dancing with us last night?" she asked.

How did she know? I felt this lady knew me to the depths of my soul. I still could not utter a word.

"Ah, Milada, you thought it was a dream? Many a dream has been known to come true!"

She called me "Milada" again!

I said, "My name is Anna," and immediately regretted it! Somehow I knew my name was not Anna, but Milada.

"We all go through many names in our life. In my tribe we all have four names. The first is our true name, the one that tells who we are inside. When we have lived three years we choose a name for ourselves. When we marry, the head of our clan, the Baron, bestows upon us another name. When we are older and no longer raising our children we spend our time helping others and working for the good of all. Then we choose yet another name because, you know, as we live we outgrow our old names and our old role in the group as we outgrow our clothes! My name is Layla. May I call you Milada?"

"Oh, yes!" I replied, "I like that name."

Layla said, "Would you like to meet my horse, Firefly?"

Of course I said yes. Hand in hand we walked across the village square. I didn't think about asking Grandpa's permission if I could go with Layla. I was too excited about meeting the lady with the radiant smile - and now I was going to meet her horse.

We were at the far side of the square sooner than I thought possible. We reached the foot of the church steps. This morning, it all seemed normal, as if the festivities of the previous night had, indeed, been a dream. Layla waved at the fiddler who remained on the steps. Had he slept there all night, I wondered? He didn't seem tired or uncomfortable.

He waved back at us and sang out his greeting, "Good day to you Layla, and good day to little Milada, too!"

He knew my name! I was happy that he did! I smiled back at his cheerful face. Passing through the south side of the village we came to the field where the gypsy band was camped. There were many horses there, none of them tied up or fenced in.

"Don't your horses run away?" I asked Layla, forgetting to be shy, or polite.

She just laughed and said, "They do not want to leave us. We treat them well and they are happy to share their lives with us."

I wondered which horse was Layla's. I looked over the horses as they serenely grazed. There was a sleek buckskin with black mane and tail, an elegant mount. Was that Firefly? One horse was jet black. I imagined that on a moonless night it would be nearly invisible with only its yellowish eyes to betray its presence. Was that one Firefly? Or was he the palomino who tossed his head so proudly?

I was so lost in thought that I was startled to feel a soft nose nuzzling the top of my head. I turned and looked up and saw Layla with her arm around a creature with eyes as kind as her own. This, of course, was Firefly.

"She likes you!" Layla said with a smile. "Want to go for a ride?"

Layla hoisted me up in front of her. She held the reigns lightly, made a soft clicking noise and we were off, gently cantering toward the forest. I watched as Firefly's reddish mane rippled in the breeze. I can't remember ever being so happy! We rode along the wide river, watching the duck and geese take their morning baths.

"Why do you call her "Firefly"? " I asked, "Do her eyes glow in the dark?" Layla's laughter was like a tinkling brook.

"Maybe they do. But that's not why I call her "Firefly". When I ride her I feel the fire rise in my blood. I want to gallop up to the stars. Together we can fly like fire, like the fire that is the stars. Maybe one day, Firefly will take me home."

I didn't understand all that Layla told me but I was satisfied that Firefly was a lovely horse, and that her eyes shone like stars, or fireflies.

We dismounted in a grove of white barked trees, their leaves just starting to emerge in springtime freshness. We sat together, not speaking, just watching the river flow by. Layla finally spoke, "Milada, my friend, would you like to come and live with me?"

Without a second thought I said, "Yes".

Looking back now I wonder why I didn't think of my Grandpa who I'd be leaving alone; why I didn't think of my playmates or the animals in the village I'd lovingly named. I think that I believed that Grandma would be coming along with us. I don't know. But I was sure that it was the right thing to go with Layla. I hugged her and said, over and over, "Yes, yes!"

On the ride back to the village I couldn't stop myself from asking questions. There was so much I wanted to know.

"When are we leaving? Will I sleep with you? Do you always live in your wagons or do you have a house somewhere? Can I ride Firefly by myself when I grow up? Can you teach me to dance like you? Can Grandpa come with us?"

At this last question I felt a change in Layla. She touched my arm gently and said, "Alas, that cannot be. But we will pass this way every so often and visit him."

Suddenly I was afraid. What if Grandpa would not let me go? Life would surly seem empty and dark when the light of Layla 's smile was no longer near. We left Firefly at the camp and hurried back to Grandpa's house. He was still sitting by Grandma's side. Layla told me to gather my few things together and went to speak with Grandpa. I couldn't make out her words. She spoke very softly to the old man. Then she called me over. I could see in her eyes that it was all right for me to go.

I looked at Grandpa and he looked at me. I saw such sadness and yet such love in his eyes. It reminded me of the blind man's song, so sad and yet so lovely. Grandpa took me in his arms and held me for a long time. Then he said,

"I'll miss you terribly, but Layla is a lovely lady. She will care for you like the mother you never knew. You are lucky to be invited to join the star children. It is best for you to do so. I will leave a candle burning in the window each night to guide you back to me when you come through the village on your travels. Go now. Learn and be happy."

We embraced once again. I glanced at Grandma, still lying silently on the bed. I felt she was already waiting for me with the gypsy band. Hand in hand Layla and I walked back to the camp, never looking back.

Chapter 5

The Secrets of the Forest

Pale sunlight filtered through the young leaves onto the beaten earth of the clearing. Layla led me across the colourful carpets laid out on the ground. I could hear music in the distance, and the beat of drums and laughter. At the far end of the clearing was a brightly painted wagon.

Layla sat on its shiny blue step, her eyes smiling at me and said, "This will be your home for a while."

She lifted me up so I sat beside her on the wagon.

"Do you live here, too?" I asked, hoping that she would tell me yes.

"No, little one," she replied, "I live on the other side of camp with my family."

"Do you have lots of brothers and sisters?" I asked, " I wish I did."

"I have one younger brother" she said, "You will meet him soon."

I felt something move behind me. A pair of green eyes peered out at us from beneath the curtained entrance to the wagon. I saw that they belonged to a large grey cat.

"Look who's here," Layla said to me. Then she said to the cat, "Hello, my friend. Where are your children?"

As she spoke a tiny white face peeked out from under the curtain, then another and another and another! Soon the mother cat and four grey and white kittens joined us on the blue step. One of the kittens curled up in my lap.

"She likes you, Milada," Layla said.

"I like her, too. Can I keep her?" I asked.

"The kittens come and go as they like. If you are good to her she'll stay here with you," she replied.

"Kittens!" I heard a cheerful voice say. I looked up and saw a little girl standing and smiling at us.

Layla said, "Tanya, this is Milada. She's come to live with us."

"Hello, Milada. Do you like the kittens?" Tanya asked.

"Oh yes!" I replied noticing that Tanya's eyes were the same colour as the mother cat's.

"I love animals," Tanya said, "especially baby animals. I have a baby hedgehog inside. I don't know what happened to its mother. I found it a few days ago under that big oak tree over there".

I didn't know which tree was an oak tree but I looked to where the girl was pointing.

"I left it there because maybe its mother would come back, but I kept watch. The next day, there was still no sign of its mother so I brought it in and have been feeding it myself. Do you want to see it?"

I looked at Layla, not wanting to leave the safety of her company, but also wanting to see the baby hedgehog.

"I'd like to see it, too," said Layla. Tanya hopped up the step and pushed aside the curtain. Layla and I followed her.

It was dark inside the wagon, but even in the dim light I could make out the shapes of strange objects that I had never seen the likes of before. Here and there a glint of gold picked up what little light filtered through the heavy drapes. Tanya moved to the back corner of the wagon and lifted a crimson blanket. There, nestled in a bed of dried leaves a tiny creature about the size of my hand lay curled up in sleep.

"He sleeps almost all day long," Tanya whispered, "I give him milk in the evening and early in the morning. When he gets big enough to take care of himself I'll let him go."

"Is he prickly?" I asked, remember that Grandma told me never, never to touch a hedgehog.

"Not yet," Tanya replied. "Touch him and see for yourself."

I was a little bit afraid in case his quills really were sharp. Maybe Tanya was trying to trick me.

"Go on," she said, "just be very gentle."

I reached out my hand and very carefully touched the sleeping creature. Its little spines were stiff but not unpleasant to touch. I felt the slow rhythm of its breath beneath its fur lifting and lowering my fingers. Tanya smiled at me and I smiled back.

We quietly left the wagon and went back outside into the sunlight.

"Do you live in this wagon?" I asked Tanya.

"I sleep here with Zora. I live in the forest and out here in the sun," she replied.

"My Grandpa didn't let me go into the forest by myself. He told me it is very dangerous," I said.

"It can be, when you don't have the knowledge of the woods," Layla said. "From the time we are babies we learn the secrets of the forest and how to live with its creatures. In time you will learn, too."

"Come with me," said Tanya, "I'll show you where the swallows nest, and where the dormouse lives and the fox cubs' hole, and…"

I looked at Layla again and saw her smile her consent. Tanya took my hand and together we ran into the forest.

And so the days passed one after another. Layla was right, I did begin to learn the secrets of the forest. Although she was not much older than I was, Tanya, knew so much about the plants and the animals that made the forest their home. Every morning we woke to the sound of birdsong in the leafy canopy above our wagon.

Before we joined the others for breakfast Tanya would make sure that all the small animals in her care had been fed. I went with her on her rounds, helping her carry dried seeds for the birds and fresh milk that came from one of the goats that accompanied the gypsy band on their travels. Zora did not come with us. She had other work to do.

I was a little bit afraid of Zora with her piercing black eyes and serious look, older than her seven years. She left the wagon early in each morning to collect wild herbs and flowers while they were still moist with dew. During the day she was busy cleaning them and setting them out to dry. I was too shy to ask her what she was going to do with them.

One cool morning I woke up with a pain in my throat. It hurt me so much I didn't want to go with Tanya to feed the animals. She went by herself but came back with Zora after a few minutes. Zora put her hand on my forehead. It felt cool and soothing.

"Open your mouth wide and let me have a look," she said,

Without another word she left the wagon only to return a little later with a cup of warm tea in her small hand.

"Drink this," she said, "it will make you feel better".

The tea tasted bitter but I drank it up. I had never tasted anything like it before. I put the cup down beside me and fell back into a dreamless sleep. When I awoke, I could tell from the streak of light coming through a small crack in the wooden roof that the sun was high in the sky. My throat felt much better.

Zora poked her head through the curtain. I had to shield my eyes against the bright sunlight.

"How are you feeling now?" she asked me, seeing that I was awake.

"I feel much better. What did you give me to drink?" I asked her.

"It is a tea made from the bark of the red elm tree," she replied.

"How did you know that it would help my throat?" I asked her.

Zora said, "The forest is full of plants that help and heal us. Our people know the ways of the forest."

"Can I learn them, too? " I asked her.

"I can teach you," she said, "but it's up to you if you can learn."

Chapter 6

Preparing for Our Journey

One morning as I lay in bed I heard other sounds, besides the chirping of the birds. I could hear horses neighing, goats bleating and people calling to one another.

I turned to Tanya and said, "What's all that noise?"

She said, "Everyone is up early. Maybe today we will move our camp."

Zora reached up and pulled back the curtain. I could smell the breakfast fires already lit and fresh bread toasting. In the dim light of dawn we saw the wide skirts of the women swishing by as they moved with unaccustomed speed.

"Yes, it was decided last night. The Baron decreed that it is time to move on".

"Who is the Baron?" I asked.

"He is the leader of our band," said Zora.

"He is Layla's father," said Tanya.

"And Dragan's," Zora added.

So Dragan was the name of Layla's brother. I still hadn't met him. I saw Layla every day. She always asked, "And how is my little Milada today?" Sometimes she took me for a ride on Firefly. Once we rode to a meadow full of flowers as red as Layla's skirt.

"Can I have a red skirt, too," I asked her. She just smiled.

That very same night Layla came to our wagon with something in her hand.

"This is for you, little one," she said, handing me a parcel.

I untied the string that bound the soft material together and saw a bright red flounced skirt, just my size. I slipped it over my head and Layla help me fasten it at the waist.

"Thank you! Thank you! Thank you!"" I said as I spun around and around until I was so dizzy that I collapsed into Layla's arms, laughing.

"Now you are ready to dance with us at the campfire!" she laughed.

Together we drew near the other gypsies who had gathered for the evening.

Through the smoke of the campfire I looked around at their faces. Where was Grandma? I expected to find her here. But Grandma was not at the campfire. There were no old people there. One or two had a touch of grey in their hair but there was none as old as Grandma and Grandpa. A boy sitting across from me smiled. He had fire in his eyes. There was something familiar about him but before I could ask Layla who he was, Tanya came and sat by my side.

A man with a huge moustache took out a viol and started to play. It was one of those bittersweet songs. I tired to keep my eyes open, to watch and wait for the happy songs so that I could dance and twirl by the fire, but my eye lids felt heavy and I felt myself slipping into pleasant dreams, my head on Layla's soft lap.

Days, how many, had passed since that summer's night. And still there was no sign of my beloved grandmother.

"How can we move without Grandma? I thought she was coming on this journey with us," I asked, returning from my memories. But Tanya had already risen to join the others in their preparation.

I jumped out of bed and ran to find Layla, unhappy and afraid for the first time after leaving my home.

I found her by a small fire, carefully balancing a big black kettle on a grill over the flames. I hardly noticed the boy from the campfire sitting beside her, warming his hands.

"Layla, is it true? Are we leaving? Where's my Grandma? Why isn't she here?" I asked in a rush of words.

Layla smiled as she poured some hot water from the kettle into a small cup infusing the fragrant leaves within.

She handed me the cup and said, "Your Grandma is on her journey to the stars. Maybe someday you will catch up with her, but, for now, you must follow a different path."

The warmth of the tea and Layla's eyes helped a little but I still felt like my heart would break. I sank down by the fire and buried my head in my arms. My tears dripped into the steamy cup.

"Watch out - you're making your tea salty." I felt a gentle touch on my shoulder and realized the boy was talking to me.

"What?"

"You'll make your tea salty with all those tears. Don't worry about your Grandma. She knows that you are well. Be happy so she can be happy for you, too. If you are sad, then she will be sad because she loves you and is watching over you from her place in the sky."

I lifted my head and looked into the boy's eyes. I couldn't look away. They were fiery brown, like Layla's, with the same soft kindness that melted away all my fears.

"Are you Layla's brother?" I asked the boy, wiping the tears off my cheek with the back of my hand.

He smiled, "That I am".

"Zora said that your father decided that we are leaving today. Is it true?" I asked him.

"Yes, the weather is changing. It's time to move to a more protected camp for the winter," he replied.

"Why does everyone move when your father says it is time?" I asked.

"They move because they trust him to know when the time is right," he said.

"How does he know?" I continued, wanting to know.

"He follows the signs. I'm learning to follow them, too, so some day the people will trust me like they do my father. Look."

Dragan pointed his long finger at the patch of sky visible between the branches of the overhanging tree. I looked up and saw some large birds circling overhead. I could hear their hoarse cries carried on the wind.

"Birds," he said.

"But there are always birds in the sky," I told him.

"Wait and watch," he said.

The circle of birds grew tighter. More birds came from all four directions and joined in the circle dance. The patch of sky grew dark with birds, their cawing loud in my ears. Then, from the circle, one bird pulled away. The others followed making a great "V" in the sky. Their calls grew dim as all together they flew out of sight.

"See," Dragan said, "the birds know when to move. When they move, so do we. The leaves on the trees are turning gold and red. Soon they will fall from the trees and return to the earth to nurture the new sprouts."

Layla came and sat beside us.

"Yes, Milada," she said, "it's time for us to move on. This is a time of adventure, a chance to learn new things and see new places. Embrace change, because, you know, everything is always changing. The seasons change, the plants and trees grow; you grow and change yourself moment by moment. Look, you've been with us only a short time, but I can see that already your shoes are too small for your growing feet!"

I looked down at my tight leather shoes. Most of the gypsies wore no shoes at all. Many of the children in the village went barefoot, too, but Grandma always said that I must wear my soft leather shoes. I hadn't really thought about it before.

"I'll find you some bigger ones and you can give those to Tanya for the journey."

I didn't want to give Tanya my shoes!

"But they still fit me!" I protested.

Dragan laughed.

"Never mind, then," Layla said as she returned to the big black kettle.

I was still looking at my feet, squished into my leather shoes, not liking that Dragan was laughing at me, when I felt hot breath on the back of my neck. I pulled away and saw the huge face of a horse, inches from my own. Dragan laughed even harder.

"I'd like you to meet Dobro" he said. "He must have missed me."

In one movement, Dragan stood up to pat his horse. Dobro's raven forelocks fell across his eyes just like Dragan's dark hair fell over his own forehead. Dobro nuzzled Dragan. Boy and horse looked content. I couldn't help laughing myself.

"That's better," Dragan said, "Why cry when you can laugh? Would you like to come for a ride with me?"

I looked a Layla for approval. She smiled and we were off into the early morning mist, Dragan holding tightly to Dobro's mane, me holding tightly to Dragan.

Chapter 7

Our Departure

When our ride was over I felt I had made a friend for life. I no longer feared moving on. I thanked Dragan and Dobro, gave Layla a big hug then ran back to the wagon to help Tanya and Zora pack up our bedding, cooking pots and other bits and pieces that were spread outside our wagon. Zora was carefully bundling the herbs that had been hanging to dry on the massive oak that over-shadowed the wagon.

"Why didn't you put those in the sun to dry?" I asked as I watched Zora's delicate hands tying each separate bundle.

"If they dry too fast they loose some of their strength," she said. "It is better to dry them slowly and gently. Don't rush things."

I felt that she was telling me off because I always ran from place to place, impatient to get where I wanted to be. I think she somehow knew what I was thinking because she came up to me and gave me a little hug and said, "Why don't you go and help Tanya with her animals."

I went inside the wagon and found Tanya holding the hedgehog wrapped in a quilt because it wasn't a baby anymore. Now it's spines were hard and very, very sharp.

"It's time for us to say goodbye," Tanya softly told the ball of prickles.

"Aren't you taking him with us? You've had him since he was just a baby," I said.

"No, Milada, his place is here. Maybe where we are going there won't be the right things for a hedgehog to eat. It's better if he stays in his own place," she replied.

"Won't you miss him?" I asked, knowing that I would miss watching him wake up in the evening and turn circles in his box in the wagon.

"Every Hello is also a Goodbye," Tanya said as she stepped out of the wagon with the hedgehog. "Goodbye, little one, may you live and grow".

Tanya gently set him down on the carpet of leaves. He looked back at us once as if to bid us farewell and then scuttled into the dense bushes and was gone.

"Bye, bye, little hedgehog," I said. I knew I'd miss that strange little creature.

"Let's go and see about the others," Tanya said, taking my hand.

Together we went into the woods to gather the small goats and chicks that would be making the trip with us.

Soon, everything was ready. The colourful wagons were hitched to the strongest horses, which would pull them across the rutted roads. The horse's silver bridles glistened in the sunlight and their bells tinkled as they pawed the earth, ready, as we were, to move on. I climbed up on our wagon, wondering if Zora and Tanya knew how to manage the huge horse that had been hitched to it.

From my high vantage point I could see that none of the others had boarded the wagons. What were they doing? Before I had time to hop down and find out Layla came into the clearing. She helped me down from my perch and said,

"Before we go we gather round the embers of our last fire and give thanks to the spirits of this place."

She took my hand and led me through the trees into the big clearing. Only a few glowing embers now remained from last night's fire. We joined our hands with the others, completing the circle. The Baron began to sing a strange and beautiful song. It sounded like the wind when it blows though the dense leaves of the forest. I could not understand his words but something in the sound of them brought tears to my eyes. The Baron stopped singing. There was no sound in the forest, not a rustle or a chirp. No horse whinnied. No dog barked. It was as if this was a moment out of time. I could not even hear the sound of my own heartbeat. Nothing. Only a silence so deep that I thought for a moment that it was all a dream.

Finally the Baron spoke. "Thank you, Spirits of this place, for allowing us this time here. Thank you for the food that your have provided for us, for the plants you gave us to help the people and animals of this place, for the earth to sleep on and the air to breath. It is time for us to move on now and leave you to your peace. Thank you and bless you all."

He reached down and carefully took up some glowing embers in a small brass box. As he stood up, he looked around the circle and said, "Let's go!"

At once the circle exploded into a whirl of activity. From somewhere came the sound of a happy flute. Soon a drum joined in. We all went to our wagons while some of the men buried the rest of the embers.

"Let's go," said Layla, almost dancing as we walked toward the wagon.

"Will you ride with us?" I asked hopefully.

"Zora can handle your wagon," she said, "I'll ride Firefly". She sensed my disappointment. "Would you like to ride with me for a while?" Would I!

The two of us mounted Firefly and joined the procession of caravans that was moving onto the tree-lined road. Soon Dragan joined us on Dobro. The sun had risen only halfway up the sky and we were on our way; away from my Grandpa and the only home I knew. Why did I feel so happy?

Chapter 8

Bora's Viol

Although we moved over and over again the excitement of the journey never wore off. The seasons turned, and with each turn we travelled to a different camp. The places were different but the pattern was the same. As we entered a new village the people came out to greet us, smiling and bringing us gifts of fresh bread, vegetables and wine. There would be music and dancing on our first night in the village. We quickly set up our camp. The Baron would take the embers from the small brass box and light several small fires and one large one to bring us together.

Tanya and I were becoming great friends and I wasn't so afraid of Zora anymore. Often she took me with her on early morning collecting trips. Now I ran barefoot like the others. I finally gave that first pair of shoes to Tanya, but we had both long outgrown them. The morning dew felt cold as the damp earth squeezed between my toes but as the sun rose I loved the feel of the warm grass beneath my feet. We collected chamomile flowers to make a fragrant tea that could calm a stomach ache and help us sleep. Zora dried the flowers and sewed them up in muslin bags to give to people who came to the gypsies for help.

"How do you know what herbs to use?" I asked her on one of our expeditions.

"I always knew," she said, "And I watch and observe what happens when people use them. I watch what animals eat when they are ill. They know what to do. And so do I. Now, you are learning, too."

And I was. When I wasn't careful and ran into a patch of stinging nettles I knew which leaf to rub on my skin so it wouldn't come up in a rash. I knew that if I tripped and cut my knee I could pound some fresh sorrel leaves and put them on the wound and it would heal faster. But, with or without shoes, I hadn't learned to slow down. I still ran while others walked.

One warm spring morning I was running through the woods looking for Tanya when I stopped in my tracks. A sound. Was it an animal crying? Or a baby? The sound grew into a song. Someone was playing the viol. Slowly at first, then the tempo picked up. I couldn't stop my feet from dancing! Who could be playing in the forest at this time? I thought all the grown-ups had gone to the village.

As I moved toward the sound, I saw Tanya, her thick brown plaits hanging down her back, walking quietly in the same direction.

"Tanya" I whispered, "Tanya, who's playing the viol."

She turned to me and whispered back, "I don't know. Let's go see!"

Together we moved toward the music. In the clearing we saw a small boy about our age. He held the viol in his stocky arms. His eyes were closed and he seemed to be listening to the sounds coming out of it with wonder and enjoyment. His foot tapped out the rhythm.

"It's Bora," Tanya whispered.

Listening to the happy music I just couldn't stay still. I clapped my hands and started to dance around Bora.

He opened his eyes and smiled at us, and continued to play. When the song was finished he lowered the viol.

"Hello," he said.

"Hello Bora, I didn't know you could play like that!" said Tanya.

"I didn't either," he replied with a shy giggle. "I've always liked to listen to music but I didn't know that I could play. Last night Radko gave me this."

Bora giggled some more as he waved the viol in front of us.

"He said, "This was my first viol. Take it and play. You know how." So I took it, and the bow, too. It felt really good in my hands. And I played. Isn't it great! Maybe you can play, too. Here, try it."

I looked at Tanya but she didn't move to take the instrument.

"I know that's not my talent," she said.

I took the viol and tried to hold it like Bora did. I held the bow and pulled it across the strings. The sound that came out was like an angry cat when someone steps on its tail! We all cringed.

"I guess it's not my talent, either," I said, handing back the instrument.

Bora took it with a grin and started to play another cheerful tune.

"How come Bora can play like that? And you know all about animals, and Zora knows about herbs and plants," I asked Tanya as we headed back to the camp.

"That's the way it is. We remember."

I was just going to ask "remember what?" But before I could get the words out of my mouth I heard a loud crash coming from the camp.

"What was that?"

"I don't know," Tanya said, "let's go see."

We hurried back to the wagons. People were gathered around one of them. One of the hitching poles was sticking up over the crowd. I saw Layla among the people.

"What happened?" I asked her.

"Radko was repairing the wheel on his wagon when the support gave way," she said.

Curious, as always, I edged my way into the crowd of people until I could see Radko, crushed under the wagon, his lifeless face with its huge moustache gazing up at the bare branches of the birch tree above us. The men carefully lifted the wagon and pulled Radko's body out from under its heavy weight.

Bora left us and went to Radko's side. He picked up his right hand and just sat quietly beside the body. A woman with a thick silver plait reaching nearly to her waist stepped forward and gently closed his eyes with the palm of her hand.

This woman, Mother Miriana, sometime went to the villages when someone died there. She danced and laughed with the others at the campfire, but when she spoke everyone listened. I knew she was older than the others, but not nearly as old as my Grandma.

I knew now that my Grandma was dead. The "journey" that she was on I could not follow. In the villages, when someone died everyone cried. Some people even pulled out their hair. They brought the body to a church and lit lots of candles and prayed. What for? For the person to come to life again? "Save his soul", they prayed. Save it from what?

It was different with the gypsies. I watched as Radko was placed next to a small fire. Mother Miriana and her friend Lazara followed.

Bora came back to us and said, "That's why he gave me his viol. Someone has to play for the band."

He took up his instrument again and began to play a haunting melody, one that made me want to cry and smile at the same time. Mother Miriana was singing softly with words I did not understand. She and Lazara sat beside the body all day, singing and swaying slowly back and forth.

Layla found Tanya and me at our wagon.

"Come," she said, "Let's go to the village to get some bread and vegetables. Tonight there will be a feast of farewell for Radko."

Already a goat was roasting on a spit and a large space had been cleared for dancing. Layla called to her brother, "Come with us, Dragan. We need your help to carry things back".

I was happy that Dragan was coming with us. His bright eyes seemed to dance as he spoke.

"A party tonight; too bad Radko's going to miss it. He loved a good party," he said.

"His spirit will be with us," said Layla. "He was ready to move on."

"He gave Bora his viol," I blurted out, "and you should hear how well he plays it!"

"We'll hear him tonight," said Layla. "And we'll dance."

In the village, everyone stared at Layla and her brother. People always stared at them wherever they went. With their shining eyes and jet-black hair they were a striking sight. But it was more than just the way they looked; it was the way they moved, easily and gracefully, almost dancing as they walked through the crowded market place.

Dragan walked between Tanya and me linking one elbow with each of us. As we walked along the cobbled street I heard the sound of hooves behind us.

"Oh, no," sighed Dragan, "It's him. He never leaves me alone."

"Him who?" I asked.

"Him." Dragan flicked his head back to look over his shoulder and rolled his eyes, "Dobro".

I turned and looked behind just as the horse got close enough to nuzzle the back of Dragan's neck.

"Well at least he can help us carry things back to camp," Dragan remarked with a grin.

We filled our baskets with onions, fresh bread and earthenware pots of pickled cabbage that the villagers prepare in the fall to last until spring. We sat down by the fountain to rest a while before the walk back to camp. I noticed Layla's attention was focused on the cheese stalls. I turned to see that she was watching a young boy, a little older than Tanya and me. His light brown hair brushed the collar of his brown felt jacket. He was talking to one of the women selling cheese.

"I need a taste before I buy. How do I know that your cheese is any good?" I heard him say.

The woman cut a small bit off the round of cheese.

"There you go," she said.

"Mmm, not bad, not bad. I'll think about it." He went to the next stall and said to the woman there, "Your neighbour's cheese is very good, but I have heard that yours is better."

"Here, have a taste," she said, cutting off a sliver of soft white cheese.

"Make a little bigger so I can taste it!" he said.

She gave him another piece, this time a bigger one.

"Very, nice, very nice. What about that other kind, that one there," he pointed to a large yellow wheel.

The woman cut off a small slice and held it out to him.

"There you are," she said, "why don't you buy some of each?"

"Maybe I will," said the boy as he ate the cheese, "maybe I will."

As we watched he went back to the first woman.

"Your neighbour's cheese is very good. Let me have another piece of yours so I can choose whose is best, and a piece of bread too if you can spare it."

The woman hesitated, then cut him another piece and handed him a chunk of heavy brown bread.

"This is such a hard choice," said the boy, "I'll have go away and give it some thought."

He turned and started to walk away from the cheese sellers.

Both of them started shouting at him, "Eh, boy - you eat my cheese and buy nothing!" said one, "If everybody were like you I would have no cheese to sell!" said the other.

"Come on," called Layla and moved to follow the boy through the crowded square.

He sensed that he was being followed and moved faster. Dragan ran ahead and caught him by the arm. He stiffened as if ready for a fight. As he turned they came face to face and his muscles relaxed when saw the smile in Dragan's eyes.

"Are you hungry?" Dragan asked the boy.

"Not so much anymore," he said with a grin, "I've had some cheese".

Layla said, "Do you have a home?"

"Not really," his bright blue eyes clouded over for a moment then the brave face returned, "I'm free. I come and go, do odd jobs for food."

"We are camped in the forest not far from here. Tonight we will have a celebration. Come with us and eat your fill," Dragan said.

"Why not?" said the boy.

We skirted the village to return to camp, followed faithfully by Dobro, his hoofs beating a rhythm on the track.

Chapter 9

Goran

I watched the boy as we walked back to camp. He and Dragan walked ahead of us, with Dobro following close on their heels. The boy was not as tall as Dragan and had to walk faster to keep up with his graceful strides.

"My name is Goran," I heard him telling Dragan.

"I grew up in the next village but when my folks died I came to live here with my uncle. He has no children of his own - but if he did they would probably run away! It's not that he is a bad man, he just forgets things. You know, unimportant things like feeding me!

"He has a flock of sheep. The *sheep* he loves! *They* never go to sleep hungry. He is out in the fields with them all day, talking to them, playing them music on his flute. Sometimes he remembers to come home and give me some supper, sometimes he doesn't. So I do odd jobs around the village, I fix fences, I help the ladies beat the rugs - that's one dusty job! But that way I get enough to eat."

I was so intent on listening to the boy's conversation that I didn't hear Layla's footsteps as she came up behind Tanya and me. I was startled when she spoke.

"What do you think? Will this boy Goran join our band?"

I looked at Layla and then at the boy. He was still in animated conversation with Dragan.

"He certainly likes to talk!" I said.

Tanya gazed at the boys as they walked and talked easily together.

"I think he's been lonely" she commented. She ran up to him and took his arm.

"I'm Tanya," she said. "Do you like animals?"

"Animals…well, sure…well, I really don't like sheep very much…" he said with a grin.

Layla put her arm around my shoulder. Her familiar sent of lavender and straw always calmed my over-active mind. All the questions that had been chasing themselves around my in head - would Goran join the band? Would he stay in our wagon? Would Tanya be his friend and not mine? All the questions melted away. None of them seemed important as Layla and I walked together down the dusty trail carrying the provisions for the night's celebration.

Another question eased into my mind. This one I would ask.

"Layla, why don't we cry when someone dies like they do in the villages? Instead we have a big party and laugh and sing?"

"We understand death in a different way. We don't see it as an end of a life, just as a pause, as a time lived in a different world, for a while," she said.

"Like when we dream?" I asked. "Sometimes when I wake up I feel like I've been on a trip to a different world. It seems so real that when I wake up I'm surprised to see that I'm in my bed on the wagon."

"Yes, Milada," said Layla, "It's something like that."

"So why don't the people in the village know it? Why do they cry and feel sad when someone dies?" I asked.

"Because they don't remember," she said.

"Mmm, that smells good," Dragan called to us over his shoulder.

"Yes, it certainly does," said Layla.

We had reached the campsite before I finished asking my questions. I guess, really, I never finish asking questions.

While we unpacked our baskets on the long wooden tables that had been set up next to the unlit central fire I saw Dragan introducing Goran to Bora. I guessed that Goran would stay in his wagon *if* he decided to stay with us. I had a feeling that he would.

The rest of the day was spent in preparation. Huge pots were hung over the cooking fires. I helped chop the onions and carrots that would go into the soup. Zora brought some dried herbs from the wagon. When she crumbled them into the broth a wonderful aroma filled the air. By the time the sun went down my tummy was rumbling in anticipation of the wonderful meal we would soon enjoy.

We cleared the long tables and then lay them with saffron cloths and placed several loaves of fresh bread at intervals along their lengths. The women brought out the small silver salt pots that were kept for feast days and placed them on the table as well. The men carved the roast kid and filled the earthenware wine jugs from the large barrel on the back of Marko's wagon.

The gypsies scattered to their wagons to change into their festive clothes, richly embroidered in red and gold, and to bring their own plates, cups and knives from their wagons. Tanya and I hurried back to our wagon to dress. I loved to get dressed up! I put on a yellow blouse and a full red skirt. Tanya wore a green dress with golden stars embroidered over it. These clothes were not new. They were passed down to us as older girls outgrew them. We would pass them on to the younger girls in turn. Each girl added some embroidery, and made any needed repairs. Some of the skirts were more patches than fabric, but the effect was very colourful. I liked the thought that another little girl, long grown up, or even the great-great-grandmother of one of the women in the band, might have worn the very skirt that I would twirl in tonight.

We dressed quickly and were soon back at the table. I put my plate, cup and knife in front of me. At first I thought that it was strange that we each had to keep these things in our wagon. At home my Grandma always set the table so it was ready when we came. But, of course, I later realized, she had a cupboard to keep things in, and many fewer people to feed. With the gypsies, even the small children took care of their own things. That's why we could move camp so quickly.

The fire had been lit. The Baron stood at the head of the table. His black hair, a little silver at the sides, gleamed in the light of the crackling fire.

"Tonight we say "Farewell" to our good friend Radko. He had decided to leave us for time. May his journey be a fruitful one. We drink to his success!"

We all lifted our cups and drank a toast to Radko. Bora took up his viol. He played a happy tune as we all sat down to enjoy the feast. I sat between Tanya and Zora. Goran sat across from us on the other side of the table. I watched him polish off a heaping plate of food before I even finished my soup.

"That boy is really hungry," I whispered to Tanya.

"My name is Goran". I felt my cheeks flush red that he had heard my comment. "This is the best food I've had in my life!"

"Thanks to Zora's herbs," I said. "My name is Milada."

"Pleased to meet you," Goran replied, "You were at the market today, too, weren't you."

"Yes, I liked watching you with the cheese sellers!" I said, with a straight face.

"You saw that?" he said, uncertain of my reaction.

Oh, oh...had I said too much? My cheeks felt even hotter.

"I really did plan to buy some cheese," he added.

"Yes, of course," I said trying to sound sincere but I couldn't suppress a little giggle.

I was happy to see Goran smile, understanding that his antics amused me.

While we ate, different musicians took turns playing. As everyone finished the meal the volume and intensity of the music grew. The men lifted the tables to the side of the clearing to make room around the fire for dancing. I joined in with the women whirling and twirling in our bright skirts. The men danced among us, taping their heels into the earth. I noticed that Dragan was a very good dancer, graceful, and for once without Dobro looking over his shoulder. Goran sat by the fire, lost in thought. I sat down next to him to catch my breath.

"Come and dance with us".

He turned to look at me. His eyes were far away. As I watched they came into focus.

"What were you thinking?" I asked him quietly.

"I was thinking by what luck or twist of fate I am here tonight among these people, people who dance at death, having eaten the best food in my life, listening to the most beautiful music, feeling accepted," he said quietly.

"Will you stay with us?" I asked.

He paused for a moment before giving his answer.

"If they will have me, yes, I will. I can't think of any reason not to," he said.

At that moment the music faded. Bora began to play a haunting melody. The dancers formed a circle around the dying fire. Everyone who was not dancing also joined the circle and we all joined hands. Goran's hand was warm and rough. He held mine tightly as we all stood watching the embers in silence. When the final notes of Bora's song faded into the night the men dropped hands and moved toward the glowing coals. We watched as they shovelled them to one side and started digging a hole. It didn't take long to dig a pit long enough and wide enough to hold a man.

Radko's body, wrapped in a pale muslin shroud was laid into the hole. No words were uttered. No tears were shed. The men quickly covered the body and patted down the earth. They then replaced the still glowing embers of the fire. Dragan came over to where Goran and I stood.

"We will move camp at first light, just as we always do when someone dies. Goran, will you come with us?" Dragan asked.

Yes," said Goran, "I would be honoured to join you."

Chapter 10

A Field of Millet

Spring came, and summer followed in the circle of the year. During the warm months we moved often, visiting many different villages. I liked the mountain villages, with their fast running streams overhung with thick canopies of fresh green leaves. One warm morning I lay in my bed enjoying the ray of sunlight pointing like a golden finger through the dust particles in the air. Zora, of course, was already up and out collecting her marvellous plants.

I looked across the wagon to see if Tanya was still in bed, but she was up already, too. The birds twittered in the trees, the air felt warm on my cheek. I stretched like a lazy cat and stuck my toes out from under the sheet and wiggled them, enjoying the feeling. Then, lots of light! Someone had pulled the curtain open. A smiling face beamed at me.

"Hello sleepy head!" Dragan said. "It's a beautiful morning! Come for a ride?"

"Oh, yes, please!" I said.

Dragan waited while I pulled a dark blue skirt over my nightdress and went outside to splash some cool water on my face.

Dobro stood behind Dragan. They were both very handsome in the morning light. "Here you go," Dragan said, handing me a chunk of brown bread and a slice of cheese. "Breakfast". He vaulted gracefully onto Dobro's back, lifted me up behind him and we were off. Slowly at first until we were away from the camp. Then Dragan made a clicking noise with his mouth and we were off.

We galloped down a leafy path, the sun filtered through the leaves turned everything into a symphony of soft greens. The smell of the earth, still moist with morning dew, rose up with the even beat of Dobro's hooves. I held on tightly to Dragan, not afraid but excited. I wanted this ride to go on forever.

As we cleared the woods Dragan slowed Dobro to a walk. I shielded my eyes from the bright sun that was before us. On all sides of us fields of ripe millet spread out as far as the eye could see. Even up on Dobro's back the flowering stalks were taller than my head.

"It's odd to see flowers bigger than people," I said. "If I were standing on the ground they'd be much, much taller than I am."

Dragan hopped off Dobro's back and then helped me down, too.

"Yes, they are much, much taller than you are!" he said.

I looked up at the tall plants. I felt like I had shrunk in size, that their feathery heads were the size of regular flowers and I was tiny.

Before I saw it, I heard the sound of a horse trotting down the road that we had come. Someone was calling out for Dragan

"There you are, the Baron is looking for you" Marko called. "He wants to talk to you. Now!"

"Come, Milada. I must go and see what my father wants," Dragan said.

I was enjoying the beautiful morning and really didn't want to go back to camp yet.

"Can I stay here? I will follow the road to camp later," I said.

"Are you sure you'll be all right?" Dragan asked.

"Yes, I'm sure," I said. We hadn't come all that far and the road led back.

"All right then. See you later," he said as he hopped onto Dobro, pulled up on the reins to turn back toward our camp and was off.

It was nicer with Dragan here with me, I thought, but I was enjoying the warmth of the summer's morning and the sound of a soft breeze rustling through the tall plants. I wandered off the road and into the field. Within the forest of thick stalks I really felt like an insect - an ant or a ladybug! Imagine being so small. How do insects see the world? We must look like giants to them. What if a huge foot were to step down and squish the life out of me! I'd be more careful when I walked from now on!

The day was getting warmer, but it was shady beneath the green stalks. I was getting hungry. I thought I was going in the direction of the road back to our camp, but after walking for a long time I didn't come to it. Maybe I should try a different direction. I jumped up as high as I could to try to see over the plants. But as hard as I tried I couldn't get high enough to see the way to go.

I tried to remember where the sun was when we were coming. It was in my eyes when we cleared the forest, straight ahead. It was morning so that would be east. I knew that I needed to go west to get back. But I could see the sun almost directly above me now. I couldn't tell which way to go. I struck out in what I thought was as straight line. Eventually I had to come to the edge of the field. Anyplace was better than this jungle of oversized, monstrous plants.

I walked and walked and walked. My hands were bleeding from pushing aside the rough stalks. My hair was caked with sweat and dust and pollen that rained down from the stalks blossoming above my head. My legs were so tired that it was an effort to lift my foot to take a step. I felt tears in the corners of my eyes. I just wanted to get home.

Finally I saw some light ahead of me. The road! The thought that I was finally to be delivered from this nightmare gave me the strength to more forward faster. At last I reached the last row of millet. The tears in my eyes started to flow for real. I wasn't at the road. I was at a stream. On the other side of the stream - more millet!

I sat on the bank and let my tears flow. This day started out so well; awakened by the sunlight, the ride with Dragan and now look at it! I was tired and hungry and lost. But what good is it to cry? I bathed my face in the cool water, took a long drink. So. I stood up and had a look around. I'll follow the stream, I thought. There was no way that I was going back into the fields.

Right or left? Left or right? Which way to go? Then I remembered something that Layla told me once when I asked her one of my many questions. She told me, "When you don't know what to do, sit quietly and take a deep breath. Don't focus on anything, let thoughts come and go as they will. Ask the question quietly to yourself and then just wait for the answer. If you are quiet enough you will hear it."

I sat down again, closed my eyes and took a deep breath. Which way to go? I asked no one in particular. At first I was thinking. West. Which way is west? Maybe if I just stay here someone will find me? Maybe they won't notice I'm not there? Maybe, since I'm not really one of them they'll move on without me? Stop! Stop all these thoughts!

I took another deep breath and tried to keep my mind quiet. There are bugs buzzing around my head, let it go… the sun feels warm on my hair, let it go…inhale…exhale…feel the breath going in and coming out…let it go…

For a moment my incessant thoughts stopped. I heard the tinkling sound of the stream flowing over the rocks. I let go of that thought, too. In my silence the gurgling voice of the water seemed to whisper the words 'go, go, go with the stream'. That's it! That's the answer. I would follow the direction of the stream. It flows to the river. The village is on the river and our camp is near the village.

With new energy I followed the direction of the rushing water. Soon I came to the end of the millet field and entered the welcome shade of the forest. I remembered how my Grandma and Grandpa always told me to stay out of the woods. With the gypsies I learned to love its darkness, its mystery and its treasures. I was so lost in my thoughts that I was startled when I heard someone call my name.

"Milada - is that you? What are you doing here?" It was Goran, sitting by the edge of the stream.

"Hello. It's a long story" I said, relieved to see him. "Tell me what you are doing here instead."

I saw Goran looking at my cut palms but neither one of us said anything about them.

"I'm watching these salamanders," he said.

I looked where Goran was looking and saw a tangle of slimy white salamanders in a shallow pool formed by river-rounded rocks. At first I didn't like the sight of them but the longer I watched the more fascinated I became.

"Look," said Goran, "here comes another one".

The new arrival skirted the writhing mass. The suction pads on its feet held it onto the rock as the rushing water tried to pull it into the flow. The salamander eased itself into the group and was lost among the others.

"Now it's one of them. It's not alone anymore." Goran said, thoughtfully. What he said next came as a surprise.

"Milada," he said, "Do you think that the gypsies really accept us as one of their group?"

"Oh yes" I replied, without thinking very much.

"Do they, though? I see them talking among themselves and then stop if you or I come near. All right, I have only been with them for a little while, but you have been with them since you were small, haven't you?"

"Yes," I said, "Since the day my Grandma died, and that was a long time ago."

"And some of the things they do are strange," he continued.

"Like what," I asked.

"They use funny words and sing those strange songs and they dance when someone dies. They are not like other people," he said, throwing a small stone into the stream.

It entered the water with a plop.

"No," I said, "They are happier. They know how to keep from getting sick, from getting old. They understand death in a different way."

"But that's strange," Goran replied.

"It may be strange," I said, "but it's good! And I can't imagine staying in one place like other people do. I like the way we move around seeing new places, visiting old friends to bring them news from other villages. It's always a celebration when we arrive in a village."

"Yes," Goran said, "I like it for now. But I don't know that I would always want to live like this. I'd like a place of my own somewhere, a little land to grow my food."

"Look!" Goran pointed at the rock pool in the stream. I'd forgotten all about the salamanders. The whole lot of them had been washed over the edge of the pool and was flowing down the stream.

"Look at that," he said, "They don't notice that they aren't protected anymore".

Chapter 11

Hidden Words

"I'm really, really, really hungry," I told Goran as we watched the tangle of salamanders disappear downstream.

"Let's go and find something to eat, then," he said as he stood up and dusted off the seat of his trousers.

He reached out his hand to help me up. I took it but then flinched from the pain. He let my hand go. We both looked at my palms. They were full of scrapes and dried blood.

"What happened to your hands?" he asked me.

I told him all about loosing myself in the millet forest.

"No wonder you looked so upset," he said. "Do you feel better now?"

"Oh, yes," I replied. "Just really, really, really hungry!"

We walked back to the camp. As we neared the clearing the scent of roasting meat made my tired legs move quickly.

"I hope the meat is ready." I said, my mouth moist in anticipation.

"Me, too" he said and we both walked faster.

We joined the others around the cooking fire. I looked around for Dragan but he wasn't there. But Tanya was, and with a new friend. Cradled in her lap was a baby lamb.

"Come and see," she called when she saw us coming toward the fire. "Her mother gave birth to two but would only give milk to the first-born," she explained. "It happens sometimes."

I reached out to touch the little lamb. Its fleece was soft against my sore hands.

"Look at your hands!" Tanya exclaimed, "What have you been up to all day!"

"It's a long story," I said. I really didn't want to be reminded of my experience with the millet field again.

"Zora's over there. Go ask her for something to help your hands mend quickly," she said as she stroked the little lamb.

I left Goran talking with Tanya and went to find Zora. When I showed her my hands I expected her to gasp and ask me what happened. Instead she just beckoned me to follow her back to our wagon. She wet a rag with the water that we kept cool in an earthenware jar. Besides the water it held a large clear stone. I always wondered why this stone was in the water. It made the jar extra heavy, especially when the jar was very full of water. While she bathed my palms with the cool water I decided to ask her about it.

"That stone is a piece of quartz crystal," she explained. "It grows deep in the earth. It has a particular energy that enlivens things around it. The crystal makes this water very special. It is healing water."

My hands were starting to feel better and some of the redness was already fading.

"Where did you get the stone? Are they just lying around? Can I find one, do you think?" I asked, wanting a healing stone of my own.

"They are not easy to come by," Zora replied. "I was given this one by Layla. Our people have several. They are entrusted to some of us for a time. They are not ours. We are only their custodians. We will pass them on to others when the time comes."

"How do you know when that will be?" I asked.

"We just know," she said. "How do your hands feel now?"

"Much better," I replied.

Zora went into the wagon then reappeared with a small, dark green glass vial. She pulled out the stopper and I could smell what was inside. It was a strong scent; like the countryside in summer.

"What is that?" I asked her.

"This is oil infused with rosemary. It will help your hands to heal," she said.

Zora took one of my hands in hers and gently rubbed the oil into it. As she did the same with the other hand my tummy made a loud grumble.

"Let's get our plates and knifes and go to dinner," Zora said with a barely perceptible smile. "I think someone is hungry."

Together we returned to the group. On the way I saw Dragan talking with his father, the Baron. The Baron had his back to me. He was bent over slightly and seemed to be studying his boots, usually shiny, but today lightly covered with a fine coating of dust. Dragan was looking down, too, deep in thought. He didn't see me. I wanted to tell how I got lost in the fields, but whatever he was discussing with the Baron seemed important. I wouldn't bother him now with my adventure.

The fragrant meat had been sliced and placed on a large platter in the centre of our eating circle. Zora and I joined Goran and Tanya, now without the lamb, in the circle. Last to join the circle, the Baron and Dragan sat down, both lost in their own thoughts.

There was an unusual silence during the meal. Even Goran kept his chatter to a minimum. Before we had eaten our fill of the delicious roast the Baron, Dragan and some of the other members of the group moved away from the table, still deep in conversation.

"I wonder what is going on today," Goran said as he watched the gypsies get up and join the other group that was gathering by the embers of the cooking fire.

"I know the Baron called Dragan to see him this morning when we went out for ride on Dobro" I told him.

"You went riding with Dragan? And he left you to get lost in that field?" Goran said, a look of annoyance appearing on his face.

"I didn't plan on getting lost," I said, wondering at Goran's sudden change of tone.

"You planned to spend the day with the Baron's son?" he asked.

"Well, I like his company. I like riding with him," I said, feeling a bit defensive but not knowing why I needed to explain myself to Goran.

"So why didn't you ride back with him when the Baron summoned him?" Goran said.

"It was such a beautiful morning. I didn't want to go back," I said. "I really didn't think I would get lost. I told you. So can we talk about something else, please?"

"All right. What do you think they are talking about over there?" Goran looked over at the Baron and the others huddled by the fire.

"I really don't know," I said, "but it must be something important. Let's go and see."

As Goran and I moved closer to the group by the fire the people lowered their voices until no one spoke at all. The Baron's baritone broke this strange silence.

"Good evening, my children" he said in a gentle voice. Although his voice was calm, his brow was lined.

"Please would you two go find Mother Miriana," he asked. "We would like some of her special tea. Tell her we need the *very special* brew. She will know what you mean."

"Certainly, Baron" I replied as I grabbed Goran's hand and headed toward Mother Miriana's wagon. "Ouch!" In my excitement to be of service to the Baron I forgot about my painful hands.

"What's the rush?" Goran asked as I ran on ahead.

"The Baron wants his tea," I said.

"I think he just wanted to get rid of us". At Goran's words I froze.

"Why do you say that?" I asked, confused. I felt honoured that the Baron trusted us to carry a message even if it was just a request for tea.

"Because it's true. Haven't you noticed that lots of times they stop talking when you or I come near? We live with them but we are not trusted as part of the band."

"That's not true!" I blurted out. "Maybe they don't trust *you*. You've only been with us for a while, but I've lived most of my life with them. Why wouldn't they trust *me*?"

"If you don't believe me just observe," he said. "They are different from us. We will never be totally accepted in their lives."

"If I marry Dragan they'll have to accept me!" I said before thinking.

"They'll never let you marry Dragan!" he said. "And besides, I always thought you would marry *me*."

"What!" I exclaimed and turned to look at Goran. His eyes sparkled mischievously. "Ah, you're joking!" I said and gave him a playful slap on this shoulder.

"Ouch!" I had forgotten my hands again. We both burst out laughing. "Let's go find Mother Miriana and see about the Baron's *special* tea.

Chapter 12

Magic Dust

As we approached the fire I saw the elder woman bent over the flames.

I was always a little afraid of her, the one they called Mother Miriana. She seemed to be the eldest of the gypsies, older than the Baron, older than anyone. The wisps of hair that escaped her dark green kerchief were silver and so was the thick plait that fell down her back as far as her waist. Her skin was like the tanned leather of my first pair of shoes and her fingers were stained dark with the juice of thousands of berries and herbs that had passed through her hands over the years. She was the one who was called when someone died or when a new baby was coming into the world.

I don't remember for sure but I think that she was there on the day my Grandma left us. I always wanted to ask her about my Grandma but I was afraid to. I don't know why. Mother Miriana was always warm and friendly with me. It's just that that day was like a dream. Maybe it *was* a dream and I was *always* a part of the gypsy band.

"Good evening, children" Mother Miriana greeted us from her campfire. There was a large black iron pot suspended over the fire with steam rising from it.

"Good evening, Mother Miriana," I said, wondering what she was cooking after we had eaten such a feast.

"I'm preparing tea," she said, as if she read my mind.

"The Baron would like you to make some of the special tea," Goran said to her.

"The *very* special tea, please." I added.

"It will be ready soon. Would you like to sit by my fire for a while until it brews?" she said.

As we settled ourselves on the worn carpets near the fire a stranger approached us from a path through the forest. He was a young man from town. He wore a crimson jacket and high riding boots although there was no sign of his horse. As he drew closer to the fire I could see that his jacket was well-cut but threadbare and that his boots, though of good leather, were old and worn.

"Good evening, Madam," he said, addressing the old woman. "I seek Mother Miriana. Are you she?"

Mother Miriana looked at him with her piercing green eyes. "Why do you seek this woman?" she asked.

"I have been told that she has magic," the young man replied.

"Magic?" Mother Miriana said, her eyes searching the man's face.

"That she can cure the sick. Help people solve their problems...," he continued.

"What you speak of, young man, is knowledge, not magic."

She spoke these words sternly to her visitor, but turned to us and gave us a wink.

"I am she. Tell me what you want and I will help you if I can," she said, turning back to the young man.

The young man knelt down beside Mother Miriana and said, "My father died two years ago. He left me an estate with much land. I have men who work the land for me, but although they seem to have enough to eat there is nothing coming in for my family or me. I have debts to pay. If I don't make some money from my land I will be ruined. I heard from my cousin that you have magic dust that can make the land produce more. Please, Mother Miriana, can you give me some of that magic dust to make my land more fertile?"

"And what will you give me if I give you this magic dust?" she asked.

"I have a gold ring that my father left me. I will give that to you." With these words he took a gold signet ring off his finger and offered it to Mother Miriana.

"Just a minute," she said, taking the ring.

She went into her wagon. From where we sat, Goran and I saw Mother Miriana climbing out the back end of her wagon with a small brass box in her hand. She bent down and scraped some dry mud into the box. What was she doing? The young man looked uncomfortably at the finger where his ring had been. He did not speak to us. Goran broke the silence.

"I think I've seen you in town. In the tavern," he said.

"I sometimes go there to hear the news from the other farmers," the young man replied, not looking directly at Goran, still preoccupied with the white stripe of skin where his ring had been.

Goran opened his mouth to say something but before he had the chance Mother Miriana reappeared from her wagon.

"Here is your magic dust," she said, handing him the brass box.

I looked at Goran to see if he was thinking what I was thinking. Mother Miriana was giving a box of dirt in exchange for a gold ring!

"Now here is what you must do with it to make it work," she continued. "Every morning as the sun is rising and every evening as it is setting you must sprinkle some of this magic dust in the four corners of your land. You must not miss even one day or the magic will be undone. Is that understood?"

"If I do this I will prosper?" he asked, hopefully.

"If you follow my instructions, yes, you will," the woman assured him.

"Thank you, Mother Miriana, I will do as you say". The young man stood up and brushed the dust off his once-fine trousers.

"One more thing," Mother added. "When the box is empty come back here and tell me your experience."

"Certainly I will. A thousand thanks!" With those words the young man hastily made his way back through the trees, relieved to have completed his business so quickly.

Mother Miriana smiled. I was confused. I thought the gypsies were all very honest. I was afraid to say anything but Goran exclaimed, "Mother Miriana, that was clever of you to take that man's gold ring for a box full of dirt! I mean *magic dust!*"

"I know of that young man. He is lazy, a wastrel. His father left him a large inheritance and he spent most of it on drink and gambled the rest away," Mother Miriana said.

"I've seen him through the tavern window playing games of chance," Goran added.

"Although his land is good he never checks on the farmers who work it. Of course they keep everything for themselves since their landlord cannot be bothered to do any work himself. There is no magic. I told him at the start, only knowledge. When he goes around his land sprinkling the *magic dust* the farmers will see him. He will get to know them and keep up with the day-to-day doings on his land. And he *will* prosper," she said, "Through knowledge, not magic."

"But that golden ring must be very valuable," Goran continued.

"To the young man it is," she said. "I could have just given him the "magic dust" but then he would not value it. He would not make a point of following my instructions to visit his land."

A wonderful aroma was wafting up from the black iron pot.

"The Baron's tea is ready. Will you help me carry it?" she asked.

Mother Miriana poured the steaming brew into three smaller pots. We each took one and headed back to the fire where the Baron was still deep in conversation.

Chapter 13

On War and Weddings

Back at the main fire, now not more than a pile of glowing embers, the gypsies were chatting in small groups. After I helped Mother Miriana serve the tea I found Tanya, re-united with the baby lamb, and Zora.

"What was going on?" I asked, trusting them to tell me the truth.

"Nothing that concerns you," said Zora.

I wondered if what Goran had told me was true. That the gypsies were not telling us everything; that we really were not considered part of their family group. I petted the little lamb, feeling as lost is it was, alone without its mother's love.

"It was something to do with our community," Tanya said.

I think that she saw how Zora's abrupt words hurt me.

"Todor is thinking of marrying a woman who is not of our group. The Baron is not sure that is a good idea," she explained.

"Do you always marry within your group?" I asked.

There had been only a few marriages since I started my travels with the gypsies.

"I thought it was up to the Baron to decide who is to marry whom," I said.

"Usually that is the case," Tanya said. "There are other bands from the same source as ours. Sometimes, in the middle of summer, we come together for a great feast. Then many matches are made."

"I don't remember ever meeting any other people like you," I told her.

"It has been many years since we all came together. Times around us are changing. Our paths have taken us farther a field. In some places there are wars that make passage difficult," she explained.

"What is *war,* Tanya," I asked. I had never heard that word before.

"War is when people from different places, or with different ideas fight each other," she said.

"Like men fight at the tavern sometimes when they drink too much wine? They yell and hit each other, but then drink together the next night as friends," I asked, always having wondered at some men's strange behaviour.

"No, Milada," Tanya continued, "War is not like that. It is more organized. There are leaders, kings, dukes or barons who make a plan of attack. The soldiers follow them into battle."

"Why? Maybe they will be hurt?"

"Many are hurt, many are even killed," Tanya said with a touch of sadness in her voice."

"So why do they fight? Why war?" I could not understand why men would do this. There were hardly any arguments among the gypsy band, let alone fights.

"There are many reasons," Tanya patiently explained. "Sometimes it is to get control of more land or more power; sometimes because one leader insulted another. Who knows what starts a war, but once one is started it is very hard to stop."

I wished Goran were here. He had lived in the town for many years. He would know better about such things. I watched him laughing with the other boys. Did they ever think about war?

"Why don't people live together, work together for the good of all, like your people do?" I asked.

"This is our way. They have their own way, their own learning," Tanya replied.

"I like your way better! I am so happy that I came to live with you," I said sincerely.

"I am happy you came to us, as well," Tanya said with a big smile. "You are a good friend, Milada. Would you hold this lamb for a minute? I would like some more tea. Would you like some? Zora?"

I nodded and Zora shook her head as I took the lamb in my arms. I felt its little heart beating fast as it slept on my lap. Its soft wool soothed my reddened palms. Poor little thing. Imagine its mother kicking it away. It was lucky to have Tanya. And so was I.

"What do you think about war, Zora?" I asked to break the silence.

"It is a fact of life among the others," she said, looking down at the sleeping lamb.

"Who are the others?" I had never heard that term.

"They are the people who are not part of our group," she replied.

"Am I an "other"?" I asked, dreading her answer would be yes.

"Yes and no," she said. "Yes because you were not born of our line. You do not remember where you came from. No because you have lived with us for many years. You sit at our fire and you follow our ways."

I remembered where I came from, the village where I was born and lived with my Grandma and Grandpa, but it seemed so long ago.

"I never want to leave my life here," I said, and I meant it!

"Never is a long time," Zora said, looking me right in my eyes. "Life brings many surprises. We can't know what we will do until life reveals itself to us."

Before I could ask another question Tanya was back with the tea - and Layla.

"What have you there, Milada?" She asked as she sat down beside me, her bright skirt spreading around her.

"It's Tanya's lamb. Isn't she sweet?" I said, as I gently caressed the young creature.

"Tanya is so good with baby animals," Layla said. "I'm sure she will be an excellent mother to small people as well."

Tanya smiled. "I look forward to my time of motherhood. I like helping the little ones."

I had not really thought about it before, but most young woman of Layla's age were already mothers of several children. I asked her,

"Layla, why have you not married and become a mother yourself?"

Stroking the lamb she replied, "In this lifetime motherhood is not my path. I love the children. I dance with them and tell them stories, as I did with you when you first joined us. But my destiny is different. The Baron knows this and so does not wish for me to marry. It is my wish as well."

"I would like to marry one day…if it is the Baron's wish," I added.

"You can make up your own mind," Layla said, "when the time comes,"

"Will the Baron choose a partner for Tanya?" I asked.

I could see Tanya smiling out of the corner of my eye. "He already has," Layla said.

I was dying to ask who it was but just at the moment Goran and a couple of the other boys plopped themselves down next to us, laughing.

"'Evening, ladies," Goran said.

"You all seem happy, boys," Layla said, laughing herself.

"What's so funny, Goran?" I was glad to see him in better spirits. How could he not feel a part of this group of boys who so obviously liked him?

"It's that Dobro," said Bora, his eyes sparking.

"Dragan's horse?" I asked. I always looked forward to hearing about Dragan.

"Yes. You know the Baron wanted to speak with Dragan today about a matter of importance to the group," Bora said.

"Yes, he was called back from our ride this morning for some important matter," I told him.

"Well, you know how much that horse loves him," Bora continued. "He kept looking over Dragan's shoulder. When Dragan told him to go, instead of going he just sat down next to the Baron and put his head on Dragan's lap!"

We all laughed at the picture Bora's words conjured up.

Then Layla said, "We've had enough talk for one night. Bora, play us a tune on your viol to soothe us into a good night's sleep."

Bora took up his viol and played. One by one the gypsies returned to their wagons. There was no moon that night and stars shone brightly high above us. Goran and I were the last ones to go. As we walked to our wagons he put his arm lightly around my shoulder. At the parting of our ways he turned to me and, very softly, touched his lips to my cheek. Then, without a word he hurried down the path to his wagon.

I continued slowly to the wagon I still shared with Tanya and Zora. What a day this had been. And how welcoming was my bed!

Chapter 14

Colours and Herbs

By the time I awoke the following morning Zora and Tanya were already up and out of the wagon. Usually I heard them moving around, putting on their skirts and embroidered blouses, but today I heard nothing. I lay in my bed, enjoying the warm air blowing through a gap in the sky blue curtain at the entrance to our wagon. I was in no hurry to get up and start my day.

Lying there I remembered the day before. My experience in the millet field almost seemed like a dream. Was it only a dream? I looked at my hands and knew that it had been real. My palms, although much better, were still marked with small red cuts from the rough stalks. And did Goran really kiss my cheek last night? Or was *that* a dream!

I liked Goran very much. I guess I loved him. But I loved him like a brother. I certainly did not expect a starlight kiss! Did he mean it when he said he wanted to marry me? No, he was just joking. The kiss meant nothing...now if Dragan kissed me...that would be different! It felt so good riding behind him on Dobro as we flew through the woods and open meadows. I was so disappointed when he had to return to the camp.

I wondered if Todor would marry that woman. I decided it was time to get up and see if there was any news. I put on a pretty blue blouse and my red skirt, quickly splashed some water on my face, grabbed my cup and bowl and went to find Tanya. Just as I stepped off the wagon I saw her hurrying in my direction.

"There you are, sleepy head!" she said, giving me a big hug, laughing. "Were you lost in your dreams?"

"Only my daydreams. Have you been up a long time?" I asked her.

"Oh yes," she said. "That baby lamb was crying for food. I had to find a ewe to give me some milk for her."

I noticed the baby lamb was beside Tanya. She followed my gaze and started to laugh again.

"Watch this," she said.

Tanya took a few steps forward, then back. Then she skipped in a zigzag line back to the edge of the clearing. The lamb followed her every move, every zig and every zag. I burst out laughing as Tanya and the lamb returned to the steps of the wagon where I sat.

"She follows me everywhere," Tanya said, "even when she isn't hungry".

"She thinks you are her mother," I laughed

"I will have to teach her to be a sheep! Baaaah, baaah!" she said, laughing, too.

"Maybe the lamb isn't hungry any more, but I am. I need my breakfast," I said, getting up from the step and starting for the main fire where we gathered for our morning meal.

Tanya and her lamb followed. We met Zora coming back the other way toward our wagon.

"I'm going into the village today to help a man who has a high fever. Would either of you like to come with me?" she asked.

"I have to watch this lamb. She is too young to leave alone," Tanya replied.

"I'd like to come with you," I said. "Do I have time for some breakfast first?"

"I have to prepare my herbs before we go, so, yes, have your breakfast. Then meet me back at the wagon and we will go together from there," Zora said, in her serious and practical manner.

I hurried to have my bread and tea. I saw Goran sitting next to a wheel of cheese.

"Are you going to eat all that cheese?" I asked him. "I remember that you like cheese, but that's a lot!"

Goran's cheeks went red. Was he thinking of our first meeting at the market when he tricked his way into a meal, or was he thinking of last night's kiss?

"Yes, I like cheese. But I'll share this with you," he said, cutting me off a generous wedge.

"I'm going to the village with Zora," I told him as I enjoyed the cheese and a piece of freshly baked bread.

"I'm coming, too," he said.

When we finished eating we went to find Zora. She was just stepping out of the wagon when we arrived.

"Ready to go?" she asked.

"Yes. Goran is coming with us, too," I said.

"Good. Please, would you both help me carry these things?" She said, handing us each a bundle. One was wrapped in dark blue cloth and the other in bright yellow, a particular shade I hadn't seen before.

As we walked toward the village I asked Zora about the unusually coloured cloth.

"It is a special colour made from the stamens of the crocus flower, called saffron. It takes thousands of flowers to get enough stamens to make the dye, and the flowers grow far from here and are hard to come by. It adds to the healing power of the herbs," she explained.

"Each colour has a particular vibration. By storing the herbs in different coloured cloths I am subtly altering their properties. It makes them work better to help people recover more quickly."

I looked at Goran to see if he understood what she was talking about. He looked confused, too.

"Zora, can you explain how a colour can help a person get over a sickness?" I asked. "I don't understand how that can be."

Zora paused for a moment, thinking. "I will try to explain it to you," she said. "Listen. Things seem solid, but they are not. Think about water. In the winter when it is very cold, we have icicles hanging off the roof of our wagon, right?"

"Yes,' I said, remember seeing glittering icicles on chilly winter mornings.

"Usually water is a liquid. It takes the form of whatever container it is in. When we put it in the pot and heat it up for tea, have you noticed the steam that rises above the pot?" she asked.

"Yes, I burnt myself on the hot steam more than once,' Goran said.

"That steam is water, too, but in another form."

"But what does all this have to do with colour and healing?" I asked. I was curious but also getting a little impatient with this long explanation.

"I want you to understand that everything that appears to be solid, like the icicle, is really not solid and static but a pattern of movement, like steam," she explained. "In things that appear to be solid the movement is slower, in liquid faster and in gas or steam even faster."

"But what about colour?" I asked.

"The colours we see are a reflection of the light on a surface. We see different colours because different colours absorb and reflect different frequencies of light," she told us.

"This is too complicated," Goran said.

"Shall I stop?" replied Zora.

"No, no, please go on," I said, getting more and more curious.

I know I felt different when I wore my red skirt than when I wore my dark green one. The red one made me feel more alive, the green one make me feel calm.

"At night we don't see colours" Zora continued patiently. "Everything seems to be different shades of gray. That is because there is no sunlight to reflect and produce the colours we see."

"What about the rainbow," I asked. "There is every colour in a rainbow!"

"We see a rainbow when there is moisture in the air while the sun is shining," she said. "The tiny drops of moisture separate the white light of the sun into all its seven colours. Each colour holds a particular vibration. When the colours are separated we see each one side by side in the rainbow."

"I always thought the rainbow was a magic sign," said Goran. "That's what everybody thinks. I don't know about this air moisture business…"

"Call it magic if you like," Zora said.

We walked along in silence for a while. Zora didn't seem upset by what Goran said. She just stopped talking. I waited to see if she would start again. When she didn't I had to ask, "Zora, please tell me how the colour makes a difference to your herbs."

"Just like everything else, our bodies are not solid as they appear but are also a pattern of movement. Different parts of our body resonate with different frequencies of colour and also of sound" she explained.

I thought about the music Bora played on his viol. How some sounds made me feel happy and others brought tears to my eyes. I was beginning to understand what Zora was talking about. Goran was kicking a little stone along the path, raising dust. Was he listening?

Zora continued, "When a person gets ill it means that their body is out of balance. It could be from something outside of them, liking eating food that is spoiled or poisoned or it could come from a strong feeling like sadness, anger or fear. With herbs, with colour and with sound, too, the body can be brought back into balance. It is a very subtle system. It responds to subtle treatment. A bit of colour applied in the correct spot, the right sound, the right tea can all help a person to heal."

"How do you know which is the right colour, sound or herb?" I asked, wanting to learn more.

"You learn from observation and experience, Milada." she replied. "I know that you have learned some things in the years you have been with us. Do you remember which tea to use for a pain in your throat?"

"The bark of the red elm tree," I replied. Many times this tea helped me.

"What about to help you sleep," Zora asked.

"Tea made from chamomile flowers. And for a tummy ache, use the leaves of the spearmint plant," I said, please to show off my knowledge.

"Very good. You are learning how to help yourself and others," Zora said, with a rare smile.

"What about the colours?" I asked, still curious. "Why this special yellow and the blue?"

"Yellow is good for the stomach and spleen," Zora said. "It helps to calm a person's worries and fear. The dark blue is for the head. It soothes a headache and can help bring down a fever."

"Zora, how do you know all of this?" I asked.

"It is the wisdom of our people. I have always known it," she replied.

"Do all the gypsies know?" I asked.

"All have some knowledge about how to heal. I seem to have a talent for it, like Bora has for the viol. But we all understand the nature of things," she said.

We arrived at the edge of the village. Several people were coming to meet us.

"There you are at last," a woman said, taking Zora's arm. "Come quickly, his fever is rising."

Chapter 15

In the Market

Quickly we followed Zora and the woman to a large house in the village square. At the door, Goran said, "This isn't a job for me. I'll find you later."

He handed me his bundle of herbs then turned and left without waiting for any answer or comment. Zora was already half way up the stairs when I ran to catch up with her. I told her Goran had gone. She made no reply.

It was hard to see in the darkened bedroom. I stood in the doorway with the two bundles of herbs waiting for instructions from Zora. She and the woman stood close to the figure lying on the bed. They spoke softly together and then the woman moved toward the door where I stood waiting. She hesitated.

Zora said, "Go now. Put two pots of water on to boil. I will do what I can."

After the woman left Zora called me over. "Milada, go and open the window. There is no air in this room."

I did as I was told. I pushed open the wooden shutters and sunlight flooded the room. I looked around and was surprised by the richness of its furnishings. There was a fine, polished wood chest of drawers and table by the bed, which was also made of carved wood. The man in the bed was covered with a thick down quilt of fine damask, the colour of burgundy.

Zora beckoned me over. She placed my hand gently on the man's forehead. It was burning hot.

"A fever is good," she told me. "His body is fighting off the infection. We must watch that he does not get too hot, though, because that can cause damage."

From the blue bundle, Zora tore off a piece of cloth the size of a handkerchief.

"Milada," she said, "please soak this in some cold water."

There was a fine china pitcher and bowl on the table. I poured some water into the bowl and dropped in the blue cloth.

"Wring it dry and bring it here," Zora said.

I did as I was told and handed her the cloth. She broke off some herbs from the bunch, wrapped them up in the damp cloth and placed it on the man's forehead. She unwrapped the yellow bundle and folded some of the herbs into the middle of the cloth. She gently pulled back the quilt and laid the yellow cloth with the herbs on the man's stomach next to his skin. Then she pulled the quilt back into place.

She sat down on a chair beside the bed and called me over as she removed something from the leather pouch she'd been carrying. There were two packets of herbs each wrapped in a large leaf.

"Milada, please take these downstairs to the woman," Zora instructed. "Ask her to put one packet in each pot of boiling water. Tell her to turn down the heat and let them simmer until I ask for them."

"Yes, Zora," I said, taking the packets. "How will you know which one is which?"

"We can tell from the smell and from the colour of the tea." Zora said, turning back to the man in the bed.

She took his hand in hers. I heard her singing softly as I left the room. Going down the stairs I smelled the herbs, first one packet and then the other. They did smell very different. One was almost sweet and the other pungent.

I found the woman of the house in the kitchen. The pots had just come to a rolling boil. I gave her the herbs and Zora's instructions. She emptied one leaf into one pot and the second into the other.

"We are so lucky that your people are here. I don't think my husband would have a chance to live without your magic," she told me.

"It's not magic," I started to say, but when I saw the look in the woman's eye I fell silent. I sensed she needed to believe in magic. How could she know that a young girl like Zora would have enough knowledge to save her husband?

"What is you name," asked the woman.

"Milada," I replied.

"Milada, would you please go to the market for me? I don't want to leave the house in case I am needed," the woman asked.

"Yes, certainly I will do whatever I can to be of help," I replied.

She handed me two silver coins and a wicker basket.

"Please buy some bread, some cheese, some onions and carrots," she said. "I will make a good soup for us all. Maybe my husband will be strong enough to taste some, too."

I took the coins and hurried to the market square. There, by the fountain, sat Goran. I raised my hand to wave to him, opened my mouth to say hello, but before any sound came out he waved his hand at me, and put his finger across his lips, beckoning me to be quiet. I plopped down next to him and whispered, "Hello! What's going on?"

He pointed in the direction of the tavern. On a bench outside Todor sat with a woman with bright red hair, talking and holding her hand.

"I think that's the woman Todor wants to marry!" Goran whispered. "Look at that hair. Have you ever seen such a colour?"

"I like it. It's red like fire," I said. "Once on our travels we stopped at a village where many people had hair that colour, men, women and children, too. The little ones were so cute with their red hair and little brownish dots across their noses. Maybe she is from that village."

"Shh. Don't let them hear you." Goran said, ducking behind the well when Todor looked our way.

"Why not?" I asked. "We all know about the woman."

"I don't know. I just think it's better if they don't know we're watching, that's all," he whispered.

"Well, I'm not watching. I'm on my way to the market place. Do you want to come with me or are you happy here, in hiding?" I showed him the two silver coins.

"You can buy a lot with that much money," he said, lightly touching the coins in my hand.

I did not have much experience with money. Usually people gave us bread, meat, vegetables, wine; whatever we needed was ours even before we asked for it. I did not know how much I could buy with the money.

"Please come with me. You know better how to buy things in the marketplace," I said.

Together we went to a stall selling bread. The smell was wonderful. As we approached a chubby man removed a round wooden cover from a large earthen oven. He pushed in a flat wooden paddle and when it came out it held three golden loafs of bread.

"I would like to buy one of those, please," I asked the red-faced lady in the front of the stall.

"That will be three Florins," she said.

I started to give her one of the silver coins but Goran grabbed my hand before I could pass the coin to the woman.

"I can see you don't know how to shop," he whispered, "You never pay the first price!"

"Madam, although your bread smells good it is hardly worth the princely sum of three Florins. We will give you one," he said.

I stood there with my mouth open. How could he speak to the woman that way?

"Young man, our bread is the finest in the village. And you can see it is fresh, it has just come out of the oven. For one Florin I can give you a loaf from yesterday. If you want a fresh loaf then you must pay the price," the baker's wife replied.

Goran continued, "Thanks for your offer, but day-old bread is not for us. I will find another baker. I've heard there is a much better one on the other side of the square."

How did Goran know that? Did he ever buy bread in this village before? This bread smelled and looked so good. I doubted we could find better. I started to say something but he jabbed me in the ribs with his elbow.

"Come on, Milada. Let's go to the other baker," he said.

As he took my arm and led me away from the stall, the woman called out.

"Come back," the woman said. "I can let you have the fresh loaf for two Florins; save you the walk to the other side of the square."

"Wait, Milada," Goran said to me as if I was the one who wanted to go to the other bakery! "Two Florins is a fair price."

I gave him the money. He passed it to the woman in exchange for the warm bread. I took the bread and put in into the basket while Goran counted the change he received back from the silver coin.

"Thank you, ma'am. I'm sure your bread is delicious; certainly the best in the village," he said with an engaging grin. The baker's wife smiled as we went on our way.

"I think I'll let you do all the shopping," I told Goran with a sigh. "This is too much work for me!"

"You'll get used to it. It's a game we all play," he said with a grin as we headed for the vegetable sellers.

Chapter 16

Zora's Healing Magic Works

Goran made quick work of the shopping. He still had one silver coin and several copper florins.

"Shall we buy some of those roasted nuts to eat on the way back?" he asked me.

"This is not our money," I told him. "We need to bring the change back to the lady."

"I don't think she would mind," Goran said. "My careful shopping saved her money!"

"No, Goran. I wouldn't feel right using her money to buy something for us," I said. "Come on, she's waiting for these vegetables to make some soup."

On our way back through the main square, Todor was still sitting with the red-haired woman. He saw Goran and me and waved at us.

"Hello there, you two," he called. "Come and meet Emilia."

Although I was anxious to get back to the house I thought it would be rude not to go over and greet Todor and his lady friend. Todor was several years older than we were, slightly older that Dragan. He played a small instrument that sat on his knee. When he drew the bow across its three strings it sang like hum of a hundred insects buzzing in the night. I saw his instrument, wrapped in a rough, rust coloured blanket by his side. Beside it was another strange shaped bundle wrapped in a similar way.

Goran and I ran over to where the couple sat, enjoying a mug of ale in the morning sunshine.

"Goran, Milada," Todor said, "I would like you to meet Emilia. I am hoping to make her my wife."

The red-haired lady smiled. "I am happy to meet you both. Are you part of Todor's clan?"

Todor said, "My clan has adopted these two. Milada has been with us most of her life, young Goran for a year or so, isn't that right?"

"Yes, just about a year, " Goran replied, looking with fascination at Emilia's flaming locks. I was more fascinated by the strange shaped bundle.

"Todor, I know that is your instrument wrapped up in the rug, but what is that other thing next to it?" I asked, unable to stop my curiosity.

Todor smiled and said to Emilia, "Milada is famous for her questions. She is always asking questions! Why don't you answer this one? "

Without a word, Emilia reached across Todor and picked up the bundle. She carefully unwrapped what was inside. It seemed to be a piece of polished wood. But when Emilia pushed back the edge of the fabric I saw that it was indeed another musical instrument.

"This is my mandolin,' she said, setting it on her lap, her left hand holding its narrow neck while her right hand played idly on the strings.

"Oh! Would you play us a song?" I asked.

"Don't we have to deliver those vegetables," Goran reminded me. He seemed to want to get away from Todor and the red-headed woman.

"Yes, we do. But can I come back later for a song?" I said.

Emilia looked at Todor. "We will be here for a while, won't we? I told my friends to come and meet us here."

Todor nodded. "This is as good a place as any to enjoy the sunshine."

Goran and I continued back to the sick man's house. We knocked, and when no one answered we went inside. Goran looked around the large room.

"These people must have a lot of money," he said, running his finger over the smooth wood of the mantle piece.

"Maybe they do, but all the money in the word won't help the man get over his fever. Only Zora's knowledge can do that," I said.

"Does Zora take money for her healing?" Goran asked.

"She doesn't ask for any," I told him. "She says she is just sharing her gift. Sometimes people insist to give her money or presents of food for our group."

The woman of the house came out from the kitchen.

"You are back. Good. Did you find everything?" she asked.

I handed her the basket and the coins that were left.

"You keep those," she said, "for doing the shopping for me."

"Oh, no, we couldn't," I said, at the same time I heard Goran saying, "Thank you ma'am. We appreciate it," as he dropped the coins into his pocket.

He took the basket and followed the woman into the kitchen. I went upstairs to see how Zora was doing.

I opened the door quietly. Zora was still holding the man's hand and singing softly. I approached slowly, not wanting to wake the man if he was sleeping.

"He's much better now, "Zora whispered. I could see that his colour had improved. His skin was no longer blotchy and red as it had been before.

"What is the cause of his fever?" I asked Zora.

"Worry, I think, "she replied. "He told me that he was worried about loosing his money. He is a merchant. He travels from town to town, buying things in one place and selling them in another. But his last trip was not successful. There are many other merchants, younger than he. His sons are not interested in helping. They prefer to stay in the tavern and spend the money he has made."

The man groaned in his sleep. "He needs a good rest, "Zora said. "The fever is his body's way to make him stay at home for a while and decide what he wants to do."

"It seems he has a lot of money" I said. "Look at these furnishings. And his wife gave us a silver coin just for going to the market. I didn't want to take it but Goran…"

"Shhhh, now. Don't wake the man," Zora whispered. "Often people with lots of money think they need even more to be happy. We know that if you are not happy with yourself, with you life, with your family and with your friends, no amount of money or goods will make you so."

The man stirred again then opened his eyes.

"Hello there," he said. "Now I see *two* angels! Am I in heaven?" At these words, I giggled and Zora smiled.

"We were sent by the angels in heaven to help you. How are you feeling now?" Zora asked.

"I guess I'm not in heaven after all," he said, "because I feel very, very hungry!"

"Your wife is preparing some soup," I told him.

"I think some soup is just what you need," said Zora. "Milada, go and tell the woman of the house that her husband is awake and ready for some soup."

I ran down the stairs, anxious to tell the woman the news. I found her in the kitchen. Goran was chopping vegetables while she readied the fire.

"Better hurry with that soup," I said. "Your husband is very, very hungry!"

At my words the woman's worried face broke into a smile. She pulled off her apron and hurried out of the kitchen to see her husband's recovery for herself.

She returned shortly with an even bigger smile.

"I don't know how Zora's magic cured him so quickly," she said. "My neighbour told me he would be dead in a few hours and here he is asking for bread and soup!"

"Let me take him a piece of bread," I said, as the lady went back to the soup pot. I broke off a chunk of the fresh bread and ran back up the stairs. The man was now sitting up. Zora was packing away her coloured fabrics.

"I brought some bread," I said.

The man looked hungrily at the bread in my hand.

"It's better for you to eat some soup first," Zora said. "It will prepare your stomach."

The man reached out to take the bread in spite of Zora's warning and stuffed it in his mouth.

"Ah, well," said Zora, packing up the rest of her herbs. "You rest now. We will go down and see how the soup is coming along."

As we walked down the stairs I asked Zora, "Why did he eat the bread after you told him that soup would be better?"

"Wise words often fall on closed ears. He thinks he knows better. And he will make himself ill once again."

Chapter 17

Zora and the Magic Rocks

Soon a delicious scent was rising from the black pot hanging over the fire. Zora had added some special herbs to the broth and my mouth watered in anticipation of the meal. The woman set places for us at the kitchen table. Besides the bowls she placed a platter of dried meat and another of cheese. She ladled us each a generous portion of the steaming soup, but she did not join us to eat. She took a covered bowl upstairs to her husband.

"Don't wait for me to eat," she said, as she went out the door. "You've all had a busy morning and must be very hungry."

As we enjoyed our meal, Goran told Zora, "We met Todor in the square...and the woman he wants to marry."

"She has really red hair," I added, "and plays the mandolin."

"Did you hear her play?" Zora asked.

"Not yet," I said. "We'll go and see if they are still there when we finish our meal."

"How did it go with the man upstairs?" Goran asked, changing the subject.

"He will recover. This time." Zora replied.

"What do you mean, this time?" Goran asked her.

"I think he really doesn't want to live anymore," she said.

"Why not?" Goran said. "He has everything money can buy."

"Yes, but his sons do not respect him for the many years he spent travelling the countryside, trading. He provided everything money can buy, like you said, but he was never there," she said. "His children do not know him. Even his wife is like a stranger to him. He is tired from all his travels, yet feels lonely and useless staying a home without the adventure of the road."

"But it's good to stay in one place sometimes, isn't it?" Goran said wistfully.

"If you are happy there, yes, I think it could be." Zora replied.

After my years travelling with the gypsies I couldn't imagine staying in one place. We had friends all over the countryside. I always looked forward to seeing our old friends and meeting new ones. Yet, sometimes I remembered the village of my birth. I wondered if my Grandpa still left a candle in the window like he said he would, to guide me home. In all our years of travelling we had never gone back to my village. I wondered if we ever would.

The woman returned to the kitchen with the empty bowl. "What magic have you worked, my girl. My husband was so hungry he ate the whole bowl of soup and is asking for more."

"One bowl is enough for now," Zora advised. "He can eat another in a few hours. Now he needs to sleep and regain his strength. And don't forget to infuse the herbs I gave you. The lighter coloured one in the morning and the darker one at sunset."

"I won't forget," the woman said.

"It's time for us to go now," Zora announced, collecting her things and preparing to depart. "Thank you for your wonderful meal."

"We really enjoyed it," I added. "Thank you."

"Thank you ma'am," Goran said.

"You hardly need to thank me, young man. You did much of the work, chopping all those carrots and onions. And one meal is not enough to thank you for healing my husband, " she said turning to Zora. "Please let me give you some coins."

She went to the cupboard and reached up to the top shelf. She took down an earthenware jug with a wide mouth, stopped with a wooden plug. She removed the plug, reached in and took out a handful of silver coins. Goran's eyes looked as though they were going to pop out. We had never seen so many coins before.

"Here," she said, "Take these. Please."

"No, that is not necessary. It is my path and my pleasure to help when I can," Zora said while moving to the door.

Goran looked at Zora as if she were crazy. I could almost hear him thinking *"take the coins...take the coins!"*

But Zora was adamant. "I really cannot take your money."

"Well then, let me give you a gift. What will it be, a china vase?" she said, picking up a delicate vase from the sideboard.

"I don't think that would survive very long in Zora's wagon," Goran commented.

"You are right, young man," the woman said, looking around the room for a suitable gift.

"We really have everything we need," said Zora, restless to leave the house now that her work was done.

"I know something you may like. It is a curiosity that my husband brought back from his travels. It's like nothing I had ever seen before. Wait here a moment." She went out of the kitchen but was back shortly, holding something small wrapped in rough grey fabric in both her hands.

The packet seemed heavy for its size as she set it down on the table.

"What is it?" I asked her, looking expectantly at the package on the table.

"Have a look," she said, as she unwrapped the fabric.

Sitting there on the cloth was what looked like a dirty black stone. I looked more closely and saw that there were actually two stones stuck together. They weren't very pretty. Not like the stones Zora sometimes used to help her heal, or some people made into rings and necklaces. These just looked like very black rocks.

"What's so special about those rocks?" Goran asked.

I blushed at the rudeness of his question although I had to admit I was thinking the same thing. There was a look on Zora's face I had never seen before. Her eyes lit up and her smile was broad. For the first time she actually looked like the child that she still, just barely, was.

"Do you know what these are?" the woman asked Zora.

"I have seen something like them once before, many, many years ago. It was at a gathering of all the gypsy bands. A woman from another band had some and showed them to me. No one in our band has any. They are very hard to come by," she said, looking with fascination at the rocks.

"Yes, they are rare indeed," the woman said, "and I insist on giving them to you."

"But what are they?" Goran interrupted, his curiosity getting the better of him.

"Try to pull them apart," the woman told him.

Goran, pulling a face, took one in each hand and pulled. Nothing happened.

"They are stuck together," he said. "If we get a hammer and awl I can get them apart."

Zora moved closer to the rocks. She took hold of them, jiggled them a bit and then pulled them hard away from one another.

"We don't need a hammer," she said, giggling.

Zora, giggling! What were in those rocks? Were they magic laughing rocks? But they only had that effect on Zora.

"Watch this," she said, turning one of the rocks the other way. She tried to put them back together, but every time that they got close it was if something pushed them away from each other.

"Let me try that," Goran said, reaching out for the rock.

"Be careful with them," Zora said, "Don't drop them!"

"This is so strange!" said Goran, trying to push the two stones close together. "Here, Milada. You try it."

He handed me the two rocks. They felt heavy in my hands. I tried to push them together one way but they just wouldn't go. I turned one around and they snapped together with a *clack* nearly catching my finger in between them. I put them back on the cloth. I wasn't sure if I liked these strange rocks or not!

"Can I really have them?" Zora asked, gently caressing the ugly rocks, and still smiling.

"Yes, my dear. They have been sitting in a drawer for years. The boys played with them when they were small, but got bored with them as they grew older. You can play with them on your travels; show them to the children. I think my husband got them from some gypsies, a long time ago. That's why I thought you might like them."

"I do. I like them very much. And I can use them in my work," Zora said as she wrapped the stones back up in the grey fabric and tucked them into the pocket of her skirt. "Thank you, so much!"

"I always knew they were magic," said the lady. "I just didn't know how to use them."

A few more words of thanks and we were out the door. I wanted to go and find Todor and the red-haired woman, Emilia, but Zora wanted to go back to the camp. I think she wanted to play with her rocks!

"You two can stay in the village, but I'm going back to camp now," she said.

She had left the bundles of herbs with the woman. Now she only had the empty cloths to carry so she didn't need our help.

"All right, we'll see you later," I said as Goran and I headed for the village square to see if Todor and Emilia were there making music in the sun.

Chapter 18

A Little Music in the Village Square

Todor and Emilia waved at us a when they saw us coming.

"We wondered if you would come back," Todor said, making room for us on the now shaded bench.

"Will you play for us?" I asked anxiously. "I'd love to hear you play."

Emilia smiled and picked up her mandolin. "And I would love to play for you!" she said with a smile.

She placed the instrument on her lap, closed her eyes and began a song, the many strings singing merrily as her fingers flew over them. Todor clapped along, holding the rhythm. When the song was finished, Emilia sighed and opened her eyes.

"That was wonderful!" I told her. "Could you always play like that?" I remembered how Bora had picked up the viol and played it beautifully.

"No, it took me many years of practice to learn. I lived with a gypsy band for some years, like you Milada. One of the gypsies taught me to play. But it never came as easily to me as it seemed for them."

"But you were a very good student," Todor said, smiling as he took up his own instrument. "Let's have another song!"

As Todor and Emilia played happily into the dusk I noticed some people at a nearby table staring at us. I whispered to Goran, "Look over there. Do you think those people are watching us?"

"I noticed them some time ago," Goran replied. "At first I thought they just liked the music. But look at their faces. They don't seem to enjoy the music at all."

I glanced over at them. Goran was right. One man with heavy jowls and greasy black hair was scowling.

"Maybe they don't like the music. Maybe it disturbs them," I said.

"Then why don't they leave?" said Goran. "There are other taverns they can sit and be miserable in!"

At the end of the song, Todor put his instrument down. "I'm ready to go back to our camp. Will you join us for our evening meal, Emilia?"

"I would like to," Emilia replied, "but Vesna has not come yet. She asked me to meet her here today."

"We've been here for hours. Night is falling. She won't come now," Todor said, "Let's go to my camp".

But just as Todor spoke we heard a voice call out.

"Emilia! There you are, my friend!" Goran and I both turned to look at the source of that loud call and nearly bumped our heads together.

"Vesna, there you are! We've been here all day waiting for you," Emilia said.

To me she sounded a little disappointed. I think she wanted to come back to our camp with us.

"Well, I'm here now and looking forward to a long chat," said Vesna, as Emilia's smile faded. "Is this that man I've been hearing about? The gypsy? Just couldn't stay away from them, could you?"

Although she was smiling Vesna's voice seemed hard and cold.

"Very good looking," she continued as if Todor were not sitting there beside Emilia. "I'd like to find a handsome gypsy boy of my own."

Her eye lit on Goran, passing right through me as if I weren't there.

"This one might turn out to be a looker when he grows up! And what's your name, boy?"

"None of your business," Goran muttered, the turning to me, "Come on, Milada, it's time to go. See you later Todor, Emilia."

"It was nice to meet you, Ma'am," I said to Emilia. "Thank you for playing your mandolin for us. I hope to hear you again sometime."

Goran was pulling on my arm, impatient to leave.

"I'd like that," she replied. Neither Goran nor I said goodbye to Vesna; nor she to us.

"I like Emilia," I said to Goran as we walked back to the camp. "She seems like one of us. I think it would be great if she marries Todor and comes to live with our band."

"They are not *our* band," Goran said, darkly. "We will never be a part of them. They see us as visitors, passing through. And that is what we are."

"Don't say that, Goran. They are the only family I have now." I said.

"How do you know that? You told me you had a grandfather. Maybe he still lives. What about aunts and uncles - or cousins your own age?"

I was so young when I left, and was so excited to join the gypsies that I had not really given much thought to my life before I came to live with them.

I remembered playing with children my age sometimes. But I didn't like to play with them as much as I liked going out into the fields with my Grandpa or all alone, to pick flowers and watch the animals. The children I remember were afraid to go into the woods. They liked to play in the village square, splashing me at the fountain, pulling my hair.

"Some children came to our house on feast days. Maybe they were my cousins," I told him.

"Have you ever been back to your village?" Goran asked me as we neared the clearing.

I saw Zora showing Layla the black rocks. I longed to go and join them, but they seemed to be deep in conversation.

"No, I haven't," I replied.

"You never asked the Baron to lead the group back there?" he asked.

"I would never ask the Baron such a thing! It's up to him where we go. He knows best what is good for us," I said.

Really, I had never considered the possibility of requesting that we return to my village. Sometimes I missed my Grandpa, but my life was so interesting, so full here that I had no thoughts of going back.

"Do you really think he does what's best for everyone?" Goran asked. "How do you know that he doesn't have his own business interests to satisfy?"

"Goran, you have been here only for a year," I said. "But even you can see that we are happy, and well cared for. Why are you so suspicious?"

"Because I know more of the real world," he said. "You are the one who is living in a dream. And one of these days you will wake up!"

Tears prickled in the back of my eyes. I felt so angry with Goran that I was afraid to say anything, knowing whatever I said would be hurtful. Without a reply I ran back to my wagon, threw myself down on my bed and let my tears flow.

After a while, there were no more tears, just an empty feeling. Was Goran right? Was my life with the gypsies just a dream that would some day come to an end? Did they see me as someone different, an outsider, one of the *Others*? I couldn't go back to my village. I knew no one there. The gypsies were my friends, my family, my everything.

I heard feet climbing the steps of the wagon and Tanya's soft voice calling my name. She found me on the bed, my pillow still wet with tears.

"Milada! Here you are!" she said. "The evening meal is ready and you were nowhere to be found."

"I'm not hungry," I said, my face still buried in the pillow.

"Come anyway, there will be music and dancing!" she said lightly.

When I did not stir she noticed my mood.

"What is it, my love," she said, sitting beside me on my bed and gently rubbing my back.

I felt her long plaits brush my cheek as she bent down to see my face.

"Crying? Oh Milada, what is it?" she said gently.

"Am I a part of your band? Goran said that we are not and that we will never be and that I'm dreaming if I think we are!" There, I had said it. It felt good to let my feelings out.

"Of course you are a part of our band," Tanya said, still stroking my back, "for as long as you would like to be."

I knew that would be forever.

Chapter 19

Natural Law

Hand in hand Tanya and I went to join the others for the evening meal. Many of the gypsies had already finished eating. Some were preparing their instruments, tuning up with each other on one side of the circle near the fire.

"Why is music so important to our people?" I asked Tanya while we ate. "Other people play music on feast days and special occasions. We have music almost every night, and sometimes in the day time, too!"

"Music is food for our soul, "she replied. "Just as we need to eat food to feed our body we need music and the joy of gathering together to feed a deeper part of ourselves."

"Is it this joy that keeps you all so young?" I asked, knowing that they were very different from other people but still not really understanding why.

"I have heard other people say that we have a secret elixir that we drink to keep young! That's nonsense. You are right. It is the joy we feel and our love for one another that makes us so different," she replied. "And our knowledge of natural law."

"What is natural law?" I asked.

"Natural law is the basis of all life on our planet." Tanya said.

"Our planet?" What was that?

Tanya giggled. 'How have you lived so long with us and you don't know about the planets, the sun, the moon and the stars?"

"Oh, Tanya," I said with a sigh, "there is so much to learn! I've learned about healing herbs and now colours from Zora. You've shown me how to take care of wounded animals. I dance with you and sing your songs, but there always is more to learn. Sometimes I think I ask too many questions and bother people; and sometimes when I ask a question I get an answer I don't understand."

"So, where do I start?" said Tanya, looking at me. She paused for a moment and then began. "You know everyday the sun rises in the east. It goes high up in the sky and then sets every evening in the west."

"Yes," I said. "Everybody knows that. The sun moves around the earth every day. We can see that."

"Most people think that the sun moves around the earth, but imagine for a moment that that is not true," Tanya said.

"How can it not be true? We see the sun come up and then go down again," I said, wondering what she was getting at.

"What if *we* are the ones doing the moving," she said. "The earth, the planet that we live on, is a huge sphere, round like the moon. It turns around itself once every day. The sun seems to rise and set because of the way our earth turns."

"So we are living on a giant ball turning around once a day?" I said in disbelief.

"That is correct. And the earth is moving around the sun at the same time. You know about the seasons. That summer is hot, winter is cold; fall and spring are in between. Didn't you ever wonder why?" she asked.

I had never really thought about it. "That's just the way it is," I said.

"Yes, and its part of natural law. By observing the way things work in nature we can understand many things on a deeper level," she continued. "Have you noticed that in summer the days are longer and the sun rises higher in the sky than in the winter? "

"Yes, I love the long summer days!" I said.

"The longest day of the year, the summer solstice, is called mid-summer," she explained. "The sun climbs highest in the sky and rises in the north-eastern part of the sky. It seems to rise in that same position for two or three days, then it starts its return journey toward the south. The days begin to grow shorter and shorter until one day in the autumn when day and night are the same length. We call this the equinox, because day and night are of equal length. The sun rises directly east and sets directly west. Some people set up stones or build wooden columns to mark these directions. If you know east and west, then you can find north and south. It is a way to understand the relation of places on our earth."

"I remember some tall wooden stakes set in a big circle," I said. "We made camp near them once. I felt there was something special there. You were all very quite. I was afraid to ask why."

"If you had asked then, you would know now," said Tanya with a smile. "These places have special meaning for our people. They connect us to where we came from," she said.

I wondered what she meant but before I had a chance to ask she continued to speak.

"After the equinox the nights grow longer than the days until the winter solstice. On that day the sun rises in the south-east and sets in the south-west.

You see that the sun in the winter stays lower in the sky. It never climbs right above our heads like it does in summer. After mid-winter the days get longer once again until the spring equinox, when once again they are the same length."

"I understand," I said. "But what can we learn from this?"

"We can understand that everything in life moves in cycles. Nothing stays the same. We may like the warm weather and long days of summer. But we know those days won't last forever. Things change in our lives all the time. We have good times and sometimes things seem bad."

"What do you mean, they seem bad? The *are* bad - like when my Grandma died!" I said, remembering the feelings I had that day.

"It's not easy to tell what is good and what is bad. We need time, and hindsight to see the bigger picture. You like living with us, don't you?"

"Yes, of course I do! I can't imagine living anywhere else," I said from my heart.

"If that *bad* thing, your Grandma's death, hadn't happened then you would not be living here with us," Tanya said.

"I hadn't thought of that," I said.

"And, as the pleasant days of summer will not last forever, neither will the difficult days of winter. When you find yourself in an unhappy situation, if you understand natural law you will know that your unhappiness will not last forever. It will pass like a season. Don't run away from your sad feeling. Stay with it, see what you can learn from it, because every difficulty in your life presents an opportunity to learn something and to grow in wisdom."

I let out a big sigh, "I have so much to learn!" I told Tanya. Just then I heard Goran calling my name.

"Milada, where have you been? I need to tell you something," he said, plopping down next to Tanya and me. "Evening, Tanya! Have you seen Zora's new toy?"

"I saw her showing something to Layla but I didn't see what it was," she replied.

"Go and ask her about it. I'm sure she would love to show you her magic rocks!" he said.

"Magic rocks?" said Tanya, raising her auburn eyebrows, "Sounds intriguing! I'm going to see."

With that she hopped up and ran over to where Zora was sitting.

"What is it Goran?" I asked, still upset with him about what he said before dinner. I wondered if he knew anything about natural law, if he believed that the earth was a ball rolling around the sun. What Tanya said made sense but it was so hard to believe!

"Do you remember those people in the tavern? The ones who were watching us?" he asked me, when Tanya was out of earshot.

I could picture them in my mind. One was heavy, with strands of greasy black hair hanging behind his dirty ears. One was thin and very unkempt, with dusty clothes that seemed too big for his bony frame. The third man was good looking but there was something that didn't seem right about him. I could not say what was wrong; maybe it was the unpleasant expression on his face.

"Yes," I said, "I remember them well. Why?"

"You know when we were in the market to buy the vegetables for the soup?" he asked.

"Yes."

"I saw two of those men with Emilia's friend Vesna!"

"Really? Where were they?"

"They were standing in an alley," he said. "They were talking, and then looking around as if to see if anyone was listening to their conversation."

"Why didn't Vesna greet them in the tavern?" I asked him.

"That's what I was wondering, too. I know they saw each other. But she ignored them totally."

"I like Emilia but didn't have a good feeling at all about her friend," I said.

"The red-haired woman is all right, I guess, but I didn't like that Vesna person!" Goran replied.

"That was obvious. You were so rude to her," I said.

"Well, now you know why," he replied. "And she was rude to us, too."

"Emilia didn't seem to like her much either, even though she called her a friend. I think she wanted to come back here with Todor."

"No wonder the Baron isn't sure if he should allow Todor to marry the red-haired woman," Goran said.

"She has a name! And she lived with the gypsies like we do. I'm sure she would fit in," I told him.

"It's the Baron's decision, not yours," Goran replied. "And you said yourself - he always knows what's best!"

Chapter 20

The Gypsies' Secret?

Time passed and soon I forgot about Vesna and the strange men in the tavern. My days were full, collecting berries from the forest. In was early fall and the brambles were heavy with sweet, fat blackberries. Many of the young people were scattered around the woods with their collecting baskets. When a basket was full we would bring it to the central area where some of the women were busy at work. Some of the blackberries were cooked with honey and stored in earthen jars for the winter. Others were squeezed through wicker nets and the dark purple juice flowed into a big vat. Some honey was added and a white powder that Goran brought from the baker was added to the juice. I asked him what the powder was.

"It's what makes the bread rise when they bake it," he said. "It makes the juice turn into wine."

"Is it magic?" I asked, "It sounds like it!"

"It's not magic, everyone knows about it," he replied.

"I didn't know about it," I said.

"Well, now you do," he said and went off with his berry basket swinging.

The juice was set aside for a few days until bubbles began to break through the layer of crushed berries on the surface. It was as if it were boiling without any fire to heat it. I touched the vat to see if it was hot, not leaving my finger there for long in case it got burnt, but it wasn't hot at all. There were hundreds of little gnats flying above the vat.

I asked Layla what was happening.

She said, "The juice of the berries is fermenting. The sugar in it is turning to alcohol. Soon we will have blackberry wine."

"How do you know when it is ready?" I asked.

"When the gnats go away," she replied. "Then we strain the juice and put it into a sealed barrel. In a few weeks it will be ready. Just in time for Todor's wedding."

"Did the Baron give his permission for Todor to marry Emilia, then?" I asked her. I hadn't heard the news.

"Yes, my father had a long talk with them both. Todor really loves the woman. He was willing to leave the band to stay with her. But we would miss him too much! And Emilia is familiar with our ways and wishes to join us."

"So it is not impossible for one of the gypsies to marry an outsider?" I asked, thinking of my own chances of marriage with Dragan.

"It doesn't happen very often," Layla replied, "but is it not impossible."

Before that information could sink in there was a loud rustle coming from the thick undergrowth. Layla and I both looked in the direction of the sound. Coming through the thicket, her long plaits full of leaves and small twigs Tanya emerged carrying a young fawn.

"Come and see," Tanya said, "I found her underneath a blackberry bush. I think her leg is broken."

Layla and I moved closer to see the fawn. One of its legs was hanging at an unnatural angle.

"Please hold her, Milada, while I go get a stick to use as a splint and some rags."

I took the fawn in my lap, cradling its head in my hand. It looked up at me with its big brown eyes and my heart went out to it.

"Poor thing," I said to Layla. "I wonder where its mother is."

Layla caressed its flank, "I don't know. She may have been shot by a hunter's arrow. Usually a doe stays close to her fawn."

Tanya returned with her supplies. Zora was with her. I held the fawn while Tanya set the broken leg. All the time Layla stroked the fawn to keep her calm. When the leg was secured in the splint Zora took the rocks from the lady in town out of her pocket. She pulled them apart and placed one rock on one side of the broken bone and the other rock on the other side.

"This is the 'magic' of these rocks," she said. "They hold a special energy that speeds up healing of broken bones."

"Will the deer be able to run again tomorrow? " I asked.

"Not tomorrow. But if her bone would mend in a month by itself, it will mend in half that time with the help of the stones," Zora told us.

"Will you leave them on her leg all the time?" I asked.

"No, I will keep them on the injury for a little while now and again in the morning. I'll do that every day until I can see it's getting better," she said.

Layla went back to the blackberries. Tanya, Zora and I sat with the fawn, in silence.

"You picked all the blackberries in the woods already? There are no more left to collect? Is that why you three are just sitting around?" Goran called out, holding a very full basket of berries.

"Shhhh! You'll wake the fawn," I said.

Goran put his basket down next to Layla and came over to where we sat.

"What happened to its leg?" He asked joining us on the mossy ground.

"I don't know how, but she broke it," Tanya told him. "I put it in a splint and Zora is using her rocks to help it mend faster."

Goran looked at the rocks and then at Zora. "How can those old rocks help heal the deer's leg?" he asked her.

"Remember the force you felt pulling the rocks back together?" she asked him.

"Yes, it was strong!" he said.

"Well that force, when it passes through the damaged bone helps it to heal faster," she told him. "Wait and see how quickly the fawn will be able to walk again."

"Will she walk in time for Todor's wedding?" I asked.

"So the Baron decided to let it go ahead?" Goran asked, shaking his head.

"I thought you liked Emilia, " I said.

"I don't trust those friends of hers," Goran replied.

"We don't know that those men even know her!" I said.

"Well that weasel Vesna does", he retorted.

"What are you two on about?" Tanya said, looking up from the injured fawn.

"Nothing, really," I said. "I like Emilia, and Todor seems to really love her."

"Sometimes it takes more than love to make a marriage work," said Zora, darkly.

"Do you have love potions to make people get on better? Gypsies do, don't they?" Goran asked, looking seriously at Zora.

"Yes, we have love potions," she said, "and wealth dust and all sorts of magic rocks."

There was a twinkle in her eye. Did Zora make a joke? Maybe those really *were* magic rocks!

"Come on lazy bones," Goran said, giving me a little punch on the shoulder, "Let's go find more blackberries before it gets too dark to see them."

He gave me a hand up, looking right into my eyes as I pulled myself from the ground. I could not read his look.

"Where's your basket?" he asked me.

I pointed in the direction of Layla. Goran ran and got my basket and presented it to me with a flourish.

"My lady's basket!" he said. What's got into him, I wondered?

When we were away from the others he grabbed my arm and started running down the path. When we were too far to be overheard he stopped and pulled me to the ground.

"What is it?" I asked, wondering at this strange behaviour.

"I went into the village today; to the market square," he said.

"Yes, and?"

"I saw that Vesna again. She was with those men."

"Did she see you?" I asked.

"No, I was careful to stay in the shadows. I pulled my cap down low over my face and got close enough to hear what they were saying."

"And what were the talking about? The rising price of carrots?"

"No, they were talking about the gypsies!"

"About us?" I wondered why.

"About the gypsies' secret."

"What secret? I don't know about any secret!"

"I told you we don't know everything about the gypsies!" he exclaimed.

"What did they say about this secret?" I asked.
"They were saying that the gypsies never get old."

I didn't know how old the gypsies actually were, but none of them looked very old. Mother Miriana had silver hair but she was fit and graceful with hardly a line on her face, not like the white-haired women in the villages who shuffled stiffly through the square as if it pained them to take a step.

"They said that the gypsies must have a secret potion that keeps them youthful. And that potion would be worth a lot of money!" he said.

"There's no secret potion!" I exclaimed.

"How do you know?" he asked.

"I just know. But I will ask Layla. She will tell me the truth."

Light was fading. I remembered what Tanya had told me about the days getting shorter.

"We better get back to the camp," I said to Goran, "it's getting dark."

I wondered if I should tell him what Tanya told me, about the earth being a ball going around the sun. I decided not to. I didn't think he would believe me.

Chapter 21

I Become a Boy

It was decided to stay in our camp near the village until Todor and Emilia's wedding. The Baron said that we would move on the day after the wedding. It was already late in the year to be in the highlands. There was much to do in the camp, both in preparation for the wedding and also amassing a good store of food for the winter that would soon be upon us. The villagers gave us bushels of onions and garlic. We dried them and strung them together, hanging them like garlands from the rafters of our wagons, adding a festive touch.

There was much to-ing and fro-ing back and forth from the village. Two or three days went by in this flurry of activity before I noticed that Goran was seldom around our camp. Even at the mid-day meal he was absent. That evening I saw him arrive at our evening fire.

"Where have you been?" I asked him, before he had time to prepare his plate of food. We both piled our plates with stew made from wild boar and vegetables then settled ourselves near the fire. The nights were cold now. It would soon be time to move on to a warmer place.

I waited as long as I could while Goran wolfed down his stew.

"So where have you been these days? I hardly ever see you around the camp." I said, curious as ever.

"I've been in the village, " he said. "I found a job!"

"A job?"

"Yes," he said. "I went to the house of the woman whose husband Zora helped. I told her I knew she wanted to stay home to nurse her husband and offered to run errands for her and do odd jobs around her house."

"But we are so busy here, now, preparing for the winter and for Todor's wedding," I said.

"There are many people here to do the work. The lady, her name is Mrs. Dushanka, needs help," he said, "and she pays me well!"

"You take money from her?" I asked.

"Why not? She has lots of it!"

"Why do you need money? Everything we need the gypsies provide for us."

"I may not always live with the gypsies," he said. "In the real world people need real money."

"Are you planning to leave us?" I asked.

Even though he had only been with us a year or so, it was hard to imagine life without him around. I had missed him the last few days.

"Not now, but one day the time will come when it feels right to move on. Maybe you will want to leave with me?" he added, looking down at his empty plate.

"I will never leave the gypsies," I said without giving it a thought.

"Never is a long time," Goran said, turning to look at me in that funny way.

Anxious to change the subject, I asked him, "Have you seen Vesna and those strange men?"

"Yes," he replied. "Every day I go to the market for Mrs. Dushanka. And every day I see the men sitting in the tavern, talking and drinking. I've never seen Vesna with them in the tavern, but I *have* seen her talking to one of the men in the alley near the market square a few times."

"Could you hear what they were saying?" I asked him.

"I wasn't able to get close enough again without them seeing me," he said. "Why don't you come to the village with me tomorrow? Maybe the two of us can find a way to get close enough to overhear what they are talking about."

The following morning we met at the breakfast fire.

"I'm ready to go," I told Goran, excited at the thought of what we were going to do, and a little afraid at the same time.

"Go back and change your clothes into something less bright," he told me. "We don't want to be noticed. You will stand out in those colours."

I never thought about how we must look to the villagers. We always wore bright happy colours. It wasn't until I heard Goran's words that I realized the people in the villages dressed much more sombrely in shades of brown and grey.

"I don't think I have anything less bright," I told him.

"Come with me!" He grabbed my hand and pulled me toward the wagon he shared with Bora and Nico. He shooed away several dogs that were enjoying the sun in front of the wagon. Many dogs travelled with us. They lounged around in the sun all day, rousing themselves only to beg for scraps from our meals. At night they slept near the wagons and warned us if any person or animal came near. When we moved, they moved with us, unlike the cats that, with the few exceptional cats that had adopted a particular person or wagon, stayed behind. When we set up a new camp, after a day or two there would always be new cats!

Goran pulled me inside the wagon, rustled around in a wooden chest under the window and threw what seemed to be a bundle of rags at me. As I caught them, Goran said, "Quickly, put them on and meet me outside."

He hopped out of the wagon as I called to his back, "But these are boys clothes!"

He called back, laughing, "Today you'll be one of the boys!"

I shook out the clothes and looked at them. Brown. *Not* my favourite colour. I took off my embroidered yellow blouse and wide red skirt. I really did not want to wear the drab boys' clothes, but Goran was right about the colour being less noticeable. But what about a girl dressed as a boy? Wouldn't that attract attention?

I put on the itchy shirt, then released my long hair from under the collar. As I pulled on the Goran's rough britches, I thought I'm never going to pull this off. I am a girl!

I stepped off the wagon, my legs feeling strangely free in the britches, but I missed the feel of my skirt swishing around my knees.

"How do I look?" I asked, "Like a *Mladen*, not a Milada?"

"With that hair? You must be joking!" he said, pulling his knife out of its sheath.

"No way am I cutting it!" I said, gathering my hair protectively.

"Just kidding," Goran said. "I like your long hair. I'll get you a cap and you can tuck it under."

He popped into the wagon and was out again with an old blue cap. "Hold your hair up, " he instructed me.

I twisted it at the back of my neck and held it to my head as Goran pulled the hat down firmly.

"There you go," he said, standing back to survey his work. "Not half bad. I think you'll pass. Can you walk like a boy?"

"How does a boy walk? " I asked him.

"Like this," he said, shoving his hands deep in his pockets and striding forward, leading with his chin.

"Like this?" I said, sticking out my chin and doing what I thought was the same thing.

When Goran stopped laughing he said, "No, not quite. I hope I don't look like that. Try it again!"

I tried the walk again, this time remembering to shove my hands deep into the pockets of my britches. But as soon as my right hand went in it came out again. There was something disgusting in there!

"What is it!" I screamed as something flew out of the pocket when I pulled out my hand!

"Oh, that's where Lizzie went!" he said running over to the thing on the ground.

"Lizzie?"

"Lizzie is a lizard I found last week. I was going to show you, but then she disappeared! I guess I forgot her in my pocket."

"Is she dead?" I asked, coming a little closer. Just then, the seeming lifeless shape turned over and ran right past me into a nearby bush. I jumped back screaming.

"Come on, Milada, you have lived in the woods for years. I can't believe you are afraid of a little lizard."

"I'm not afraid of them," I replied. "I just don't like when they make sudden movements like that - or when I stick my hand in a pocket and touch something I don't expect to be there!"

"Let's get going. You can practice walking like a boy on the way to the village. And if we run into any lizards, snakes, bats, whatever, remember you are a *boy*!"

The two of us strode off down the path toward the village. I was glad we didn't have to pass through camp. I suppose I could say we were just playing a game. But it wasn't usual for us girls to go around pretending to be boys!

Chapter 22

A Conversation in the Alley

I strode along, confident that I was mastering the *boy walk* until we neared the edge of the village.

"I'll never fool anyone with this outfit." I said, ready to turn around and go back to the safety and bustle of our camp.

"Come on. Milada, I mean *Mladen!*" Goran said, "You'll be fine".

He moved to grab my arm, then remembered that I was supposed to be a boy and let his hand fall to his side.

"Come on Mladen! I'll race you to the fountain!"

And away he went. I ran after him, nearly tripping as I tried to run like I thought a boy would run. In the end I just ran like I always did while keeping one hand firmly on my cap.

We blended in with the other children playing at the village fountain. Goran pulled me behind it and without saying a word indicated the tavern. I saw the three men sitting in the tavern in the same place they were the day we met Emilia.

As if he read my mind, Goran said, "They always sit at that table."

"Quick," Goran said, "here she comes. And here comes the Baron and some of the other men of the band".

I pulled my cap farther over my eyes and we both slumped down as if fascinated by the water in the fountain.

I heard Vesna's nasal voice.

"Good day, Baron," she said. I could see her image reflected in the cascading water of the fountain. She stood very close to our Baron, with one hand on her hip and the other fingering a lock of her thin hair.

"And what brings such a handsome man to our village square this day?" she continued. "Looking for someone to show you around? I'd be happy to."

"Thank you, madam," he said, quickly putting more distance between them, "but I have many tasks to attend to."

As he and the others of our band passed the tavern one of Vesna's friends spat on the ground and muttered some words I couldn't catch.

"How can they be so disrespectful of our Baron?" I whispered to Goran.

"To them he is a 'dirty gypsy'," he said. "They cannot fathom his wisdom and kindness."

"Where did Vesna go?" I asked, noticing that she was no longer in the square.

"Look, there are only two men now in the tavern. The skinny one is gone. I bet you we'll find him in the alleyway with Vesna," Goran said. "Let's go and see if we can find them. But first we need a plan."

We sat on the steps of the fountain, trying to work out how we could get close enough to hear what they said.

"You could pretend to be a beggar," said Goran, thoughtfully. "You could sit in the alley and pretend you are blind. Set your cap out for people to put coins in."

"That won't work," I told him, "for two reasons. First no intelligent beggar would sit in a quiet alley. It's much better to sit in the square where lots of people pass. And second, if I take off my cap my hair will fall down and it will be obvious that I am not a boy!"

"You're right," he said. "Let's think of something else."

He sat in silence for a couple of minutes then said, "What would make two boys linger in an alley?"

"They could be trying to catch something. Or to collect insects?" I suggested.

"That might work in the woods, but not in an alley," he said.

We thought some more.

"I have another idea," I said. "What if the two boys dropped the coins from their pocket? They would stay to pick them up."

"What if Vesna and the man tried to pick up the coins the boys dropped?" he said. "It seems something they would do."

Yes, Goran was right. They would want to take the coins for themselves.

"But stopping to pick something that we drop would give us a reason to stay in the alley. It has to be something that wouldn't interest the others, though, definitely not coins!" he said.

"What do we have that we can drop?" I asked. "Not our caps..."

"We don't have anything, but I have some coins. We can buy something and then drop it," Goran told me.

"What shall we buy? Apples?" I suggested.

"We would pick them up too fast, unless we bought more apples than we could carry. We need something that would take time," he said, scratching his head thoughtfully.

"What about grapes?" I suggested, "They're small and will roll off in every direction.

"The ones that come off the stem will roll all right. I guess we could take them off the stem before we go into the alley. But it might seem strange and attract attention. And grapes squash so easily. When you drop grapes you often just leave them."

"Let's walk around the market and see if we get any ideas," I said. "And we can pass in front of the alley and see if they are there. Maybe they aren't even meeting today, so we'd better buy something that we can really use."

We walked to the market square. The red-faced baker's wife called out, "'Morning Goran! Your usual today?"

"No, thank you!" he called back.

"Who's the lad?" she asked with a smile.

The *lad* was me!! I was happy that my disguise was working.

"A friend from the camp," he said. "I'll see you tomorrow."

As we went past the cheese sellers, several vendors called out their greetings to Goran.

"Does everybody in the market know you?" I asked him in astonishment.

"Most of the vendors do," he replied. "They know I'm helping Mrs. Dushanka. And they know that she has money to spend."

"Why is money so important to these people? The gypsies never worry about money?" I asked him.

"People give the gypsies gifts of food, wine, tools, clothes, everything. In the villages, people need money for those things. Sometimes they exchange things they make or food they grow for other things that they need. But money makes trading easier. You don't have to find someone who has what you need and also wants what you have to offer," he explained.

The alley was just to our right. From the far side of the square, where we were, we could not see anyone there.

"Maybe they are farther back, in the shadows," I said.

"Let's not walk over there to look," said Goran. "If they are there it might make us look suspicious."

"All right, let's see if we can find anything good in this part of the market." I agreed.

We continued to the area of the fruit sellers. We passed over the apples, pears and other large fruit. There were berries, but they presented the same problem as grapes would. Then we passed a stall displaying dried fruit and nuts.

At the same time, Goran and I exclaimed, "Walnuts!"

"Walnuts won't break when we drop them," he said.

"And they don't get squishy!" I added. "And they roll really well."

"And we can buy a lot of them, they are not expensive," Goran said.

"And I love them, so even if Vesna and the men aren't there we can enjoy eating the walnuts!" I added.

We bought a large bag of nuts and walked slowly toward the alley.

"Walk quietly and don't talk too much," Goran said seriously. "I think I can see them over there, a little way down the alley. When we get close enough I'll drop the nuts. You go after the ones that roll away. I'll stay close to Vesna and the man."

"Then you'll be able to hear them, but I won't." I complained.

"If you stay too close they might see that you are a girl," he said, "Don't worry. I'll tell you everything I hear. Now, try not to talk. Follow my lead."

I took a deep breath and followed Goran into the alley. The tall houses on either side prevented much light from reaching the surface of the narrow street. There was an unpleasant sour smell, like the when four cats were trapped in Goran's wagon all day. I was going to say something about it, but then remembered we'd agreed that we wouldn't speak to each other.

Just then a huge rat ran across our path. We were very near Vesna who was deep in conversation with one of the men. I was ready to scream, but Goran jabbed me in my rib with his elbow and mouthed the words, *"You're a boy!"*

We were too close for me to feel comfortable. The man, who I remembered as being thin, from this close looked like a skeleton wearing clothes. He smelled even worse than the alley. I wondered how Vesna could stand so close to him and still be able to breathe, let alone speak.

They did not seem to notice us as we walked by. Just as we passed them Goran let the nuts run out of the bag. They made a loud noise as they dropped, the clacking sound each made as it hit the cobblestones echoed off the nearby walls.

The bony man looked over his emaciated shoulder. Goran was crouched just behind him while I was already moving away, chasing a nut. I wasn't too far to hear the man tell Vesna, in a gravely voice, "Clumsy children! Now, where were we?"

I followed the nuts out of earshot, but I knew Goran was near enough to hear everything that was said. Luckily, Vesna and the man took no notice of our presence.

As I picked up the last nut, one that had rolled half way down the alley, I saw Vesna leaving in the direction of the market square. The skinny man walked by past me towards the other end of the alleyway. I kept my head down and could smell him as he went by.

With my pockets full of nuts I ran back to where Goran was still crouched. His face was white. I could see he was very upset.

Chapter 23

A Dark Plot?

"Goran, tell me what they said". From the look on Goran's face I knew it was nothing good.

"Not now," he said, standing up slowly.

Some walnuts dropped from his lap as he stood. Their clacking on the cobbles broke the silence. I ran to collect the nuts. Goran stood still in the shadowy alley.

"Come on, let's go," I said, forgetting I was supposed to be a boy and taking him by the arm. "You can tell me when we get to the woods."

He shook off my arm and headed out of the alley to the square. We walked quickly passed the fountain. I saw Todor and Emilia sitting in the tavern. Vesna sat with them. They were laughing about something. I pulled my hat down more firmly and quickened my pace. I didn't want Todor to notice me and wonder at my attire.

Luckily he had eyes only for his bride-to-be and Goran and I passed unnoticed. As soon as we left the village for the safety of the woods I pulled off my cap and shook down my hair. My head was hot and itchy. I looked forward to changing back into my own comfortable clothes, but not before I heard what the people had said in the alley.

"Tell me, Goran," I said. I sat down on a mossy bank at the side of the stream that led to our camp. "It can't be *that* bad."

"It can be *that* bad, and worse," he said, "they are determined to find out the gypsies' secret. They will stop at nothing to get it."

"But there *is* no secret," I said.

"Maybe there isn't," he said, "but those people think there is and they will kill one of the gypsies to get it!"

"Kill one of us?" I exclaimed. "How can we tell them a secret that doesn't exist?"

"Apparently, Vesna asked Emilia to get it out of Todor. But Emilia told her there was no secret."

"Is Emilia in on the plot with Vesna?" I asked, hoping the answer would be no.

"I don't think do," Goran replied. "Vesna said that Emilia was a fool to believe there was no secret when it's obvious that there is, and that they will have to try another way to get it."

"What other way, did they say?"

"They will kidnap one of the gypsies," Goran said. "If they find out the secret the gypsy will be released. Otherwise…"

"Did they say which of us was the target?" I asked.

Goran hesitated then said, "No. I didn't hear any names mentioned."

"Maybe it will be Todor, since he goes to the tavern everyday it would be easy to trick him into a house and lock him in. Should we warn him?" I asked.

"No, I don't think we should say anything yet," Goran replied. "Maybe they are just talking and will not do anything."

Something felt strange. I thought to myself *Goran knows more than he is telling me.*

"I think even if it is only a possibility we should tell someone what we heard. We should tell the Baron."

"Do you think he would believe us?" Goran said scornfully. "We are not a part of their band."

"Why would we say something that wasn't true? We should tell him what we heard."

Goran still looked uncertain.

"We'll tell him tonight after the evening meal," I insisted and went to change my clothes at last.

But that night the Baron and his son were absent from the campfire. I asked Tanya if she knew why.

"The Baron heard that there was another band of gypsies related to ours camping in a nearby valley. Todor's brothers travel with that band. The Baron went to tell them about Todor's wedding and Dragan went along to keep him company," Tanya told us.

"When will they be back?" I asked.

"I don't know exactly, a week maybe," Tanya replied. "For sure they'll be here in time for the wedding."

"Goran and I went to the village today," I said. I wanted to tell her what we learned, but Goran interrupted me.

"And bought some lovely walnuts." He took some out of his pocket and handed them to Tanya. "Try one!"

While Tanya cracked the nut's hard shell, Goran gave me a look that said *don't say anything!* I gave him one back that said *why not?* He just shook his head. I hadn't heard what was said so really it was for Goran to tell and, for some reason, he didn't want to.

"This walnut is delicious," Tanya said. "May I have another one?"

"Certainly," Goran said, handing her another one. "I'm going to see what Bora is up too. Maybe we will have music tonight."

He got up and went over to where Bora sat by the fire.

"Do you think it's a good idea for Todor to marry Emilia?" I asked Tanya.

"There are always problems when someone from our band marries an outsider," she said. "There was some trouble today because Emilia's parents wish for her to be married in their village church."

"Why is that a problem?" I asked.

"Because Todor is not of her faith. Her priest will not allow it," she replied.

Tanya could see that I did not understand what she told me.

She continued, "The people in the villages call their church the *house of God*. On Sundays they all visit God at his home and pray and sing together."

"I've heard the sound of singing coming from the church. It was pleasant but the songs didn't seem happy like ours," I said.

"I know what you mean," Tanya said. "I like the church bells, though."

"Yes, so do I," I said. "But why can't Todor marry Emilia there?"

"Their priest will only marry people of the same faith. Todor, like the rest of us, believes that God is everywhere, and we can pray everywhere, beside every tree, every mountain, every stream, not only in a church built by human hands, and not only on a Sunday! Everything we do is a prayer, is an honour to the Great Spirit and the goodness in everything."

"So what will they do?" I asked.

"They love each other and want to be together. Since Emilia will be travelling with us she decided to marry here, in our way, and then we will bring a feast to the village square to share with her friends and family."

"The other day, Zora said that sometimes love wasn't enough for a successful marriage. What did she mean?" I asked.

"When two people come together it doesn't affect just them. Their families marry each other, too, in a way. When people join in marriage and especially if they have children then the families are forever connected. The way we live, travelling all the time, maybe this isn't so important. But for the people in the villages, if the members of the families don't like each other there can be big problems!"

"Tanya, do you know who the Baron has chosen to be your husband?" I had been dying to ask her this question, and this seemed like a good chance.

"I think I do," she replied. "But I cannot speak his name."

"Is he someone from our band? Someone you like?"

"Oh, Milada, marriage is still a long way off. Let's enjoy being young a while longer!" she said jumping up and running toward the goat pen.

I followed her over to see the kids, still suckling their mother's milk. I wondered about telling her what Vesna and the man had said. But seeing Tanya so happy playing with the baby goats I thought, *why upset her.* Maybe Goran was right, maybe it was just talk and would come to nothing.

I went back to the fire and saw him sitting with Bora and the other boys. I wondered if he would tell them what he heard. I started to go over to them, but my feet were dragging on the ground I was so tired. I turned the other way and went to my wagon. With a last look up at the stars I pulled the curtain closed and curled up in my bed, exhausted from my long and strange day as a boy.

Chapter 24

Preparing for the Wedding

I woke up to the unusual sound of bustle in the camp. The smell of food cooking, the clatter of metal pots and rasping sound of knives being sharpened were ordinary enough, but not going on all at the same time and not at this early hour of the day. I looked over at Tanya's bed. It was empty. Of course she was already up, feeding her animals and lending a hand in the wedding preparations. I wondered why, after so many years living with the gypsy band I still could not rise like they did at the first light of dawn.

I got out of bed, feeling a little chill in the air. Summer was coming to an end. Tanya had left a pitcher of water for me outside our wagon. I splashed my face and felt ready to see what this day would bring. Despite the festive feeling in the camp as people all worked together to prepare for Todor and Emilia's wedding feast I felt uncomfortable with the knowledge of what we overheard in the alley. I helped myself to some soup from the heavy iron kettle that simmered over a low fire, and went to look for Goran.

I heard the boys shouting to one another at the edge of the camp. Following the sound of their voices, I found them erecting a wooden frame that would make a canopy for the wedding.

"'Morning, Milada!" Nico called to me from his perch high on the corner of the structure.

"'Morning!" I called back. Although there were several boys involved in this project Goran was not among them.

"Have you seen Goran?" I asked, to no one in particular.

Nico replied, "I saw him when we had our breakfast. I think Layla asked him to go with her to the village."

I decided to go to the village to find them. We could tell Layla what we heard. She would know what to do. As I passed through the centre of the camp to reach the path to the village, Mother Miriana called out to me.

"Milada! Would you come and help me with these apples, please?" Oh no. If Mother Miriana asked, I was obliged to obey. Usually I would relish the opportunity to help. But not right now!

As we sat side by side peeling basketsful of sweet-smelling apples I thought about the danger we were in. I wondered if I could tell Mother Miriana about Vesna and the plot to kidnap one of us. No, not without Goran…ouch! A million miles away from what I was doing, I nicked my finger with the sharp blade of the paring knife.

"Milada, where are you, my child? I've never seen you so quiet! And now look what you've done! Let me see."

I held out my bleeding finger. It didn't hurt but blood was dripping onto the sliced apples. I looked down at their white flesh dotted with bright specks of red and felt a chill go down my spine.

"Let me put some salve on that. It will prevent the wound from festering and help it to heal quickly." Mother Miriana produced a clean handkerchief from her apron pocket and quickly wrapped my finger, holding tight to stem the flow of blood.

"Hold you finger and follow me to my wagon', she said, setting aside the bowl of apples from her lap.

At her wagon, she washed my cut in fresh water then applied a strange smelling paste that she spooned out of a small brass box that was kept on a high shelf above the window of her wagon. I'd seen her use this salve on many wounds in the past, but never before thought to ask her what it was. This time my curiosity got the better of me.

"What is the paste that helps wounds heal quickly," I asked her as she bandaged my finger in a bit of white linen, "and why does it smell so odd?"

"This paste is very precious," she replied. "Some of the ingredients come from a long way away, from special trees that only grow in hot places far south of here."

"How do you get it if it from trees that don't grow here?" I asked, surprised at my own boldness.

Mother Miriana smiled. "Now our Milada's back - back to her questions, always questions. I was wondering when you would ask me about my medicines. I see that you are interested, but you are shy around me."

Blushing, I replied, "Yes, I guess I've always been a little bit afraid of you. You know so much. And you are so much older than the others and so wise. I didn't want to waste your time with my silly questions."

"Wanting to learn is never silly, Milada," she said looking right into my eyes. "I am older because I have much knowledge to share. I am teaching Zora and some of the other young girls the secrets of healing plants. I would be happy to share some of my knowledge with you, too, if you would like to learn."

Maybe Mother Miriana has the secret that Vesna and the others want so badly. "Yes, I would like to learn, very much! But why are these things secret?"

"They are not really secret," Mother Miriana replied. "It's just that not many people make the time and effort to learn. I know many things. Some of them you will learn and remember."

"Do people from outside the gypsy bands know about the healing plants?" I asked.

"They know about some of them," Mother Miriana replied. "They know about the remedies that can be made from plants that grow where they live. Since our people travel we can learn about and use plants from far and wide. When we have gatherings with other bands we exchange our knowledge and our ingredients, too. That is how I came by the special substance in this salve."

She indicated the brass box, now back in its place on the shelf.

We walked together back to where we'd left the half-peeled apples. I felt more comfortable now and decided to ask Mother Miriana one more question.

"Mother Miriana," I asked, with just a little hesitation, "Do the gypsies have a secret that only they know?"

"Yes," she said, with her head bent down to the apple she was peeling.

"Can you tell me?" I asked, also looking intently at my apple.

"No," she replied, "I cannot tell you."

I felt tears welling up in my eyes. So there *was* a secret. Vesna was right! And it was a secret from *me*, too. So Goran was right, too, when he said that we were not considered part of the gypsy band.

As if Mother Miriana knew what I was thinking she put her knife down and rested her hand on my shoulder.

"There will be a time for you to know the secret of the gypsies. But you will find it out for yourself." She smiled, but it was a sad smile, a smile of someone who knows too much.

Chapter 25

To Tell or Not To Tell

With most of the wedding preparations complete we gathered around the fire for our evening meal. In spite of the days of hard work getting ready for Todor and Emilia's wedding and collecting and preserving food to serve us through the coming winter months spirits were high. There was a buzz of chatter as various groups of friends discussed the events of the coming day. I heard the first strains of music rising as the instruments were being tuned. But I was not in a festive mood at all, sitting beside Tanya and Zora, nibbling on my meal, still concerned that the Baron and Dragan had not returned and did not know about Vesna's plot.

"Tomorrow is the wedding," I said to them. "Will the Baron be here?"

"If he is not back, there will be no wedding," Zora replied.

I knew that the Baron conducted the wedding ceremonies. It was up to him to give the couple his blessing and confirm their union as married people.

"I'm surprised that he and Dragan aren't back yet," I said. I missed having Dragan at the campfire, with his smiling eyes always ready for a laugh. When I sat beside him I could feel his warmth; not only the warmth of his tall, strong body but also the warmth of his heart. I had a similar feeling when I hugged his sister, Layla. Layla who had made me feel welcome and safe when I first came to live with the gypsy band.

"I'm sure they'll be back tonight or tomorrow morning in time for the wedding," Tanya said with a sweet smile.

I really wanted to tell Tanya what Goran and I heard in the alley. But we promised each other that we would only tell the Baron. Maybe there was nothing to tell. I surely hoped so!

I got up and went to where Goran sat with the other boys. When he saw me he rose and met me by the fire.

"What if the Baron isn't back before the wedding?" I asked him. "We won't be able to warn him."

Goran replied, "The more I think about it," he said, 'the more I think we ought to mind our own business and keep our mouths shut."

"Are you saying that we shouldn't tell the Baron?" I asked, shocked.

"Can we be sure we heard right? We don't know that the gypsies have a secret. And anyway, why would the Baron believe us?" Goran replied.

"They *do* have a secret!" I blurted out. "What if we don't tell him and then someone is hurt? We have to tell him. It's up to him if he believes us or not."

"Well, we can't tell him if he isn't here," Goran said.

"We can tell someone else. We can tell Mother Miriana," I told him.

"If we tell her, what will she do? She'll tell us to tell the Baron," he said.

I knew he was right. The Baron was the one to tell. Tomorrow was the wedding. The Baron would be back for sure and we would tell him what we heard. He would know what to do. Until then we would just have to wait and hope that nothing would happen. No point in worrying the others. Tomorrow would be a happy day, the big celebration, and then we would be moving our camp further south for the cold winter months.

"We'll be leaving this camp in a day or two," I said, trying to convince myself and Goran that there was no danger from Vesna and her cohorts. "What can they do tomorrow? It's the wedding. We will all be together so how can they kidnap anyone? And then we leave. Maybe you are right and we won't have to tell anyone."

"Let's enjoy this evening and the wedding tomorrow. I'll be sorry to leave this place and my job with Mrs. Dushanka. But I won't miss Vesna and her "friends"," Goran replied as he took my hand and led me closer to the spirited music.

I found Layla next to the musicians, tapping her foot and swaying to the rhythm. When she saw me she put her arm around my shoulders.

'Hello, Milada, my friend. I see you've been busy helping Mother Miriana…and asking lots of question, as usual!" she said.

"I hope I didn't bother her," I said, 'but she told me if I don't ask I won't learn."

"She told me you asked about the secret." Layla was looking at the fire. I was happy that she didn't see the look in my eyes.

"I heard there was a secret. And that people wanted to know it," I said softly.

"Where did you hear this," she asked, still gazing into the fire. 'We don't speak of such things among ourselves."

"I heard it in the village," I said. I hadn't promised Goran that I wouldn't talk about the secret, only about Vesna's plan. "Some people were talking and I overheard them."

"People in the villages talk about a lot of things that they do not understand," Layla said, thoughtfully.

"But Mother Miriana said there *is* a secret," I said without thinking, "but she wouldn't tell me what it is.'

"It's not really a secret. It's something we all know," Layla said. "And someday you will know, too, without anyone telling you."

"That is what Mother Miriana told me, too," I replied.

Of course I wanted to know *now*, but at least I felt confident that I would learn the secret sometime; that I *was* considered one of the gypsy band.

"Enough talk of secrets. I know you love to dance as much as I do. Come!"

Layla led me to where the others were dancing around the fire. As I twirled and spun, feeling the heat from the flames, my anxieties melted away. My body took on a life of its own. My mind did not direct its motion; it was free to soar with the rising music. I felt the rhythm of my bare feet touching the earth and drawing up its energy. I never tired when I danced. Only when the music stopped did I realize that I'd been dancing for hours and could barely walk the short distance to the wagon I shared with my friends. Sometimes, like tonight, they would be lost in the dance, too. Other times I would come in as quietly as I could so I wouldn't disturb their peaceful slumber.

Tomorrow would be an exciting day. It had been several years since the last marriage in our band. I looked forward to eating all the delicious food that had been prepared and other, different delicacies that Emilia's family in the village would offer. If only Vesna and those men would just disappear!

As I lay in my bed that night, listening to the faint chirping of the last crickets of summer, I wondered if it would have been better never to have overheard that conversation. But we did hear it and we had to do something about it. If only the Baron were here.

Chapter 26

A Wedding Day

The morning of the wedding I woke to the sound of plates clinking and laughter tinkling. Tanya gently nudged my shoulder.

"Wake up, sleepy head," she said with a laugh. "It's nearly time for the wedding."

I opened my eyes and saw that Tanya's long hair was braided with brightly coloured ribbons and that she was wearing a skirt of her favourite colour, green with golden embroidery. Her bright green shawl brought out the green in her eyes, sparkling even more than they usually did.

"I'm awake," I said, not really sure if I was or if I was still asleep and dreaming. How could I have overslept today, the day of the wedding?

"Come on and get ready for the celebration! I brought you some herbal tea; breakfast has long been cleared away!'

I didn't usually oversleep. It must have been all that dancing! Tanya helped me into a festive red skirt with an extra flounce. Layla had recently given it to me as she did each time I grew too big for the previous one.

"Here is a new red ribbon for you hair," Tanya said, holding out a long strip of red satin.

"Thank you!" I told her, as I gathered a small section of hair and tied on a bow. Tanya loved her plaits, but I liked to let my hair flow free, adding the ribbon only as a festive touch.

I drank the tea and felt happy and ready to greet the day. But then I remembered. I remembered what Goran and I must tell the Baron.

I ran to catch up with Tanya and asked, "Did the Baron and Dragan return?"

'Oh yes," she said, "They arrived late last night just as the last embers of the fire were fading."

"I must find the Baron. Goran and I have something important to tell him." I said.

"The Baron will be preparing for the wedding. What ever it is will have to wait until later," Tanya said and stopped in her tracks. "What do you and Goran want to say to the Baron? Are you two thinking of getting married?"

"Tanya! If I'm thinking of marrying anyone it certainly isn't Goran!" I said, shocked at the thought.

"Well the way he sometimes looks at you I'm sure that the idea has passed through *his* mind!" she said with a giggle. "And you do spend a lot of time together."

"He's my friend," I said, "like you, like Bora and the others."

"If you say so," she said with another giggle as we continued to follow the sound of happy voices.

Imagine Tanya thinking Goran and I will marry someday! At least she didn't ask me again what we had to tell the Baron!

As we neared the centre of the camp I saw that the wedding canopy had been completed. The wooden frame was now decorated with boughs of golden leaves from the forest's trees. Garlands of wild vines lined the square frame with many brightly coloured ribbons strung at each of the four corners fluttering prettily in the gentle breeze.

I looked for Goran in the crowd, and for the Baron. Goran saw me and started to come in my direction when suddenly the wedding music begun. A clattering of drums and tambourines announced that the bride and groom were on their way.

The bride's party approached from the east; a line of women walking two by two beating a compelling rhythm on their tambourines. At the end of the procession the bride sat on a white horse, looking radiant in a splendid green dress that complemented her auburn hair.

At the same time, the groom's party came from the west. The groom, seated on a jet-black horse, came forward surrounded by the men in a loose mob, playing drums in a counter rhythm to the one that the women played. The sound was mesmerizing and all conversation ceased as people began to breath in time with the rhythm and each other.

Although I'd been to weddings before this was the first time I noticed the effect the mingled rhythms had on us. I could feel the earth vibrating with the nuptial drums like the heartbeat of an unborn child. We were all vibrating to this same heartbeat, inhaling and exhaling together, stepping together as one being. It was as if we were all being united, not only the bride and the groom.

The hypnotic rhythm drew us all toward the canopy. There, the Baron waited for the couple to dismount and join him on the raised platform beneath. When the three of them stood under the canopy the drums dropped in volume but still continued to beat an accompaniment to the Baron's words.

"Friends," he began. "This is a joyful day! With the wide sky above and the sacred earth below these two people come to join as one for this time of marriage. I invoke the spirit of the earth to give them structure and support in their life together and provide for their physical needs. I invoke the spirit of water to give their life a steady flow and to quench their thirst. I invoke the spirit of fire to give them passion and to keep them warm. And I invoke the spirit of air to connect them with all beings and to give them the breath they need to live."

He took Emilia's right hand, raised it to his lips and gave it a gentle kiss.

"Welcome to our band," he said softly.

Then he took Todor's right hand and brought it together with Emilia's. Looking at the couple he said, "As leader of this band I give you to each other, to love and to protect come what may. May you be blessed with the bounty of the earth and grow old in happiness together."

With tears glistening in her eyes Emilia looked up at Todor. He pulled her close to him and embraced her as the beating of the drums rose in volume. As if on cue the other instruments began to play and everyone let out a whoop of joy. I heard the cry come from my mouth as well and found myself crying and laughing at the same time.

Over the music and the drums and the joyful noise of the people the Baron's powerful voice rang out, "It is done! Come now to the feast!"

As I turned to go toward the village my joy was suddenly deadened by the sight of Vesna and her three friends standing on the edge of the crowd. They were the only ones not smiling. They talked among themselves, not even looking at the happy couple moving in their direction.

Chapter 27

Kidnapped

People were climbing on wagons that were already loaded with food for the feast. The whole band was going into the village to celebrate the marriage. I knew I had to find Goran and then go and tell the Baron what we heard. Since I saw Vesna at the wedding I had a sinking feeling in the pit of my stomach. I ran between the wagons, hoping to find Goran before they started to move toward the village.

Tanya called to me, "Come on Milada, hop up here with me."

'I'm looking for Goran," I told her.

"Are you?" she said with a wink and a giggle. "I think he went on the wine wagon up front. He seems to have developed a taste for it."

I could see that the wagons had already started to move so I climbed up with Tanya.

"Wasn't that a wonderful ceremony?" I said.

"As yours will be with Goran!" she laughed.

"I told you we were friends!" I said.

Then I asked something I had been wondering.

"Tanya, will the Baron choose a husband for me? He didn't choose Emilia for Todor, he found her for himself."

Tanya replied, "I don't really know. I know that some of us have a destiny within the band to marry as the Baron directs us. You know my husband has been decided. But since you joined us, that is, you were not born into the band, I don't think that you have that responsibility."

Should I tell her that I dream of being Dragan's wife? How I imaged the two of us standing under the canopy receiving the Baron's blessings. No. I will keep that dream to myself. Dragan would have to marry someone born in the band. But if he loved me? The way he takes me on his horse and rides with me through the fields; the way he comes and sits beside me at the fire and sometimes picks me up and twirls me when we dance; the nice things he says to me; the smile in his eyes. But, if I think about it, he is charming with everyone. Yet maybe there is hope.

"Milada, Milada," said Tanya, shaking me out of my reverie, "where are you?"

"I'm right here," I told her. But I didn't tell her what I was thinking, even if she *is* my best friend!

Soon we stopped in the village square and unloaded the provisions on the long trestle tables that the villagers had set up for the feast. As soon as my wagon was unloaded I ran to find Goran.

He was at the wine cart, tapping the barrel into earthenware jugs to go on each of the tables. There was a very strange look in his eyes.

"Hiya Milla," he said. He had never called me "Milla" before.

"Come on Goran," I said pulling him away from the cask. "We have to go and find the Baron. Now. I saw Vesna and the others at the wedding. It's going to happen today!"

"Now, now, Milla. Don't you worry your little head," he said stumbling to the wooden bench at a nearby table.

"Goran!" What's the matter with you?" As I said the words I realized what the matter was. He had been sampling the wine! All the way from our camp by the looks of it.

"Oh Goran, what have you done?"

"I'm celebrating!" he said with a lopsided grin. "Have a glass yourself! Don't worry, no one's gonna kidnap our Layla."

Layla! Oh no. That is what Goran was holding back. He knew that if I thought that Layla were in danger I would not be able to hold my tongue. I looked at him and realized that he would be no help now and ran off to find Layla and the Baron.

I returned to where I left Tanya.

"Have you seen Layla?" I asked her as she put the finishing touched on the table decorations.

"I saw her a little while ago with Dragan, heading to the field by the square. She's probably trying to reason with Dobro, his horse, to stay in the paddock with the other horses instead of at Dragan's side."

I ran off in the direction of the field. At least if she was with Dragan she would be safe. When I got there I saw Dragan, patting Dobro's velvety nose.

"Now, my friend," he was saying to his horse, "today you must stay here. Keep the others company. I have things to do in the village and the people will not accept a horse, even such a wonderful horse as you, in the middle of their party."

When he saw me he laughed and said, "You know how he is. It's nice to be loved but sometimes his attentions are just too much!"

As he spoke he, I could see that he had sensed that something was wrong. He opened his arms and I flew into them, tears of fear falling freely from my eyes.

I felt momentarily comforted by his warm embrace but knew there was no time to lose. I looked up at him and said "Oh, Dragan. Where's Layla?"

"She was here with me. A lady from the village came and said that a friend of hers had fallen and twisted his ankle. Of course Layla went to help."

"What did the woman look like," I asked with mounting fear.

"She was about so tall," about as high as Dragan's shoulder, with light brown hair, thin, pretty in a hard sort of way."

Vesna.

"Where did they go?" I asked him.

"Back toward the village square," he said. "Someone must have seen them there."

Without thinking I ran in the direction of the square. Looking back I should have told Dragan everything and asked for his help but I was so scared all I could think of was finding Layla as soon as possible.

I reached the square. Many tables were laid out and ready for the feast but people were still milling around, talking to each other and watching the sheep roasting on spits over the open fire. In my haste I nearly ran into Zora.

"Have you seen Layla?" I asked her, breathlessly.

"I saw her with Emilia's friend, the one who came to the wedding. They went into the alley over there." I looked where she was indicating and saw that it was the same smelly alley where Goran and I overheard the plan.

I ran off in the direction of the alley, reaching it just in time to see Vesna pushing Layla into a doorway at the far end. I was about to shout out, but luckily for once I didn't follow my first impulse. Calling out would do no good. It would only alert them that someone knew what was going on. I wished that Goran were here. He would have a plan to get Layla out of there!

I remembered what he told me, if you have the information, you have the upper hand. Slowly and quietly I made my way down the dark alley. The house on the end had no window onto the road but as I turned the corner I could hear voices coming from a grilled opening high up the wall on the far side of the house.

There was a pile of rocks beneath the window. I climbed up, careful not to dislodge any stones that might slide down and betray my presence. What I heard brought fresh tears to my eyes.

Chapter 28

A Friend in Danger

My fingers scraped on the rough stone wall as I pulled myself high enough to be able to gaze into the room. A lantern was lit and by its dim light I saw the large man push Layla onto a divan on the opposite side of the room. Vesna was locking the door.

"You thought we couldn't do it, didn't you? You and your people think you are so clever, with your travelling and your tricks," said Vesna, almost spitting the words into Layla's surprisingly serene face. "Well, you're not so clever, after all, now, are you?"

When Layla didn't respond the large man stepped toward her with his arm swung back, ready to give her a slap. I held my breath. Vesna saw him. She held up her hand and indicated for him to hold off.

"Wait Xeno. We don't want to hurt her," she told him, "Not yet." She turned back to look at Layla. "No, we don't want to hurt you. We just want to know the secret."

Layla stayed silent. She didn't look frightened or even concerned at the situation she was in! Not me! I felt hot tears rolling down my cheeks. Oh, why didn't we tell somebody? Why didn't Goran tell me that it was Layla that they were after? I felt that I could have stopped this. That it was all my fault!

The fat man, Xeno, said, "Let me beat it out of her. We haven't got all day."

"Silence!" she said. "How can she talk if she is beaten? You remember what happened the last time." Xeno hung his head.

"I remember," he said and slunk off to a dark corner where he sank down onto a stool that seemed too small to carry his heavy frame.

"Well, my dear," Vesna said looking back at Layla and trying a different tactic. She smiled and said, "Will you tell us? Tell us the secret of how you gypsies stay so young."

Layla looked Vesna directly in the eye and said, "There is no secret. We stay young because we are happy. We live simply, off the bounty of the land and from the generosity of others. We don't rely on money, houses or possessions for our happiness. We love and support each other and we end each day together in dance and in song. Living like that keeps us young."

"I know you have magic potions made from special plants that heal people. You must use something to keep you young?" Vesna hissed.

"Our people have knowledge of the use of many plants and herbs. Some of your people do, too. This is not magic. And each person, each illness needs special consideration. There is no one "potion" that will heal all," Layla calmly replied.

I could tell that Vesna was losing her patience and not satisfied with Layla's response. She started pacing up and down the small room, her eyes glancing in Xeno's direction.

'Maybe we *will* have to encourage her to talk," she said as she paced.

There was a loud wrap on the wooden door. Vesna opened it a crack and asked, "Who's there?"

"It's me, Lako," the skinny man said as he pushed his way in. "Emilia is asking for you. All the women are gathering for the bridal dance. You'd better go so she doesn't send someone to look for you."

"The last thing I want to do now is dance! I want the secret of youth!" Vesna spat.

At these words a tiny laugh escaped from Layla's lips. Her eyes were merry. Without thinking, Vesna slapped Layla's face with her open palm. I gasped then ducked my head down quickly in case someone heard me.

"What do you have to laugh about?" I heard her shout at Layla. "We can kill you, you know!"

Layla replied, "You say you want the secret of youth, but you won't dance. I told you the secret. You didn't listen."

I heard another slap. "Silence you insolent wanton! I'll give you until tonight to think about what will happen. If you don't tell us the secret we will kill you. Slowly. Xeno, you stay away. This is a job for Lako and his blade."

I pulled myself up, wanting to see what was going on and not wanting to all at the same time. My fear made my fingers slippery on the stones but I managed to regain my perch. When I saw what was happening I almost ran, but I steeled myself to look so I could report back to the Baron.

In the dim light, I saw that the skinny man held something in his hand and was approaching the bed where Layla had fallen back against the cushions from the force of the slap. He twitched and a long shiny blade appeared in his hand as if out of nowhere.

"Tonight, Vesna hissed, we'll put you somewhere safe. And tomorrow you will tell us the secret. If you are reluctant to do so, my friend Lako here will give you a little encouragement." She beckoned him closer. "Give her a little sample."

I held my breath and watched in horror as the man gently, almost lovingly, took Layla's hand then ran his blade the length of her forearm. A thin red line appeared. Layla sat up and looked at it, watching as her blood started to run down her arm and collect in a pool in the palm of her hand.

"What a lovely face you have," Vesna said, softly touching Layla's cheek. Suddenly she pulled back her hand and slapped the cheek hard. '

"What a shame we'll have to cut it. And if you don't tell us," she continued, "we'll start with these lovely fingers, one by one they'll fall, and then the toes. No more dancing then."

She cackled at her own wit and looked at the men to see if they got the joke. The heavy one just sat with his mouth hanging open staring at Layla.

The skinny one, Lako, cackled, "Ya, no more dancing, heh, heh," as he flicked away the blade of his knife.

"And speaking of dancing, I had better go before I am missed," Vesna said as she picked up her shawl and headed for the door. "Put her downstairs. And don't hurt her - *yet!*"

Vesna unlocked the door and hurried out. I wondered if anybody was looking for me. I needed to find the Baron, but I didn't want to go and leave Layla like this.

"Come on then," Lako said pulling Layla to her feet. You can cool off in the cellar".

I wondered why Layla didn't try to fight him. I'm sure she was stronger that the skinny man and could fight her way out of his grip. But then I remembered the heavy man, Xeno. He looked slow but there was so much of him, the two men together would be hard to take on.

"Come on you lazy one!" Lako shouted to Xeno, "Come and open the door to the cellar."

Xeno took a key from the peg beside a low door on my left. He put the key in the lock and turned it. The door swung open and Lako pushed Layla towards it.

I wished that I could tell Layla that I was here, that I had seen what had happened and that I would bring help. Just as that thought was in my mind, Layla turned and looked up, right at me at my perch behind the grill. I will never forget the look of love and sadness in her eyes.

Chapter 29

Light in the Darkness

As Layla disappeared through the dark doorway, I scrambled down the stones and looked to see if there was a low window in the wall to left of where I'd been. The path sloped down toward the river. A little way along the wall I saw another grated opening, barely above the ground. I knelt down and carefully looked through the rusty grate. When my eyes adjusted to the darkness within I saw Layla sitting on a pile of hay in the far corner. She was alone in the room. I heard the heavy wooden door slam shut and the key scraping in the lock.

I waited, holding my breath for a moment in case the men came back in. When they didn't, I called out to Layla, my voice barely above a whisper.

"Layla, Layla! Look up. I'm here!" I said, "I'll get help. Don't worry!"

Layla looked up at me. "Milada, child; how did you come here?"

"Goran and I overhead Vesna's plan to kidnap one of the clan. We wanted to warn the Baron but he did not return until this morning and now it's too late! I didn't know that she planned to kidnap *you*! I would have warned you to stay away from her!" I said as tears filled my eyes once again, seeing the red mark of Vesna's palm on Layla's lovely face.

"There was nothing you could do, Milada. Some things are meant to be. All things happen for a reason, even though we may not understand what that reason is," Layla said, coming over to the window.

"Still, I'm glad that you came," she said, reaching up to rest her fingertips on mine as they clung to the grimy grate.

I looked at her tapering fingers and remembered what Vesna had said about cutting them off. More tears came at the thought and I couldn't look at Layla. As if she knew my thoughts Layla said, "Don't worry my child, no one will hurt me."

"But they said that they would kill you if you won't tell them the secret!" I said through my tears.

"You know there is no secret to tell," she said.

"But there *is* a secret! Mother Miriana told me, and Tanya, too!"

"Did they tell you what it is?" Layla asked me, with a smile in her eyes.

"They said I would find out for myself! And if I knew it I would tell Vesna if it would save you!" I said without thinking.

Of course, that's why they didn't tell me! I'd do anything to help Layla. Anything.

"Milada," I heard Layla's voice as if through a thick fog. "There is something you can do for me."

'Anything,' I told her, "I'll do anything for you."

"Take this," she said, untying a pouch that was attached to her leather belt. She handed it to me and said, "Please give this to Tanya. Ask her to keep it for me. She'll know what I mean."

I took the small pouch. It was heavier that I expected it to be. For a moment I was hurt that she asked me to give it to Tanya instead of letting me keep it for her. I banished the thought and said, "Yes, of course I will give it to her."

"And here is something for you," she said, reaching up and lifting a leather thong from her neck. She handed me the necklace of golden amber beads strung onto the narrow leather band.

"Do you know where these stones come from?" she asked me.

"I know they are called "amber" and come from a tree, not from the ground like other stones." I said, proud that I knew it.

"Yes, pieces of amber are like tears of a great tree that have been preserved by pressure and the passing of time. If you look closely you will see tiny insects inside of some of the beads. These were stuck on the resin and preserved in it. The substance is living and holds some of my own life force because I've worn this necklace for many years," she said.

I remember seeing it on her. She wore it against her skin so it only showed when her blouse fell open at the neck while she was riding or dancing. I looked at the beautiful piece as she laid it in my hand.

"Wear it and think of me', she said as I put the amber around my neck. "Know I love you and I will always be with you. And that one day we will meet again."

She said these words with such a feeling of love, my tears stopped and my heart felt warm. For a moment I understood. But then the moment was gone and the tears came again.

"What are you saying? Are you going to run away?" I asked, hopeful that she had a plan to escape.

"In a way, yes I will run away," she said, "So don't worry about me, little one. All will be as it should be. Go now. Someday you will understand."

"Oh, Layla," I said and reached out to squeeze her hands, "Thank you for the beautiful necklace. I will wear it always and think of you. I love you so much, thank you for everything!"

I could see a touch of pain flicker across Layla's eyes, and then it was gone and her familiar smile returned.

"Go now," she said. "Enjoy the feast. Everything will be as it should be."

Layla looked up at me and gave my hands a last squeeze. She mouthed the word "*go*" as she let go of my hands and moved away from the window. With her pouch safe in the depths of my pocket and her amber hanging from my neck I slowly stood up and moved away from the window. It was hard to leave her alone in the dark room but she told me to go. I needed to find Goran and then tell the Baron what had happened.

I walked to the corner where the path met the alley and looked to see if anyone was there. It was deserted. I ran down the alley and back to the village square where the feast was in full swing. The music played, people laughed and enjoyed the food that was piled high on the long tables.

I saw the Baron sitting at the high table with the bride and groom. I started to go that way when a felt someone's hand on my arm. It was Bora.

He said, "Milada, where have you been? Goran's been looking for you everywhere! Come on!"

He took my hand and pulled me to a table at the edge of the square. Goran was sitting there with his head resting on his hands.

"I found her," Bora said as he plunked himself down on the bench next to Goran.

Goran looked up at me, his eyes red and sad. "Milada, I'm so sorry. I don't know what happened."

"What happened is what happens when somebody drinks too much blackberry wine!" I said. Bora laughed.

"I told you to stop," Bora said. "That happened to me once. The wine tasted so good, but it's not like drinking too much juice! It makes you crazy and then comes the headache."

Goran just groaned. I looked at Bora and said, "Please go get some water for Goran. I think it will help his head."

As soon as Bora left I whispered to Goran "They've got Layla". Why didn't you tell me it was she that they were after?"

"I really didn't think they were serious," he said. "How do you know they've got Layla?"

"I saw it all!" I told him. "They've locked her in a basement room, they slapped her and cut her arm. Vesna said that they will cut her face and then cut off her fingers and toes tomorrow if she doesn't tell them the secret. We need to tell the Baron!"

"Let's go," he said. Suddenly his head seemed clear.

Chapter 30

A Parting

We rushed back toward the sound of the voices raised in celebration. Todor's friends were competing with each other to offer the most colourful and sometimes embarrassing toast. People laughed and clapped their hands to the rhythm of the spontaneous rhymes. I could just make out that top of the Baron's head where we stood next to the groom, right in the centre of the crowd.

"How will we get to him?" I asked Goran.

"Let's go around and see if we can get there from the other side," he said.

As we skirted the crowd the band struck up again. The tight group of merrymakers spread out as some people began to dance while others settled back at the tables for another round of food and drink.

"Where is he now? I can't see the Baron?" I said.

It seemed that the whole square had erupted in a frenzied dance. Goran and I stood on the sidelines watching people twirl by. A group of Emilia's friends passed. Among them was Vesna. For a moment, our eyes met. I felt a chill run down my spine. Did she recognize me? But the momentum of the dance carried her out of my vision. Just then, Tanya grabbed me and pulled me into the dance.

"Where have you been, my friend?" she asked, with her arm around my shoulder. "You're missing the fun. It's a lovely wedding!"

As I looked into Tanya's smiling eyes I knew what I was about to say would take the shine right out of them. In that moment I could see that she sensed there was something wrong. She stopped dancing and we quickly moved away from the musicians.

"What's the matter, Milada?" she asked, "Has something happened?"

"They've got Layla!" I said, no longer to hold back the tears that welled up from my heart. "They're going to kill her tomorrow if she doesn't tell them the secret."

Tanya took me in her arms while I sobbed and sobbed. I tried to stop so I could tell her what happened but the words would not come. I felt her fingers touching Layla's amber necklace and saw a tear run down her cheek.

Suddenly, Goran was at our side, "There you are!" he said, "You disappeared!

"Did you find the Baron," I asked him.

"No, I was looking for you."

"Please tell me what has happened," Tanya asked, hastily brushing away the tear.

Goran started, "A couple of days ago we overheard some people talking in the village."

"They've got Layla!" I said at the same time. This was not time to tell long stories!

"Who has Layla? And why? You said before that they want to kill her? Whatever for?"

"They want to know the secret herbs that keep the gypsies young," Goran replied.

"There are no secret herbs," said Tanya.

"There is a secret, though," I said, feeling hurt that Tanya thought I didn't know that.

"It isn't something that can be told," Tanya said very seriously as another tear escaped her eye.

"We have to find the Baron and get him to save Layla before it's too late," I said, trying to pull myself together. "Let's all go and look for him."

The crowd was a lively as ever. Goran stood up on one of the wooden tables and looked over the bobbing heads of the dancers.

"Can you see him?" I shouted.

"No, I don't see him anywhere," he answered.

I climbed up beside him. Looking toward the fire I saw him. "There he is - over there!"

"That's not the Baron," Goran said, "It's Dragan."

I looked again and saw that he was right. "Let's tell Dragan, then. He'll know what to do," I said as I jumped down from the table.

I grabbed Tanya and Goran's hands in each of mine and we ran in the direction of the fire. When we neared the place I saw Dragan sitting on a wooden bench with his legs outstretched, drinking and laughing with a group of men from our band.

As we approached the fire he looked up as if he sensed that we were there. He smiled up at us, but instantly his face dropped. He excused himself from the group and came to join us. He put his hand on my shoulder and steered me away from the fire. Tanya and Goran followed.

"What is it, Milada? Has something happened?" he asked.

Before I could reply Goran said, "Layla's been kidnapped. We heard them planning it but didn't think it would actually happen."

There he goes with the long stories again. I interrupted him, "Dragan, you've got to come now, quickly. I know where they are keeping her. You've got to get her out of there tonight!"

As I said the words I noticed the first hint of pink in the eastern sky. It was nearly morning already. "Come, now. We have to hurry." I grabbed Dragan's arm, looked into his eyes, pleading with him to move.

"Don't you think we should consult the Baron," Goran said, as if Dragan's authority were not enough.

"We don't have any more time," I shouted. "Come on. Please! We have to save Layla."

There was a far away look in Dragan's eyes.

"I think it is already too late," Dragan said, as he gently touched the amber necklace I wore. I knew that recognised it as Layla's. "I think she has decided to go."

"Go? Go where?" I said. I felt I was loosing control of myself. Tears slid down my face. Why were they not moving?

"Come on!" I said, pulling on Dragan's arm. "They sliced her arm once and said they will cut her again and then kill her," I shouted. "I can show you where she is." This seemed to shake him into action.

"Let's go," he said, and the four of us took leave of the square and headed toward the darkened alleys of the town.

The sky was getting lighter by the minute as we hurried through the narrow streets. I led the group, still holding Dragan's hand. Its warm strength gave me some comfort, though the pit of my stomach felt knotted and cold.

"This is the place," I said, showing them the alley with the low window.

Dragan and I knelt down to look in, our heads close together. The others crowded in beside us to try and see through the small opening. It was very dim inside, with only the light was from the candle, now burned down to its base.

As my eyes got used to the light I saw Layla sleeping peacefully on the divan. How could she be so relaxed, after what Vesna had said and done! Her arms lay by her sides, palm facing upward. I looked for the long cut that

Lako had made with his sharp blade, a foretaste of what was to come, but there was no sign of any blood or mark.

Suddenly, voices echoed in the silent street. Someone was coming! Before we had a chance to move, I heard the front door creak open on its hinges. The voices were muffled now as the people moved inside. Soon the basement door was flung open and Vesna entered followed by Lako with Xeno bringing up the rear.

"Shut the door," Vesna hissed. "It's time to do this before all those fools go home to bed."

I held my breath, hoping no one would look up toward the grated opening. I expected Dragan to be on his feet, charging around the corner and into the room to stop them from hurting Layla, but he was still by my side.

"Wake up, my girl!" Vesna said, poking at Layla roughly, 'It's time for us to talk. Well, actually, it's time for *you* to talk!" she cackled.

When Layla did not stir Vesna shouted, "Wake her up, Xeno!"

Xeno stomped over to the divan and whacked Layla's face. I gasped; I couldn't help myself. I felt Goran shudder at my side. Dragan, though, did not move. Layla's head flopped over to one side, but nothing else moved. What was happening?

Vesna gasped. "She's dead!" She grabbed the skinny man, Lako, by his collar, "You idiot! I told you not to kill her before she told us the secret. Or maybe she told you the secret and then you killed her before she could tell us. Xeno, get him!"

Xeno held Lako easily in his bear-like grip. They were all yelling at each other.

Lako said, "If I killed her, where is the blood?"

That shut them all up. Then Vesna said, "Maybe she took poison. We should have searched her before leaving her alone. She's no use to us now."

Dragan pulled me away from the window just as Vesna looked over her shoulder in our direction. He put his arm around my shoulder and whispered, 'It is over". Come."

He took my hand in one of his and Tanya's in the other and led us away.

Goran turned to look at us, then indicated that he would stay, Dragan nodded and then led us away. I was numb. What happened? Was Layla dead? How? Why?

I looked up at Dragan, wanting to ask him all my questions, but the look in his eyes told me that this was not the time for questions and answers. It was the time for silence.

In silence we walked back to our camp, hand in hand. When we reached our wagon, Dragan let my hand go. He lifted me up and placed me up on the wagon's porch.

Resting his hand on my shoulder he said, 'I know you don't understand this now; maybe someday you will. Know that Layla made her choice and that we will see her again. For now, keep her alive in your heart".

He gently took my head between his two hands, bent my head toward his and kissed the centre of my forehead.

"Go now, lay down and rest. The band will move now, away from this place of sadness."

In a daze I opened the curtain, went inside and lay down on my bed, still in my festive red skirt, the ribbon now lank in my hair. I could hear Dragan and Tanya softly talking outside the wagon. Their voices were too low for me to follow. What were they saying? Layla had said that someday I would understand. I wondered if I ever could.

Chapter 31

Another Move

I don't think I slept at all that short night. I lay on my back, tears running down my face, unchecked into my ears. After a while, Tanya came in, but then went out again without a word. I remembered the pouch that Layla had given me for Tanya. I reached into my pocket and took it out. It felt heavy in my palm. I wanted to open it and see what was inside. Should I?

Before I had a chance to, Zora pushed open the curtain of the wagon. She saw that I was awake.

Before I could speak she said, "I know what happened. They're bringing her body home. We will bury it beneath the fire and then move our camp today. Come, there is much to do."

Zora was no longer wearing her festive clothes. When had she come in to change? Maybe I did doze off after all. I rose from my bed and changed my clothes. I felt sad looking at the red skirt, once my favourite, but which now would always remind me of loosing someone I loved so much.

I found Tanya and Zora packing up the many pots and kettles that were used for the wedding preparations. A quiet emptiness took the place of yesterday's festive anticipation. I looked around for Mother Miriana. She might have some wise words to help me understand why and how Layla died. I didn't see her anywhere.

"Tanya, have you seen Mother Miriana today?" I asked.

"She is with Layla," Tanya replied. "They will be back soon."

The way she said it made me forget for a moment that Layla was gone. Just then I head Goran calling me.

'Milada, there you are. Come here, I want to tell you something!" he called.

"Go on," Tanya said. "We are almost done. Zora and I will finish this."

I ran over to Goran. "What happened after I left?" I asked him, as I sat down next to him on a wooden chest waiting to be loaded onto the nearby wagon.

"They talked about taking someone else, but Vesna thought it would be too dangerous now. They were going to take Layla's body and throw it into the river but then decide just to leave it where it was. They have no idea we know about them."

"What will they do now?" I asked.

"Nothing. The townspeople will think we just moved on. Maybe they think Layla won't be missed? There is nothing to connect them to her," he said.

"Nothing except us! Does the Baron know?" I asked.

"Yes," said Goran. "Vesna and the others didn't stick around for long. If they had, Mother Miriana would have caught them."

"Mother Miriana?" I asked, puzzled. "What does she have to do with it?"

"Maybe Dragan or Tanya told her," he said. "But she arrived very soon. Almost before the others fled."

"And the Baron?" I asked.

"He arrived to take Layla's body just as Mother Miriana was finishing," Goran replied.

"Finishing what?" I asked him.

"She and two other gypsy women entered the room. They each had two wax candles about as long as my forearm. They put Layla's body in the middle of the room."

"On the floor?" I asked.

"Yes. They put a candle at her feet and two on each side of her body. One woman sat on each side. They were whispering something together. I could feel the rhythm but could not make out the words. They sounded very strange. Mother Miriana lit the sixth candle from the ember she always carries. She used that candle to light the others and then placed it at Layla's head. She knelt down beside it, gazing down at Layla's face with the palms of her hands facing down."

"Then she started to sing a strange song. Her voice was very low. Maybe I was just tired but I thought I saw light coming from Layla's body as Mother Miriana sang, moving her hands down the body and back up again three times. Then all the singing stopped. Mother Miriana placed her hands on Layla's head and bent down close like she was kissing it. Maybe she was kissing it. But then something really strange happened! All the candles went out! All by themselves! I'm sure no one blew them out," Goran said.

"Maybe there was a draft? Did someone open a door?" I asked.

"No," he continued. "They just went out. Then Mother Miriana and the others got up, took the candles and left. Just like that."

"And left Layla there?" I asked in disbelief.

"Yes, but almost as soon as they went, the Baron arrived with two men. They wrapped Layla up in a blanket and brought her back here. They are digging the pit under the fire now."

"How did Layla die?" I asked, not really expecting Goran to know.

"Maybe she *did* take poison. You know they know all about herbs. I bet there are some that can kill you," he said.

"Layla wouldn't kill herself. She loved life. Why would she carry poison leaves around, anyway? She didn't know she would be kidnapped," I reasoned.

Maybe she knew she was going to die, though, when she gave me the necklace and the pouch for Tanya. But, what did she say? She said to tell Tanya to keep it for her. Why would she say that if she knew she was going to die?

"Move along, children. It's nearly time to go." The men had come to load the crate that we'd been sitting on.

"Time to move on," said Goran. "They just throw her in the ground and leave. I don't know if I'll ever get used to the ways of the gypsies."

"I am sad and I am confused," I told him. 'But I know the body that we are leaving behind is not Layla. Her spirit is somewhere else, free, maybe travelling with us. Somehow I feel I'll see her again."

"When you die, you die. End of story," Goran said.

Somehow those words did not ring true.

PART 2

THE FIRST QUARTER

Chapter 32

Of Heaven and Hell

Once again we moved on, leaving the village. The first months were strange for me. I'd come to expect to see Layla several times a day, always with a smile on her lips. At night, there was music at the fireside as before, but Layla was not there to pull me into the dance. I always wore the amber necklace that she gave me. It made me feel like she was still close by, somehow.

Todor's new wife travelled with us for a few weeks, but she missed her comfortable life in the village and soon returned to her family there. Todor went with her at first but after a while he returned to our gypsy group, telling people that he preferred life on the road with them. Nothing was said about Layla's passing. How could everyone have forgotten her? I felt sad, and also angry.

One day, not long after we moved on I asked Goran, "Why didn't the Baron do something? We knew who took Layla, we told him, but all he did was to have her body brought back to us and then we left. Didn't he care?"

"That's what they always do when one of the gypsies dies. In the villages people cry and tear their hair in mourning. They bring flowers to the graves of the people who have died. They remember them and pray for their souls," he said.

"What's a soul?" I asked.

"I don't really know. I remember my mother saying that you have to be good or your soul will burn in hell when you die," he said.

I didn't understand what he was talking about.

"What is "hell"? How can you burn when you are dead? Maybe a soul is something people get when they grow up and people burn it when they die. But what does that have to do with being bad or good?" I asked him.

"When you are good, your soul goes to heaven," he said, not paying attention to my questions.

"Heaven? Where is heaven?" I asked, not really expecting much of an answer.

"It's up in the sky. The angels live there. They sing sweetly all day long," he said, "That's what people say, anyway. I've never seen an angel. I don't think that they are real. I think people just say these things to make children do what grow-ups want them to."

"Children here don't know anything about hell and heaven. We do what we are told because we understand that the grown-ups know better and want to help us to learn," I said. "Isn't it funny to tell children their souls will burn up if they aren't good!"

I still didn't know what a soul was. I still wondered!

That evening I saw Mother Miriana with some of the other women preparing vegetables for the evening meal. I went up to her and asked if I could help.

"Of course you can, little one," she said handing me some turnips. "Be careful with the knife!"

When I finished cleaning the bunch of turnips I cut them in pieces like I saw Mother Miriana doing and placed them in the pot with the other vegetables.

"Mother Miriana," I said, "Can I ask you a question?"

"Of course you may, my child," she said. "I was wondering when you would!"

"Mother Miriana, what is a soul?"

"A soul is the part of you that gives life to your body. The part that lives on after you die," she said.

"So when a person dies, a part of them lives on?" I asked.

"Yes, my child. The body is the temporary home of the soul. The soul creates it, uses it for a while and then moves on to other worlds."

"To heaven?" I asked.

"The other worlds can be called by many names" she replied.

"Can a soul burn in hell? Does it hurt?" I asked, still confused.

"Who told you about burning in hell, my child?" she asked with a smile.

"Goran said that the people in the villages say that," I replied. 'He said that if a person is good their soul will go to heaven and if a person is bad then it will go to hell. Is there a hell?"

"Yes, my child, heaven and hell exist, but here, for the living, not after the body dies."

"Where is heaven?" I asked her, "and where is hell? I hope we don't go anywhere near it!"

Mother Miriana laughed. "They are not places. They exist in the minds of the people. People make their own heaven and their own hell by the way they choose to engage with the world around them."

"What do you mean?" I asked her.

"As you know, my child, things are always changing. Things are the way that they are. Nothing is good or bad. When we eat a chicken for dinner, you could say it is good for us and bad for the chicken!"

I never really thought about that. "But when those people took Layla, that was bad," I said.

"It was sad for us to loose our sister, but we cannot know the bigger picture and what part Layla's passing has in it. Of course we feel sad because we miss her presence, but some day each body will die, just as the trees loose their leaves each winter and the grass dries and perishes," she said.

"But being angry about what happened will not bring Layla back. Anger is a way that people create their own hell. Fear is another way. If you live without anger, fear and desire your life will be happy. You will live in heaven."

"But the leaves come back in the spring. The grass grows again," I said.

Mother Miriana just looked at me and smiled.

Chapter 33

Layla's Gift

And so the winter passed; our camp moving from place to place, while we helped to make the lives of the village folk lighter with our music and our healing herbs. One day in early spring there was a festival in the village near where we were staying. For the first time in months I remembered my pretty red skirt. As I lifted it from the chest where it was thrown it that morning so many months ago, I felt something heavy in the folds of its fabric. It was the pouch that Layla had given me for Tanya. I ran out to find her.

Tanya was sitting under a tree with a mother cat and her five small kittens. Their eyes had just begun to open and they were starting to explore their world.

"Milada, come and see!" she said when she saw me coming. "Look how this one is so curious. There is one brave kitten in every litter, and one that is very shy."

I sat down beside her and watched as the kittens played in front of us. Their mother watched them and also watched us to make sure that we would not hurt her babies.

"Tanya, I'm so sorry! I forgot all about this," I said as I held out the small leather pouch. "Layla gave it to me to give to you, that day." I couldn't bring myself to say "the day she died".

"Thank you, Milada," she said as she gently took it from my hand.

"Layla said to tell you to keep it for her. She said you would know what that meant. Maybe she isn't really dead?"

Suddenly my heart leap with the possibility that we would meet Layla again somewhere on our travels; that she had only pretended to die; that an empty blanket was buried under the fire, not Layla's lovely body.

Tanya did not reply to my question or confirm my hopes. She said, "I know what this is. It is very precious. Shall I show you?"

"Oh, yes, please!" I said, and moved closer to Tanya as she drew a clear crystal sphere out of the pouch. It sat in the palm of her hand, catching the sunlight.

'It's beautiful," I said, looking at the clear stone.

"Yes, it is very beautiful and very precious. There are only a few of these in the world. Mother Miriana has one. They are kept within the gypsy bands, never traded or sold."

"It is very pretty but what do you do with it?" I asked.

"There are many ways to use a stone like this," Tanya replied. "Look at my hand through the stone."

I looked. I could see all the small lines on Tanya's palm.

"What do you see?" she asked.

"I see the lines on your hands; really clearly," I replied.

"Do you know you can tell a lot about a person by the lines on her hands?" she asked.

I nodded. I'd seen some of the gypsy women looking at people's palms in the villages that we passed through.

"The stone helps us to see things more clearly. Look," she said as she gently picked up the bravest kitten. She held the stone near the kitten's head. Looking through it I could see all the details of its fur and markings and even a tiny tick that was lodged behind its eat.

Tanya handed me the stone while she removed the tick. 'See how useful it is!" she laughed.

"What else can it do?" I asked.

"Watch this," she said. She placed the kitten down next to its mother and went over to a sunny spot among the trees. She gathered some dry leaves and made a small pile of them surrounded by a circle of stones.

"Let me have the stone, please," she said.

It felt comfortable in my palm, almost as if I were holding a person's hand; maybe Layla's hand. Reluctantly I passed it to Tanya. She placed it on a small tripod that she had made out of twigs. It was a warm day so we sat down under a nearby tree.

We sat in silence for a while. Tanya closed her eyes and seemed almost asleep. I was too excited, wondering what was going to happen with Layla's stone.

I heard a noise coming from the thick part of the forest. Then I heard Goran's voice, "Hello Milada, Tanya! What are you doing out here?"

Tanya opened her eyes and smiled. 'We're watching Layla's stone," I told him, realizing as I said it that it was a strange thing to sit around watching a rock!

Tanya said, "Let's go have a look".

The stone looked the same, but as we got closer I noticed smoke coming from the pile of leaves under it.

Goran said, "Did you take an ember from the fire this morning?"

Tanya said, "No, I made the fire with this crystal."

My eyes opened wide. "It's a magic crystal! That was the secret that those people wanted! Layla could have given them the stone and she would still be with us today!" I felt angry that Layla would leave us, just to protect this magic rock.

Tanya put her arm around me and said, "No, my friend, this is not a magic rock. Its round shape gathers the rays from the sun into a small point. It becomes very, very hot and that heat makes the dry leaves burn."

She carefully removed the stone from the twigs and put it on top of the pouch in a shady spot. Then she put out the fire by covering it with soil.

"It is very useful to have one of these in case you need to make a fire and don't have an ember. But it doesn't work at night or on a cloudy day!" she said as she wiped the stone on her skirt and put it in its pouch.

"I was looking for you to tell you that we are moving on now. We should be at our new camp by nightfall," Goran said.

Tanya went back to the cat family and gathered the kittens in her wide skirt. "Somebody please bring the mother cat?" she called as she walked back toward our wagon.

I picked up the mother cat, who was not very happy about it. I very nearly got a scratch from her sharp claws. Goran followed me.

As he caught up and walked beside me he said, "Nobody told us about these stones before. See, they still don't think of us as a part of their group."

"Don't be so sensitive," I told him, struggling to hold on to the writhing cat. "We just didn't have the opportunity to see one."

"How did Tanya know what to do with it, then? Someone must have shown her," Goran said.

"Maybe she saw Layla using it, or Mother Miriana. Tanya said she has one, too," I replied.

"I don't like Mother Miriana. I think she's a witch," Goran said. "She's always talking in riddles."

"Don't say such things!" I told him. "She helps so many people with her knowledge."

It was getting very difficult to walk and hold the cat. I held it out to Goran. "Here, take this cat, will you?"

He tried to hold it but it arched its back and jumped out of his arms. "Stupid animal!" he yelled. "It scratched me! Look, I'm bleeding."

"Come on. Tanya will have some salve for it. Hopefully the cat will find her way to her kittens and not get left behind."

Chapter 34

Moon Time

I found Tanya in our wagon, securing the last of our things before moving off. The kittens were asleep together in a wicker basket. Their mother was beside them, glaring at Goran with her shining yellow eyes

"Look," I said, pointing at the cat, "she knew exactly where her kittens were!"

"Stupid cat,' he said, now looking at Tanya, who was smiling. "Look what it did to me!"

He showed Tanya the scratch. It had stopped bleeding but was red and swollen. She went to the chest and took out a small vial.

"Sit here," she said. Goran did as he was told. She applied some of the creamy substance to the wound and immediately the swelling went down.

Goran smiled at her. "That's better," he said. "I'm going to ride with the boys." And with that, he was off.

The mother cat settled down to sleep with her kittens. I wrapped my green shawl around my shoulders. There was a chill in the air that would get stronger when we started off then settled down on the seat next to Tanya as she clicked the horse into motion.

"We are so lucky to know about healing plants," I said to her. "When the people in the villages are hurt or get sick they don't know what to do."

"They have some knowledge," she said. "We have so much more because for many years our people have travelled and learned the ways of many places. We meet and share our knowledge and our plants. Then we are able to help others," Tanya said.

I felt happy to be a part of this group. The rest of the wagons and people on horseback joined the road and formed a colourful but dusty column as we moved along at a steady pace.

After travelling for a few hours I had an uncomfortable sensation. I felt dampness between my legs. I thought that maybe I needed to relieve myself and went to the wagon to use the chamber pot. I thought to myself that it was a good thing that this was a smooth stretch of road.

When I took down my underclothes I saw blood. I didn't do anything that would make me bleed. I wondered where it had come from, if there was something wrong with me. I changed my underclothes and went back to Tanya.

"Tanya," I said, "I found blood on my underclothes. I feel fine, but is something wrong with me?"

Tanya looked at me and smiled. "There is nothing wrong with you," she said. "You are just growing up. This is moon-blood. It is part of being a woman. When we camp tonight you will join Zora and the others in the tent of the moon-time women."

I wondered why sometimes Zora did not travel with us in our wagon anymore. In the last few months it was not unusual. She was not with us today.

"What do the women do in the moon-time tent?" I asked.

"I can guess," Tanya said, "but tonight you will know."

Part of me felt a little frightened, but of course I was very curious and couldn't wait until the riders and wagons gathered in a flat clearing for the night.

While Tanya was unhitching the horses I ran off to find Zora. When I ran I felt a little pain in my abdomen. I wondered if that had to do with the bleeding and slowed to a walk. I found Zora with many other women off to the side of the main camp.

"What are you doing here?" she asked when she saw me. "Is someone looking for me?"

"I'm looking for you," I said. "Tanya told me to come and join you and the moon-time women."

I saw a smile slowly breaking over Zora's serious face. "Have you seen your moon-blood?" she asked.

"Yes. Is there something wrong with me? Is something hurt inside?" I asked.

She took my hand and then pulled me into her arms and gave me a big hug, something very unusual for her to do!

"Milada, welcome to our sisterhood. The moon-blood is the mark of your coming of age. Once it begins, you stop being a child and become a young woman, able to have a child of her own. Come and join the others."

What did she mean by "once it begins"?

"Will I keep bleeding all the time?" I asked.

131

"No, not all the time," she replied. "Your moon blood will come for a few days every month."

She led me to a large tent that had already been set up under some tall trees.

Beside the tent was a line hung with long strips of pinkish cloth, blowing in the light breeze like festive flags. I'd noticed these flags before and wondered about them, but it was one of those things that nobody mentioned. Zora took one of the cloth strips off the line and showed me how to fold it into a small rectangle.

"We use these to catch the blood," she said. "When it is soiled, wash it in cold water and hang it out, then take a clean one from the line."

I felt more comfortable with my cloth padding, but still confused as to why I was bleeding and why Zora seemed so calm about it.

"Come," she said. "Let's go inside."

From the outside, the tent looked like one of the usual large ones that we used for meals and gatherings, but when I stepped in it was like entering a different world. Maybe this was the heaven on earth that Mother Miriana told me about!

Outside, the tent was a drab brown; inside the walls were made of fine carpets coloured rich reds, patterned with deep shades of green, blue and gold. All around the walls were thick cushions upholstered with lush rugs, the same style as those that covered the earthen floor. A dozen flickering oil lamps lit the tent. In the golden light I could see most of the women of the gypsy band. They sat or lay on the cushions, some speaking quietly, others fingering the jingles on tambourines.

Zora indicated one of the lovely cushions. I sat down and sank into its softness.

"I am sure that you have many questions, as usual," she said, in a way that was much more gentle than her usual brusqueness.

"Maybe we should explain first and then if there is anything more you would like to know you can ask us," she said, as some of the other women gathered around me.

"It's so beautiful in here," I told them.

In spite of my usual curiosity I felt at peace just sitting there in the glow, enjoying the new sensations all around me.

"Yes, it's a very special place," said Seneka, a woman slightly older than Zora. "We all love to come here during our moon-time."

"I never really noticed that the women were all gone," I said. "Zora, I know you seemed busier than before and travelled less frequently with us in our wagon but you never told us about this place."

"It's something for you to know about when the time is right," she said.

Maybe this was the gypsy's secret!

"Do only the gypsy women have a moon-time?" I asked. The women around me all laughed.

"No, every woman has a moon-time, but few of them celebrate this time the way we do," Seneka said.

Chapter 35

The Tambourine

Surrounded by the warm comfort of the moon tent I felt very relaxed. I settled back sleepily on the soft cushions, but ever curious I couldn't help myself from asking more questions.

"What do you do while you are here?" I asked, "Why don't you always stay in this beautiful place?"

"Our special time calls for a special place," Seneka said.

"Do men ever come here?" I asked. "Or is it only for women?"

"A man may come in if he wishes but the few who have tried have not felt comfortable to stay. They can feel that it is a special place for us. They have their own places and their own special ways," she said. "We respect theirs and they respect ours."

I looked around again, and realized that there were no children, only women in the tent.

"Where are your children?" I asked Annika, another of the women who had joined our group.

"They are playing with the other children. The women who are carrying new life inside them and older women whose moon-time has passed watch over them for us," she replied.

"Please tell me about the moon-time. What does it mean?" I asked.

"When a girl child reaches a certain age her body begins to change, to ready itself to become a mother," said Annika. "Her breasts begin to bud in anticipation of the day she will provide milk for her child."

"But why do we bleed?" I asked, thinking of how lately my blouse had become a little tight.

"You've seen how a woman's body grows round before giving birth to a baby, haven't you?" Zora asked.

"Yes," I said. 'I know that the child is growing within its mother's belly."

"Well every month a woman's body readies itself to nurture the seed that will grow into a child. Every month a woman's body releases a seed, but the woman's seed alone will not grow into a baby," Annika continued.

"In this world there is a balance; light and dark, day and night, summer and winter, male and female. Although they may seem like opposites, they are actually extreme aspects of the same thing. Without one, the other cannot exist. For a seed to grow into a new person in a woman it needs to receive a gift from a man. The union of the two create a third, new, being."

"So, why do we bleed?" I asked, not making the connection between day and night, dark and light and what was happening to my body.

"If the seed has not received its gift then no baby will grow and the place that has been prepared is not needed at that time," Annika explained patiently.

"The blood you see is the womb cushion. It is not needed so it comes out through an opening in your body. At this time our bodies are cleansing themselves. It is a good time for us to be quiet and to connect with the earth, the great mother of us all."

"If my blood makes a cushion for the baby," I said, "then it must be all red inside me, like it is in this tent".

"This tent represents the womb of the mother, we come here to honour her, and honour ourselves at this time," Seneka said.

Zora got up and returned a moment later with a tambourine.

"This is for you," she said as she handed me the instrument.

I loved the joyful sound of the tambourine when it was played to accompany our fireside dances. But when I shook it the sound seemed to jar in the placid atmosphere of the tent. The women around me giggled when I tried, unsuccessfully to silence it.

"There are different ways to play this instrument for different occasions," Seneka said.

I remembered the way the women played at Todor and Emilia's wedding and understood what she meant.

"During our moon-time we play to honour the elements and the natural rhythms of the world," Seneka said, as she picked up her own tambourine.

"There are four strokes that we play," she said as she showed me how to hold the instrument balanced in my left hand, just in front of my heart, with my fourth finger resting lightly on one of the jingles.

"The first stroke is called KA and represents the earth," she said. She struck the centre of the tambourine with her five fingers, producing a flat full sound.

With my right hand, I tried to do the same. The force of the blow made the jingles ring. The women giggled.

"Good try, Milada," Seneka said. "Angle the head of the tambourine down a little bit so the jingles stay silent."

I tried it again and was surprised that I managed to produce a sound similar to Seneka's.

"Excellent!" Annika said, clapping her hands together.

"The next sound is DUM," Seneka said. "DUM represents water".

She struck the skin of the tambourine with her index finger. It made a low, resonant sound.

"You try it, Milada," she said.

At first it felt awkward. My finger touched the skin and made a very weak sound, nothing like the vibrant one that Seneka had made.

"Don't worry," she said, "it takes some practice. The next sound is TAK, the sound of fire. Use your fourth finger just on the edge of the drum."

Seneka demonstrated the TAK.

"It sounds so different from DUM!" I said. "I never noticed that the tambourine could make so many different sounds."

"It's a sign of your growing maturity that you can hear the difference," Annika said. "Try to play the TAK".

I hit my fourth finger on the skin of the tambourine. "It sounds like a DUM," I said, because it did!

"You hit the skin; too close to the centre of the drum. Try again but aim to hit the rim," Seneka instructed.

I tried again. It still sounded like a DUM, but on my third try I got it!

"It's funny, but I felt different things in my body when I played TAK and when I played DUM," I said.

"That's because fire is a very different energy from water," Zora said, with a touch of her usual impatience.

"The last stroke," Seneka continued, "is called CHA. CHA represents the element of air."

"How do I play the air?" I asked her.

"To play CHA," she said, "use the pad where your fingers meet the palm of your hand to hit the rim of the drum and make the jingles sing. Like this!"

Seneka hit the edge of the tambourine, not touching the skin at all. The jingles rang out. Some of the other women joined in on their tambourines and I did, too, playing an even rhythm - one- two- three- four -one- two- three- four one- two- three- four one- two- three- four !

As we played the air sound I thought I could here voices singing. When we stopped I asked Seneka, "Who was singing? No one seemed to be but I heard some beautiful voices."

"You heard the overtones," she said.

"Overtones?"

"When different frequencies of sound meet they create a third, higher sound, called a harmonic overtone," Seneka explained. "Rather like when the essence of a man and a woman meet, a new life is created."

"Some people call them the voice of angels," Annika added.

Maybe this really was heaven!

Chapter 36

Creating a New Life

Because the women's moon-time had come we spent a few days in our transient camp. Although no one said that we had to stay in the special tent it felt like such a privilege to be there I didn't miss my bed back in the wagon. Every few hours we were brought food to eat and fresh water. At first I didn't feel very hungry. The strange ache in my belly was still there. I asked Zora about it.

"It is part of the cleansing process," she told me. "The muscles are pushing to loosen the blood to come out. Wait a minute," she said as she went out of the tent. In a few moments she returned with a steaming cup.

"Drink this tea made from the flowers of the chamomile plant. It will help," she said. "Then lay on the floor with your feet propped up on the cushions".

I followed her instructions and soon dozed off into a gentle sleep. When I awoke I felt much better and hungry! I helped myself to some of the dish of dried fish with herbs. Now the questions started to bubble up in my mind. I didn't want to disturb the peacefulness of the tent but there were so many things I wanted to know.

I sat down next to Zora and Seneka.

"Feeling better now?" Zora asked.

"Yes, thank you," I replied.

"Do you have some questions for us?" Seneka said, with a smile. "I know you always have questions, Milada. You have always been famous for your curiosity."

"Yes, I have lots of questions!" I said.

"Here in this special tent we have lots of time," Seneka said. "Now and every month. It is our time to rest from the many physical jobs we do. It gives us the time to do another important job."

I looked around the tent. None of the women seemed to be doing much of anything. Maybe they will do their jobs later, I thought.

"What jobs do you do in here? Sewing?" I asked. The women giggled.

"No, we do not sew," Zora said. "We quiet our bodies and our minds. When they are very quiet we can hear the wisdom of the elements, the earth, the water, the fire and the air whispering to us. We use this knowledge to guide the Baron on the decisions that he makes for our band."

"It is our most important job," Seneka added. "The survival of our people depends on it."

"Can't the Baron do it for himself?" I asked. I thought the Baron was very wise and knew everything.

As if she could read my thoughts Seneka said, "The Baron is a wise man, but no one person is all knowing. Working together as a group of women we can tune into the great truths of nature and beingness."

"Can't men do it if they sit together?" I asked.

"How often do you see men sitting together?" Seneka said with a smile.

"They have different ways, different skills. A man's path is more focused on a goal. He fixes a point and gets to it. That's why it is the men that hunt to provide us with food. The men build and maintain the wagons."

"We women, because we need to protect our children, can be aware of many things going on at the same time. We can prepare food while we chat and also watch what our children are doing. We are more sensitive to our environment in order to sense danger before it comes so we can bring our children to safety," she continued.

"Of course there are female aspects in men and male aspects in women. We all can do each task if we must. But by doing the things that fit our basic nature we have less stress and can lead happier lives," Annika added.

"You said that a woman cannot make a child without a gift from a man," I said. "What is that gift and how does he give it to her?"

"I'm sure you have seen the animals coupling in the fields at certain times of the year," Zora began, "and male cats waiting in turn to mount a female".

"Yes," I replied, "I've seen them and heard them yowling all night when it was that time."

"Then you know that the female will grow fat and then give birth," Zora continued. "We watched many of Tanya's animals give birth together."

"Is it the same with people?" I asked, thinking that it didn't sound very nice!

"People are not cats!" Zora said, "We do not only follow our instinct."

"Some people do, Zora, " Seneka said, "but we look at things a different way."

"Yes, in the villages men and women often come together to join their bodies out of lust, just to feel the release that comes when a woman's body joins with that of a man," she said.

Now I was getting very confused. It must have shown in my face. Seneka took my hand and said, "You know that many of our ways are different from the ways of people in the villages. Our way of coming together - woman and man - is one of those."

"In a way, we are like the animals. When our bodies mature to the point of being able to create new life we get the feeling that we want to mate, just like the animals do. But we have more consciousness than the animals. We know that we are more than our physical bodies and everything we do has an impact on every other part of creation," Seneka told me.

"Do you mean we have a soul?" I asked her.

"You can call it that," she said. "These things are often beyond the scope of words. You will know after you learn to sit in silence."

"Can you teach me the way of the gypsies?" I asked.

"When an animal mates, the male shoots his life-fluid into the female while they are coupled together. They then separate and the male looks for another female to couple with. For animals, their instinct is to mate as many times as possible to insure that there are offspring," she said.

"For a man and a woman, things are different," she continued. "Often, people who are not aware of whom and what they truly are, couple only for the pleasure it brings them. A woman will conceive a child that is not really wanted or that the family does not have the resources to care for."

"For us, the union of a man and a woman is a sacred one. Our coupling brings balance to ourselves and balance to our community as well as the world beyond. The men in our band are taught how to enter into a woman and not shoot their life-fluid. Instead, the energy rises in him and mingles with the woman's energy to lift them both into a state of grace."

Seneka patted my hand. "I don't expect you to understand this now, Milada," she said, "As you grow, so will your understanding."

"When a man and woman decide to make a child it is a very special occasion. They come together in joy and love. The man offers his gift, his life-fluid to the woman, whose body is prepared to receive it. That's why the children here are so special and so happy."

I wondered if, when my mother and father made me, they felt that joy.

"We will talk more in the coming months," Seneka said. "Your understanding will deepen as you have more experience with life and as your body matures. Work with your tambourine, it is a good tool of understanding and experience."

Seneka picked up her instrument and started playing a pattern of DUM, interspersed with quick jingles with her left hand.

DUM tic tic DUM tic tic DUM tic   DUM tic tic DUM tic tic DUM tic

As she continued to play the other women joined in. I felt shy at first but Seneka smiled at me.

"Come on, Milada," Zora said, "you can play the DUM's. Leave the jingles for now."

I picked up my tambourine and tried to remember how to hold it. It felt awkward at first but soon I was managing to hold the drum and play DUM, the sound of water.

The women swayed back and forth together as they played. Annika looked at me and smiled. Some had their eyes closed. As I felt more comfortable I let my eyes close as well. And then, once again, I heard the voices of angels.

Chapter 37

A Familiar Village

I passed another two days in the moon-time tent. Some of the women had already left when I noticed that my bleeding had stopped.

I asked Zora, "I am not bleeding any more. Is it time for me to leave?"

"Yes, she said, "We will all be leaving soon."

"Do all women have their moon-time together?" I asked her.

"Woman who live closely together and close to nature do, yes," she replied. "Did you notice the phase of the moon when you started to bleed?"

"I can't remember seeing the moon the nights before," I replied.

"That is because our moon-time comes when the moon is near the sun, that is what they call a 'new moon'," Zora said. "When the moon is full a woman's body is ready to receive a child, if the woman's cycles are in tune with nature."

I bid goodbye to the women who were staying and went off in search of Tanya.

"Hey! Milada! Where have you been?" It was Goran.

He came running toward me.

"I was worried about you, but the old witch said you were with the women. What have you been up to?" he asked. "Learning new tricks?"

I looked at Goran. Although he was older than I, he suddenly seemed very young. I didn't know what to tell him. What would he understand about what it means to be a woman?

"I spent some days with the other women," I said, "now that I am old enough. Do you ever spend time with the men?"

"Todor asked me if I wanted to join them one time. I stayed for a while but the things they talked about were so strange I left and did not return," he said, looking down at his feet as if he did not feel comfortable looking at me.

"They say we will be moving on tomorrow," he said, brightening as he changed the subject. "Are you hungry? Let's go see what's cooking."

"I want to go to my wagon and see what Tanya is doing," I replied. "I'll meet you at the fire."

When I reached our wagon I found Tanya playing with the kittens.

"Hello, Milada," she called out, "have you been with the women?"

"Yes," I replied.

"You look different these days, more grown up. Oh, you have a tambourine! Let me see it, please."

I handed her my instrument. She held it in her left hand, close to her heart and started to play a rhythm with DUM, TAK and CHA.

"How do you know how to play?" I asked her, "Have you been to the moon-time tent?"

"No," she said with a far away look in her eyes, "but I remember," she said as she handed back the tambourine. "Keep this safe," she said. "It will be your teacher and your comfort."

I took the tambourine and stowed it next to my bed. Tanya settled the kittens and we went to find the others already seated around the fire, eating the evening meal. I saw Seneka and Annika sitting together along with their children. They smiled at me. I smiled back, now as a friend instead of as a child.

Goran was sitting with the boys, throwing bits of wood on the fire. I thought I heard the fire singing TAK, TAK, TAK-TAK-TAK.

After we finished eating the Baron announced that we would be moving on the next morning. Some people stayed where they were, talking and laughing together while others started packing the cooking pots and long tables on to the kitchen wagon.

Although I had not done much for the past few days I felt very tired and was looking forward to my bed in the wagon. I saw Goran get up and head in my direction but I pretended I didn't and hurried to my wagon, my bed and my dreams.

The next morning I felt Tanya gently nudging my shoulder.

"Wake up, sleepy head, the sun is getting high. It's time to go!"

Zora was just finishing hitching the horse to our wagon when I emerged.

"The Baron has already sounded the call," she said. "Let's be on our way."

I had a quick wash and hopped back on the wagon. Tanya handed me a piece of bread and some cheese.

"Thank you," I said. "I was sleeping so soundly I didn't hear you get up. Thanks for getting some breakfast for me."

"You looked so peaceful," she said, "I didn't have the heart to wake you up."

We travelled all day through a deep forest. The sun could hardly reach us. Tanya, Zora and I sat close together on the driving bench with our thickest blanket covering our legs.

Towards dusk, our wagon emerged from the woods and followed the road through fields or ripening wheat dotted with bright red poppies I felt a strange familiarity. I asked Zora, who held the horses' reigns, "Have we been here before?"

"Once," she said. "It was many years ago."

The sun was setting as we approached the village. "I think I know this place," I said as we set up camp in a cleared field just outside the village walls.

Even before the fire was lit some of the village people had come to greet us, bringing with them baskets of wild greens that they had collected and sausages and chickens to roast. Although people were usually happy to see us arrive in their village, this was a spectacular welcome. Goran came to find me as Tanya and I let the horse free to graze.

"Come on," he called, "this looks like a great village. Let's go and explore."

Tanya nodded. "I'll finish off here and come and find you later," she said as Goran and I ran off in the direction of the village gate. As we entered the gate and reached the main square it all came back to me.

"This is my village, Goran! This is where I was born. I'm going to find my grandfather. He said he would leave a light on in the window for me!"

I wasn't sure which way to go. I don't know how long it had been since that day so long ago when my Grandma died and Layla offered to let me come with the gypsy band. When I looked down at my feet on the well-worn cobblestone road, I could picture how small they were when I left that place.

I took a deep breath and kept walking, trusting that my now larger feet would remember the way home. We walked and walked but I did not see any window with a candle beckoning me home. There was one house on the square that felt very familiar.

"I think that this is the one," I told Goran.

"Knock on the door and see who lives there," he replied.

We approached the heavy oaken door. It looked familiar but much smaller than I remembered. Timidly, I rapped on the door. There was no answer.

"Maybe they went out to greet the gypsies," Goran said. "They don't expect the gypsies to come knocking at their door!"

He knocked harder on the door. Still it remained firmly shut.

"Let's go," I said. "There's no one home."

Just as we turned to go I heard the door squeaking on its hinges. A young girl, about my age stood there. 'Who's there?" she asked, looking right and left.

Goran looked at the girl, then looked at me, then looked back at the girl in the doorway. He had a puzzled expression on his face.

"What's the matter?" I asked him.

"That girl," he said, "she looks just like you."

I look at the girl again. Yes, she was about my age and my height, but she looked so serious! Her hair was a similar colour but most of it was covered by a white kerchief. She was thin and pale. I'd see my reflection every morning in my washing bowl. I knew what I looked like and it wasn't like the drab girl in the doorway.

"She doesn't look like me!" I insisted, but I don't know if Goran even heard me. He was already heading back towards the house.

"Good evening," he said to the girl. "I am Goran. I travel with the gypsy band. This is my friend, Milada. She thinks she remembers this house."

The girl smiled at Goran, then looked me up and down. "I'm Dunia," she said. "This is our house."

"Who lived here before you did?" I asked.

"I don't know why I should tell you," she said.

"Go on," said Goran. "Was it an old man?"

"Well, yes. Actually this house belonged to my great-grandfather," she replied.

"Is he at home, can I see him?" I asked, trying to see beyond her into the house.

"Granddad died years ago. We moved in here when I was a little girl," she said, shifting her body to block my view. "I live here with my parents and pesky little sister.

Goran took me by the shoulders and stood me next to Dunia. 'You two must be related. You could be sisters."

"The only sister I have is the one inside," she said. "Yagoda, come out here a minute," she called over her shoulder.

A second girl appeared in the doorway, a little younger than Dunia with a cunning look in her eyes.

"This is my sister, Yagoda. Say "hello", Yagoda".

"Hello Yagoda," she said with a sigh and disappeared back into the house.

"There was talk of a cousin. My father's brother had a daughter. When his wife died he left the village. He came back once, a long time ago, looking for his daughter but by that time Granddad had died. I don't remember what happened to the girl. I think she was called Anna," Dunia said, ignoring her sister's rudeness.

I felt a chill run down my spine. Goran looked at me and said, "Well then Milada, maybe you're from some other house, or some other village. But you sure look like this girl."

"Let's go," I said, taking Goran's hand. "This has been a long day. I'm tired and hungry."

Goran tipped his hat in Dunia's direction, made a little bow and said, "Good night, then. We'll be staying here a while. I look forward to making your acquaintance."

Dunia smiled at him and waved as we walked back towards our camp.

"She seems nice," Goran said. When I was silent, he continued. "Too bad it's not your grandfather's house...or is it?"

He turned to look at me. The night was dark and I hoped he wouldn't see the tears in my eyes.

Chapter 38

With Dragan in the Moonlight

I didn't feel like saying anything on our way back to the clearing where we had set up our camp, but Goran wanted to talk.

"I can't get over how much that Dunia girl looks like you; and the younger one, too. She looks like you did when I came to live with the gypsies. Seeing her made me realize how long I've been travelling. And you've been with them even longer. Can you remember your life before that?" he asked.

"A little," I said.

"Like what?"

"I don't know. Playing in the fields. Hating to be cooped up in the house. Sitting in my Grandma's lap and feeling warm and loved," I said.

"I don't think I ever met my Grandparents". Goran told me. "I can't even remember my father. My mother worked hard, cooking for the tavern. We slept in the back room, on a mattress of straw on the floor. At least it was warm there."

"Why did you leave?" I asked him, realizing that we had never talked like this before.

"When my mother got sick and died the landlord of the tavern told me to go. I stayed with my uncle for a time, but when summer came I lived by finding odd jobs in other villages, helping at farms or just from the charity of people I met and sleeping wherever it was when night fell. In autumn when it was starting to get cold I was lucky to meet the gypsy band; and I've travelled with them, and with you, ever since."

"It's hard to remember the time before you came," I told him. "One year is so much like the next, moving, following the seasons. Only we get too big for our clothes and need to get bigger ones."

"I don't know how much longer I will stay with the gypsies. It's time for me to think of my future, of what I want to do with my life."

"Why not stay with us?" I asked.

Goran stopped in the middle of the path. He put his hands on my shoulders and looked me in the eye.

"What do you mean with 'us'? You are not one of them any more than I am," he said. "We are different. We will always be different. Why can't you understand that?"

I pushed him away. "You joined later. I was just a baby. I don't want another life, stuck in one place all the time!" I shouted.

"You weren't so young that you don't remember your life before the gypsies," he said, "that house, your Grandpa..."

So that's why he asked, so he could trick me. I said, "Just leave me alone!" and ran on to our camp ahead of him.

Usually the smell of grilling meat would make me feel hungry and anxious to join the others by the fire. But this evening even it did not temp me. I skirted the group by the fire, intending to go to the wagon while the others were out and let the tears that had been welling up inside me flow unchecked.

I felt one tricking down my cheek when a hand came to rest on my shoulder. I had been looking down, watching my step in the dark forest and hadn't heard anyone coming. I stopped, startled to see Dragan at my side.

"Where are you off to, Milada? Surely you would like to partake of the wonderful food the villagers brought for us?" he asked.

I turned to look at him, to tell him I was not hungry but instead of words, my tears came pouring forth. He said nothing, but enfolded me in his arms and let me cry. I don't know how many minutes passed in this way but slowly the tears stopped.

"You had better go," I managed to say at last, "Before all the sausages are gone."

"There are tears in my pretty Milada's eyes and you think I am concerned with sausages?" he said, with a smile in his dark, shiny eyes. "Come, let's sit here a while. Tell me why you are crying on this lovely spring evening."

We sat down on a mossy bank, leaning on an ancient oak tree. "I think that this is the village that I came from." I told him.

"And that makes you sad?" he asked, gently. "Are you remembering your people here? Your mother and father?"

"No, I don't remember them at all. I remember my grandfather and my grandmother; how she would hug me and sing me to sleep at night. It was after she died that Layla offered to take me with the gypsies."

The thought of Layla set of my tears again. Dragan held me close and stroked my hair.

"You miss Layla, of course. We all miss her. She had a very kind soul. But she is near us still. Be very still and you can feel her presence here with us."

I felt so confused, so sad; missing the love of my Grandma and of Layla. But it felt so good to be in Dragan's arms. I felt protected and yes, loved. Was it Layla's love I felt through her brother or was this something else. My tears dried, but I wanted to stay forever in Dragan's warm embrace.

We stayed together under the tree until the moon rose over the clearing.

"Come now, little one," Dragan said, brushing his hair off his forehead with the back of his hand. "Let's see if there is any food left for us. I can see you feel better now, and maybe even a little bit hungry."

He was right. I was feeling both better and very hungry. Hand in hand we walked toward the fire.

"Goran says we'll never be a real part of the gypsy band. He's thinking of leaving, but I want to stay with you forever. I won't have to go, will I?"

"My child', he said, "it's up to you if you want to stay with the gypsy band or not. Only you know what is in your heart."

"Then I'll stay forever!" I said, knowing that what was in my heart was love for Dragan.

Chapter 39

A Ribbon for My Hair

Dragan and I joined the others around the fire, helping ourselves to a bowl of the fragrant vegetable and sausage stew from the iron pot hanging over the fire. Dragan lead me to join Tanya.

"This meal is delicious!" I said, starting to feel better.

"We grilled the sausages first," Tanya said, "It makes all the difference. Where have you been? We missed you."

Beyond the fire I could see Goran watching me. I felt bad that I had pushed him away. I smiled at him. He got up and started to make his way to where we were sitting.

"I had a little shock," I said. "This is the village where I lived before".

"I knew it!" said Goran as he sat down beside me. "Those girls are so like you. I knew you had to be related. Why didn't you stay and talk with them? Why didn't you tell them that you were Anna?"

"I was just so surprised," I said, "and shocked. What do I have in common with them now? I don't remember them at all."

"Dunia is your age," Dragan said. "Didn't you play together?"

"There was one girl who was often in our house," I said, "but she liked to stay indoors and I hated to stay in the house. I was always outside unless the weather was so bad that my Grandma would not allow it."

"Let's go back tomorrow and tell them," Goran said.

"I don't think I want to do that," I told him.

"Why not?" he asked.

"Soon we will be moving on again," I said. "What difference will it make if they know I am their cousin? They don't know me at all."

"What if your father comes back again?" Goran asked. "Don't you want to meet him?"

"I never knew my father," I said. "The gypsies are the only family I need."

The look in Goran's eyes told me what he was thinking; that I was fooling myself thinking that I was one of them. He remained silent, though, in the company of Dragan and Tanya.

"Let's all go meet them," Tanya said. "Maybe when you get to know them you will want to tell them that you are cousins."

Dragan smiled at Tanya and took her hand.

"That is a wise suggestion," he said. "It's usually preferable to let a situation develop and then respond rather than forcing it."

So the next morning Tanya, Goran and I went into the village. It was a market day and the main square was thronged with people buying and selling their wares.

"Remember how you used to steal the cheese?" I asked Goran, laughing.

"I never stole any cheese," he said with a cheeky grin, "Those nice ladies where happy to give it to me! Look over there, it's Dunia and her sister."

We looked where Goran was pointing and saw Dunia at a stall selling brightly coloured ribbons.

"Look at those pretty ribbons!" Tanya said, stepping up to the colourful stall. "I think I have a few coins. I'll buy some for our hair."

"I like those bright red ones," I said.

"I like the green ones," Tanya said, reaching out to feel the texture of the ribbon.

"Hello Dunia, hello, uh…I'm sorry, I've forgotten your name," Goran said to the two girls.

"Hello. You are back," Dunia said to Goran. "Her name is Yagoda. Say 'Hello', Yagoda".

Yagoda ignored her sister and Goran, busying herself with the ribbons.

"Hello! I'm Tanya," Tanya said brightly. "Aren't these ribbons lovely. Which colour do you like best?"

"I don't like all these bright colours," she said. "Yagoda wanted to come and have a look and it's my job to keep an eye on her."

"I think they are beautiful," I said. "The brighter the better."

Tanya asked the vendor for a red ribbon for me and a green one for herself. They were very long.

"I will cut mine into two pieces, one for each plait," Tanya said as she handed over two copper coins.

"I may leave mine long to flow when I dance or cut off some small pieces to make bows," I told her as she handed me the pretty red ribbon, "Thank you so much".

Tanya wore her thick auburn hair in two plaits that hung down to the middle of her back. I never liked to tie up my hair. I sometimes put ribbons in it, just for fun, but only when I was helping prepare our food or doing some other job where it gets in the way would I tie it back like the tail of a horse.

Thinking of horses, I said, "Do you have another coin? We can get a ribbon for Dobro's mane?"

"Who or what is Dobro?" Dunia asked.

"Dobro is our Baron's son's wonderful black horse," I replied.

"You will spend money to buy a ribbon for a horse?" she said with disbelief. "It's bad enough buying them for yourselves, but ribbons for a horse, well I never heard of such a thing."

Tanya and I looked at one another, barely able to hold back our laughter at the girl's serious expression.

"What colour do you think Dobro would like," Tanya asked me, fingering an orange ribbon, "the orange one or the blue?"

"Definitely the blue," I said suppressing a giggle.

Goran was looking at the two of us, looking rather puzzled as if to see what we found so funny.

He turned to Dunia and said, "You are from this village, show us where we can find the best cheese."

"The best cheese comes from the shepherd who takes his sheep to high pastures. It is early in the year, though. There is still snow up there. But he may have some cheese from the last season preserved in brine," she told him. "I'll show you where to find his stall."

"Come on, Yagoda," she said, tugging on her sister's sleeve.

"Can't I buy a ribbon?" she asked her sister.

"Do you have any money?" Dunia asked her.

"No," she replied.

"Then how to you expect to buy a ribbon?"

"You have money," Yagoda replied.

"I was given money to buy food, not frivolous things," she said. "Let's go".

Yagoda looked wistfully at the ribbons. She ran her fingers over them, then grabbed a handful and gave them a tug. Several fell onto the dusty ground. The stall keeper came over quickly and started to pick them up us Yagoda skipped off after us.

"If I had stayed in this village," I said quietly to Tanya as we followed Goran and Dunia to the cheese stall, "do you think I would act like these girls? They don't seem very happy at all."

"Staying in this village was not your fate," Tanya said, "but even if you had you are of a different temperament. You would have found your way."

"I'm so glad that I found the gypsies - or that they found me!" I told her.

"I'm glad, too," said Tanya, putting her arm around my shoulder as we walked companionably through the crowded market.

We caught up with the others at a stall stocked with many different varieties of cheese.

"I wonder if Goran is up to his tricks!" I said to Tanya.

The cheeses really did smell good. I was feeling hungry!

"Try this one," Dunia handed as small piece of cheese to Goran.

"Can we have a taste, too," I asked.

Dunia looked at me but before she could speak the woman behind the counter said, "You are from the gypsy band, yes?"

"Yes, we are," I replied.

"Here, have a taste of these two. Tell me which one you like and I'll give you a piece to take to your camp."

"Thank you very much," I said as I took the samples.

"Thank you, madam, you are very kind," said Tanya as she accepted hers.

Both of the cheeses were delicious.

"Which do you like best?" I asked Tanya.

"I like the soft one," she said. "It is only made at this time of year when the young lambs are being born and the ewes have much milk."

The woman behind the counter smiled. "Good choice! Here you are. When will the gypsies come and play music in the village square?"

"Thank you, so much," Tanya said. "I don't know when we will come but it will be soon, I'm sure. Thank you for your kindness and generosity."

Dunia made her choices and purchased three small pieces of different cheeses. I heard her saying to Goran as we walked away,

"We in the village have to pay for what we buy, but your gypsy band gets everything free".

Goran replied, "I am not one of the gypsies. I am just living with them for a while. Not all villages are as welcoming as this one."

"Our village isn't always so welcoming. Yours is the only group that gets such treatment," she said.

Tanya heard her and said, "Do you know why that is?"

"No," Dunia replied.

"Many years ago, they say," Tanya began, "the people of this village were very ill. Many had died and many more lay in their beds close to death. Our group arrived in the camp near the village. When we came to the square it was deserted. The streets were deserted; the market had closed down because vendors feared catching the illness."

"One of our elders knocked on the door of the headman of the village to find out what was happening. Up until that time people mistrusted the gypsies, but the situation was so bad that the headman explained about the illness that was decimating the village."

"Later that day many gypsies came into the village with a broth made from healing plants and roots. They went from house to house, giving people the rich soup and tending to anyone who was already suffering from the illness. After three days, people started to recover. After a week everyone in the village was fine."

"A feast was held to celebrate and thank the gypsies. And from that day forward the people in this village have always welcomed us."

I heard Dunia murmuring under her breath, "magic…"

"When did that happen, Tanya?" I asked.

"It was a long time ago," she replied. "Mother Miriana was a young woman then. She must remember."

"I will ask her if she does," I said. It was strange to imagine Mother Miriana as a young woman!

Chapter 40

Fresh Bread

When we had finished in the market Tanya said, "I am going back to camp. I'll bring the cheese to the cooking tent. Milada, Annika took the bread dough to the baker this morning. Why don't you pass by there and see if she needs help carrying the loaves back to camp."

"Alright," I replied, "I'll see you back there in a little while."

I asked Dunia, "Can you tell me where the baker's shop is?"

She started to explain.

"Go down that street, turn left at Rico's house, then turn right until the cross street…"

I was getting very confused, who is 'Rico', how would I know which house was his? Yagoda spoke up.

"I'll show you the way," she said.

I was surprised. She didn't seem to be very interested in us.

"Thank you," I said, "that will be very helpful."

"And I'll walk Dunia home," Goran said, "I'll see you later at the camp."

They turned and started back across the market square.

"Come on," Yagoda said, "the bakery is this way."

"Don't mind my sister," she said as we walked. "Sometimes she gets so full of herself. Our mother works hard in the fields and she thinks she has to take care of all of us."

"That's a big responsibility," I said. "Do you help her?"

"She thinks she doesn't need my help. She treats me like a baby, but I do what I can," she said. "It's nice to be out of the house for a while."

"Do you like to play outside?" I asked, thinking of how I loved to roam in the fields when I could escape my Grandma's watchful gaze.

"Yes, I do," she replied. "But Dunia like me to stay at home. She says it isn't safe to go out of the village, into the woods. She says I will get lost."

"I love wandering in the fields and in the woods," I told her. "I've lost my way sometimes, but I always found it again and learned something in the process."

"I like to watch the animals," she said. "I like the way the horses gather together at the end of the day and seem to watch the sunset together. But the day I saw that, when I got home my father beat me with his belt. They didn't know where I was and thought something bad had happened to me."

"He beat you?" I said in disbelief.

"Yes, that time and other times, too, when I do something bad," she replied.

"Watching horses is bad?" I asked.

"No, I don't think so. But going out in the fields when they tell me to stay at home, that's bad. I guess I'm a bad child because I sneak out whenever I can," she said.

"The gypsies never beat their children," I said, "or tell them to stay close by."

"How do they make them behave?" Yagoda asked.

"Everyone keeps an eye on the little ones. As we get older we learn how to keep ourselves out of trouble," I told her. "Sometimes children get hurt by being too adventurous, but the gypsies know ways to make them heal quickly."

"Here we are." she said, "This is the baker's shop."

I saw Annika inside. "Wait here a minute," I told Yagoda as I went into the bakery.

"Hello, Milada," Annika called out cheerfully, "have you come to help me?"

"Yes," I replied, "Tanya said you might need some help."

"Yes, I do," she said. "There are many warm loaves here to bring back to camp."

While the rosy-cheeked baker loaded our baskets I asked if I could use the big knife on the counter that he used to cut the large crusty loaves into pieces.

He said I could. I removed the new red ribbon from where I had tied it around my neck and cut it into two long pieces.

"I'll be right back," I told Annika and went out to find Yagoda who was waiting for me outside.

"This is for you," I said, handing her half of the red ribbon. "I hope you like the colour."

"Oh, yes," she said. "Thank you!"

She gathered her hair in her hands and used the ribbon to tie it together at the nape of her neck.

"Shall I make in into a bow for you?" I asked her.

She smiled and turned with her back to me so I could form the ribbon into a large red bow.

"There you are," I said. "Maybe one day I can take you to see our camp in the forest. If you are with me, you won't be in danger. You can go out of the village without sneaking away."

"I would like that," she said. "Now I had better get home, before I get in trouble for being away too long. Thank you again for the ribbon."

"Thank you for being my guide," I said. "I'll see you around!"

I went back into the bakery. The baking bread smelled delicious. Annika and I collected our baskets filled with the crusty brown loaves. I could not even wait to get out of the shop before breaking off the end of one and popping the still warm bread into my mouth.

"Who was that girl?" Annika asked me as we walked back to our camp." She looks a lot like you."

"Her name is Yagoda. She has a sister called Dunia. They live in the house where I used to live with my Grandma and Grandpa. I think that we are cousins."

"That doesn't surprise me," Annika said. "There is a strong resemblance."

"She told me that she likes to roam in the fields," I said, "like I used to love to do. But her family wants her to stay at home."

"I guess that they are trying to protect her," Annika said.

"But how can she learn anything is she stays in the house all the time?" I asked, feeling myself getting angry at the thought of keeping someone a captive in a house.

"She will learn how to tend a house," Annika said, "how to cook and keep things clean; how to take care of the chickens and the pigs; things that are necessary for survival in a village."

"We learn those things, and lots more things, as well," I said.

"Milada, try not to pass judgment on others whose ways are different from ours. What is good for us might not suit them at all," she said. "Many people do not like the way we live, always moving from place to place, never being sure of where our next meal will come from".

"But we always have enough to eat," I argued, "and the gypsies never beat their children!"

"Yes, our ways are different," Annika said.

"I am so happy I came to live with you," I said.

"You would not consider staying here with those of your family?" Annika asked me.

"No, never!" I said, "The gypsies are the only family I need or want. I love being with you, travelling with you, learning your wisdom."

"And we love you, too, Milada."

Chapter 41

The Sun and the Moon

The Baron announced that we would be staying in this camp for two turns of the moon. Then it would be summer and we would travel to the highlands where the sheep were taken to graze.

Now that my blood had begun to flow I took more interest in the changing face of the moon. I noticed that when the moon was a thin crescent it appeared just after sunset and followed the sun down in the west. When the moon was getting bigger it appeared high in the sky after sunset. When the moon looks like full circle I saw it come up just as the sun was setting. The last quarter appeared to rise above the horizon late in the night.

One night, at that time of the cycle, as I sat waiting for the moon to rise, Tanya came and sat down at my side.

"What are you thinking?" she asked me.

"I'm looking at the stars," I told her. "Look at how many there are up there!"

"Some of them have names," she said, "Did you know that? They help guide us on our journeys. That's why we often travel at night, especially when we are going a long way in places where there are no village roads to guide us."

"Do you know their names?" I asked.

"Some of them," she said. "That bright one over there; that is the North Star. The others seem to move around it, but it is always in the same place."

"Over there is the group called the Big Bear. It looks like a huge square. And over there is Orion, the hunter. See the three bright stars in a line," she asked, pointing over her head. "That is called "the belt of Orion', he who hunts the bear".

"He will have to cross that river of stars to get to the bear!" I said. "Isn't it beautiful?"

It was late and the moon was just coming up, slowly rising above the eastern horizon. It was a startling bright white, like half a slice of the fresh cheese.

"I was wondering why the moon comes up at different times, depending on how full it is," I said to Tanya.

"Think about it," Tanya said. "Does the moon actually change shape, do you think?"

"I don't think so," I said. "Isn't it the shape of a ball?"

"Yes," Tanya replied. "So why does it look different at the different times of the month?"

"Because of the way earth goes around the moon?" I asked, not sure that was the right answer.

Tanya said, "The earth goes around the moon?"

"I remember learning that the earth is round and it goes around the sun even though it seems like the sun is moving around the earth." I said.

"Yes, the earth is moving around the sun, but the moon is moving around the earth," she said, "circles within circles."

"The moon is not as shiny as the sun, but it is very bright," I said, watching the moon move higher and trying to understand.

"The moon has no light of its own," Tanya said. "It reflects the light of the sun. If you look closely you can see the whole circle of the moon even though only half of it looks bright."

I looked up at the moon and realized that she was right.

"So if the moon is reflecting the sun's light, where do you think the sun is now?" she asked me.

"It must still be down below the horizon," I said.

"And where is it when the moon is full?" she asked.

I thought about it for a moment and then said, "It must be just opposite! That's why when the moon is coming up the sun is going down."

"That's right," she said. "And every so often the path of the earth comes right between the dance of the sun and the moon and we can see the earth's shadow pass across it."

"I remember one time, a long time ago when the moon turned red and then seemed to disappear. I was little and felt afraid, but then the moon came back again. Do you remember that?" I asked her.

"Yes, I do," she said. "It's a very special event."

"Does the sun ever seem to disappear?" I asked her.

"It is a more rare occurrence," she said. "Sometimes the moon travels between the earth and blocks the sun. It seems to vanish. All that remains is its fiery crown. The birds think night has fallen and all is silent."

"Have you ever seen this happen?" I asked her.

"I have a memory of it," she said, "but I cannot say from where or from when."

~

Soon it was again the time of the new moon, when the night sky was dark. Once again my moon-blood flowed. I took my tambourine and made my way to the moon-tent. I felt more comfortable there this time. I knew to put my legs up and just let myself relax into the soft cushions.

The following day, as I lay enjoying the soft sounds of the other women chatting I heard a familiar laugh. I opened my eyes and saw Tanya entering the tent.

She saw me and smiled. I got up and gave her a hug.

"Have you started your moon-blood as well?" I asked.

"Yes, she said. Now our wagon is empty at this time. I will have to come and go to keep and eye on my little ones, but I will find a young girl and teach her to tend the animals when I come in the future."

"It's time for you to tend to more grown up things now," Zora said, joining us. "Maybe have your own little one to care for."

Tanya smiled. "I'd like that," she said.

When evening fell and most of the women had gathered in the tent one by one they picked up their tambourines and started to play. No one seemed to lead or follow, but the rhythm subtly changed as we played. At first I was confused, and played the wrong sound at the right time or the right sound at the wrong time, but after a while I forgot my fingers and just heard that my playing matched the others. If I thought about it I lost the rhythm and then had to struggle to get started again.

The playing came to a natural end and the women all stood up and raised their drums high in the air. I followed their movements. At a silent signal, we shook our tambourines, making the jungles sing loudly. At the same time we brought them down the front of our bodies until our arms were straight. Then we took a breath in unison and raised the drums again. Smiling, with an exhale, we shook the tambourines and brought them down again. One more breath, drums up. Smile, exhale, shake, drums down. Our session ended in laugher and bright spirits as we put our drums away for the night.

Chapter 42

The Four Elements

The next morning Seneka called me over.

"Would you like to know more about the four sounds we make on our tambourines?" she asked, "and why they are so important for our health and that of our band?"

"Yes. I'd like that very much," I said sitting on the carpet at her feet.

"What do you know about the four elements, Milada?" she asked.

"I know we walk on the earth. We use pots made of clay, that's earth. People make houses out of stone or bricks made from earth. When someone dies we bury the body in the earth," I said.

"What are the characteristics of earth?" she asked.

"The ground is hard. It's mostly cold and dry. It's always there beneath our feet holding us up!"

"What about water?" she continued.

"Water moves. Water falls down in rain and in melted snow. Water flows in rivers and streams," I answered.

"What shape is water?" she asked me.

I stopped to think about it. "It doesn't really have a shape," I said. "It takes the shape of whatever container it is in."

"What about fire?" she asked.

"It doesn't really have a shape either," I said. "When I look at it, it moves and flickers. It is never the same. It can destroy forests when it comes from the sky as lightening and it can cook our food and keep us warm".

"And air?"

"I don't know," I said, puzzled, "I know we need to breathe it to live, but I can't see it. But when I put my jug into a pond to fill it with water there is a 'glug, glug' sound and bubbles come out of it. So though it looked empty it was really full of air."

"That is a very good observation, Milada," Seneka said. "What about the wind?"

"The wind is air in motion. It can be very strong," I said.

"Air connects all living things," she said. "We all inhale and exhale the same air. We can pick up scents in the air and also thoughts if we are very, very still."

"We also have all four elements within us," she continued. "What do you think the earth is in your body?"

I thought for moment and then said, "Is it my bones? They are the most solid part of me, they hold me up like the earth does."

"Very good, yes," she said. "What about water?"

"My blood," I said.

"What else?"

"My water when I relieve myself, my tears when I cry, the goo that comes out when my nose is runny". I thought to myself, "what a lot of water!"

"And air?"

"Air is the air that I breathe!" I took a very deep breath and stuck my tummy out.

"See, air!" I said, patting my tummy and trying to hold my breath and talk at the same time.

Seneka laughed. 'What about fire?" she asked me.

I really had to think about this one. "Sometimes when people get ill they get very hot. That's a kind of fire," I said.

"Yes," she agreed. "Have you ever touched someone or an animal that has died?"

I remembered many of Tanya's kittens that for one reason or another not survived. "Yes," I told her.

"Did they feel warm, like this?" she asked, taking my hand in hers.

"No," I said, "They felt very cold".

"So," she said, "you see that the fire in your body is the essence of life itself. When we are alive we are warm, it is the spark of spirit within each one of us."

"When you play the four sounds on your tambourine, think about the four great elements," Seneka continued. "Think about bringing them into balance within yourself and within our community."

"I am beginning to understand," I said. "Too much fire can destroy a forest, to much water makes a flood..."

"And anger is like a fire that burns and destroys friendship," Tanya said, joining us. "I've been listening to what you've been talking about," she said. "Understanding nature helps us to understand ourselves."

"When the elements of our body and of our emotions are in balance we can stay as we are meant to be, healthy and happy," she said.

"You say that anger is like fire," I said. "Which emotion is like earth?"

"If the element of earth is too strong a person may be over serious and heavy, slow to take action or always wanting to do something the same way, unable to try new ideas," she replied. "If there is too much water a person may be lazy, just following the easiest course of action without considering if there is a better way or what might be the consequences of following the path of least resistance."

"And if there is too much air?" I asked, puffing up my tummy again.

"Well you know what happens if there is too much air!," she said with a grin and puckered her lips to let out the sound of passing wind.

When we'd finished laughing at her antics she continued, "Too much air and a person can have many ideas but never put them into practice. Before she starts on one thing she is thinking about something else. She will talk and talk but seldom take action."

"We all have some of each element in us. Observe yourself and see where you have too much or too little and then try to bring yourself into balance," Seneka said.

I thought to myself that I had too much air and not enough earth. I liked to keep moving and trying new things but I didn't stick with any one thing for any length of time. It was something I could work on to bring myself into better balance.

"How is it when an element is in balance?" I asked.

Seneka replied, "When the element of earth is in balance a person feels grounded. She knows who she is and feels confident with what she does. She can make a plan and follow it through, but not in an overly rigid way. She will take into account the changes that always occur."

"When the element of water is in balance a person will know how to handle life's constant changes. She will respond to them with grace but be able to stay focused on her path and knows how to give and receive love."

"When the element of air is in balance a person will be open to new ideas and have the ability to communicate them to others, to follow them through and bring them to fruition."

"When the element of fire is balanced a person will have passion and enthusiasm for what she does. She will have the will to persevere if the situation is difficult. When in balance, she will not become dogmatic or fanatical in her passion."

Tanya said, "I observe my animal friends, how they live and move in grace and balance through the changing cycles of their lives. I wonder why it seems harder for humans to do the same."

"I watch them be born, grow up and die," she continued. "I bury them in the earth, and their bodies decay like the fallen leaves in autumn. The year turns, from the cold of winter to the heat of summer and back again," she said.

"The moon goes around the earth and the earth goes around the sun," I said, "Everything is moving."

"Many, many years ago," Seneka said, "all the people moved around like we do. There were no villages. People followed the wild animal herds to get food to survive."

"Then some people learned how to tame the animals and keep them in one place. They learned to grow grain where they lived so they didn't have to travel far and wide to find good things to eat," she continued.

"It does seem easier, in a way," I said. "But I like the way we move around."

"It's not bad to live in a village or a town," Seneka said, "if you don't forget where you came from, that you are a part of nature."

"It is important to understand natural law," said Tanya. "When you do, you are not afraid."

"You will learn, my dear Milada, that being afraid makes people do terrible things to one another," Seneka said, sadly.

"Like have wars and kill one another," Tanya said.

"Why would they do that?" I asked.

"Because they are afraid that there is not enough food or money for everyone so they want to make sure that they will have everything that they need," she said.

"But how can they know that?" I asked. "A fire can burn a village, its fields; animals can get sick and die or run away."

"We understand this and take from the land only what we need for now," Tanya said. "We know how to find food when others might not recognize it. We trust that there is enough for us all."

"In the towns and villages they have forgotten their place in nature and how to survive in harmony with it," Seneka added. "Part of our work is to hold this knowledge and teach people if they have ears to hear the wisdom of natural law."

I felt very lucky that fate had led me to the gypsy band and their ancient knowledge. We passed the rest of our moon-time companionably together, sometimes singing, sometimes playing our tambourines and sometimes just dozing on the soft cushions. I was sorry when the time came that our moon-blood had stopped and it was we folded away our special tent until the next month.

Chapter 43

Sore Ears and a Rabbit

While we had been in the moon-tent Annika made the suggestion that on the day of the next full moon we could have a festival in the main square of the village. Now that day had come and preparations were in full swing.

I was helping Mother Miriana and the other women prepare food for the feast when a woman from the village approached us, out of breath,

"Please, can you help me?" she panted. "I was told that the woman with the silver hair could help me!"

Mother Miriana wiped her hands on the square of muslin tied around her waist and approached the woman, indicating for her to take a seat on the wooden bench near the cooking table.

"Of course I will help you if I can," she said. "What is the problem?"

"It's my child," she said, "He is crying all the time and holding his ears. They seem to be causing him great pain."

"It sounds like he has a blockage in his ears," Mother Miriana said. "There are ways to help."

Then she went back to the cooking table.

"Won't you come now?" the woman asked, looking distressed. The boy is too ill to bring here.

"I have preparations to make. Milada, bring this woman a beaker of water," she said to me. "Wait a few minutes and I will come".

While I fetched the water, Mother Miriana picked up a fat rabbit that one of the hunters had caught early that morning. She took its skin off like a jacket and then scraped the layer of fat into a small metal bowl. She went over to the cooking fire and placed the bowl on a tripod so the fire was underneath it.

"Milada," she said, "please find me a piece of clean calico and cut into two squares with the sides the length of my forearm."

I ran off to our wagon to find the calico. I was sure that there was some there because Tanya used it to make bandages for wounded animals. I found a long piece about the right width and tore of two pieces that were almost square. I hoped that they would do.

When I returned to Mother Miriana she was standing over the bowl of melted rabbit fat. I handed her the calico pieces.

"Are these all right?" I asked her.

"They are excellent, my child," she said.

I wondered what she was going to do with them. Maybe put them around the child's head? But why the rabbit fat? Maybe that was something for a dish for the feast?

I could see that the woman was getting restless. She asked me, "Why is she still cooking when my son is in pain?"

I told her, "Mother Miriana will do what she can to help. Please be patient, since she said to wait".

Mother Miriana laid the calico flat on the table. Using a wad of cloth so she wouldn't burn her fingers, she carefully took the bowl of rabbit fat and poured some on each piece of fabric.

"Watch these for a minute, please," she said, "while I go and get Mugwort to make some tea to ease the boy's pain."

When she returned with a small bag of the herbs, the fat had almost cooled. She rolled up each piece of fabric into a cone.

"Let's go," she said. "Milada, see if you can find Zora or Tanya to come with me."

"Can I come, too?" I asked, a little sad that she wanted to bring one of the other girls instead of asking me.

"Yes," she said, "of course you may come. But I would like one of the others to come as well to learn what I am going to do to relieve this boy's earache."

I had seen Zora near our wagon. I ran back calling her name.

"What is it, Milada?" she asked as I neared the place where she was collecting wild herbs.

"Mother Miriana wants you to come and see something," I said. "Now!" I added, thinking of the woman's distress and impatience.

"Let me just put these herbs on the wagon's bench to dry," she said.

We hurried back to find Mother Miriana following the woman out of our camp already on the path leading to the village.

As soon as we reached the house we could hear the boy's cries.

"He must be in a lot of pain," I said quietly to Zora as we entered the darkened house.

"Put some water on the fire to boil," instructed Mother Miriana. A young girl, probably the sister of the sick boy poured some water from an earthen jug into a copper kettle and hung it on a hook over the fireplace.

Mother Miriana went over to the young boy who lay on his side on a low couch beside the fire. He held his ears and wailed. Gently, she put her hand on his shoulder and breathed in and out, slowly and rhythmically.

After a few moments the boy's crying ceased and his breath took on the same rhythm as Mother Miriana's.

"Don't be afraid," she said to the boy, keeping her hand lightly on his shoulder. "I know how much your ears hurt and I am here to help you. Do you trust me?"

The boy's eyes opened wide and he slowly nodded, keeping his hands on his ears.

"Zora, come and see what to do. Milada, please light this taper from the fire and bring it to me."

She handed me a long, thin candle and I did as I was told. She gently placed her hand over the boy's hand and moved it away from his ear. She then took one of the calico cones from her pouch and placed the thin end into the boy's ear. I heard his mother gasp when she lit the top of the cone with the taper.

I listened as she explained to Zora, "The fire creates a gently heat and suction that warms and clears the inside of the ear. It makes a gentle pulse that will release pressure and lessen the pain."

When the cone burnt down to about a palm's width from the boy's head Mother Miriana removed it and asked Zora to toss the rest in the fireplace to burn itself out.

"Does that feel better now?" she asked the boy. He nodded.

"Please turn on your other side so we can treat your other ear," she told him in a soft voice.

"Here, Zora. You do this one," she said, handing Zora the second cone.

I lit the taper again and handed it to Zora. She lit the cone and held it steady until it burned low. Then she removed it and threw the remaining bit into the fire.

"Excellent work," said Mother Miriana. "Ask Milada to explain how I made the cones."

Mother Miriana smiled at me as if she knew how proud I felt that I knew something that Zora didn't!

She put her finger to her lips and moved away from the boy, whose rhythmic breathing showed that he was now fast asleep.

"This is good," she said to the boy's mother. "Let him sleep. He should feel better when he wakes".

She handed the bundle of herbs to the boy's mother and said, "Soak a spoonful of this in boiling water until the water is cool enough to drink. Then strain it and give it to the boy. Make it for him in the morning, then again when the sun is high and once more in the evening until the pain is gone."

"Thank you, thank you so much!" the woman said taking both of Mother Miriana's hands in her own. "I don't know what I would have done if your band had not been here. I am not rich but I would like to give you something for your work."

"I require nothing," Mother Miriana said. "Yet there is much work to do for the festival this evening. May I borrow your daughter to help us for a while?"

"I would be pleased to come and help you," said the girl before her mother could answer.

"Yes, of course," she said. "I would come and help too, but I need to stay here in case my boy wakes."

"Of course your place is here. Hopefully your son will feel well enough to join in the festivities. Now it is time for us to go," Mother Miriana said.

On our way back to the camp we got to know the boy's sister. Her name was Janka and she was a little older than I.

"Thank you so much for helping my brother," she said. "Much more of that crying and I would have had an earache, too!"

We arrived back at the cooking table. There were two cooking fires, one with a whole lamb turning on a spit and the other with a great earthenware pot propped up in a bed of glowing charcoal in the centre of the fire. Men tended the cooking meat while the women prepared vegetables.

There was plenty of work for us all to do, cutting, chopping, mixing and carrying. But it was pleasant to work together and chat.

"I remember when you came before," Janka said. "I was little but I remember the feast! How everyone danced by the fire. I wanted to, but I was shy."

"Will you dance tonight?" I asked her

"Yes, I think I will!" she said, "now that I've met you".

"Here come the boys," I said when I saw Goran and his friends approaching the fires.

"Hello!" I said. "Have you been hunting?"

"Only hunting for hollow logs," he said, "filled with honey!"

Each of the boys held out a pail full of the sweet golden liquid.

"Come give us a taste!" I said.

He came over to where we were cutting up some onions for the stew. I reached out to put my finger into the pail of honey, but Goran pulled the pail away.

"I don't need onion flavoured honey!" he said, dipping his own finger into the pail and holding it out towards me. I took his finger in my mouth, anxious to get at the tasty honey, but then noticed the way Goran was watching me, with a sort of far away look in his eye. Something felt different between us. I didn't know what it was but it didn't seem right for me to be sucking honey off his finger, even though I'd done it many times before.

Zora said, "Go fetch a ceramic pot for the honey and let us get on with our work".

"He's cute," Janka said rolling her eyes in Goran's direction, "Is he your boyfriend?"

"No!" I said, "we've been friends since we were little, but he's not my boyfriend".

"He seems to really like you," she said.

"We are friends," that's all." I told her. "Neither of us was born into the gypsy band. We both came to live with them when we were children".

"Can anyone who wants to travel with the gypsies?" she asked me.

"There are not many who do; just Goran and I, as far as I know".

I told her about Todor's wife, who lived with us for a while but then left.

"It seems like a nice way to live," Janka said, "but it must be hard, too."

"There is a lot to learn," I said, "but I love my life with the gypsy band.

Chapter 44

Two Butterflies

As dusk approached most of the cooking was done. We all helped to load the food onto one of the smaller wagons. Goran helped to hitch up the horse and take the food to the village square.

Janka went home to see how her brother was doing and to put on her best clothes for the feast.

I was heading back to my wagon the do the same when I saw Dragan outside of his wagon busily polishing his boots. I thought of the ribbon that we had bought for Dobro's mane. I still had it with me in my pouch.

He was so intent on polishing his boots that he was startled when I called his name.

"Oh, Milada," he said, looking up at me, still rubbing his left boot, "Are you ready for the feast."

"The food is ready, but I'm not dressed yet" I said. "It looks like you will have the shiniest boots at the festival!"

"I'm not that concerned with the way they look," he said, seeming only now to realize how shiny they were. "I just seem to loose myself in thought when I polish them".

He brushed the hair out of his eyes as he sat up and looked at me directly. For a moment I was lost in his eyes before I remembered the ribbon.

"Here," I said, holding out the blue strand of satin.

"For my hair?" he laughed, holding a piece of the ribbon in each hand and pushing his hair off his forehead.

"It's not for you!" I said, giggling. "It's for Dobro's mane! Tanya and I bought some ribbons in the market and I thought Dobro would look very smart with a blue ribbon in his mane!"

"We will have to ask him," Dragan said, "but I think he will like it!"

He stood up and gave me a quick hug. I wanted to melt into his arms, but it was over as soon as it began.

"Go now and make yourself even more beautiful for the feast," he said, "while I go and have a word with a horse about a ribbon!"

I hurried back to the wagon and found Zora outside, wearing her purple and gold skirt, ready to go.

"There you are!" she said, "Hurry now, it's almost dark. I'll wait for you and Tanya and we can go together".

"I'm ready now" Tanya said, pushing open the curtain, "but I'll wait for you!"

At first I didn't recognize Tanya as she emerged from the wagon like a butterfly out of a cocoon. Her auburn hair was unbound from its usual plaits and framed her face like a halo. She wore a bright green dress decorated with golden stars. I recognized it as one that Layla used to wear.

"You look so beautiful in Layla's dress," I said, wondering where she had got it.

As if reading my mind she said, "I always loved this dress. Layla said that one day it would be mine. Mother Miriana gave it to me today. She said that I was growing and that it was time for me to have it."

She spun around and the full skirt opened into a circle.

"It makes me feel beautiful," she said, with a smile.

"You look beautiful," I said. "And grown up!"

I entered the wagon and took my red skirt out form the chest. When I pulled it over my head and tried to tie the cord around my waist I saw that it was too tight. I tried the spangled green one but it was very short. It had been a while since the last festive occasion. I didn't realize that I'd grown so much.

As I came out of the wagon Zora called to me, "Are you ready?" Then she saw my short skirt and laughed.

"It looks like you have grown up as well!" she said. 'Let me see if I have something pretty you can wear."

I thought of Zora's preference for sombre colours and my heart fell. I wanted to look festive and pretty this evening. Zora entered the wagon and dug into her chest. I could only see her back, not what she was holding when she said to me, "My mother wore this dress. She loved it so much that I never passed it on, but it's too bright for me. I think you might like it, and the size might be right, if it isn't a little too big."

Zora stood up. When she turned around she held up the most beautiful dress I had ever seen. It was red, my favourite colour, with golden suns and silver moons embroidered all over it.

"Oh, Zora," I exclaimed, "Can I really wear it? It is so beautiful!"

"Let me help you put it on," she said. "There are many laces to do up."

Zora pulled the laces as tightly as they would go and the dress fit me fine.

"There is room for you to grow with this dress," she said.

"You mean I can keep it?" I asked her, thinking it was not possible for such a beautiful dress to belong to me.

"Wear it as long as it makes you happy and then pass it on to someone else who will love it as you do," she said.

I threw my arms around her, without thinking of her usual reserve.

"Thank you, thank you, thank you!" I said. "I will always think of you when I wear it!"

"Come on, let's go while there is still some food left," she said with a smile as she pulled the curtain open. "Tanya, look! Here comes another butterfly!"

I felt as pretty as a butterfly as I emerged from the wagon.

"Wow!" said Tanya, "look at you! Where's your red ribbon? Let me tie it on your hair and then we can be off."

I popped back into the wagon and handed her the ribbon.

"It's shorter than mine," she said.

"I gave part of it to Yagoda," I told her. "She actually is a nice girl."

"Let's go," Zora said.

I knew that there was plenty of food, but still I was anxious to join in the celebration and to see if Dragan would notice how pretty I looked in my new red dress.

Chapter 45

Dancing by the Fire

The full moon had risen by the time we reached the village square. Long tables were heaped with food and we helped ourselves to a plate of meat and cabbage stew spiced with garlic and onions and even some cinnamon from Mother Miriana's special pouch.

"This is so good!" Tanya said, licking her fingers. "We haven't had such spices for a while. Mother Miriana said that she used the last bits of the spices she had for this feast. She will replenish our stocks at the great meeting of the clans in Midsummer".

"We've been collecting herbs on our travels for the exchange all year," Zora added.

"It is wonderful how the gypsies all work together," I said.

Just then I heard Bora strike up a tune on his viol. Others joined on their instruments and people near the music began to dance.

"Come on, Tanya," I said, taking her hand and pulling her toward the music.

"I'm still eating!" she said. "I'll come as soon as I'm done."

"Don't eat so much that you'll be too full to dance!" I said, laughing.

"There will be plenty of time for dancing," she said. "We watched the moon come up; we'll still be dancing when it goes down!"

I found Goran standing near the musician, clapping his hands in time to the rhythm.

"Milada!" he exclaimed when he saw me, "You look beautiful! Where did you get that dress?"

"Thanks," I said. "Zora gave it to me. It belonged to her mother".

"I wouldn't expect to see Zora in something so...red!" he laughed.

"She said that it is too bright for her," I said, and did a little twirl. "But it's just right for me!"

"Let's dance," I said and took Goran by both his hands. He came more willingly than usual.

We danced to the lively music, our faces flushed in the light of the fire. After a while I needed to catch my breath.

"Let's go get a drink of water," I said to Goran and we made our way back to the tables.

Dunia and Yagoda were sitting there with some other children from the village.

"Hello Dunia," Goran called. "Will you join the dance tonight."

"I prefer to sit and watch," she said.

"Can I get you something to drink?" asked Goran. "A cup of blackberry wine, maybe?"

"A cup of water would be nice," she said.

"Can I bring you a cup, too, Milada?" he asked.

"Yes, please," I said, "the dancing has made me very thirsty."

I sat down on the bench next to Dunia. I saw she was wearing a pretty dark blue skirt and white blouse with embroidery covering the sleeves. Over the skirt she wore a heavily embroidered apron, definitely for decoration, not to keep her skirt clean. She would need an apron over her apron, I thought! I noticed that Yagoda and the other girls wore the same things but with slightly different embroidery. None was as intricate as Dunia's.

"What beautiful embroidery!" I told her gently fingering her apron. Without thinking, she pulled it from my hand as if to protect it.

"It has taken me many hours to make," she said.

"You all have similar dresses," I said.

"That's so when we go to festivals in other villages people will know we come from this village," Yagoda said. "I'd rather wear a red dress like yours, but then people would think that I am from Havida village instead of Richuka. The women here have always worn blue."

"Does it matter so much to know who comes from which village?" I asked.

"Oh yes," said one of the girls in blue. "We are very proud of our village and want everyone to know that we are a part of it."

"And boys from other villages know that ours is rich," added another of the girls. "So when they see our clothes they know we will make good brides."

"They can see from the embroidery on our aprons that we can sew well and have the skills to keep house," said the third girl.

I had never considered such things. "Are there people from other villages here tonight?" I asked.

"There is a group of boys from Havida over there," Yagoda said, pointing at some young men at the far side of the fire.

"The village is not far away," she said. "I think they came to have a look at the girls!"

I saw that one of them was speaking with Meli, one of the girls from the gypsy band. They were both smiling.

"I see that Stefan has found a friend," Dunia said pointedly to the girl on her right. "I thought he had his eye on you".

"I thought so, too," she said, "Until that gypsy wench put her hooks in him".

"What do you mean?" I asked. "Meli is a lovely girl. They are just talking".

"You are very young and naïve," Dunia said. "The village boys are often tempted by the gypsy girls while we look on".

"Well maybe if you were friendlier or would get up and dance and have some fun they would like to be with you!" I spurted. As I got up I nearly collided with Goran as he returned with the water.

"Slow down, Milada," he said. "You nearly made me spill the water."

"I didn't make you do anything," I said, "Watch where you are going!" I took one cup from his hand and drank all the water down in one go.

"Thank you," I said. "I'm going back to the music. Are you coming?"

"I'll sit this one out," he said.

"I'll come with you." I was surprised to hear Yagoda say.

"Stay where you are!" her sister insisted.

"I am just going to watch the dancers," she said, getting up from the bench and standing a little behind me as if shielding herself from her sister's steely gaze.

"Suit yourself," Dunia said, "but you may have to suffer the consequences if our father sees you."

I took Yagoda's small hand in mine and started back towards the fire, the music and the dancing.

"Why would your father not be happy to see you having fun?" I asked her.

"They say that good girls don't dance by the fire. We have our special dances of the village. Those are acceptable, but to dance with the gypsies, even with your band, is not considered proper," she told me.

I thought about her words and realized that generally we did not celebrate or dance with people of the villages. This was a special occasion in one particular village. I had joined Layla in the dance here many years back, but I was so little I didn't pay attention if any of the other villagers had joined in.

We stood at the edge of the people dancing.

"Are there steps to these dances?" she asked me. "Everyone is moving to the rhythm but is doing something different."

"We listen to the music and follow where our bodies tell us to move," I said, again never having given it much thought. "Come and give it a try".

"Oh no," she said, "I don't think I can. I'll just watch."

Listening to the pulse of the music, I could not keep my feet still and moved off to join the other dancers. I soon lost myself in the music, closing my eyes and letting my body go with the rhythm.

I felt someone's arms around me. I opened my eyes and saw that it was Dragan.

"Who is this beauty in the shining red dress?" he asked me with a smile in his eyes.

I looked at him, surprised. He looked so handsome in the firelight, his black eyes shining.

"You shouldn't close your eyes when you dance," he said, drawing his finger tips lightly over my eyebrow and resting them gently on my cheek. "It cuts you off from people. Let them share in your joy."

He spun me around and then was gone in the crowd of dancers. I could still feel the warmth of his arms around me and sense a lingering scent of leather and boot polish where he had held me for that magical moment.

I continued to dance and move around with the flow of dancers. Now, with my eyes open, I saw Yagoda tapping her foot and swaying with the rhythm. I danced over to where she was standing and held out my arms.

"I know you want to dance," I said. "Come dance with me. Let yourself go!"

Without a word she took my outstretched hands and joined in the dance. At first her movements were a little stiff as if she were trying to do dance steps she remembered, but then she relaxed into the rhythm and let the music carry her to another place where the mind is quiet and there is nothing but rhythm and movement.

The music became faster and faster. I saw the musicians laughing as the tempo increased as if they were challenging each other and the dancers to keep up. It reached a crescendo and then abruptly came to a halt.

The following silence was quickly broken by the sound of the dancers' laughter and laboured breathing.

Yagoda's cheeks were red and she was wearing a big smile.

"That was wonderful," she said, "I've never felt so free!"

I gave her a little hug and we went in search of a much-needed drink of water.

Goran was still sitting with Dunia and the girls.

"Looks like you had fun," he said.

Dunia gave Yagoda a disapproving look but said nothing.

"I'll get us some water," I said, taking the two beakers from the table. I went to the big earthenware jar. In a clearing a little ways distant I saw Tanya. Her bright green dress looked grey under the moon but its embroidery sparkled as it caught its stark white light. I started to go over to her but then realized she was deep in conversation with a man. It was Dragan. The two held each other by both their hands. The moonlight shone down on them like a beacon through a break in the overhanging branches. It didn't feel right for me to disturb this moment so I turned back, filled the cups then returned to Goran and the girls.

Chapter 46

The Little Bird

We did see the moon set that night and the sun cast its rosy light in the east before we collapsed in exhaustion. I fell onto my bed without even taking off my red dress. It dazzled in the sunlight that came through the wagon's curtain when Tanya came in later that day.

"Good morning, Milada!" she said, "Or should I say good afternoon! The sun is already past its zenith!"

Tanya was still wearing her bright green dress from the night before.

"Have you been up all night?" I asked her. She looked fresh with bright eyes and rosy cheeks.

"No," she said, laughing. "I was too tired to come back to the wagon so I just curled up with a blanket under the trees. The night was not cold."

We changed out of our festive frocks. I placed mine carefully away in my chest hoping that I would have another occasion to wear it soon. We had a wash and then headed into the village to help clean up the remains of the feast.

"Where are the tables?" I said as we entered the square?"

"I guess we are too late to help," said Tanya. "It looks like everything has been done."

"Did the feast last night really happen?" I asked, "Or was it just a beautiful dream?"

"Sometimes it's hard to know what is real," Tanya replied.

Though at first the square seemed empty compared to the activity there the pervious night I began to notice that there were groups of people here and there. I saw Mother Miriana and Lazara and some other women sitting in a sunny corner chatting. On the other side of the square I saw Goran with some of the boys from our band gathered around in a circle with some of the village youths.

"I'm going to say 'Good morning' to Mother Miriana," said Tanya as she headed off to the sunny corner.

"Tell her 'Good morning' from me, too," I said and went to see what the boys were doing.

I made my way across the square and into the tight circle next to Goran. Two boys crouched on the cobblestones throwing a hand full of knuckle-bones. There was a moment of silence then the toss and many of the youths started to clap and shout.

"What are they doing?" I asked Goran, who was watching the game so intently he didn't notice I had joined the circle.

"Good morning, Milada," he said. "Someone throws the bones and how they fall determines how many points the throw is worth. Whoever get the most points in three throws wins."

"Wins what?" I asked.

"At each round the players put in a coin. If someone had a good score they might put in an extra coin or two. To keep playing the other player must match the coins. The player who has the best score after three rounds wins all the coins," he explained.

"Why are the other people all so excited?" I asked.

"We make bets on who will make the highest score," he said, "so when one of the players wins, some of us win as well."

"And the ones who loose?," I asked. "What about them?"

"Maybe they will win next time," he said.

"And maybe they will loose all their money," I said, not really understanding why this form of game was so popular.

"No one thinks they will loose," Goran said. "If they did, they wouldn't play."

"Look, here come Dunia and some other girls," I said as I saw a group of girls coming across the village square.

Goran put his hands in his pockets and turned to greet the girls.

"Good morning, ladies," he said with a little bow and a tip of his cap.

The girls giggled. They we dressed in their everyday clothes now, not in their blue festive dresses. The bluebirds had turned back into drab brown house wrens. The only touch of colour was the red ribbon still tied fast in Yagoda's hair.

One of the girls was holding something in her two clasped hands.

"What do you have there?" Goran asked her.

"It's little bird," she said. "I think it fell out of its nest".

"If you give it to my friend, Tanya," I said, "she will make sure it will be all right."

"I have a better idea," said one of the boys who had come over to see what we were doing. "Give it to me."

I didn't like the way he demanded the bird, but the girl demurred and handed it over.

"We can play a trick on the old witch," he said.

"The old witch?" I asked. "What old witch?"

"The gypsy witch," he said. "I was having some fun with my mates yesterday, just teasing one of the mongrel dogs that hangs around the butcher shop."

"What do you mean 'having some 'fun'?" I asked, feeling more and more uncomfortable.

"We were trying to see who could hit him with a stone using our sling shots," he said. "I was the best at it. It's just harmless fun. We get to practice our aim. We do it all the time," he said.

"It's not harmless to the dog!" I said.

"It's a useless dog," he said, "good for nothing. So we are enjoying our sport when all of a sudden out of nowhere comes the witch swishing her broom at us and yelling to high heaven to stop and 'leave the poor beast alone'."

"Of course the dog was as startled as we were and ran off, so that was the end of our fun," he said. "Everyone says she is so wise. Now we'll see how wise she really is."

"What do you mean?" I asked him.

"We'll use this here little birdie," he said. "I will keep it like this in my hands so she can't see it. Then we say 'here is a bird - is it alive or dead'?"

"And what will that prove?" I asked, thinking it was a stupid idea.

"If she says it's dead I will open my hands and show her that it is alive," he said.

"And if she says it's alive?" I asked.

"Then I will squeeze my first in a split second before I open my hand and bye-bye little bird. Either way and she'll be wrong!" he said. "Come on, who's coming to watch?"

Most of the children trooped off after the boy.

"What a mean thing to do!" I said to Goran, who was still by my side.

"It's a clever idea, though," he said, "Let's go and see how Mother Miriana handles it.

"I hope he won't kill the little bird," Yagoda said. She placed her hand in mine and smiled up at me as we walked across the square where the others had gathered.

"Over here, Goran," Dunia called as we approached.

I noticed that Janka, the girl whose brother Mother Miriana had helped had joined the group of older women sitting in the sun. We smiled, acknowledging each other.

"So, Grandmother," I heard the boy saying to Mother Miriana. "We have all heard about your wisdom. Here is a question for you".

He held his closed hands out in front of him and said, "I have a little bird in here. Is it alive or dead".

There was silence in the group surrounding Mother Miriana as the young people anticipated her answer and what the boy might do.

Mother Miriana looked at him coolly and said, "It is in your hands". She turned back to the women and they continued their conversation.

The boy looked disgusted. He arm tightened as if to make a fist but Janka reached out with lightening speed and knocked the bird out of his hand. It fell to the ground. She picked it up and held it gently.

She gave the boy an angry look and said, "Why are you always looking for trouble. Don't you have anything better to do?"

Tanya went over to Janka's side.

"Let me see," she said, gently stroking the bird's soft feathers.

"Here, take it, " Janka said, placing the small creature in Tanya's hand. "See if you can save this poor little creature."

Tanya took the bird and said, "I'll see what I can do" and headed back to our wagon.

"Have you had anything to eat yet?" Goran asked me as we watched her go.

"No," I said. "I ate so much last night but I am rather hungry again".

"Dunia has asked me to come to lunch," he said, "Why don't you come, too. If it's all right with you, Dunia," he added.

"I suppose we have enough food," she said.

That was not the most welcoming of invitations and I was thinking to go and find Tanya when Goran linked his left arm with my right so I couldn't leave without making it into an issue. He linked his other arm with Dunia's and we set off for the house where I had once lived.

Chapter 47

An Unpleasant Meal

When we reached Dunia's house I could see that there was no one at home. The shutters were closed and the door locked tight. Dunia took a large iron key from her pouch and unlocked the door.

"Yagoda," she said, "open the shutters so we can have some light. The day is bright enough. I will put the food on the fire to warm".

Yagoda did as she was told.

"Where are your father and mother?" I asked.

Dunia replied, "My father is the village blacksmith. He is busy at his forge. He may come home in a while if there is not too much work to do."

"Our mother is probably still out in the fields," Yagoda said. "At this time of year there is much work to do tending to the crops as they ripen for the harvest. I would have gone with her but I did not wake up until the sun was high."

"I'm surprised that she let you sleep!" Dunia said, "The rest of us managed to do our jobs today".

"She is young and needs more rest," I said.

"She would have had enough rest if she hadn't used so much energy dancing like a mad cat last night" Dunia snapped.

"Ladies, ladies," Goran interceded, "we are here to share a lovely meal that Dunia has prepared, let's not bicker."

Dunia smiled at him as she stood over the big iron stew pot.

"Will you help me put this pot on the hook, Goran?" she asked, "It is very heavy".

"Yes, of course," he replied. I could see the muscles in his arms tensing as he picked up the pot and carried it to the fireplace.

Dunia took some cheese from the cooling cupboard and put it on the polished wood table. She took a loaf of bread and sliced it into thick wedges.

"Yagoda," she said, "fetch the plates and spoons and put them on the table".

"Is there anything I can do to help?" I asked.

"No," said Dunia, "today you are our guest. Just sit down and wait until the stew is warm."

I watched Yagoda set six places at the oaken table. I tried to remember how the cottage looked when I was a very little girl living there with my Grandma and Grandpa. I remembered it as being bigger. The table seemed to stretch on forever. I loved sitting beneath it with a blanket thrown over the top and pretending I was living in my own private cave. I had forgotten about that game!

When I lived here the front door seemed so high. Now I saw that it was barely tall enough for Goran to enter without stooping. Looking at Goran, I realized that he had changed. He was much taller now and had a light dusting of brown hair growing on his upper lip. Seeing him every day, I hadn't really noticed the changes, but looking at him here in unfamiliar surroundings he seemed very different from my childhood playmate.

Yagoda finished her job and sat down besides me.

"Look at this," she said placing a strange rock in my hand.

"Where did you find this?" I asked looking at what at first looked like a snail but was actually a stone.

"I found it in the field last year when we were preparing the ground," she said. "Isn't it strange?"

"I've seen one or two similar ones," I said, "but they are rare".

"What kind of stone is it?" she asked me.

"A stone like this is called a fossil," I told her. "A long time ago that snail-like creature lived and died. There was probably a sea here a long, long time ago. Over the years the sea dried and soil was compressed over it. Some of the creatures that lived and died there were preserved in the stone that formed."

"Let me see," said Goran, coming over to take a look. "That's interesting!"

"Very pretty," said Dunia, "but it is still is stone that needs to be cleared from the fields. The important thing is to have a good harvest".

Just then the front door opened and a tired looking woman entered the house.

"I'm very hungry!" she said, "Dunia, did you prepare the meal?"

"Yes, mother," she said. "The stew is just warming up. I invited Goran and his friend to join us."

Dunia's mother looked around the room as if she hadn't noticed that we were there.

"Oh, hello," she said first looking at Goran and then at me. "Do we have enough food for guests?" she added quietly to Dunia.

"Yes, mother, we ate so much at the feast last night that we didn't touch the stew. I made enough for two meals. Shall we start now or wait and see if our father comes?"

"Let's eat now," her mother said. "I have been in the field since sun up and feel weak with hunger".

We gathered around the table. Goran said, "Shall I bring the pot?"

"No, thank you, Goran," Dunia said, "I'll put some into a bowl for the table. She ladled the stew into a large ceramic crock and placed it on the table.

"Pass me your bowls," she said. One by one she filled our wooden bowls. "Help yourself to some bread and cheese".

This stew was filling but lacked the fragrance and flavours of the ones that I was used to eating at the gypsy camp. Before we had finished, the girls' father returned.

His large frame blocked the light form the doorway.

"What is there to eat?" he asked in a booming voice, "I am very hungry."

"Dunia made a good, hearty stew today," their mother replied.

"Who are these young people?" he asked looking at Goran and me as he took his place at the head of the table. "Did you bring gypsies to eat at my table?"

Dunia said, "This is Goran and his friend, what was your name again?" she asked me.

"Milada," I said, more quietly than I intended.

"We are not gypsies," Goran told the tall man. "We have no parents and the gypsies let us travel with them for a time."

The man looked at me and then at his own daughters. "Come closer, girl," he said. "Let me get a better look at you".

Timidly I got up and approached him. There was something familiar in his eyes.

"This girl looks like one of my own," he said, "but she cannot be my daughter."

His wife stared at him, then at me and then back again.

"She does look like our daughters," she said. "and they both resemble your mother, God rest her soul".

"When did you go to live with the gypsies, girl?" he asked me.

"When I was little," I replied. "I feel like I've always lived with them. They are my family now."

"She said she used to live here," Dunia said, "with her Grandparents".

I wished I had never come to this house. I wished I could crawl beneath the table and be safe in my private cave!

"This was my parents' house," the man said. "You must be my brother's little girl. He will be shocked to find you so grown up."

"Little Anna," the mother said, "I remember her. She was always wandering off into the fields. How many times one or the other of us would fetch her home!"

The old man should have taken a strap to her," the man said. "She was lucky a bear didn't get her."

"Anna, you must stay here until my brother comes again," the man said, holding me tightly by the shoulders.

"I couldn't do that," I said. "My place is with the gypsies now. I will travel with them."

"Come now, Anna," the woman said, "You are no longer a child. It is time for you to learn the ways of our women, to tend the house and plant the fields. It is time for you to start thinking about finding a good husband and raising a family of your own".

"My name is Milada," I said, loudly, "and I am learning the ways of the gypsy women".

"I can't let my own flesh and blood abide with the heathen gypsies," the man said, tightening his grip. "I say you will stay here!"

I pulled away from him and stood behind Goran. I could see that he was also upset by the way this man had spoken to me.

"These gypsies saved your village with their knowledge!" I said. "I am learning much more important things than how to keep a house clean!"

Before he could say another word or grab me again I ran to the door, heaved it open and ran as fast as I could back to our camp.

Chapter 48

An Unexpected Proposal

I was out of breath when I reached our camp. I sat panting on the seat of our wagon. Tanya poked her head out from the curtained entrance and said, "Hello, Milada, you're back."

I was too out of breath to speak. When she saw my face she said, "What has happened?"

"He grabbed me," I said as soon as I could speak. "He called me 'Anna' and said I must stay here in the village until his brother returned."

"Who grabbed you?" Tanya asked. "Who could insist you stay if it is not your desire?"

"I went with Goran to Dunia's house; the house I remembered. It was her father. He said his brother is my father," I explained, "but I never knew him. He is nothing to me."

Tanya sat beside me on the wooden seat.

"He gave you the gift of life," she said gently. "I'm sure he would be proud of the young woman you have become".

"I don't know about that," I said, "I don't know how to keep a house or work in a field".

"You know what to do when someone has a fever or a sore tummy," she said.

"Or an earache," I added. "I might like to meet my father. But I don't want to stay in the village."

"Why not?" asked Goran who had heard what I said as he approached the wagon. "Dunia's mother has a point. It's time to think about your future."

"My future is here with the gypsies," I said. "They are my friends, and my family."

"We love you and would miss you if you left us," Tanya said, giving my hand a little squeeze. "I must go and check the horses now. You are safe here with Goran".

She hopped off the wagon and went off in the direction of the pasture.

Goran and I watched her go. Then he said, "You have found your real family now and they want you to stay here with them."

"I couldn't stay here," I said. "I would miss moving from place to place; the dancing, the singing by the campfire, the happiness of our people…"

"I'm getting tired of moving from place to place all the time and of being an outsider," Goran said. "I think I would like to learn a trade, settle down and have a place and a family of my own."

"You are still young," I said.

"I've seen fifteen summers," he replied. "It will take time for me to make a start in the world."

"You know how to do many things," I said, "things you've learned from the gypsies."

"I know how to help out with many things," he said, "but not to do one thing well."

"The gypsies always work together," I said. "That's why things run so smoothly".

"In the villages people do one craft well and then exchange their work with others or else for money to buy things at the market," he said.

"How do you know so much about the ways of the village?" I asked.

"I lived in one for a long time before I travelled with the gypsies, remember?" he said, climbing up onto the wagon and sitting beside me.

I found it hard to remember the time before Goran joined the band. We had been good friends for such a long time.

"Look, Milada," he said, taking both my hands in his, "let's stay here together and make a new life for ourselves."

He looked directly into my eyes in a way I had never seen before.

"What do you mean?" I said, letting my hands rest in his.

"Milada, I love you. I have loved you since the day we met and always dreamed that one day you would love me. I know you are still young, but not too young to be a wife. Marry me and let's start a new adventure together, here when you belong."

I could not speak. What Goran said was so unexpected. I held his hand and looked at his hopeful face and waited for some words to come.

"Could you love me," he asked, when I did not reply, "do you think?"

Could I love him? Did I love him? "Goran, dear Goran," I said, knowing what I had to say would hurt him. "Of course I love you. You and I have grown up together, travelled together, learned about life together. But I never thought about marriage. I love you like a dear friend, like a beloved brother."

His eyes fell. "Can you consider my offer?"

"You know I want to travel with the gypsies. I really do not want the life of a villager," I said.

"If you could love me I would stay with you and the gypsies," he said quietly, still looking down at our joined hands.

"Could you be happy," I asked him, "if you stayed with our band?"

"I don't know," he answered, truthfully. "You know I've always felt that I was different from them. I would rather have a more settled life," he said raising his eyes to mine, "but I don't want to loose you."

Before I could say anything more, he moved close to me and kissed me tenderly on my lips. He let my hands go and hopped off the wagon.

"Think about it," he said, "please." And he was gone.

I sat on the bench of the wagon with Goran's words swimming around my head. He loves me… He wants to marry me. No. But the kiss was sweet. No boy had ever kissed me like that before. But it did not compare to the way I felt when Dragan held me in his arms.

At our evening meal I avoided Goran. I noticed he kept looking at me, but every time he came in my direction I moved on. I didn't know what to say to him. I needed more time.

That night as we lay in our beds in the wagon Tanya asked me, "Is there something troubling you, Milada? I know about your experience today in the village; you are safe here, yet you seem tense."

"Oh, Tanya," I said in the comforting darkness of our wagon, "it's Goran. He has asked me to marry him!"

"We always knew he would," Zora said.

"Did you?" I asked, incredulous.

"Yes," said Tanya, "haven't you notice the way he looks at you?"

"And the way he always gives you the best pieces of meat when he serves the stew," Zora said.

"And how he fetches the water for you to wash in the morning?" Tanya said.

"We all use the water," I said, "and what do you mean 'the way he looks at me'?"

"Like a lovesick puppy!" Zora said. "You must have noticed it!"

"I've noticed Dunia looking at him like that," I said. "It's goofy!"

"We'll that's the way Goran looks at you!" she replied.

"Since when?" I asked, still not believing them.

"Since he first came to us," Tanya said. "He was always more comfortable with you."

"That's because I came to live with the gypsies, too," I said.

"Maybe that's part of it," Tanya said, "but everyone knows he's in love with you."

Everyone except for me.

"I love him like a brother," I said. "I can't image being his wife."

"Only you know what is in your heart," said Tanya.

As much as I cared for Goran, I knew that my heart belonged to someone else.

Chapter 49

Yagoda

I avoided going into the village. Goran came and went, often bringing cheese from the market or a dish that Dunia had prepared. He didn't mention the subject of love or marriage again, but I felt a new awkwardness around him. Once again the moontime came around and I was happy to find a reason to avoid seeing him for a few days.

On the second morning in the moon tent Tanya said to me, "You look happier today than I've seen you for a long time."

"I am enjoying the peace here," I replied. "I feel uncomfortable staying near this village, and also uncomfortable around Goran".

"You two were always such good friends," Tanya said.

"I'd like too keep it that way," I told her, "but after he kissed me everything changed and became strange."

"Our moontime gives us the chance to remove ourselves from our everyday life and bring ourselves back into balance," Tanya said. "Use these days to quiet your mind so you can better hear your heart."

Over the next days I tried to follow Tanya's advice, but found it very hard to still my mind. I thought about my friendship with Goran and the years that we spent with the gypsies. I wondered if he was right about us never really fitting in. But then I looked around and saw the other women, sharing this time together and I could not imagine myself living in the village where people did not have an understanding of nature or such a deep connection with it.

When the moontime passed it was decided that we would move our camp. Summer was coming and the great meeting of the clans. We still had a long distance to travel to arrive at the meeting place in the highlands by Midsummer's day.

Returning to my wagon, I saw Goran sitting in its shade. In his hand was a bunch of wild flowers. I felt a pull in the pit of my stomach.

"Hello, Milada," he said, "I've been waiting for you".

"Hello, Goran. Those are pretty," I said, indicating the wildflowers.

"I picked them for you," he said, handing them to me.

"Thanks," I said, feeling a blush rising to my cheeks.

"Have you thought about what I said?" he asked, his eyes cast downwards. I think if he were looking at me he would know my answer.

"Dear Goran," I began, "you have been my best friend, my brother for many years. I love you dearly, but I cannot be your wife. We are too different, we want different things from our lives."

"Are you sure?" he asked, now searching my eyes with his.

I felt a tear escape my eye as I said, "Yes, I am sure."

"I'm sorry that you feel that way," he said, almost angrily. "In that case, if there is really no chance for you to be with me, I will stay here and make my life in this village. Dunia's father has offered to teach me the craft of the blacksmith."

"You will stay here?" I asked, beginning to feel the impact of his decision. "You'll be a blacksmith? That's hard work!"

"Yes, it is. But it is a good living. Horses always need new shoes," he said, with just a shadow of his cheeky smile.

And that smile moved my heart. "Oh, Goran," I said, "I'll miss you so much!"

"Then say you'll marry me and I will stay," he said.

"I wish I could," I said, "but it would not be true to my heart."

"You think that Dragan will marry you?" he spat.

I was shocked by what he said and by his tone and by his words.

"I see the way you look at him, all moon-eyed," he continued. "But he will never marry outside of the gypsy band".

Before I had a chance to say anything Goran jumped up and ran off through the woods.

I looked at the wilting flowers in my hand and let the tears that had been building up in my eyes flow.

I don't know how long I was sitting there, my head in my hands before I heard a small voice beside say, "Anna, why are you crying?"

I looked up and saw Yagoda standing beside me holding a large bundle.

"Yagoda," I said, "what are you doing here?"

"Goran said the gypsies are leaving tomorrow. I want to come with you," she said.

"You want to come with the gypsies?" I asked.

"Yes," she replied. "They seem so much happier than the people in the village. I like to dance, to be free like you, not always stuck in the house."

"Let's go and see what Tanya thinks about you joining us," I said, taking her hand. "What's in that bundle?"

"Clothes and things," she said, heaving the heavy bag over her narrow shoulder.

I found Tanya with the other women preparing some vegetables for the evening meal.

"Tanya," I said, "This is Yagoda. She would like to travel with us".

"Hello, Yagoda," Tanya said, squatting a little to look the child in the eyes. "I remember you from the feast. You joined in the dancing."

"Yes," said Yagoda, "I loved it! That's why I want to come with you!"

"There is more to our life that dancing," Tanya said, "It is hard work moving from place to place. There is much to learn."

"I don't mind," she said. "I hate my life."

"Your life comes with you where ever you go," Tanya said. "If you are not happy in your heart you will not be happy with us".

"But I can learn to be happy with you. You are all happy. My family is not! They shout at each other and are not kind," she argued.

"You do not have to follow those ways, if you see that they are not yours," Tanya said. "You can be their teacher and bring peace to your home".

"I would rather not be there at all!" Yagoda said.

"We must ask the Baron if you may join us, then," Tanya said.

The three of us went to the Baron's tent. As we approached we could see the bent backs of the Baron and his son. They each had one foot on a log, companionably polishing their boots.

They didn't hear us coming. Tanya gently placed her hand low on Dragan's back.

"Excuse me," she said. "May we have a word with you and your father."

Dragan dropped the boot brush, swept Tanya into his arms, swung her around in a circle then placed her gently on the log.

"You girls would like a word?" said the Baron, straightening up and smiling down on us.

"Yes, sir," I said. "This is Yagoda, my cousin," it was strange to hear myself say that, but I thought it might make a difference in the Baron's decision to let her stay. "She would like to stay with us and travel with the gypsy band".

The Baron sat down on the log and looked at the child.

"She looks very much like you," he said to me. Then he looked at Yagoda and said, "Child, do you have a family? Mother? Father?"

"Yes," she said, "I do. But I am not happy with them."

"My child, we take in those children who have no family of their own to care for them. We cannot deprive your parents of such a lovely girl," he said.

"They have my sister!" Yagoda said boldly.

"You are very different from your sister. You have your own special gifts to offer," he said. "I cannot allow you to come with us now. You are very young and your place is with your family".

"Please, please let me come!" Yagoda begged.

Tanya gently took her arm and said, "The Baron has spoken, my child".

"But Anna has a father!" Yagoda blurted out. "Make her stay with us!"

The Baron looked at me and said, "Is this true, Milada?"

"They tell me that it is, Sir," I replied, "but I have never met him."

"I remember when you came to us," he said, "so many years ago. My daughter Layla spoke with your grandfather. He was happy to let you come with us and learn our ways. You were very, very young."

"You won't make me stay in the village, will you?" I asked him, feeling the tears coming again.

"No, my child," he said. "You may stay with us as long as you wish. But for now, please take your cousin back to her home."

"Yes, Sir," I said. "Thank you".

The Baron caressed my hair and smiled. Dragan put one arm around me and the other around Tanya and gave us both a little squeeze.

"See you at dinner!" he said with a smile.

Chapter 50

A Caged Bird

Yagoda shuffled her feet, kicking up dust as we walked toward the edge of our camp.

"What a mean man!" she said.

"Who? The Baron?" I asked her, incredulously.

"Yes, him," she replied. "Why did he let you stay and not me?"

"I had no one to raise me," I said. "You do."

"As soon as I get old enough, I'll run away," she said.

"When you get older you can do as you please, but now you have to go home," I said as we neared the village. "Can you find your way home from here? I will not go any closer to your house."

Before she could answer I saw her father coming toward us. "There you are!" he shouted. "Where do you think you are going?"

Before I could turn and run I felt his hand close like a vice around my wrist. He had Yagoda by the other hand and he was dragging us back toward his house. Around us, the people were staring as we passed.

"Let me go!" I shouted, but his grip only tightened around my wrist.

"I'll not let you go," he said sternly. "Not until my brother returns. Then he can have you and do what he wants. I don't care what happens to you after that. For all I care you can run back to the gypsies, but at least I have done my duty."

"But, you, my little thief," he said looking down at Yagoda and the large bundle she still held on to, "you have disgraced our family and you will pay the price with my belt."

He pushed us into the house and slammed the door shut behind us. The girls' mother looked on as he grabbed Yagoda's bundle and shoved her harshly down on the oaken bench. He still held my arm and even though I fought as hard as I could, trying to pull away from him, his grip held me fast. I looked at Dunia and her mother and appealed to them for help.

"Please tell him to let me go!" I sobbed. "You know I don't belong here".

Dunia's mother lowered her eyes and Dunia looked away as her father slapped my face.

"Be silent," he said and pushed me into the cold storage room. "You will stay in there until you cool off."

He pushed me so hard that I felt my knee scrape on the cold stone floor. Then I heard a key turn in the lock. I was shaking with fear and anger. What if he kept me in here and the gypsies went on without me? How would I find them? I looked for a way out. It was very dark in the small room. There was an odd smell of cheese and dried meat. In the dim light that came through the cracks in the door jam I could see some dead birds hanging from the rafters.

Then the screams began. I heard Yagoda crying, "No, please, not with your belt, please!"

I heard something making a swishing sound, then Yagoda's scream. Was her father really beating her? Why didn't her mother or Dunia make it stop? Was I next? I had to find a way out of here!

The whooshing and screaming seemed to go on forever. Then there was silence. I heard the front door open and close and then the sound of crying. At least he wasn't coming for me.

"It's you fault," Yagoda shouted, banging on the door to the cold room. "If you'd taken me with you this would not have happened!"

"It was not up to me!" I said, "Yagoda, open the door and let me out of here."

"He took the key," she said as my hopes of escape fell, "and even if he hadn't I wouldn't let you out. If I have to be stuck here, you can be stuck here, too."

I heard her footsteps moving away from the door.

"Please let me out of here!" I called, "Dunia! Please!"

But no one came. I could hear no other sounds from the kitchen now. It seems like everyone had gone. The light was fading from the crack in the door. I sat in the dark and felt my heart was breaking. The gypsies would leave without me. It would be my fate to stay with this family until they chanced this way again. I felt hot tears falling from my eyes. I let them fall until they turned into heaving sobs.

At first I didn't hear the tapping. I quieted myself and listened. Yes, there was a noise. At first I thought it was a rat and gathered my legs close under my skirt. As the tapping continued I thought it was too regular to be an animal, too even a rhythm. Then I heard a whisper.

"Milada, Milada, can you hear me?"

The voice was coming from high up on the back wall. I had to push aside the dead birds to see that there was a boarded up window above my head. I found a tin bucket that I could use to stand on to get closer to the window.

"Yes, I can hear you," I said. "Who is there? Can you help me get out of here?"

"It's me, Goran!"

Dear Goran! "Can you get me out?" I whispered back.

"I'll try to pry the boards loose," he said, "but we have to hurry before they get back. Can you push from the inside on the board that I tap?"

He tapped on the lower board and I pushed as hard as I could without falling off the bucket. Slowly the board came away. I reached out my hand and Goran took it in his.

He squeezed it and said, "That's my girl! Push on the next one now".

I pushed and he pulled and the second board was free. Goran removed it. "Can you get out through the hole?" he asked.

"No," I said, "It's still too small. And it's very high".

"Let's get one more board off and then try," he said.

With the third board removed the hole was big enough but it was too high for me to reach.

"Let me find something else to stand on," I said. The hole let in a little more light, although I could see that the sun was just about to set. I saw a wooden crate to one side of the door. I tried to lift it but it was very heavy. Using all the strength I had I managed to push it over to the window. I climbed up on it but was still too low to raise my body out. Maybe if I put the bucket on top of the crate I could jump out.

As I climbed down to get the bucket I heard footsteps in the next room.

"Let's see if she has cooled down by now," I heard my uncle say.

"Maybe she is hungry," Dunia mother said.

"I'll let her get hungrier," the man replied, "maybe then she will be grateful for what we are offering her."

I rushed to put the bucket on the box and as quietly as I could clambered up the pile. I was just able to reach the bottom of the hole with my knee and pull myself up into the window. Goran was waiting outside. I was so happy to see him!

"He's back," I said as I let him lift me down from the window ledge.

"Quick, hand me those planks. I'll put them back so they won't guess how you got out!" he said. "They'll think you learned a gypsy trick to disappear."

I handed them to him and he quickly fixed them back on the window.

"Go now," he said.

"You will not come?" I asked, looking into his eyes.

He looked at me a moment, then pulled me into his arms. I heard him whisper into my hair, "You know I'll always love you". He opened his arms as if to release a bird into the air. "Go," he said. "Live your life and be happy".

I could hear more shouting coming from the house. Maybe they discovered that I had gone.

"Go," he said. "Now!" and gave me a little push that woke me from the dream of the moment.

He ran down the alley toward the village square. It would not serve him if the man discovered his part in my escape. I made for the dense forest. I could skirt all the way around the village and make it back to our camp where I would be safe.

As I arrived at our wagon Zora was already hitching up our horse, Kizi. "Where have you been, Milada? It is decided that we will leave tonight!"

"Would you have left without me?" I asked.

"If you are not here when we go, there is some reason for you to stay," she said.

"Let's go!" I said, not wanting to think too deeply about the meaning of her words.

PART 3

THE FULL MOON

Chapter 51

On Our Way to the Meeting of the Clans

It was a long journey taking several turns of the moon before we reached the high pastureland where the clans met every year at Midsummer. I was happy that we moved far from the village of my birth but as the weeks wore on I found myself missing Goran and his cheeky laughter.

The days passed much as they always had, in routine tasks; collecting and preparing food, caring for the animals, moving from village to village, helping where we could and then moving on.

During my time in the moon tent I learned that this year the gathering of the clans was to be a very special occasion. Each year members of the clans that were in the vicinity met, but every seven years all the clans, with their chiefs made a point to be there.

I had never given too much thought to the gathering of the clans. I looked forward to the festivities, the music and the dancing and unusual variety of foods. But, now I was curious about who these other clans were and why we all met.

I thought about asking some of the older women in the moon tent, but when I was there I felt so relaxed that I forgot about life outside and just enjoyed that special time.

One day when we were on the road I asked Zora, who sat on the seat beside me guiding Kizi.

"I know when we meet with the other clans we exchange herbs and things that we each have been collecting," I said, "but who are these other clans? Are they your relatives? Why don't we meet them at other times?"

"It's question time with Milada again," Zora said with a sigh.

"Do you mind answering my questions?" I asked her.

"I suppose not," she replied. "It's just that you seem to have so many!"

"Years ago someone told me that if I don't ask, I won't learn!" I said, looking at Zora and smiling.

She smiled back at me and said, "Let me see where I can start."

"There are four clans that belong to our group," she began, "Each one follows a particular direction, which is why we generally do not meet on the road."

"What do you mean, each follows a direction?" I asked.

"From the place where we meet each Midsummer one clan travels north, one travels south, one goes east and the other goes west."

"Which way do we go?" I asked.

"We are the Band of the West," she replied. In the autumn we follow the setting sun until midwinter, then we turn and have the sun on our face as we travel back to the meeting place," she explained. "Some years our travels take us farther a field so we do not return for the meeting. But it is a good thing when we can. And on the special years we must."

"And this is a special year," I said, not sure what was so special about it.

"Yes," Zora said, "it is the seventh year since the last one.'

"Why every seven years and not five or ten?" I asked.

Zora paused a moment and then replied, "I really don't know why, Milada. Let's ask Mother Miriana when we stop to camp this evening. Can you remember the last time we had a special gathering? You were very young."

"I don't remember any particular summer meeting being different," I replied.

"Do you remember when Boban and Nitsa joined our group?" she asked me.

"It was a long time ago," I said.

"And Likos left".

Likos? I sort of remembered a boy a little older than me with that name. I hadn't thought about him for years.

"I think that was at the time of the last special meeting," Zora said.

"So we exchange children as well as herbs?" I asked.

"I think we might," was Zora's reply.

"I don't want to join any other clan!" I said. I had escaped staying in the village, now the thought of having to go and live with a strange clan made me apprehensive.

"Maybe you wouldn't mind if you met a nice young man!" Zora said with a grin.

"We have enough nice young men in our own clan," I said, thinking of my handsome Dragan.

"Do you think so?" Zora replied. "Anyone in particular you have your eye on?"

I felt my face growing warm, "No, no…"

"With Goran gone I've noticed a few of the boys paying you special attention," she said.

It was true that some of the boys had been more attentive. Bora brought me little gifts and I saw him smiling at me sometimes while he played his viol.

"As for me" Zora continued, "our boys all seem too young and the men too old. Maybe I will find a suitable young man to love this summer."

"How can you tell when you are in love?" I asked, thinking about the time that Goran said he loved me.

"You just know," she replied.

But had she ever been in love? How could she know?

The shade was getting deeper, signalling the end of a long day. I was happy when we pulled up in a clearing and saw the others unhitching their wagons. The cooking fires were already lit with the stew in copper pots bubbling away.

We went to find Mother Miriana who sat warming her hands at the fire.

"Mother Miriana," I said, "may I ask you a question?"

"Yes, my child," she said, patting the bench beside her. "Come sit a while and I'll tell you what I can."

"Zora and I were talking about the gathering of the clans," I told her. "Zora didn't know why all the clans met every seven years. Can you tell me?"

"We meet every seven years because our lives run in seven year cycles," she said.

"What do you mean, seven-year cycles?" I asked.

"From the time a child is born until she is seven years old is one phase of life," she said. "It is a time when a child gets used to being in this world. The next seven years are spent growing and learning the ways of the clan and about the place where one lives."

I thought for a moment and then said, "I'm not sure how many years old I am," I said. It seems a long time between Summer Gatherings and I feel like I've been with the gypsy band forever. What is the next phase?"

"The next phase is the time when boy and girls start to look at each other in a different way. It is when they start to think about love and starting a family of their own and finding their purpose in the world," she said.

"You are just about to begin this phase of your life, Milada," Mother Miriana said.

"Will it be hard?" I asked, not really wanting things to change.

"Each phase of life has its difficulties and its rewards," she said. "For now, let's enjoy the warmth of the fire and the tasty food our sisters have prepared.

Chapter 52

The Great Meeting of the Clans

After we had eaten our fill I had some more questions to ask.

"Mother Miriana," I asked, "what are the next phases of life?"

"Well, my child, the next phase is maturity. It is the time to raise our children, to find our place within the clan and to help and serve other people," she said.

"This phase lasts four times seven years. After that our body tells us that another phase is beginning, a phase when we can rest in the wisdom of our experience."

"Is that the phase that you are in, Mother Miriana?" I asked, "Is that why you don't come to the moon tent?"

"Yes, my child," she replied. "My body is passed the time of accepting new life."

"Did you have any children?" I asked her, realizing that I had never considered the possibility before.

"Yes, Milada," she replied. "I bore three children. One son died in an accident a long time ago. He was a fine viol player. When Bora plays his viol sometimes I think it is him, come back to us again."

"And the others?" I asked, vaguely remembering the accident with the wagon many years ago. I had no idea that the man who died was Mother Miriana's son.

"My two girls are travelling with other bands of our clan," she said.

"Will you see them at the gathering?" I asked.

"It has been many years since I have set eyes on them," she said. "But since this is a special year, if they are well they will be there."

"Do you miss them?" I asked, thinking of how much I would miss the others if we were parted.

"One girl left when she was very young. She was chosen to be the bride of the Baron of the Eastern Band. She was raised by them, to learn their ways. But that was a long time ago. I know not if they still reign. My second daughter grew up with me, then fell in love with a young man from the band of the North. I have met her and her children a few times over the years at the Summer Gatherings. They are grown now with families of their own."

"But you are alone, now," I said. "Don't you miss your children? And where is you husband?"

"You are all my children," she replied. "My husband and I loved each other deeply for a time and then our paths diverged. He joined the Northern Band and is still with them as far as I know."

"Mother Miriana," I asked, "how can you tell when you are in love?"

She smiled at me. "Do you think that you are in love?" she asked.

"I don't know what I'm supposed to feel," I said.

"When you are in love, you will know it. There will be no question in your mind," she said.

That is what Zora told me, but coming form Mother Miriana I believed it.

~

The next morning it was still dark when Tanya returned from breakfast with some food for me to eat.

"Wake up, Milada," she said, "The horses are hitched and we are ready to move"

"Why are we going so early?" I asked, not excited about having to get up before the sun.

"We are near the meeting place," she said. "An early start will get us there by nightfall."

Tanya seemed exceptionally cheerful, even for the early hour. She hummed to herself as she open the curtains and tidied the wagon.

I dragged myself out of bed and splashed some cool water on my face. Once I was more awake her enthusiasm was contagious. I started to hum along with her and by the time that Zora arrived back from the breakfast fire we were both singing at the top of our lungs.

"You two are going to wake up all the birds!" she said as she climbed up onto the wagon.

"I am excited about the gathering," Tanya said. "I have a feeling that something special is coming."

"There will be plenty of good food, that's for sure!" I said, "and music and dancing."

"So don't wear out your voices with so much singing now," she said.

"Come on, Zora," Tanya said, "for once get in the spirit. How are you going to find a lover if you are so serious?"

"I don't want to find a fool!" Zora said. "I want a man with his feet on the ground".

"Try to smile now and again, anyway!" Tanya said. "*We* know what a lovely girl you are but if you look so serious your sensible man won't notice you. You will scare him off with that frown."

"You can talk," she said, "you who already have a husband chosen for you."

"Yes, I am lucky," Tanya said, "and I'm sure you both will find wonderful partners, too."

I wanted to ask Tanya about this chosen man but she started singing again, and surprisingly Zora joined in with her deep sonorous voice. The song was a happy, upbeat song. I popped into the wagon and brought my tambourine to keep the rhythm as we sang.

The day passed quickly as we ascended higher and higher into the hills. We stopped briefly to let the horses rest and enjoyed a picnic of bread and cheese and then continued our journey.

As the sun was going down we crested a hill and saw before us circles of wagons around four separate fires, looking like petals of a huge flower. The music was already playing as we pulled up alongside the wagon in front of us. Zora let Kizi go off to graze and Tanya and I ran to join the fire of our band.

I had never seen so many gypsies together at one time before. We approached our fire. The Baron sat in a high backed chair that was only brought out on very special occasions. Dragan stood behind him speaking with a woman who I had never seen before. Her hair was long and auburn, her eyes a brilliant green. She had a regal bearing and looked at home with the Baron and Dragan. When Tanya saw the woman she let off a small cry and then ran in their direction.

I thought she was running to Dragan and started to follow her but then I saw her throw herself into the woman's arms. I wasn't sure what was happening. I felt a hand on my shoulder. I looked around and saw that Mother Miriana stood beside me.

"Who is that woman?" I asked her. "Does Tanya know her?"

"That woman," Mother Miriana replied, "is Tanya's mother. She is the Queen of the Southern Band."

"Is she married to their Baron?" I asked.

"No, my child," Mother Miriana replied. "The Western and Eastern bands are led by Barons, the Northern and Southern bands are led by Queens. In this way there is a balance."

"And Tanya's mother is a Queen?" I asked, confused.

"Yes, she is," Mother Miriana replied.

"But Tanya grew up with us; just like one of us!"

"In this way she can learn the ways of our people so she can understand their needs," Mother Miriana said.

"Will Tanya be a queen one day?" I asked, realizing how little I understood what was going on around me.

"No, my child, that is not her destiny," Mother Miriana replied. "She will marry the Baron's son and support and guide him in his work."

"Which Baron? The Baron of the East?" I asked, with a sinking feeling in the pit of my stomach, fearing her answer.

"No, my child. She will marry our own Baron's son, Dragan. That is why she has been living with our band."

Tanya marry Dragan? I felt dizzy. It couldn't be. I loved him and I knew he loved me. How could he hold me like that and comfort me if he didn't share my feelings? Those times I saw them talking together…I thought they were friends, like Goran and me. Maybe they didn't love each other; maybe they just had to marry because they were told to. Surely Dragan can marry whomever he wants.

Tanya knew all along that Dragan was to marry her, yet she never told me. How could she keep it to herself? Suddenly, the festivities made me feel both angry and sad. Who were these people? They all seemed to know things that I didn't. Maybe Goran was right after all. Right now I missed him so much. I longed to talk to him, to hear him joke and make light of the situation. But he wasn't here anymore; because I told him to go. How stupid could I be?

I couldn't stay by the fire any longer. I ran back to our wagon, hoping the others would not come until morning, and cried myself to sleep.

Chapter 53

A Meeting With a Queen

I awoke to the sound of the birds singing. Sunlight filtered through the thin summer curtains that hung at the windows. From the angle of the sun's rays I knew that it was well into the morning. Tanya pushed aside the curtain and saw that I was awake before I had time to shut my eyes and pretend to still be asleep.

"Well, good morning!" she said brightly. "Where did you disappear to last night? Were you not feeling well? Are you feeling better now?"

I didn't feel like speaking so I turned and faced the wall without a word. Instead of going away as I hoped she would Tanya came and sat besides me on the narrow bed. She put her hand on my shoulder and said, "What is it Milada?"

"It's nothing," I said.

"If it were nothing you would have danced last night," she said. "The music was spectacular. It's not at all like you to miss such festivities. Is something wrong?"

"Mother Miriana said that you are going to marry Dragan," the words spilled out of me in spite of my desire to keep them to myself.

"Yes, we have been betrothed for many years, since my birth, I think. He has been waiting for me to grow up. We will be married soon."

"Do you love him?" I asked.

"What I feel for Dragan is more than love. He and I are one. When we are together I feel truly myself - complete and whole. I can't think of another way to explain it," she said.

"I love him, too," I said softly, almost hoping she wouldn't hear me.

"I think everyone loves Dragan," she said, gently stroking my hair. "He is very kind. He will have a hard job to do in the future, leading our band. It is my destiny to be by his side, not necessarily my choice."

"And what is *my* destiny?" As I said it I heard the bitterness in my voice.

"I cannot tell you," she said, "Only you know what is in your heart".

I felt hot tears welling in my eyes. I thought I knew what was in my heart. Now I would have to see.

When I did not respond Tanya said, "Come, Milada, come and join the others. Listen to the stories they have to tell from the far off places they have travelled."

"Has your mother travelled far? How could she leave you with strangers for year upon year?" I asked.

"The people of the other bands are not strangers," she replied. We are all one people, coming from one source. She had her work to do, as I have mine. Among us this is not a strange custom," she said.

"All elder women are our mothers and men are our fathers; we are sisters and brothers, one large family based on love and respect. We will be the mothers and mentors to the next generation, teaching them our ways as we were taught."

"You seem to know a lot without being taught," I said, thinking of the many things the gypsy children just seemed to know.

"Sometimes we remember things," she said, "and we build on our experience".

I was beginning to understand what Goran meant when he said that we were different. I didn't like the feeling at all.

"Come on, Milada!" Tanya said, pulling the blanket off of me. "It's too nice a day to worry about such things. Come and help me with the animals. The young horses are beginning to explore their world. We can introduce them to the young ones from the other bands and see how they like each other."

They exchange children like they exchange horses, I thought to myself as I reluctantly got out of bed. If I had a child, could I let her go with another band for years and not have the joy of seeing her grow, I thought as I splashed cool water on my tearstained face. Was this the trade off for a life of travel and adventure? Was it not possible to have it both ways?

"What are you thinking?" Tanya said, watching me as I dried my face and replaced the towel on an overhanging branch.

"I was thinking how some of your customs are pretty strange," I said, looking directly into her eyes to see her reaction to my criticism.

To my surprise, Tanya started to laugh. She took a step toward me and gave me a big hug.

"Milada," she said, "you have lived with us for most of your life. Our connection with one another goes back a long, long time; longer than any one lifetime. Don't expect to take it all in or understand our ways. Take what works for you and let the rest go."

"But I thought I was one of you," I said, feeling the tears coming again.

"We love you, Milada," Tanya said, still holding me close. "But you were not born into the band. There is a reason that you joined us. One day you may learn what it is. Do not distress yourself about what was or what may come. Today is a beautiful day. You are here with us, part of our family and part of these festivities. Come, let's have a smile!"

She held me away from her so she could see my face. I could see the love in her eyes. Even thought I felt sad and disappointed, in the light of that love I could not hold back a smile. I knew Tanya was right. Why should I loose the pleasure of this sunny day with worry about things I could not know or control?

"That's better," she said when she saw the beginning of a smile on my face. "Get dressed. I want you to meet my mother."

I hurried into the wagon and threw on my dark blue skirt with golden starbursts embroidered around the hem. I had never met a queen before and could not image what I would say to her. I felt comfortable with Dragan but always shy when I was in the Baron's presence even though I knew he was a very good and gentle man.

I hopped down from the wagon and followed Tanya to the main part of the camp where the cooking fires burned day and night. The smell of roasting meat greeted my nostrils long before we reached the area that had been cleared for the gathering. We left the camp of our band and entered that of the band of the South, following the sound of instruments playing a lively tune.

In front of the biggest, most brightly painted wagon I have ever seen a group of musicians played odd shaped instruments. One looked like a fat pumpkin with a stork's neck with many strings stretched along its length. Another long-necked once had a small body and was played with a bow. A young woman blew through a long reed-like pipe. The sound she made was sweet but had a touch of sadness. Once again I felt like I had to hold back my tears. As if she could sense how I was feeling, Tanya took my arm and gave me her brightest smile.

"Come on," she said, pulling me up the high steps to the doorway of the wagon.

"What do I say to a Queen?" I asked. "I've never met one before?"

"Just be yourself," she replied.

Entering the wagon from the bright summer's day it took my eyes a moment to get used to the dimness inside. At first I couldn't see anyone inside. I looked around, not believing my eyes. There were many shelves along the walls, some laden with leather bound books and other with fine china patterned in red, black and gold. The windows were hung with burgundy velvet curtains edged in gold. Where they opened I could see there was a lighter gold woven fabric that let in the light, charged with an unearthly brilliance.

At the far end of the wagon, a woman reclined on a carpeted divan. The golden light shining through the mesh curtains brought out the gold highlights in her long auburn tresses. Tanya ran up to the woman and jumped onto the cushion beside her. Tanya's hair flowed loosely over her shoulders. It had the same golden tint as the woman's. I stood frozen in the doorway, stunned by the beautiful picture and unfamiliar scene before me

"Come, my child," the woman beckoned to me, "come and sit beside me." Tanya sat on her left side. She patted the cushion on her right. "Come!"

As if in a trance I approached the divan and gingerly sat down. The woman smiled at me and then gathered me in her arms.

"You are Milada," she said, "I have heard so much about you!"

I felt myself relax into her embrace. I no longer felt fearful; instead I felt comforted and safe. I wanted to stay in her arms forever and ever, with my head resting on her breast. I felt Tanya snuggle up beside us. The three of us cuddled like a mother cat and her kittens until the sun was high above us dimming the light and turning the wagon into a sheltering cocoon.

Chapter 54

Vasa

The sound of footsteps jarred me out of my pleasant reverie. Light streamed in for a moment but then was blocked by the silhouette of a man standing in the doorway. Tanya's mother relaxed her embrace and sat up.

"Excuse me if I am disturbing you, my lady. I did not know you have guests," he said.

"Come in. These are not guests, these girls are family". I felt honoured at her words.

"Girls," the woman said to us, "this is my consort, Vasa. Vasa, meet my daughter Tanya and her good friend Milada."

Tanya and I stood to greet the man. His warm smile made me feel at ease. He looked at Tanya and then at the still seated woman.

"I can see that this one is your daughter," he said, "there is a strong resemblance between you".

He smiled at Tanya, "I am pleased to finally meet you," he said, "I have heard about you, about your love and care for animals and your skills in healing. I had no idea that you were such a beauty, although it is not surprising, knowing you mother."

I was surprised to see Tanya's cheek's flush to a becoming pink.

"I have heard tell of you, as well, Sir," she said, "that you are a fine man who has brought prosperity to the clan and much happiness to my mother."

Vasa smiled once again at Tanya then turned his eyes toward me.

"And Milada," he said with a grin, "the girl who asks a thousand questions."

I felt my own cheeks growing red but could not contain a smile.

"Vasa, my love," said Tanya's mother, "would you please ask Adela to bring us some hot water. I will make the girls some tea."

"Certainly, my lady," he said. He gave a small bow to us before he turned and left the wagon.

Tanya's mother patted the divan. "Come back here my chicks," she said, "it is pleasure to have you near me."

We joined her on the soft cushions. I really did have a thousand questions but didn't know where to start, or even if I ought to ask anything. While I was thinking about what to say, Tanya beat me to it by asking, "Mama, I have heard only a little about Vasa. Can you tell me about how you met?"

"Vasa and I first crossed paths a long way south of this place, maybe five, maybe six years ago. It was one of the years that our band did not return for the gathering. We had travelled a long way. At first times were good for us. We settled near a town by the sea where ships came and went with precious cargo from places that would take years to travel by land. Our people helped load and unload the ships. In this way we acquired many unusual and precious items."

I followed the woman's gaze across the wagon. "See those china dishes and cups?" she said, indicating the heavily decorated pieces I had seen when we entered the wagon.

"Yes," I replied, "they are beautiful. I have never seen anything like them."

"They come from a land far from here," she said, "a land that has many beautiful crafts and much ancient knowledge".

There was a faint tapping on the wooden doorway. "Adela," the woman said, "is that you?"

"Yes, my lady. Shall I bring the water?" a soft voice replied.

"Yes, please come in," the woman said as she rose from the divan and moved gracefully to the doorway. "Let me help you."

She pushed aside the heavy curtain to let a young girl, of about eight or nine years enter the wagon. She was very slight, with small bones like a bird. She had shining dark eyes and a mop of raven black curls that framed her heart-shaped face.

"Put the pot there on the table and have a seat. You may join us for some tea."

The girl smiled and did what she was told, moving with a confidence that belied her small stature. She sat down next to me on the divan.

"Hello," she said, "I'm Adela."

"Hello, Adela," Tanya said, "I'm Tanya, Madam Eleeza's daughter".

"I thought you were," Adela said. "You are so much alike."

"And this is my friend Milada," Tanya said, scooting deeper into the divan so that Adela could see me.

"Hello, Adela," I said. There was something familiar about the girl but I could not put my finger on what it was.

"Hello!" she replied.

While we were making our introductions Madam Eleeza had taken a beautiful teapot and four of the precious cups and saucers from the shelf on the wall. I noticed that each shelf had a fabric pad and a narrow guardrail to protect the precious china when the wagon was moving along the rutted roads.

I wondered why she didn't keep these valuable things safely packed in a trunk so the would not be damaged in the gypsies' travels.

As if she knew what I was thinking, Madam Eleeza said, "There is no point in having beautiful things if you cannot see and enjoy them everyday."

As she spoke she swished some of the hot water in the teapot then poured it out into her washbasin. She sprinkled a few leaves from a small silver canister into the warm teapot and then added the boiled water. The three of us had fallen silent as we watched her slender fingers placing a cup in each saucer.

"Shall I continue my story while the tea is brewing?" she asked?

"Oh, yes, my lady," I said, anxious to hear more.

"One day when our band was camping by the town on the coast a flotilla of sails appeared on the horizon. People rushed to the docks to greet the ships but instead of trading ships they were warships. Hundreds of men poured out of the ships brandishing swords, cutting down anyone in their path. They overran the town, taking anything they could lay their hands on."

"Our people sensed what was coming and all escaped back to our camp without harm. We quickly loaded the wagons and moved farther inland, away from the coast. The townspeople who could ran to the countryside, but many stayed in the city to protect their homes and were killed. After the invaders had taken everything of value they sailed away again on their ships, but before they went they burnt the city to the ground".

As she spoke she poured some tea into each of the cups. She offered one to each of us and then sipped her own.

"Mmmm, I do like this tea," she said. "It, too, comes from far away".

I lifted the delicate cup to my lips. The fragrance of the tea was like nothing I had ever smelled before. It was like a spring morning, when the dew lay heavy in the newly sprouted grass. Its taste was just as exquisite.

"Where was I?" she asked as if coming back from a dream.

"The town was burnt to the ground," Tanya said. "Please go on."

"One of our band returned to the town after we had seen the ships sailing away. He saw that there were still a few people alive but many of them were badly hurt. It seemed that it was safe for us to return and help the injured people.

"We gathered our supplies and whatever useful herbs we found growing in that place and moved our wagons as close as we could to what was left of the town. We went to any houses left standing and brought the injured people to our camp.

"In all, there were forty-five, maybe fifty people still alive. Many were badly burned. Some had broken bones from when their house collapsed over them. We did as much as we could to make people comfortable and tend to their wounds but the townspeople's grief was overwhelming. So many had lost their lives, their friends, members of their families. Their homes were gone and all their possessions.

"I was setting the leg of a small girl when I heard people screaming. I went to see what the commotion was all about. Most of the people who could still stand on their feet were massed together yelling, "Kill him! Kill him!"

"I asked someone of our band what was going on and was told that one of the invaders had been found. I gathered the others of our band and moved closer to the mob. When the people saw us they stopped yelling and parted to expose the man they had captured.

"One of the bolder townsmen kicked him and yelled, "His people destroyed our town, now we will have our revenge on him!"

"I could see that the man was hurt and was trying to speak but every time he spoke someone shouted so I could not hear his words. I asked our strongest men to go to him and get him. Because the townspeople respected us for our healing skills and the help we had given them they let the men bring him to me.

"Blood ran down his face from a wound on his head. His clothes were filthy with soot and mud. I asked him who he was and what he was doing there. The people had all fallen silent, waiting, many with sticks and knives in their hands, to take their revenge.

"The man spoke quietly. He seemed to be in great pain. "I am not one of them," he said, speaking the language of the coastal town but with a heavy foreign accent. "Those people took me from my home because I am skilled in the healing arts. I thought I could escape when they landed here but I was caught up in the fighting and injured. And now you want to kill me."

"The men of the town raised their weapons. "Why should we believe you?" one of them yelled. Before they could set upon him I raised my arms.

"Stop, now, all of you!" I said. "This man is injured and needs help, just as you do. Leave him to us for now."

"There was grumbling but the men moved away. Some of our band helped him to my wagon where I cleaned his wounds and gave him some broth. He took a long sip and then slumped back into a deep sleep. When he awoke I could see that he was much better.

"Thank you for saving my life," he said. "Maybe I can help save some others. I have some very potent herbs in my pack. If there are people that your knowledge cannot help, maybe these herbs can."

"There were two people that seemed beyond hope. One was a young child and the other an old woman. Both had high fevers that didn't respond to the treatment that we tried. I asked that the two be brought to me. Soon the child was carried into my wagon, but the old woman had already died. The man touched the child's forehead then lifted her eyelids and looked into her eyes. Without a word he went to his pack and took out some small packets of herbs. He took a pinch from one packet and then another and put them into a small mortar.

"Do you have some boiled water?" he asked.

"I gave him a cupful. He added a few drops of the water and mashed the herbs into a paste with a pestle. "Do you have a spoon?" he asked.

"I handed him one and he gently spooned the concoction in to the girl's mouth. Almost at once I could see her colour changing and feel her temperature drop to a safe level. Her breathing became easier and so did mine as I realized that two lives had been saved that morning."

"The man was Vasa?" Tanya asked.

"Yes, my child," Madam Eleeza replied. "And the little girl…"

"That would be me!" said Adela with a shy grin.

Chapter 55

In a Cave

When we finished our tea Madam Eleeza said, "Adela, would you and Milada go and see how the preparations are coming along. I would like to spend some time alone with my daughter."

"Yes, my lady," Adela said.

"It was a pleasure to meet you," I said, not really wanting to leave this special place. There was one question still burning in my mind.

"It was a pleasure meeting you, as well," she said. Then, as if she could sense my question, Madam Eleeza added softly, "Ask me, my child."

"If Tanya will stay with our band, who will be the next Queen of the South?" I asked.

Madam Eleeza smiled as she stood up. Her golden gown flowed, unbelted from her shoulders. She put both of her slender white hands on her rounded tummy. "She will be our next queen," she replied, indicating the child I now could see was growing inside of her.

Adela and I climbed down the wagon's steps. We walked in silence toward the centre of the camp. I saw a group of women huddled together. They seemed to be all looking at something.

"Come, Milada," let's see how the wedding dress is coming along," Adela said, taking my hand and pulling me toward the group of women.

"What wedding dress?" I asked her.

"Tanya's, of course," she replied. "Our women have been working on it for some time. I was asked to do some of the finer embroidery because my fingers are still small," she announced proudly.

"Do you know when will the wedding be?" I asked. "At next summer's gathering?"

"No," she said, "It will be much sooner than that. It will take place at the next full moon, next week, I think it is"

"Next week?" I said.

"Yes, we are all looking forward to the day!" Adela said.

We pushed our way through the crowd of women until we stood next to the ones who were putting the final touches on Tanya's wedding gown. The material was a little rough to the touch, but had a sheen to it that changed from bright green to deep blue depending on how it fell. It was covered in golden embroidery, stars, suns and crescent moons.

"See those tiny stars," Adela said, pointing to minute shining dots around the neckline of the dress. "I made those! The thread is of real gold!"

"It's beautiful," I said, thinking how Tanya would look in it and how Dragan would look at her. I needed to speak with him, to tell him how I felt. If he loved me he could stop this wedding now.

"I have to get something from my wagon," I said to Adela and abruptly left the group.

I ran back to where our band was camped. Some of the boys were playing musical instruments, practicing for the night's festivities. At the grand gathering, every night was festive so I could hardly imagine what the wedding would be like. I had certainly never seen a dress as beautiful as the one that Tanya would wear. I wished that the dress were mine and that I would stand beside Dragan from that day forward.

I sat for a while; listening to the music and dreaming about the life I would have with Dragan. Maybe he would have to leave the band if he married me. We would travel together, just the two of us, having adventures and helping people we would meet along the way; he riding his black horse, Dobro, and I on a pure white mare. What a picture we would make riding along the crest of a hill! People from the villages would greet us and bring us their finest food and wine and offer us a place to stay in their warm cottages. We wouldn't need to have a wagon because everything we would require would be provided for us. In exchange we would heal their sick and bring them news from the wide world.

"Hi Milada," Bora said.

I jumped at the sound of his voice. I was so lost in my thoughts I didn't notice that the music had stopped and that he had come up beside me.

"Where were you?" he asked with a smile. "Your body is here but your mind was miles away."

"I was listening to the music," I replied, "and sort of drifted away with my thoughts."

"That is one of the things that good music does," Bora said. "It releases the mind to fly, to see far vistas and bring in new ideas."

"Well then, your music was very good!" I said, having thoroughly enjoyed my daydreams. But now, back to reality, I felt lost.

"We are going to go explore the caves near here," said Bora. "Do you want to come along?"

"I'm too old to go poking around in the dark," I said.

"You always liked exploring before," said Bora, "Don't tell me you are getting boring now that you are getting so beautiful. Are you turning into one of those village girls who spend their days fixing their clothes and daydreaming?"

A blush rose to my cheeks. He thinks I'm beautiful! And he's accusing me of being like a village girl. I had to show him that I was still myself, Milada, the curious one, always up for an adventure!

"Let me get a candle and then I'm coming!" I said. At least I could get my mind off the wedding for a while. And if Bora thinks I'm beautiful, maybe Dragan does, as well.

Bora waited for me while I ran to my wagon to fetch a candle. I also grabbed my shoes, remembering that the floor of a cave was often littered with sharp stones. Then together we ran toward the riverbank where a few of the others were waiting.

"Do you remember where the entrance to the caves are?" Milosh asked Bora.

"I think they are down a little farther, around that bend," he said.

It had been several years since we had visited these caves. As we approached the entrance it seemed much tighter than I remembered.

"Here it is!" Bora said, and disappeared within. "Come on!" His voice sounded muffled even though he was just beyond the cave's entrance.

The others quickly followed but I hesitated before going in. Something did not feel right.

"Milada," came a voice from within, "are you coming or not?"

When I didn't answer I heard somebody say, "She's probably daydreaming again".

That was enough to make me ignore the feeling of apprehension and crouch down end enter the dark cave.

The others had already lighted their candles. I crawled down the narrow entry passage toward their light. When the ceiling was high enough to stand I said to Bora, "Here I am! Can I have a light?"

He held his candle close to mine. I had forgotten how beautiful it was inside of the cave. The candlelight reflected off the crystalline surface of hundreds of stalactites and stalagmites. The domed ceiling rose high above us in the centre of the cavern. A dark stream ran along one side and many small passages led away into the dark.

"Let's try this one," Milosh said.

"It seems very dark and narrow in there," said one of the girls. "I think I will stay out here."

Milosh had already disappeared into the darkness. Bora was following him. He looked over his shoulder, "Are you coming Milada?"

Once again I heard a small voice inside saying, "Stay here," but I didn't want the others to think I was afraid so I silently followed. It was hard to hold the candle while crawling along the passage. At times I could not see the light of the others ahead of me. I thought about turning back but the passage was too tight. I made up my mind that as soon as I found a place that was wide enough I would return to the main cavern.

Suddenly the space around me opened up. I felt a cool draft and my candle went out. It was pitch black in the cool stone cavern. I could see nothing, not even my hand in front of my face. I knew I should not panic. I sat very still thinking that I could feel my way back to the narrow passage and then on to safely. Then I felt a warm hand on my shoulder.

"Bora, is that you?" I said, feeling relieved that I was not alone in the dark space.

He did not answer. Instead I felt the hand sliding down onto my breast.

"What are you doing?" I yelled. Before I could pull away I felt another hand on my other breast and warm lips kissing my neck.

"You are so beautiful, " I heard a thick voice say. It didn't sound like Bora. The boy, whoever he was turned me to face him and pressed his lips against mine.

"No!" I shouted and pushed him away. I tried to get away from him but the caves walls felt like they were closing in around me.

"Come on," said the voice, "surely you are old enough now to kiss and be kissed".

"Maybe I am," I shouted, but not like this." I took off my shoe and hit out in the darkness in front of me. I figured that if I couldn't see then he couldn't see either.

"Hey, that hurts," said the voice, but I heard laughter in it and felt more and more helpless.

My fingers finally found the opening of the passage. The boy was on the other side of me so I could crawl away if I was fast enough. Kicking out behind me I made my way into the passage, feeling its sharp stone edge cutting my palms and tearing my skirt in my haste to escape.

When I reached the large cavern the others had gone. I saw the entrance to another passage close to the one I came out of and crawled into it as fast as I could.

In the faint light I saw the boy, with his nose bleeding, emerging from the passage.

"Where are you, you little vixen?" He wiped the blood off his face with the back of his hand. "Look what you did; a small price to pay for that kiss. Where are you?"

It wasn't Bora or Milosh or any boy from our band. I had never seen him before. I felt relieved that none of my friends had attacked me like that. I kept very still so he wouldn't see me. There was a little bit of light coming from a fissure in the rock high above us. I could see from the angle of the sun that it was late in the day.

"I know you are here somewhere," said the boy, "and I can wait."

And wait he did. I was getting very cold sitting still beneath the stones. Where were the others? Maybe they went out another way? I wanted to leave but I was afraid to move out of my hole. Certainly he would get bored and leave, I thought. Instead he took an ember out of a metal box in his pocket and lit a candle.

"You must be getting cold," he announced to the cavern. "Why not come out and let me warm you up?"

I huddled in my hole, making myself as small as possible to hold in my body heat. I don't know how much time had passed. Maybe I even dozed off from the cold. I looked out where the boy was sitting beside his candle and saw that he was fast asleep. Here was my chance. His body was near the passage but not blocking it. If I was very quiet I could make it.

I realized that I had lost one shoe. I took off the other one and slowly and silently tiptoed around the edge of the cavern, hugging the deep shadows. Although I often went barefoot in the long summer months the cave's floor was peppered with sharp stones. Several times I wanted to cry out when my foot tread on one but I held in my cries as I held my breath.

When I was close to the entrance of the passage the boy stirred. I froze, lucky to be in the shadow of a deep overhang. I rested my fingers on a ledge for balance and felt something soft. At first I thought it was a rat, but then realized that it was too cold to be a living thing and to soft to be a dead one. I let my fingers move over the object. It seemed to be a small pouch.

I saw the boy settle back to his deep slumber. I closed my hand around the object, slipped it into my pocket and then silently dashed into the passage. I crawled as fast as I could. There was only one way to go. I could see a faint light in the distance. There was no sound from the cavern behind me. As I reached the mouth of the cave I stood and shook the dust from my hands and my torn skirt. I looked around me for the others but there was no one in sight. I followed the river in the direction of the camp, as fast as my bleeding feet would carry me.

Chapter 56

Dragan's Destiny

I could see the light of the campfires in the distance and hear music and laughter. I needed to see to my feet and change my ruined clothes before joining the others. I hoped that boy would sleep the whole night in that damp cave. I hoped he would never come out! Could he have been one of the boys from another band, or was he a local youth who just happened to be in the cave at that moment? I'd never known a boy to behave like that.

I was so lost in my thoughts, with my head down to watch the ground so I would step only on the soft soil of the path and not on any more stones that I ran head on into someone coming the other way.

"Milada! Where have you been? The others were looking for you".

I knew that voice, it was the voice I longed to hear, but not now, not like this.

Dragan took a step back and lifted my chin so that our eyes met.

"Milada, what is the matter? Are you hurt?" he asked.

I tried to formulate words, but once again all I could do was let my tears fall and enjoy the comfort of Dragan's embrace. He took me in his arms and then led me towards a mossy bank. When he noticed that I had difficulty walking he picked me up in his strong arms then set me gently beneath a tall tree. He sat down beside me and took one of my hands in his.

"This is bleeding," he said, "and this," as he took my other hand.

"I know," I said, "I'm sorry I am getting blood on you".

He took out his handkerchief and gently wiped the blood from my palms then from the soles of my feel.

"May I?" he said, indicating my skirt.

I nodded and he lifted my skirt to wipe the blood form my knees. I looked down at the soiled skirt, my bruised shins and dirty feet. I didn't feel like a beautiful woman now, but like a foolish child. I could not imagine Tanya ever being in this situation.

The tears once again began to flow. Dragan sat beside me. He cradled me in his arms and waited until I my tears stopped.

"I wish we could stay like this forever," I said, not sure if I said it to myself or out loud.

"My little Milada," Dragan said, "you are a very special girl. Life will bring you many adventures".

"I thought I'd have an adventure today," I said, "But it turned out not to be a good one. I wanted you to see me as a woman, not as a foolhardy child."

"I see the beautiful woman you are becoming," Dragan said. "It is a lovely moment, watching the young girls blossom like flowers."

"They say that you will marry Tanya," I said, quietly.

"Yes, we will wed when the moon is full," he said.

"I love you so much," I said. "I always dreamed that someday we would be together, and now I learn that you will marry Tanya."

"Everyone knew that Tanya and I would be wed," he said.

Yes, I thought, everyone but me! Even Goran knew, but I didn't want to believe it.

"I've loved you since I was little and we rode through the fields of ripe millet."

"I'm surprised you remember that day so long ago," Dragan said with a smile. "You know I love you, too, but Tanya is my destiny."

"What do you mean?" I asked, as I wiped the last tears from my face.

"Look up there," Dragan said, pointing at the clear night sky.

I looked up and saw the constellations glittering above us.

"Do you see those stars to the north-west that form a zig-zag path?" he asked.

I looked for a moment and then saw the stars he meant. "Yes," I said, "over there".

Follow the path and you will see a cluster of stars. There are seven of them."

I saw the stars, but wondered what this had to do with him and Tanya.

"They are called 'The Seven Sisters'," he said.

"I know the names of some of the other stars," I said. "But I've never heard of 'The Seven Sisters'".

"They are where our clan comes from," he said softly. "They are our home".

"You come from the stars?" I asked with disbelief. Was he making up fairy tales for me, as he would for a child? "If you come from the stars, how did you get here?"

"We came in the form of energy. It was decided to come and bring our knowledge to the people of the earth," he said. "But we are learning that the people find it difficult to understand and accept us."

That wasn't surprising, I thought, people from the stars, indeed. "Why are you telling me this now?" I asked, surprised by the anger rising from deep inside.

"I am telling you to help you understand about Tanya and me," he said. "We have been together through time and through space. In each lifetime we find each other and reunite. We are two halves of the same being."

When I remained silent, he continued, "And I am telling you because some how, some place in some future time you will write our story."

Few people in the clan knew how to read and write. We carried the knowledge in our heads, one person teaching another. I couldn't imagine that I would ever write their story.

We sat in silence for a while, both looking up at the stars and thinking our separate thoughts. I felt an emptiness descending upon me. Things would never be the same. It was bad enough when Goran left. Now with Dragan and Tanya marrying I felt as if I was loosing both my best friend and the man I loved. I liked the others but not in the same way. Maybe I should have stayed in the village. No! That would be even worse. I felt lost and ill at ease. The music was getting louder but I didn't feel in a festive mood at all.

"Milada," Dragan said after a while, "Don't worry about the future. Tonight you are here among your friends and people who love you for who you are and for who you are becoming. Go and put on a pretty dress. Put some salve on your hands and feet and join us around the fire."

"I understand now why I will never be a part of your clan," I said.

"But in a way you are one of us. You have travelled with us for many years and learned our ways. And now you know the secret of our origin," he said. "Very few people outside of the clan do."

Dragan got to his feet and helped me up. "Can you walk?" he asked," or shall I carry you to your wagon?"

My feet felt better for having rested them. "I can walk now," I said, thinking that I would rather be in his arms, but finally understanding that he and I had no future together. I wondered if there was someone, somewhere for me; someone who was my destiny.

Chapter 57

Changes

I took off my torn clothes, changed into the first thing I picked up and then dressed my wounds. I realized that I hadn't eaten since breakfast and was feeling very hungry. What a day this had been! Part of me just wanted to crawl into my bed but my hunger pangs were too strong so I gingerly made my way to the fire. The delicious smell of roasting meat and the sound of laughter began to work their magic on my low mood.

When Bora saw me he ran to my side.

"Where did you go?" he said. "When you didn't come out of the cave with us I thought you had gone back to the entrance, but when I returned to the fire Dania said that neither she nor the other girls who had waited there had seen you."

I wasn't sure how much to tell him about what happened in the cave. "Did you know all of the boys who were with us?" I asked.

"No," he replied," There were some I knew from other bands and a few local boys who like to play tricks, like hiding in the shadows and blowing out our candles. Why? Did something happen?"

"My candle went out," I said, not wanting to share the details, "Look how I cut my hands on the stones when I couldn't see where I was going."

I showed him my hands then he laughed and showed me his. They were cut as well.

"This is what happens in caves!" he said. "Come and let's get some of that fine meat while it's nice and hot".

Sitting with the young people I felt at home. Dragan, as usual, was right. I needed to focus on the present time. It was Midsummer; I was with interesting, knowledgeable people who cared for me. I spent the afternoon drinking tea with a queen in her golden cocoon. As my gaze travelled from face to face I thought about what Dragan had told me, that they had come from the stars, to bring their learning and their healing skills to the people here. It still seemed very hard to believe, but then again how did the members of the clan have so much more knowledge than other people?

Bora was drinking blackberry wine. He offered me a glass and I accepted.

"Bora," I said, noticing that the wine was making him jolly.

"Yes, my beauty," he answered.

"What are those stars up there?" I asked, pointing past the zigzag line to the bright cluster that Dragan had shown me.

"Those?" he said. "Those are our home."

Before I could ask him what he meant by that, the girl, Adela, came up beside me.

"Hello, Milada," she said. "Madam Eleeza would like to speak with you".

"Right now?" I asked, wishing I had put on a fresher skirt.

"Yes," Adela said. "She asked that you come with me now."

I finished my wine, patted Bora on the head and followed Adela to one of the long tables by the fire. At its head sat Madam Eleeza with Vasa on her right side and Tanya on her left.

"Good evening, Milada," Madam Eleeza said. "Come and sit with us".

There was place on the bench next to Tanya, and Adela and I both sat down.

"Good evening, my lady," I said. Tanya took my hand and gave it a little squeeze but dropped it when I winced in pain.

"What happened?" she asked.

"I'll tell you later," I whispered.

"Milada," Madam Eleeza began, "My daughter has told me so much about you. How you are a kind girl well versed in our healing arts."

I felt myself blushing. "I try to do the best I can," I said.

"Now that Tanya will be wed she will have other duties to attend to," she continued. "I have decided that Adela will travel with your band for a time and that you will guide her in her learning, just as you were guided by those farther along the path than yourself."

I felt honoured to be asked this, but also a great sense of responsibility. Did I have enough knowledge to teach someone else?

As if she sensed my thoughts Madam Eleeza smiled and said, "Do not worry, my child. The others will still be there to help and support you. And you know more that you think you do!"

"You and Adela will have to raise my little ones," Tanya added. Did I hear a touch of sadness in her voice?

"Will you not be with our band?" I asked, hoping that she and Dragan were not leaving us, although it might be easier for me not to be seeing the two of them together every day.

"I will be with you but I will have much to do in my new role," she said. "And I will need your help with preparations for the wedding," she added.

I remained silent, still not happy at the thought of Dragan and Tanya's marriage.

"I can't wait until the day!" Adela said, her enthusiasm reminded me of my own. Where had it gone?

~

The next morning the preparations began in earnest. Women from the four bands worked together to prepare the many dishes that would be served at the wedding feast. The full moon was only five days away and there was much to be done.

I did not see Mother Miriana among the woman. When there was a break I went off in search of her. I found her sitting in the sun outside of her wagon, deep in thought. I started to leave without disturbing her but she called to me.

"Milada," she said, "come and sit by me for a moment".

I did as I was told. Getting closer I could see a strange yet beautiful radiance on Mother Miriana's face.

"Are they looking for me?" she asked me. "Do they need my help?"

"I don't think so," I replied. "I missed you! I am used to being at your side when we are preparing for a feast so I came to see where you were."

"I am here," she said, "enjoying the sunshine and preparing myself for my journey home".

"Are you leaving us?" I asked.

"Yes, my child," she replied. "It's time for me to move on."

"Are you going with a different band?" I asked.

"No, Milada," she said with a gentle smile, "this time I'll be travelling alone. Run along now. I'll come in a while."

She closed her eyes and seemed to doze off immediately. I got up quietly and went back to our wagon. Tanya was there, packing her clothes and few possessions into a wooden trunk.

"What are you doing?" I asked her.

"Getting my things together," she said. The men will come later to take them to Dragan's wagon."

Of course Tanya would be leaving the wagon we had shared for almost all of my life. Why hadn't I thought of it before?

"I'm going to miss you," I said.

"You'll have Adela to keep you company," she said, "and Zora for a while longer".

"Where's Zora going?" I asked.

"She is thinking of marriage as well," Tanya replied.

"Who will she marry?" I asked. I knew she did not have her eye on any of the boys in our band.

"When the time is right, the man will appear," said Tanya.

"How do we know when the time is right?" I asked. "And how do we know when it is the right man?"

"Ah, Milada and her questions!" said Tanya as she put the last items in the trunk.

She didn't say it in a mean way but I felt as if I'd been dismissed. I had thought about telling her what had happened in the cave but saw that she was busy with her preparations and had enough of my childish questions. When did she suddenly get so grown up?

Chapter 58

The Beautiful Book

Tanya finished her packing and the two of us returned to the centre of the camp. Adela met us on the path.

"There you are!" she said, out of breath, "I've been looking for you everywhere! Madam Eleeza would like to see you in her wagon."

Tanya took Adela's hand and the two of them headed toward the brightly painted wagon.

"Come on. Milada," Adela said. "She wants to see you, too."

I was happy that I would have the chance to visit that special place again and to spend some time with Tanya and her mother. It felt like a great privilege to be in the Queens presence.

We climbed the high steps, pushed aside the curtain and were once again in that magic golden place.

"Greetings!" Madam Eleeza said, holding out her arms. Tanya ran to her mother and was enveloped in her embrace. Adela and I followed and her arms widened to include us as well. "Come and sit beside me, Milada. Adela, run and get us some water and we can all have some tea."

"Yes, My Lady," Adela said and skipped away.

Madam Eleeza took one of the leather bound books off the shelf and sat down on the divan between Tanya and me.

"I want to show you this book," she said. "It is very special and very precious."

Carefully, she opened the heavy cover. Inside, the pages were made of thick vellum. The first page was covered with strange shapes and squiggles.

"This is written in a very old language," Madam Eleeza said. "It is not one that I can read. This book has been in Vasa's family for many generations. Even he does not know how to read this script, but the story in the book has been passed down from one generation to another."

Madam Eleeza turned the page and both Tanya and I said "ahhh" when the beautiful painting on the next page was revealed.

"Look at that!" said Tanya. "The colours are amazing. I've never seen anything like it!"

Madam Eleeza said nothing as she turned to the next page.

"What a beautiful picture!" I said. The back of the first page was covered with more of the squiggly writing. On the right-hand page was a picture even more beautiful than the first. Whereas the first page had shown a young man in mid-step, smiling and looking over his shoulder, not noticing that he was about to step off a high cliff, the next page showed a man in flowing robes surrounded by flying symbols in a myriad of colours.

It was not just to colours that made the pictures so special. There was so much detail in each one. I had a feeling that the pictures told a very deep story.

Silently, Madam Eleeza turned each page, revealing more and more fantastic images. The third page illustrated a regal looking woman sitting on a throne flanked by deeply painted curtains. Once by one we marvelled at the pictures. There were twenty-two in all.

Adela had returned with the water, but the tea was forgotten as we looked through the magical book. In the last illustration a beautiful woman with long flowing hair danced naked in the sky surrounded by stars and mythical creatures.

"This one is about going home," Madam Eleeza said, then shook her head, as if pulling herself out of a dream. "I suppose the water has gone cold now," she said with a smile.

"I'll take it back to the fire and warm it up," said Adela, hopping up from her place next to Tanya.

"That's an amazing book!" I said. "What is the story about?"

"It is the story of the journey through life," Madam Eleeza said. "We come into this world for a purpose, to live, to grow and to learn about who and what we are. This book is like a map, a guide to help people to unfold their consciousness while in this world."

I did not understand what she meant.

"Where did this knowledge come from?" Tanya asked. "It is not from our people."

"No, Tanya, our people know the way," Madam Eleeza replied. "This comes from Vasa's country, a very ancient place.

"Did he tell you the story?" she asked.

"Yes, Tanya, he did," she said, "As I shall tell it to you. Do you see that red leather box, on the top shelf?"

"Yes," Tanya replied.

"Go get it and bring it here," her mother said.

Tanya did as she was bid and soon returned with the small leather box. It was in the shape of a chest and just fit in Tanya's two hands.

"Open it," Madam Eleeza said. "It is my wedding gift to you".

Carefully, Tanya set the box on her lap and opened it. Inside was a bundle wrapped in deep green silk. Tanya unwrapped it gently. Inside was a pile of cards made from similar heavy vellum as the book. On each card was one of the beautiful pictures!

"Oh, Mama!" Tanya said with a gasp. "Did you make these for me?"

"Yes, my child," her mother replied. "I spent a good part of this year copying each picture for you."

"They are even more beautiful than the ones in the book! Look at these colours. Thank you so much!" Tanya said as she carefully laid the cards aside and hugged her mother tightly.

"Each picture has a meaning," her mother explained. "These cards will help you and all your people. When you have a difficult situation or are not sure what to do you can draw a card. Its meaning will help point the way to the solution."

"The pictures are very beautiful," I said, without thinking, "but how can picking a card help you decide what to do?"

"The symbols in each picture carry deep truths," Madam Eleeza patiently explained. "When you quiet your mind, the answers to difficult problems will often come. The cards are a tool to help show what your mind already knows. The images work with your inner knowledge."

"But the gypsies always know what to do!" I said.

"Generally, yes, our people are sensitive to our inner knowing," she said, "But in the times to come this might not always be true. And tools like these are a big help to people who do not carry the knowledge from birth; to people like you."

I was silent, reminded once more that I was not part of the gypsy band.

"Come now," Madam Eleeza said, "I shall make us some tea and we will enjoy these last moments together before the wedding feast begins.

Chapter 59

Midsummer Wedding

The day of the wedding arrived. The morning sunlight streamed in when Tanya pushed aside the curtain. Outside, the birds were chirping merrily. I looked over to see Zora's empty bed. She must have risen very early, I thought. From the low position of the sun I knew that it was not long since the sun had risen.

The wedding was to be at noon, of Midsummer's day, the moment when the sun was at its closest point to the earth. I could hear Tanya outside the wagon, washing her face and humming to herself.

"Milada," she called, "shall we go down to the river and have a swim before breakfast? The morning is warm and the air smells so sweet."

There was a deep pool just bellow a small waterfall not far from our camp. In the afternoon the children loved to play there, yelling and splashing each other, but early in the morning the place was an oasis of peace.

"I'm coming" I called, as I hopped out of bed.

We walked together down the narrow path through the forest that led to the river. Leaving our clothes in a patch of sun we dove into the pool. Tanya surfaced under the waterfall. I joined her there and we washed each other's hair under the flowing water as we had often done before.

"Will all this change once you are married?" I asked Tanya as we sat side by side on the bank drying our hair in the sun.

"I really can't say what changes marriage will bring," she said with a sigh.

"Do you really want to get married?" I asked her, searching her eyes for an answer.

"Of course I do," she replied. "I've known my destiny all my life. Maybe it is a little soon, but Dragan has waited a long time for me to come of age."

"He could have married someone else," I said. "Someone older."

Tanya smiled, looking off into the distance.

"No," she said. "He needed to wait for me. Let's get back and see how the preparations are coming along."

The main camp was full of activity. The cooking fires were hung with huge cauldrons full of delicacies for the wedding feast. Lambs turned on their spits, slowly roasting over the coals. Tanya went into her mother's wagon to prepare herself for the ceremony while I joined the other women from our band.

Zora said, "Where have you been, Milada! Run and get your tambourine. We are going over our rhythms for the wedding."

"Shall I change my clothes now or will I have time later?" I asked her, noticing that she was already wearing her finest dress.

"Change now so that you will be ready," she said, "but be quick about it!"

I ran back to the wagon and changed into the red dress that Zora had given me. I twined some red ribbon in my hair, grabbed the tambourine off its nail on the wagon's wooden wall and hurried back to the group of women.

As I got closer I could hear the sound of the tambourines, those of our band and, at a distance, different rhythm coming from different parts of the forest.

I joined in, playing a familiar repetitive rhythm that we had learned in the moon tent. It was a joyful rhythm, one that made me want to dance. As we swayed together from side to side I felt myself slipping away from myself, from my feeling of separation. My eyes closed and in a moment we were one; one sound, one body, playing one rhythm together.

Without opening my eyes I felt the group beginning to move. We stepped as we played, right, left, right', left. I felt the strong summer sun shining on the top of my head and knew that it was time for the wedding. We naturally formed a line, two by two and stepped toward the centre of the camp where a dais surmounted by a flowing canopy had been set up.

I could hear other rhythms being played by the women from the other bands. As we approached the dais, one group came from each of the cardinal directions our rhythms coming together, merging in rhythmic counterpoint with each other. Each group of women spread out toward their left, forming a circle around the centre. As we continued to play the men, playing a heartbeat rhythm on their big drums followed us and formed a large circle behind us.

I don't know how long we continued this way, stepping right and left in a big circle when the cue to stop was sounded. As one, we all stopped playing and stepping and there was silence, total and profound silence.

Simultaneously, from each of the four directions came the leaders of each band. Tanya, resplendent in her blue-green gown, accompanied her mother, approached from the south. I caught my breathe at the sight of Dragan, looking more handsome than ever, walking proudly with his father, the Baron, from the west. The Queen of the north was a stately older woman with a kindly face. The Baron of the East was a young man, not much older that Dragan, with a beautiful, black haired woman on his arm.

The six people mounted the dais. Tanya and Dragan stood in front of the others, facing each other.

The Queen from the South spoke first. Facing south, she lifted her arms and intoned, "Ye Winds of the South! Home of the Sun! Bless this couple with your shining light. Spirit of the Water, bless them and let them live in your natural flow!"

Next, our Baron turned to the west. "Hail, ye Winds of the West! Land where the sun sets. "Bless these children with the knowledge of the two worlds. Let them know your ways and walk the rainbow bridge between the worlds, finding your wisdom for their people. Spirit of the Earth, bless them and their people. May they live long and prosper!"

Then the Queen from the North looked to the north and said in a voice surprising strong for her stature, "Oh you Winds of the North, you the keepers of ancient wisdom. Grant these children your knowledge. Let them take their place in the lineage of our ancestors, to pass down their wisdom from our forbearers to our children. Spirit of the Air, teach them to communicate directly with you and with all others who can benefit from their knowledge."

Last to speak was the young Baron of the East. As he spoke in our language, his partner in a strange and lilting tongue echoed his words. "Winds of the East, from the land where the Sun is born. Teach this glorious couple to always become, as each new day becomes. Teach them to see clearly what is and what can be. Show them how to lead their people for the highest good of all. Spirit of Fire, show them the way of passion and of life. Bring them joy in all they do!"

Then all six knelt down and the Queen from the North said, "Mother Earth, we know that our life comes from you, the mother who will never leave us. We, your children, love, honour and thank you."

Then they all stood and raised their arms to the heavens. The people on the ground also raised their arms. We held our tambourines high in the air and listened as the Baron said, "Great Spirits of the stars. We are your children. Bless us always as we aspire to live as a reflection of your light."

We shook the tambourines as we brought them down in front of us. The Baron and Tanya's mother stood beside the couple.

The Baron said, "Today, in the presence of the united bands my dear son Dragan and the Lady Tanya will be wed. This is their destiny, as you all know, and is a great day for all of our people."

At his words, a cheer went up all around me. I shook my tambourine with the others, but I still felt a deep sadness in my heart. I loved Tanya like a sister, but the love I felt for Dragan still burned deep in my heart. From this moment on I knew that he would never be mine. I felt tears moisten my eyes but willed myself not to cry.

Throughout the ceremony Dragan and Tanya had not taken their eyes off one another. They were both smiling. Adela mounted the dais and handed the Baron and Madam Eleeza two wreaths of wildflowers joined by a ribbon. The Baron placed one wreath on Dragan's head while Madam Eleeza placed the other on Tanya's.

The Baron took Dragan's right hand and Tanya's left and joined them. Dragan reached out and took Tanya's other hand in his.

The Baron spoke: "Under the wide sky and above the sacred earth these two people come to join as one. Be with each other, love and protect each other, come what may. May you be blessed with the bounty of the earth and grow old in happiness together."

The Baron continued, "From this day forth Dragan will be know as 'Iovan'. This is his name as a man and the future leader of the Band of the West."

Madam Eleeza spoke, "And from this day forth, my Tanya will be known as 'Radha', a name fit for the Baron's wife and leader of her band. 'Iovan' dropped his wife's hands and pulled her close to him in a tight embrace, then lifted her off her feet and swung her around and around.

Once again, the drums began to sound, this time in one rhythm. I joined in on my tambourine. I could not keep the tears from falling, but I kept playing. Over the noise of the drums Baron's powerful voice rang out, "It is done! Come now to the feast!"

Chapter 60

My First Student

The feasting went on all afternoon. As the sun set and the full moon rose great logs were piled on the fire. Musicians from all four bands played together in the clearing near the fire and we all danced in celebration of the great event. When the moon was high in the sky the music stopped for a moment. A huge drum started to pulse out the rhythm of a heartbeat. The drummer walked out of the clearing, though a path in the forest. The musicians began to play again as they surrounded the laughing bridal couple. They followed the drummer along the path and we all trailed along behind them. The drummer led us to Dragan's, now Iovan's, wagon. It was hung with vines and bunches of wildflowers tied with ribbons, silver in the moonlight.

Iovan picked up his bride and lifter her on to their wagon. The couple waved to us as the music continued and then disappeared behind the wagon's curtain. A small group of musicians from our band stayed near the wagon to play for the couple inside while the drummer lead us all back to the fire where we continued to dance until the moon set in the west and the first light of dawn painted the sky a rosy pink.

One by one the musicians packed up their instruments and went to their wagons to sleep. Many people were asleep beneath the trees. I found Adela curled up with a little brown puppy, one of the ones that Tanya had been caring for. I gently tapped Adela's shoulder.

"Adela, come with me to the wagon," I said. "It's much more comfortable than the hard ground."

"Is it morning already?" she asked, looking around sleepily.

"It's morning, but not time to get up!" I replied, helping her up and then scooping the pup into my arms.

We found Zora fast asleep in the wagon, still wearing her dress from the night before. We undressed quietly, not to disturb her, closed the curtain to shut out the brightening sunlight and settled in our beds for a long nap.

It was strange to see Adela asleep in Tanya's bed. Would Zora be leaving the wagon soon? And what about me? I couldn't imagine sleeping anywhere else than my cosy bed here in the wagon. Nothing would change for me. I would stay with the gypsies, travelling with them and learning their ways, helping people we meet along the way.

But without Tanya, without the hope of being with Dragan, something felt missing, empty. I didn't even have my dear friend Goran to cheer me up. Did I make a mistake by letting him go?

I knew that we would pass through that village again. Maybe Goran would come with us if I asked him. I felt better at the thought of being with him again. Maybe I did love him. Maybe I was just blinded by my feelings for Dragan. I lay in my bed, looking at the familiar ceiling thinking that while nothing had changed, everything felt different.

The next few days passed in a blur. We cleaned up the remains of the feast, constantly accompanied by music and song. Every night we danced by the fire and people from the different bands shared stories of their adventures over the past year. Herbs and potions were exchanged between members of the various bands, restocking their supplies from the four directions.

Zora was very busy sorting the various preparations, the dried herbs and infusions that she'd collected on our travels and the new ingredients that she had just received. I helped her to separate the seeds from the stalks of some of the dried herbs. I explained their properties to Adela as we worked and was surprised to realize how much I knew, which herb was helpful for which condition.

"What is this one?" I asked Adela, holding up one of the herbs we'd collected on our travels.

"Is it watercress?" she said, a little uncertainly.

"That's right," I said.

"What can we use it for?" she asked.

"We can dry the flowers and make a tea that is good for to relieve a tummy ache," I said. "When it is fresh we can crush the leaves and use it for skin problems."

"And this one," Adela asked picking up a tall stalk with tough, fuzzy leaves, "what is this one good for?"

"That is verbena," I told her. "A tea made from it will relieve headaches and help you sleep."

"There are so many different plants!" she exclaimed. "And they look different when they are growing from when they are all dried up. I don't think I'll ever remember which is which!"

"You will be surprised how you will remember," Zora said, looking up from her work.

"When we use them and see the results, see how they make people feel better, it's easy to remember. It just takes some time, that's all," I added.

"Hello my friends!" said a cheery voice. I felt someone standing behind me, and a warm arm thrown around my shoulder. "Are you teaching Adela about the herbs?"

"Tanya!" I said, turning with a smile to greet my friend.

"Milada, you must call me 'Radha' now," she said, "a new name for the new phase of my life."

"But I've always called you 'Tanya'!" I said. "You are still the same girl!"

But as I said those words, I looked into her eyes and saw that she wasn't the same at all. Her shining smile was still there, but there was also a deeper knowingness that I had never seen in her eyes before.

She said nothing, as we looked into each other's eyes, but took my hand in hers and gave it a squeeze.

Adela grabbed Radha's other hand and pulled her toward the board where the herbs were laid out to dry.

"Look at these!" she said, "This one is watercress and this one is verbena! I'm not sure what the rest are, but I will learn."

"Zora and Milada are excellent teachers," Radha said, "I'm sure you will learn well."

Zora and Radha smiled at each other, then Radha said. "I've come to tell you that we will be moving on tomorrow."

"Oh, can I come and say good bye to your mother?" I asked. "I have not seen here since the wedding. We've been so very busy these days, what with all the new herbs and things."

"Yes, do come. I'm sure that she will be pleased to see you."

"Can I come, too?" Adela asked, quietly.

I looked at her and saw a tear in her eye.

"Of course you can," Radha said.

Zora looked over and noticed Adela's tears.

"Don't cry on the herbs, Adela," she said. "They are almost dry. We don't need to get them all wet now.

Adela obediently stepped back from the drying board, but tears continued to steam down her face. I think that she had just realized that she was leaving Madam Eleeza, a woman who had been like a mother to her.

"Does Adela have to come with us?" I asked Radha. "Maybe she should stay with your mother's band.

"I don't know the reason for the decision," Radha said, "but it has been made." She gathered Adela in her arms.

"It will be alright," she said. "You know, every 'hello' is also a 'good bye'. Sooner or later all our paths diverge."

I was shocked by these words, although they seemed to calm Adela. I didn't want our paths to diverge! I wanted us all to stay together!

"We will all meet again," Radha said, as if reading my thoughts. "But maybe not in the way you expect."

Chapter 61

Farewell

As soon as we had bundled all the herbs and hung them on a long stick that fit into a rack in our wagon we headed to the centre of the camp to see Madam Eleeza.

When we neared the clearing I could see many people huddled together but there was no sound, none of the usual cheerful banter. I asked someone at the edge of the group what was going on.

"It's the elder woman from the Band of the West," she said. "She has decided to stay here and not move on with us tomorrow."

The elder woman from the band of the West? That's my band. Who did they mean? And what did they mean?

"Radha," I said as she and Adela approached, "who is the elder woman from the band of the West?"

"Mother Miriana," Radha said quietly. "So she has decided to stay?"

"That's what that woman said," I told her. "How did you know? And what does it mean?"

"We must speak with her," Radha said, with a look of concern on her face, "and say goodbye."

She kissed Adela on the cheek and then said, "Milada, follow me".

She gently pushed her way through the dense crowd of people. When people saw who she was, they parted to let us both through. There was a small clearing at the centre near the embers of the fire. Mother Miriana lay on a thin mat. Madam Eleeza, the Baron and his son were all by her side.

Radha crouched down beside her husband. "How is she?" she asked in a whisper.

Although her voice was low, the sound was enough for Mother Miriana to open her eyes.

"Radha, my girl, and Milada," the old woman said, reaching out her hands to us.

Radha took her right hand and I held her left. Her fingers felt thin and fragile in mine, like the tiny bones of a bird.

"They say you will stay here," I said. "What will you do here by yourself?"

"Milada," the Baron said, "this is not the time for such questions".

I felt like I had been struck. The Baron spoke gently, but the meaning of his words made me feel like an outsider, like a child, like someone who didn't know how to behave.

Mother Miriana gently squeezed my hand. She looked into my eyes and said, "My child, do not worry about me. This is my choice. Someday, maybe you will understand. You are a fine girl. It was good to know you."

I had no words to say. Tears were falling down my cheeks. I felt a hand on my shoulder. I looked up to see Zora looking down at Mother Miriana. I gently let go of her hand and moved over so that Zora could sit close beside her.

"Ah, my child," she said to Zora, "you have come just in time. I would like to give you something special."

She dropped Zora's hand and reached into her apron pocket. Slowly she drew out a small pouch.

"Take this, Zora, it is yours," she said, placing the pouch in Zora's hand.

Zora pulled the strings that released the opening. She turned the bag and seven brightly coloured stones dropped into her palm.

Zora gasped at their beauty as they caught the sunlight.

"You are leaving these with me?" she asked.

"You know what to do with them," Mother Miriana said.

"I've seen you use them," Zora said. "I think I know."

"You know," she said with a weak smile, then looked over at the other girl. "Radha, I have something for you".

Mother Miriana put her hand in her pocket again. She took out a clear crystal sphere, like the one that Layla had left us, but a little bit bigger.

"You are old enough now to have one of your own," she said, placing it in Radha's hand. "It will help you to steer a good course for the band.

"Thank you, Mother," Radha said, "I will look to your wisdom for guidance. Good-bye for now. May your way be smooth."

The older women gathered around Mother Miriana. Some of them held drums in their hands. It felt right to move further away and let them surround her. Madam Eleeza and the leaders of the other two bands had drawn close as well.

The crowd had naturally formed concentric circles, with the older woman closest to Mother Miriana, interspersed with the leaders of the four bands, each holding their own cardinal direction.

The women started a slow rhythm on their drums. The Baron said some words in a language I could not understand. The others repeated what he said in a rhythmic chant. I could not understand what was being said, or what was happening. I could see Mother Miriana laying in the centre of the circle of people with a smile on her lips, her eyes closed.

I felt myself moving right and left to the rhythm of the drums. We were all swaying together like reeds in a field. The chanting ceased and the drums began to beat at a faster rhythm. Faster and faster they went, then suddenly stopped as one.

Mother Miriana's head had fallen to one side. She was dead! No one cried or called out. Silently, people began to drift away. Men pushed aside the ashes from the fire and began to dig a grave, right there where the fire had been. I stood, in shock, with Zora and Radha.

"Mother Miriana is dead!" I said, "Why didn't anyone try to help her?"

Radha said, "We did help her take the first steps of her journey."

"But nobody helped her not to die! She wasn't that old - Not nearly as old as my grandmother was! No one made her teas or used our special healing herbs or the lode stones," I said, looking at Zora, "or any of the other things we have that make people better."

"She was ready to leave," Madam Eleeza said, coming up behind me. I felt the firm bulge of the life growing inside of her as she drew me into her arms. "It was her decision. We will miss her, but we need to respect her wishes."

"Come, let's have a last cup of tea together and wish all of us a good journey," she said. "Here comes Adela. Ask her to bring me some hot water, one last time."

It was hard to turn away from Mother Miriana's body. But I knew that her spirit, the part of her that made her who she was, was no longer here.

Chapter 62

Radha's Crystal Ball

By now, the sun was low in the sky. We climbed the steep steps of the Queen's wagon. Madam Eleeza leaned on her daughter's arm as she ascended. She sighed as she entered the wagon and took a seat on the divan.

"My little one has awakened," she said with a tried smile, putting her hand on her belly. "Come and feel her turning".

Radha and I sat on either side and gently rested our hands on Madam Eleeza's belly. What a strange sensation to feel the tiny child moving inside of her. We kept our hand still and the child became still, as well.

"She feels your presence," Madam Eleeza said. "You have soothed her restlessness. I think she felt our friend's passing."

"I don't understand why Mother Miriana died," I said. "She was never ill. She wasn't even that old."

"Our people generally choose not to live into old age," Madam Eleeza said. "Mother Miriana stayed longer than most."

"She stayed long enough to teach us," Radha said, "long enough to pass on her knowledge."

Radha took out the crystal sphere.

"It is like the one that Layla gave you," I said, reaching out to touch it. Radha placed it in my hand.

"Layla gave me the crystal to keep for her. It is not mine," she said.

I thought to myself, but Layla's gone, how can she ever claim it back. Maybe when we pass the same camp again Radha would bury it where her bones lay. I was afraid to ask any more questions, after being told off by the Baron, so, silently, I handed the stone back to Radha.

"Can you see anything within the sphere?" Madam Eleeza asked her daughter.

Radha cupped the stone in her palm and looked intensely into it.

"No, my lady, I cannot see anything but my palm and the last of the day's golden light reflecting in the stone" she said, gazing into the crystal in her hand.

Madam Eleeza smiled. "You are trying too hard! Take three deep breaths and don't look directly at the stone. Look a little to the right of it so you see it from the corner of your eye."

Radha breathed deeply and I did, too. I tried to look at the stone like Madam Eleeza said, but all I could see was the dying light and the wagon's shadows. Every now and then there was a flash of rainbow light when the sun sank a little lower and changed position in relation to the crystal sphere.

My eyes grew tired of looking at, or trying not to look at the stone, so I watched Radha instead. She was breathing slowly and rhythmically, her eyes cast down. There was a small smile on her lips.

"Can you see anything?" I whispered.

"I can see light shining through a clearing in the forest. There are some women there, but I cannot tell who they are," she whispered back.

Then her smile faded.

"What is it?" I asked.

"One of the women is giving birth," she said, "but the others seem concerned. Something is not right."

"Can you tell who it is?" I asked. "Is the woman Madam Eleeza?"

"No," Radha replied. "I can't see, but I can feel that it is not she".

"That's enough now," Madam Eleeza said, placing her hand over the sphere. "You know now how you use this gift. Use it wisely. If you see something that concerns you, breathe love into the sphere and let it go. We cannot change what is, but we can change how we allow things to affect us."

I heard someone tapping on the doorframe.

"May I come in?" Adela had arrived with the water for our tea.

"Yes, dear!" Madam Eleeza said. "Radha, would you please prepare the tea? I think I need to keep my feet up for a while."

"Yes, my Lady, I'll be happy to," Radha said as she rose and put the sphere back into its pouch. I got up as well. Madam Eleeza stretched out on the divan, her back propped up by the large carpeted pillows.

"Shall I bring the cups?" I asked.

"Yes, thank you," Radha said as she took the porcelain teapot off the shelf.

I followed her and took down four saucers. I reached to the higher shelf to take the cups. Somehow I lost my grip and one of the lovely gilded cups dropped from my hand. I watched it fall, as if time had stretched. I thought, 'don't break, don't break!!' willing it to stay intact. The cup hit the carpet and seemed to bounce up. I tried to catch it but it fell to the floor again, this time landing on the wooden floor, shattering into many pieces.

I reached down and picked up the larger pieces with tears in my eyes. I knew how precious and rare these cups were. How could I be so clumsy!

"I am so sorry," I said, afraid to look Madam Eleeza in the eye.

"Don't worry about it my child, it is only a piece of clay".

"But it was so beautiful!" I said, "and now it is gone".

"We enjoy these lovely things if we have them," Madam Eleeza said, "but in themselves they don't matter at all. What makes them special is the memories that they bring, of the people who gifted them to me, of the moments shared over cups of tea. There are other cups, and if they break we can get others. Maybe not as fine as these, but the important thing is for us to be together, not what we drink or the quality of our cups."

I listened to the Queen's words but still felt like a clumsy ox. Madam Eleeza held out her arms to me.

"Come here, Milada," she said.

I approached her and knelt on the red patterned rug next to the divan. She put her arms around me and smiled.

"I'm glad that I met you," she said, "and that you are my daughter's good friend. You have a kind heart, my child, but you are very hard on yourself. Love and respect yourself the way you love and respect others."

I felt comforted being in Madam Eleeza's embrace. Love myself? I never thought about that. I liked some things about myself, my free spirit, my dancing, the way I learned to help people with herbs and all, but love myself...well, that was something new.

"The tea is ready," Radha said, "Where are those cups?"

Madam Eleeza relaxed her arms. She smoothed my hair and as I sat up, our eyes met. We both smiled.

"I'll get them," I said, and carefully took one more cup from the shelf and placed it on its saucer.

Radha poured the fragrant tea. Adela took two cups and sat on the edge of the divan. She gazed at Madam Eleeza with love and longing as she passed one cup of tea to her.

"I will miss you, little one," Madam Eleeza said to her.

I could see that Adela was using all her strength and will to hold back her tears.

"And I will miss you!" she said. "I'll miss you so much!"

Radha sat beside Adela and put her arms around her.

"We will miss our Lady together," she said. "I will be here for you, and so will Milada. Pretty soon you will be so busy learning new things and travelling to new places, you won't have time to miss anyone."

"And we will meet again at the Summer Gatherings. Next time we meet, you will also meet this little one!" Madam Eleeza said, placing Adela's small hand on her rounded belly.

Adela said nothing but I saw a tear fall into her teacup. I thought I knew how she felt, having to leave the people she had grown to love and trust. Why did she have to come with us if she didn't want to? Some of the ways of the gypsies seemed to be very unfair!

"There is a bigger picture, Milada," Madam Eleeza said, dreamily, "We follow our guidance, sometimes even we do not know the reason. It is about trusting a higher wisdom."

Had I said something out loud or did Madam Eleeza know my thoughts? She looked over at me and smiled.

Chapter 63

The Last Rites

The sun was now low in the sky casting a deep golden light into Madam Eleeza's wagon. There was a tap on the doorframe and then I heard a man's voice say, "May I enter, my Lady?"

"Enter," she replied.

Vasa entered with Dragan following behind him. I still could not think of him as 'Iovan'.

Vasa went over to Madam Eleeza and said, "It is time".

He took her empty cup and placed it on the table. The cup and saucer looked tiny and fragile in his large, strong hands.

"We will perform the rite for your elder," he said to Radha, "together. Come."

Vasa helped his partner to rise from the divan and climb down the wagon's steep wooden stairs. I took Radha's cup and my own and placed them on the table. She and Dragan followed the older couple.

Adela said, "I will wash these cups for my Lady, one last time," and skipped away to fetch more water to rinse the china.

Alone, I took one last look around the room. The light was fading; the golden sun had set. I sighed at the thought that I might never be here again, never drink from these exquisite cups, never rest in Madam Eleeza's embrace. How did I come to be there in the first place, as a child from a small village? How was it that I was travelling with these unusual people, people with so much knowledge?

I wondered what the future held for me; to live all my life with these people that I loved but who would always see me as an outsider and, someday, to be buried under the fire and left alone, or to go back to my old village and stay with Goran and make a life there? That choice didn't seem as bad as I had once thought, but how could I stay in one place when there was so much more of the world to see?

Lost in my thoughts, I didn't hear Adela returning with a bucket of water, warmed on the fire.

"Milada," she said, placing the bucket on the floor and turning up the flame on the small oil lamp that burned on the table. "Are you still here? The ceremony has already started."

"I didn't realize I stayed so long," I said. "I'll go now. I'll see you later".

I clambered down the steps and joined the others. Several small fires were lit. I saw Radha standing beside Iovan and the Baron at Mother Miriana's side. The leaders of the other bands each stood at one of the cardinal directions around the body.

Mother Miriana's oldest friend, Lazara was lighting the last of six tall candles that surrounded the corpse. She and some of the elder women sat in a circle and began to chant a strange sounding song in a language I could not understand. All the other people stood in silence, encircling Mother Miriana's body. After some minutes passed the women fell silent. Lazara bent over Mother Miriana's head and seemed to whisper something to her. She sat back and a moment later, all the candles went out. I did not feel any wind. No one moved to blow the candles out. They just died as if someone had snuffed them out.

Lazara stood up and the other women followed. The musicians picked up their instruments and began to play an upbeat tune. Something shifted in the atmosphere. One moment there was solemn silence, the next there was music playing and people chatting to one another about getting the meal ready and packing to leave the next day.

The women disappeared to prepare the feast. I thought I should go and help as well but I stayed to watch what would happen next. Four men gently lifted the body and place it carefully in the hole that had been prepared. They filled the hole and patted down the soil. Other men brought small, dried branches and the larger logs and placed them on top of the fresh grave. Then the Baron lit a dried stick from one of the small fires and held it to the dry branches. A great flame rose up with a whooshing sound. The musicians took their usual places close to the fire and people started to return with their brass plates stacked with food.

Zora found me staring at the fire.

"Milada," she said, "come and eat something. We will make an early start in the morning and the road ahead is long. Let's eat well and then sleep well tonight."

"Did you know Mother Miriana was going to die?" I asked her, still looking into the fire, rather than meeting her eyes.

"Let's say that I was not surprised," she replied.

"Won't you miss her?" I asked.

"Yes, of course I will," she said, "She taught me so much. And she loved me like a daughter."

I looked at Zora, watching the blazing fire.

"And she left you," I said. "Doesn't that make you upset?"

"One of the things that she taught me is to know when it is time to go," she replied.

We didn't speak for a moment. We just stood side by side, our faces warmed by the flames.

Then I remembered the gift that Mother Miriana had given Zora as she lay dying.

"What do you do with those stones she gave you?" I asked.

"They are for healing," she said. "Each has a particular colour that supports a different part of the body. I will show you sometime in daylight when you can see their beautiful colours."

"Tomorrow?" I asked, thinking it would be something to look forward to.

I could see Zora's look softening. I think she understood how confused I was feeling.

"Yes, Milada," she said. "Remind me tomorrow and I will show you. Go now and get some supper. Tomorrow will be a long day."

"Thank you, Zora," I said and went in search of something to eat. I wasn't very hungry, but I knew that when we were on the road meals could be scarce and irregular. This was the last feast of the gathering, as well as Mother Miriana's farewell, so the food tonight would be plentiful and rich.

I filled my plate then sat down at the long table. While I was eating Dragan, I mean Iovan, came and sat beside me.

"Hello, little one," he said, "This has been quite a day. I hope I'll see you dancing by the fire tonight."

"I don't really feel like dancing," I said, "or eating". I realized that I'd just been pushing the food around my plate.

"Are you sad because of Mother Miriana, or because we are moving on?" He asked.

How could I tell him I was sad because he had married my best friend and I felt that I had lost them both? So I said nothing. Let him think what he wanted to!

"Or because of Tanya and me?" he added, softly.

I remained silent, looking down at my plate. He gently touched my chin and raised my head so that we looked into each other's eyes.

"There is someone special waiting for you," he said. "One day, when the time is right, you will meet."

That doesn't help me right now, I thought. But the sincerity in his eyes made me believe his words were true and for the first time in days I felt better.

He could see it in my eyes and smiled. I smiled, too.

"Now that's my Milada," he said with a laugh, "You look much too serious when you aren't smiling. Life moves along. If you try to keep everything the same you will only bring yourself misery. Find each day's happiness, be it in a robin's song or a rainbow. When you are happy, you bring the light of happiness to others. So, eat up and then come and dance with Radha and me and let's start a new chapter of our lives with joy."

Chapter 64

The Rainbow Stones

I did dance that night, and well past the time the moon had set. I felt like I had only just rested my head on the pillow when I heard Zora saying, "Milada, Adela, its time to go".

I saw that the sun was already past the top of the window. I rose quickly and went outside. Zora had thoughtfully brought water for us to wash. Adela waited for me to finish splashing my face with the cool water. She handed me the towel and then splashed her own small face. I thought how young Adela looks today. Was I that small when I came to stay with the gypsies? I must have been much younger. I was far too young to make tea!

Zora had already hitched Kizi to our wagon.

"There's no time to have breakfast," she said. "I thought you would rather have the extra sleep. I brought you some bread and apricots to eat on the way."

"Do I have time to say one last goodbye to my friends?" Adela asked.

"No dear," Zora said, seeing the sadness in Adela's eyes. "The others have already started their journey. We are the last to go."

I poured the remaining water in the basin at the base of a tall oak tree and looked around to make sure that we had collected all the bits that we had strung on the overhanging branches. I saw a small puppy asleep beneath our wagon.

"We don't want to leave this one behind! Adela, this is one of Tanya's pups, a little black ball of fur with huge paws for its size. It is up you to care for him now."

I bent down and took the puppy in my arms and said, "Adela, climb up to the wagon and I'll hand him up to you."

Zora helped Adela climb up. I handed her the pup and then climbed up myself. Zora clicked and Kizi stepped lightly in the direction of the other wagons that were gathering on the dusty track that would take us back to the west.

We joined the line of wagons on the road. The horses pawed the beaten earth as if they were anxious to get moving. A cheer went up from the front of the line and was passed from one wagon to the other. The people in the wagon in front of us called out "Huzzah!" and we repeated it as loud as we could so the one behind us would hear and pass it on.

I heard the sound of beating hooves and saw Iovan on Dobro, who, in spite of his advancing years, still looked sleek and full of life.

"Ready to go, ladies?" he asked as Dobro danced, restless at being reigned in so Iovan could greet us.

"Yes, my Lord," Zora said. I wondered at her formality.

"And you, Milada, and the little one?" he said looking at Adela's downcast eyes. "Do not be sad. Life is a grand adventure. Keep your eyes open so you don't miss anything!"

Without another word he continued riding down the line of wagons, making sure, as he always did that everyone was ready to move on. Moments later, he passed us like a dark streak, returning to bring word to the front wagon that all was well and we could start on our way.

As always, I could see dust rising in the distance ahead as the first wagons moved off. A few minutes later, the wagon in front of us pulled away. Zora didn't need to signal the horse. Kizi moved forward, following the others, of her own accord.

We passed by the clearing where the night's fire had been, I thought of Mother Miriana's body lying beneath the grey embers, but I didn't feel like we were leaving here there. I felt her presence in the gentle warm wind that lifted my hair as we moved down the road.

I took Adela's hand in mine, but we did not speak. Our horse's hooves beat a rhythm as we travelled on. The sun rose high in the sky and then started its journey back down towards the west before the signal was given to stop and let the horses rest.

We came to a halt on a shady stretch of road. Zora went inside the wagon and came out with a basket full of food for us.

Zora said, "Milada, there's a jug of water inside. Would you please bring it?"

"Is there anything I can do?" Adela asked.

"Please bring out the blanket and we can have a picnic under that tree," Zora replied.

We settled ourselves on the soft earth beneath the tree. People from the other wagons greeted each other and shared food from their baskets.

After we had eaten, I remembered the stones that Mother Miriana had given Zora.

"Zora," I said, "will you show us the stones?"

Zora reached into her apron pocket and took out the pouch.

"Hold out your hand," she said.

I did as I was told and seven sparkling stones fell into my palm.

"They are so beautiful!" I said. "I have never seen Mother Miriana use them. What are they for?"

"I have seen her use one or two of them at a time," Zora said, "but not all of them together."

"Can I have a look?" Adela asked. I was pleased to see her looking interested. She seemed so sad most of the day.

"Look at this yellow one," I said, picking one polished stone up carefully and offering it to Adela.

"It looks as bright as the sun," she said.

It was true. These stones seemed to capture and hold sunlight. They had radiance like of the colours of the rainbow. I looked at them one by one and realized that there was indeed one for each of the seven colours of the rainbow.

"Remember how Mother Miriana showed us how to help healing by using different coloured fabric on different parts of the body?" Zora asked me.

"Yes, I do," I replied. "One time she said that the gypsies were so healthy because we wear such colourful clothes!"

"Well these stones carry a very high vibration of colour," Zora said. "They will help healing on many levels."

"How?" I asked.

"Let me show you," she said.

She turned to Adela and said, "I know you feel sad being parted from Madam Eleeza and the others of the Band of the South. Lie down on the blanket and let me try to help you to feel more balanced."

Adela handed Zora back the yellow stone and stretched out on the blanket.

Zora said as she took the stones from my hand, "Sadness dwells in the heart. I will put this green stone called malachite on Adela's heart."

"I will put this yellow stone, a citrine, on her tummy to help her to relax and this dark blue one, a lapis lazuli, in the centre of her forehead to help her understand and be open to the changes that life brings."

Zora placed the stones and said to Adela, "Breathe deeply and let the stones do their work."

We sat in silence until we heard the horn signalling that it was time to move again. I thought Adela had fallen asleep. She seemed so relaxed. She opened her eyes and smiled.

"Is it time to go?" she said. "I can't wait to see the new places on the road ahead!"

I looked at Zora and smiled as she collected the stones and returned them to the pouch. Adela hopped up and gave Zora a big hug. Then she grabbed my hand and pulled me to my feet.

"Come on, Milada. It's time to go," she said, with the spirit of the girl I had met in Madam Eleeza's wagon. "I'm still hungry, are there any more apricots?"

"Yes, I think there are some in the wagon," I said. "Go and see."

Adela ran to the wagon and clambered up the steps.

"Those stones really made a difference to Adela's mood," I said to Zora.

"Yes, they work very quickly when the cause of a person's problem is not in her physical body but rather in her thoughts or emotions," Zora replied.

"Will they help to heal the body, as well?" I asked.

"Yes, they offer very good support to the healing process," Zora said, "in addition to herbs and eating the right foods."

"Do you know where Mother Miriana got the stones?" I asked.

"I don't know," Zora replied.

"Maybe she collected them over the years, receiving them at the gathering of the bands," I suggested.

"Yes," said Zora, thoughtfully. "Or maybe another wise woman gave the set to her as she gave them to me. Either way, I feel honoured."

"You have a great talent for healing people, Zora," I said, as we mounted the wagon.

"I am happy to be able to help," she said. "And you, Milada, you have much knowledge in the healing arts."

"I am so grateful to you and the others for teaching me things that I would never have known," I said.

Zora clicked to Kizi and we were on our way once again.

Chapter 65

Adela's Tale

We travelled for several days, stopping only to sleep and to prepare food that would last us until the next evening's camp. Breakfast was taken in our wagon, since we left our camp as soon as the sun had risen. Lunch was a picnic while the horses were watered and rested.

We chatted with Adela as we travelled along the road.

"What was it like in the place you lived before?" I asked her. "Madam Eleeza said it was by the sea."

"Yes, my parent's house was right on the harbour. My father was a fisherman. He would leave the house before the sun came up and be back in the morning with baskets full of fresh fish to sell at the market," she said.

"My mother cleaned the fish and she and her sister took turns selling them at the market or staying home and caring for us children."

"Do you have brothers and sisters?" I asked, not having given that a thought before.

"I had an older sister and a baby brother," she replied, "and two cousins, my mother's sister's daughters. We all lived together in the house by the harbour."

"Where are they now?" I asked without thinking. Adela's face dropped and a tear slid down her cheek.

"I don't know," she said. "So many people were killed in the raid. Maybe they managed to hide, or get out of the city and were saved like I was. Maybe they didn't survive."

"I was so lucky," she added quietly, "to end up with the gypsy band, and all of you."

"Will you go back and look for your family?" I asked.

"I wouldn't know where to look," she said. "The gypsies are my family now."

"Tell me about the sea," I said. "I have seen a lake and wide rivers but I have never seen the sea."

"Oh, Milada," she said, "The sea is beautiful. It goes on as far as you can see."

"What colour is it? " I asked.

"It changes colour all the time!" Adela replied. "If there are clouds in the sky it can look grey. On a sunny day it looks deep blue. If a storm is coming there are white crests on the waves. Then the fishermen know not to go out until the storm has passed. In the early morning and at sunset the sea can look pink or even red, taking the colour of the setting sun."

"Sometimes, big ships would anchor in the harbour. My father and the other fishermen would row out and bring the sailors and their cargo ashore. I saw some amazing things come off these big ships!" she told me as we rode along.

"What did you see?" I asked, curious as ever, and a little envious that this little girl had seen things that I had never, and might never ever see in my life.

"One time, there were beautiful silk fabrics, with rich patterns woven with gold thread," she replied.

"Like Radha's wedding dress?" I asked.

"Yes," she said, "something similar. There were piles of pieces of many different colours."

Did people from your village have the money to buy such rich fabrics?" I asked.

"Some of them did, but mostly they were traded with goods from inland, precious stones or preserved provisions for the sailor's onward journey. Travelling merchants bought the goods and then traded them for other things. Our town was a centre of trade."

"What else did the sailor's bring?" I asked.

"Animals!" she replied, stroking the sleeping puppy on her lap. "There were tall, noble looking brown mules from an island far to the east that is famous for that breed. Once I saw a really tall animal with a funny hump on its back. It looked odd but people said it was excellent for carrying things over long distances because it did not need to eat or drink very often."

"Did somebody buy it?" I asked her.

"Yes, a merchant who planned a long trip through dry lands," she said. "It must have been lonely, being the only one."

When we stopped for our mid-day break, word came down the line that we would be making camp for a few days. We travelled a little farther down the road and the wagons gathered in a large clearing beside a fast flowing stream.

Zora unhitched the horse and said, "This is a pleasant place to stop. It is still early in the day. I will light a fire and heat some water."

"For tea?" I said, "I'd like some tea!"

"I was thinking about hot water to wash some clothes," Zora said. "Since we've been on the road we haven't had a chance."

"We can rinse them in the stream, and go for a swim, too" I said.

"And we can have some tea," Adela added, "since the water will be hot".

While Zora prepared the fire, Adela and I went into the wagon to find our dirty clothes and the tea kettle.

I had thrown some clothes that needed washing in a basket at the foot of my bed. As I emptied the basket I felt something hard. It was the small fur pouch that I had found in the cave.

"What's that?" Adela asked.

"I don't know," I replied. I had forgotten all about the strange thing that I found on that awful day.

I took my dirty clothes and the pouch and went outside. Zora had already prepared a cauldron of water. It was warming on the fire. She added some ash and lye and stirred it into the water.

"Put your white clothes in," she said. "I'll go get mine".

I dropped my clothes on the ground and picked up the light ones, put them in the water and stirred it so that they would all be covered with the water. One time I was not careful and put an orange skirt in hot water. All the clothes turned orange! I thought Zora would be angry, but she, Tanya and I just laughed for the next few months when we put on our orange underwear.

The others added their clothes to the big pot. The water in the kettle had come to a boil. Adela brought a basket from the wagon and set it on the ground beside the fire. One by one, she removed three beautiful golden cups and a matching tea pot.

"A gift from Madam Eleeza," she said, when she saw me staring at the china.

"That was very generous of her," said Zora, picking up one of the cups and examining it in the sunlight. "These are very rare."

"She told me to enjoy them with my new friends," Adela said.

"Let's ask Nenard to make us a shelf like Madam Eleeza had so that we can enjoy looking at them," I said. "And I will be very, very careful not to break any!"

We settled in the shade with our tea in the lovely cups. Then Adela said, "So what was that thing that you found?"

"What did you find, Milada," Zora asked, as I took the pouch out of my pocket.

"Is it an animal?" she said, looking at the fur.

"No," I said. "I thought it was when I touched it in the cave. The pouch is made of fur. I can feel that there is something in it."

Seeing it in the light for the first time, I realized that it was very old. It felt heavy in my palm. The leather was stiff and hard and the fur was missing in places. I tried to open it but the leather was stuck closed.

"I can't open it," I said, "but I can feel that there is something inside".

Zora took out the sharp knife that she always wore on a leather sheath on her belt.

"Shall I cut it open so we can see what is inside?" she asked.

"Yes," I replied and handed her the pouch.

Zora carefully made a slit on the side with less fur. She squeezed the pouch and something dark emerged, as if it were being born, coming into the world for the first time.

"What is it?" I asked, impatient to see what it was that I had found.

"I think it is a woman," she replied and handed me a small dark brown ceramic figure.

It seemed to be a woman with very wide hips. The top part of the body was long and narrow, the neck as wide as the head and shoulders. It had two small breasts and lines etched over the belly and legs.

"What a strange thing. Do you know where it came from?" I asked Zora.

"I have never seen anything like it, She said. "We have stopped to camp here because it is the time of the moon tent. Bring it with you. Maybe one of the women will know what it represents."

Chapter 66

A Colourful Day

We finished our tea and Adela carefully washed the china and placed it back safely in the basket.

Zora and I took the cauldron off the fire. We removed the wet clothes and brought them down to the river to rinse. When the water cooled off we would wash our more colourful clothes. In the mean time, we took off our clothes and waded into the river. The little black puppy splashed along beside us.

"Be careful, Adela," I said, "The current is strong. Stay near the bank. And keep an eye on the puppy!"

We dipped into the water, giving ourselves a good wash along with the clothes. Zora had brought the jug with a herbal preparation to wash our hair. It made it shiny and bright and prevented small insects from making their homes on our heads.

After we rinsed our hair, we rinsed our clothes. We took turns helping each other to wring out the excess water and then hung the clothes on the low branches of the trees to dry in the afternoon sun.

We spent a pleasant afternoon, doing our wash and splashing in the brook. When we hung our colourful clothes to dry our camp took on a festive atmosphere, like a village fair.

The sunlight shown through the bright fabric and was reflected in the water of the stream and back up into our faces.

"You look green!" Adela said, laughing at me.

"And you are purple!" I retaliated. "And look at Zora! She's red all over!"

Zora sat on a stone by the edge of the stream, combing out her long hair. She had become a beautiful young woman, no longer the awkward, gangly child.

Adela paused from her pursuit of trying to catch small fish in her hands.

"Have you seen the puppy?" she asked.

"No," I replied, "not since we finished washing the clothes."

I followed Adela as she ran, dripping, to our wagon. "Blackie! Blackie, where are you?" she called. But there was no sign of the pup.

"Do you think he went down the stream?" she said, rushing back to the bank.

"I don't know," said Zora. "The last time I saw him, he was with you."

"Let's go and look for him," I said, pulling on my clothes.

"If he went into the current he could be far away by now," she said. "I'm supposed to take care of Radha's animals, not loose them!"

Adela was dressed and we were ready to start our search when I heard a familiar voice.

"Milada! Zora! Adela! Where are you?" It was Radha!

"Here we are," I said and ran to greet her.

She looked lovely. Her red hair glowed in the early evening sunlight. And, there in her arms, was the puppy!

"There you are!" said Adela, running up to Radha and holding out her arms for the pup. "Where did you go?"

"I guess he missed me," Radha said with a laugh, "and I missed him, too."

Zora, wrapped in a sheet, and carrying a big pile of multicoloured clothes greeted Radha.

"Good evening, my Lady," she said.

"Zora!" Radha said and ran to embrace her friend. "I know that it is proper, but please, you are like my sister, do not be so formal with me."

"Yes, my Lady," Zora replied, and then both girls began to laugh.

I took the pile of clothes and put them in the wagon while Radha and Zora chatted. Adela fussed over the puppy, giving him titbits to eat.

After some minutes Radha said, "Come, it is almost time for the evening meal. We will have music and dancing tonight.

We waited for Zora to dress and then the four of us, and Blackie, too, made our way to the campfire. We helped the other women prepare the meal.

"This seems like a lot of food," I said to Annika as we cut basketfuls of vegetables.

"It is nearly time for the moon tent," she said. "We are preparing extra so there will not be so much work for the other women."

It seemed like a long time had passed since the last moon tent. So much had happened over the last month. I enjoyed the evening's meal and dancing to the music of the viols, pipes and drums.

When we returned to our wagon, I lay in my bed and held the small figure I'd found in the cave. There was something strangely comforting about it. I awoke in the morning still clutching it. There was a dampness on my sheet that told me it was time to go to the moon tent.

I got up to rinse out my things in the stream. Zora was already at the fire.

"Here's a cup of tea, for you," she said, handing me a cup of steaming herbal brew. I noticed that it was in one of our usual earthenware cups, not the precious china.

"Then we can go to the moon tent together," she added.

"What about Adela?" I asked, "I don't think we should leave her all alone."

"Radha came by earlier this morning. She will take care of Adela, and the puppy".

"But Radha will be in the moon tent with us," I said.

"Not for some months," Zora said.

"Why not?"

"Because she is with child," Zora replied. "For the nine months the baby will grow in her womb she will not have a moon time."

"Tanya is having a baby!" I exclaimed.

"No," Zora said, "Radha is having a baby. The child you knew as Tanya is no more. Come, finish your tea and gather your things. I will put out the fire and we can go."

I drank the rest of my tea and went to get some clothes and my tambourine. I put the small figurine back into its fur pouch and put it in my pocket.

This time next year, I thought, Radha will be a mother. She has experience taking care of small animals, I'm sure she will be fine at taking care of a baby.

"Are you coming?" Zora called, impatiently.

"Yes," I said climbing down the wagon's steps and following her to where the moon tent that been prepared.

Chapter 67

The Little Figurine

It was good to be back in the cosy surroundings of the moon tent. Many women were already seated on the low divans and cushions, smiling and chatting together. I saw one or two new faces, women from other bands who had joined us after the solstice gathering.

One of the unfamiliar women was very dark, with curly black hair like Adela's. I wondered if she was from the Band of the South. Annika sat beside her and was showing her and another woman I didn't recognize the basic strokes of the tambourine.

I heard the dark haired woman say, "We play it differently, like this".

She played a few strokes. It sounded good, but different from the way we played.

Annika said, "That is very nice, but now that you have joined our band, we all need to play the same way to keep the sound strong."

"I have been playing for many years," the dark haired woman replied, "I will try to play your way but it may take some time."

"When we all play together, I'm sure that you will find it easier," Annika said.

"Yes," the dark haired woman replied, "I know that when we all play, after a while we become one."

"We always are one," Annika said, "but when we play we remember."

I took my tambourine and sat next to the dark haired woman.

"Hello," I said, "I am Milada".

"I am Ramani," the dark haired woman replied.

"Did you come with the Band of the South?" I asked, thinking, no, *hoping* that this woman was a lost relative of Adela's.

"No," she replied, "I am from the Band of the East. People in the villages where we travel play the tambourine in a very different way. I don't know if we took our style from them or if they learned from us."

"No one in my village played the tambourine," I replied without thinking, giving away the fact that I was not born into the gypsy band. "I'm glad that I have learned. I always feel better when I play."

Zora joined our little group.

"Zora," I said, "this is Ramani. She comes from the East. Ramani, this is my friend, Zora."

They greeted each other and then Zora said, "Have you shown the others what you found?"

"Not yet," I replied, surprised at Zora's curiosity. I was a little hesitant about the object, since remembering how I found brought up memories of that awful boy putting his hands on me.

"What is it, Milada?" Zora asked, seeing the expression on my face. I hadn't told her or anybody else about what had happened in the cave.

"When I found the pouch, I was hiding from a boy," I said, quietly.

"What boy?" Zora asked. "And why were you hiding from him?"

"It was in the cave," I told her. "I don't know who he was. He was not of our band. It was dark."

"Did he hurt you?" Ramani asked, with concern.

"He didn't really hurt me, I guess," I said. "He frightened me because I didn't know what he was doing."

"What did he do?" Zora asked, taking my hand in hers.

"Like I said, it was dark. I didn't hear him coming up behind me. I felt a hand on my shoulder, and then it slid down," my voice faltered.

"Did he touch your breasts? " Ramani asked.

I nodded.

"How did it feel?" she continued.

I wasn't sure I wanted to talk about it, but the look of love and concern on the women's faces encouraged me to express the confusion I'd been holding inside myself.

"At first, it felt good," I said. "I felt a flush of warmth going all through my body. But then I was afraid. And before I could even think about what was happening the boy turned me around and kissed me on the lips.'"

"It was not a gentle kiss," I shuddered to remember, "but a demanding kiss. He was pushing himself close to me. I didn't like the way that felt, or the bad smell of his body".

"What did you do," Annika asked.

"I hit him with my shoe and then hid until he fell asleep," I replied, still upset at the thought of what had happened.

I saw that Zora was trying to stifle a laugh.

"Why are you laughing?" I asked, feeling angry at her reaction to my ordeal.

"I'm sorry, Milada," she said, "It's just that I pictured you attacking that lout with your shoe!" She mimed the action and the others dissolved in laughter.

"Off, off!" Annika said, hitting the air with her slipper.

For a moment, I hung on to my anger and indignation, but then, even I could see the humour in the situation. I was not hurt, only a few scratches that were now healed. I could keep my anger inside, carried like a heavy burden, or join the others and let it go with a laugh.

I smiled, "All right," I said. "Yes, I must have looked funny. But I got away from him, didn't I?"

"Yes, you did!" Annika said. "But it won't be too long before you *want* a boy to kiss you."

"I want it to be a boy I like!" I said, thinking of Goran and the sweet kiss he gave me when we parted.

Zora said, "Show them what you found in the cave".

I took out the pouch and let the little figure be born again from the slit that Zora had made. The women passed it around from one to another. As each woman held it she became quiet. Soon there was not a sound in the moon tent.

When the clay figurine came back around the circle to me, I held it in my hands for a moment in silence.

Ramani broke the silence, but not with words. Instead, she started to hum a long sustained note. Shortly, another woman joined in, and then another and another. I felt shy at first, not knowing what was happening or if there was a form to follow, but soon I relaxed and hummed along. I passed the little figure on to Zora. Once more she was handed from woman to woman around the tent. When she returned to me the humming slowly faded away.

After a few moments of silence, Ramani reached out her palm to receive the figurine. She closed her eyes and said in a low voice, just loud enough for everyone to hear her in the profound silence.

"This is a representation of the great mother, the one who gives form to all life. She is the ancient one. The woman who crafted her lived long, long ago, before our people came to this earth. She understood the creation mysteries and left some of her knowing within this figure. She was of the last of the wise ones, who set things in motion here. This small statue celebrated energy coming into form. The idea of life becoming life."

Ramani opened her eyes and handed the little figure back to me.

"Take good care of her, Milada," she said, "She was made by the wise ones and has now chosen you to be her guardian. Keep her safe".

I put the strange form into its pouch.

"I think she belongs to all of us," I said. "She should stay in the moon tent. It is very comforting to hold her."

"It's good you could feel that," Zora said. "Thank you for your suggestion to share her with this gathering."

"She belongs to all women," I said, not sure where the words had come from.

Chapter 68

Winter in A Cave

The days in the moon tent passed in companionable contemplation, music and rhythm. When our moontime had passed we rejoined the others to learn that we would be moving on in a day or two.

We enjoyed those days, swimming in the brook and collecting fresh wild berries and herbs from the woods. Radha often joined us for a swim and a chat and Adela seemed at home in our company.

Through the rest of the summer and into the autumn we retraced our route, stopping at villages along the way. I was looking forward to returning to the village where Goran had stayed.

Each moontime we would pass around the ancient figurine of the "Great Mother" and feel her presence growing among us and further uniting our spirit. One day I showed her to Radha and Adela.

"I saw something like this once before," Radha said, fingering the small figure in her hand. "It was not exactly the same, but it was similar".

"Where did you see it?" I asked her.

"My mother showed it to me," she replied. "She said it was a treasure from a long time ago".

"I will show her this one when we meet again," I said.

"I'm sure she will be happy to see it," Radha said, "but next summer's gathering seems a long time away".

The golden glow of autumn faded to winter's grey, as the snows came on early. It was a good thing that we had worked hard in the fall, grinding wheat into flour for our bread and preserving cabbage in large barrels. Apples and other fruit had been sliced and dried in the last of the summer sun. We had sacks and sacks of nuts from the wild nut trees. It seemed as if the forest had been especially generous this year, as if it knew that the winter would set in sooner than usual.

The Baron decided to make our winter's camp at a spot on the south side of a high mountain, beside a small lake. There was a large cave carved out of the base of the mountain. We grouped the wagons near its entrance and used the cave itself as our meeting place. The men built an enclosure for the horses so that they would be protected from the cold and snowy nights.

We spent much of the day inside of the cavern, sheltered from the cold wind. I could not remember such weather. When coming and going to the wagons an icy wind cut through the fabric of my clothes and I felt chilled to the depths of my bones.

The wagon was warmed by a small brazier, stocked with hot coals from the main fire in the cave. We each had a quilt made from woven wool fabric filled with soft down feathers collected from hens that had been our food. The gypsies never threw anything away. They found a use for everything. Plucking a chicken for the pot in Midsummer, I wouldn't have thought to save the soft feathers to keep me warm in the depths of winter!

Generally, we all stayed in the cave where the fire and good food provided warmth for our bodies and good company, music and laughter provided warmth for our souls. As the weeks of winter passed I could see Radha's belly swelling as the child within her grew.

The time of the shortest days had long passed but it was still bitterly cold. The men had to travel farther and farther from our camp to find wood for our nightly fires. There was still much snow on the ground, making it difficult for the band to move on.

I was sitting by the fire, listening to Bora playing his viol, when the peaceful atmosphere was shattered by the sound of clattering hooves. Nenard, one of the strongest men in our band had entered the wide mouth of the cave, still sitting on his horse. He held the reigns of two other horses. Three mules with half empty packs followed behind them. They stood just outside of the cave.

Nenard quickly dismounted and said, "Where is the Baron? I must speak to him now!"

The Baron and Iovan were there, sitting near the fire with the rest of us. They had been shining their boots, companionably, side by side. The Baron rose immediately and approached Nenard.

"What is it, my friend?" he asked, placing his right hand on the man's shoulder.

Nenard was shuddering. Radha brought him a cup of hot herbal tea. He took it from her hands, without a word of thanks. He took a deep breath, then a sip of the hot brew. After another deep breath, he collected himself and spoke.

"We were looking for firewood," he began. "We went as far as the last village, about a morning's ride from here. When we were close to the village, we saw smoke rising; much more than is usual for a village, even in winter.

We rode closer. We could see the wall around the village. It looked like a ring of stones around a fire pit. The entire village was on fire."

He paused and took another sip of the herbal tea.

"We started to ride closer, in case anyone was in need of help, but as soon as we broke the cover of the forest, a group of men rushed through the gate, firing arrows upon us."

"Who were these men?" The Baron asked.

"I couldn't say," Nenard replied. "Their clothes looked strange, not like anything I've seen in these parts. Warm, they were, of leather and fur with helmets of iron."

"Boris, of the band of the North, told me that there had been raids in some of the villages of that region," the Baron said. "Then what happened?"

"We turned our horses and ran into the forest, but not fast enough. Palé and Niku were hit. Joska and I were farther ahead with the mules. He told me to stay put and he rode back to help them," he continued.

"I saw Palé and Niku fall from their mounts. Before Joska could get there, men had dispatched them with their short swords. Joska pulled back into the woods, and was able to signal the horses to return to me."

"I saw there was nothing more I could do there. Some of the men had spread out through the forest to look for us. So I took the animals and returned by a roundabout route. Has Joska returned?"

"No, not yet," the Baron replied. "How many men did you see?"

"There must have been at least thirty, maybe more," Nenard replied.

"It is not safe for us to stay here," said the Baron. "We must make preparations and leave tomorrow. Come, my friend and have something to eat. Let's hope that Joska will make it back soon".

"Palé and Niku were my good friends," Nenard said, sinking down on a cushion by the fire. "I will miss them."

"We all will miss them," Radha said, taking Nenard's empty cup and replacing it with a bowl of steaming stew. "It is always hard when our friends leave unexpectedly".

Some of the other men had led the tired horses and mules to their enclosure. They started to unload the wood from the mules' packs.

"Just unload what we will need for tonight," the Baron said. "Tomorrow we will be off."

I was sorry to leave the shelter of the cave. The warmth of the fire brought us all closer together. I enjoyed listening to Bora play his viol. Zora was spending a lot of her time with Maxim, a young man who had joined us from the Band of the North. Maybe he would know something about these strange men.

A while later, once again there was the sound of hooves. Joska had returned! Nenard jumped up from his warm spot by the fire and hugged his friend as he descended from his mount.

"Joska! I am so happy to see you!" he said.

"And I you!" Joska replied, tightening his embrace. His look of happiness at seeing his friend then faded.

"I could not bring their bodies," he said. "The men took them. I guess they were looking for things of value."

The Baron approached Joska and embraced him.

"Welcome, back, my friend," he said.

Radha brought him a dish of stew and invited him to sit down by the fire.

Lazara approached the Baron.

"We will perform the ceremony when the moon rises," she said.

"That is well," the Baron replied. "Then we will dance by the fire. And in the morning we will leave this place and thank the Earth that has provided shelter for us throughout this dark winter."

Chapter 69

The Lovers Card

As we travelled west, then southward the days became longer and warmer. I hoped that we would soon return to the village where Goran had stayed. I would not go and look for him in case that man tried to hold me again, but I would send word for him to meet me at our camp. I was sure that everyone would be happy to see him once again.

The puppy, Blackie, has grown into a very large, very active dog. He was nearly as big as Adela. Dog and girl were inseparable, keeping each other warm during the snowy nights. Radha's body was getting rounder each day. Her eyes glowed in anticipation of the new life. Iovan was often at her side, making sure she was comfortable.

Mother Eleeza must have given birth to her baby by now. I looked forward to seeing her again and meeting the future Queen. During our time in the cave, Radha and I had often looked at the cards that her mother had given her. Radha knew all their meaning and was teaching them to me. While the wagon bumped along the muddy road I remembered the picture that she had picked the morning before we had to leave our cosy winter home.

It was a picture of a tower being struck by lightening and falling down. She told me it predicted a big change in all our lives, something that might seem very bad, but that in the long run was needed to move us along in our development. I hadn't thought about it until now. We lost two of our friends that day. We had to move early because the Baron was concerned that those men might find us, there in the cave. Was that what the picture indicated? And how did a few sheets of vellum know what was going to happen to us?

We stopped to make our camp for the night. As soon as Kizi was unhitched and settled I went to find Radha to ask her about the pictures. I found her adjusting the herbs in the big stew that would be our evening meal.

"Radha," I said, "remember that you picked the tower picture on the day we had to leave the cave?"

"Yes," she said, "I was thinking about that, too."

How do the pictures know what is going to happen?" I asked her.

"Milada!" she said, "the pictures don't know anything! *We* know. The pictures just help us to get to our own knowing and to understand it better."

"Did you know that we would have to move that day? That it wasn't safe for us to stay?" I asked.

"I can't say that I knew," she said, "but I *was* feeling restless. I thought it was because of the baby. Sometimes I get the feeling that he doesn't want to be here."

That seemed a strange thing for her to say, but she continued before I could ask her why?

"Remember that Iovan and his father were polishing their boots when Nenard arrived back?" she asked.

"Yes," I replied, thinking of the many times I'd watched Dragan's hair falling over his eyes while he polished.

"Well, they generally do that the day before we move on," she said.

I thought about it and she was right.

"Do you think that the Baron had already planned to move on?" I asked her.

"No, I don't think so," she replied. "Iovan would have told me".

For a moment I felt envious of the closeness between the two of them. a closeness that I would never share.

"My mother told me that the picture that we are drawn to is the one that will give us a clear picture of what we know," Radha said.

"But we didn't look at the pictures when we choose one," I said, not understanding how that could work. "We turned them the other way round."

"If we looked at them we might pick what we want to see, not what we need to see," she replied. "By choosing one without looking, our subtle self will pick up the energy of the picture that will help us the most."

I didn't understand what she was talking about!

"Do you think that having to move on was the big change shown by the Tower?" I asked.

"I think it was the start of it but there will be more to come," she replied. "The Tower is the sixteenth picture. Its effect can last sixteen turns of the moon."

I thought about the meaning of her words.

"These may be difficult times, but the energy of the Tower gives us the opportunity to let go of anything we no longer have use for, any old ways that keep us back for moving forward or deepening our love and understanding," Radha explained. "But enough of this, Baby and I are hungry and this stew is ready!"

After we finished our evening meal, I asked Radha "May I choose a picture tonight? I want to see what is in store for me."

Radha smiled. She looked over at Iovan who was deep in conversation with the Baron and some other men.

"It looks like Iovan will be here for some time," she said. "Come to my wagon and let's see which picture you will choose".

I had not been to the wagon that Radha shared with Iovan. It was a new one, one specially built for the young couple. Outside it was painted bright green with red yellow and blue flowers framing the door and windows. We climbed up the wagon's steps. There was a wooden door rather than the hanging curtain found in most of the wagons. When Radha opened it a flood of warmth emerged. Heavy velvet curtains kept the light out and the heat in.

"Have a seat," she said, "while I get the pictures."

I sat at a small table. An oil lamp provided a weak light.

"Shall I turn up the lamp?" I asked.

"Yes, do," she said, "so we can see the pictures!"

Even though she was very round, Radha moved more gracefully that I had ever seen her move. She reached up to a high shelf and brought down the wooden box that contained the pictures.

She spread them out on the table, face down. I reached out to pick one up.

"Wait!" Radha said.

I stopped, my hand in mid air.

"What?" I asked.

"Before you choose a picture, close you eyes and take a few deep breaths," she said.

I put my hands in my lap, palm upturned as I had seen her do before choosing a picture. I inhaled deeply, feeling the air fill my belly and then my lungs.

"That's it," she said softly, "one more time."

I kept up my slow and steady breathing.

"Feel yourself sinking into the chair," she said. "Yes, that's it. Relax. Feel the soles of your feet on the floor, making a connection with Mother Earth."

I felt the bottoms of my feet tingling gently, remembering that my body is made of the same elements as the earth and feeling a deep connection with her.

"Good," Radha said. "Now imagine the energy that you feel in your feet rising up to your heart."

"See a bud just over your head," Radha continued. "Feel your connection with the stars and see the bud opening into a flower. Let the sun warm its petals and move down to your heart".

I could sense the warmth from above meeting the energy of the earth with in my heart. I felt very calm and at peace with myself.

"Now open your eyes enough to see the cards," Radha instructed. "Take one more breath and see which one attracts you to it,"

I half opened my eyes, took a breath and reached my hand in the direction of the picture I was thinking of before. As my hand neared the picture I felt something pushing my hand away, but there was nothing there! I moved my hand slowly over all of the pictures. Some of them seemed to push my hand away while others seemed to draw it closer.

"What a strange feeling," I said to Radha. "It reminds me of playing with Zora's load stones. One side of them pulls them together while the other side pushes them apart."

"That's right," Radha said. "You are beginning to feel their energy. Choose the one that pulls you most strongly."

At first I was confused. Several of the pictures seemed to pull my hand toward them. I took another breath and this time, when I passed my hand over the table I felt a strong pull in one direction. My fingers came to rest on a picture and I knew it was the right one.

"This one, Radha," I said. "This is the one I choose,"

Radha put the picture to one side and gathered the others up and replaced them in their box. Then she turned it over.

It was the cards of the Lovers.

"Ah," Radha said.

Ah, in deed!

"This picture indicated a coming together of male and female. Either the duel aspects of yourself, for you know each of us has both a masculine and feminine side," she said, "or a partnership of love."

"What is it like to be with a man?" I asked her. Here in the darkened room, with the picture of the Lovers before us it felt natural to ask.

"It is not easy to put into words," she said. "When we are together I feel completely like myself, relaxed and happy. It's like all the world is contained in us and we in it. The union of our bodies has produced this child, growing within me, but our union is much more than that. It is a union of our spirits. We can accomplish things together that we cannot on our own."

"Sometimes I feel the longing to be with someone," I said. "I have been happy here, with you and my friends, but lately there seems to be something missing."

"This feeling is very natural," she said. "We are no longer children. We are young woman. Your body is ready to take the next step in your journey."

"You see," she added, pointing at the picture. "of all of them, your inner knowing chose this one. It is time for you to find love, to find your partner."

I thought about Goran. I was anxious to get to the village and tell him what a mistake I had made. I knew what the picture meant! That Goran would come with us and we would dance together by the fire again. This time, when he kissed me, I would kiss him back!

"Why are you smiling"? Radha asked me, with a smile of her own.

"I'm just thinking about the next step in my journey," I said.

Chapter 70

Back to My Village

I knew where we were as soon as we rounded the bend. I remembered the way the trees looked, with their fresh new leaves, the ground carpeted with bright young grass, watered by the melted snow. We skirted the village and the wagons stopped one by one in the clearing where we had camped the previous year. It seemed much longer than one year since we had been here, since Goran left our band. I felt excited at the thought of seeing him again and telling him how much I missed him. *I know he will come with us if I ask him to,* I thought. How could he be happy here? Last year, he said he loved me. Now I realized that I loved him, too. I must love him; I've missed him so much!

Zora guided the wagon to a place in the shade of a huge oak tree. Blackie jumped down from the wagon, anxious to run after staying in the wagon since sun up. Adela followed behind him. I helped Zora unhitch the horse; anxious, too, but in a way I could not explain.

"Do you think Goran will have changed?" I asked Zora as she lifted the bridle and let Kizi free.

"A year is a long time," she said. "I'm sure he has grown taller; become more of a man. Look how much Bora and the other boys have changed".

"We see them every day," I said, "so I hadn't really noticed, but I guess they have, now that I think about it".

"The villagers saw us arrive," Zora said. "I'm sure they are preparing to feast us as they always do."

"Do you think Goran will come to see us?" I asked.

"I'm sure he will come to see you," she replied, "and the whole village will be at the feast."

"I don't think I will go," I told her, thinking about the man who locked me in the storeroom. I could not risk being caught again.

"It's up to you," Zora said, untying the jug that hung on the side of our wagon. "I am going to get some water so we can have a wash. If Adela comes back, tell her that there will be a feast in the village tonight."

Zora walked towards the centre of our camp, humming to herself. I would love to go to the feast, but I was afraid. Maybe, if I tied up my hair and wore one of Zora's more sombre dresses the man would not recognize me. It would be dark, after all. There would be many people so if he touched me I could call out for help.

I heard a rustle in the thicket behind our wagon. I felt my heart beating fast, thinking maybe that it was Goran. But, a moment later Blackie's hairy face poked through the bushes.

"What are you doing there?" I asked the dog.

"He found a short cut back," said Adela popping out right behind him.

"Come and let me take those twigs out of your curls," I said. "There will be a feast in the village tonight to welcome our arrival".

"Have you been to this village before, then?" she asked.

I explained that I was born in this village and how the gypsies had helped the people here.

"It's nice to be somewhere and feel safe and welcomed," she said. "Not all the villages like having us around."

I thought about what she said. I had noticed that something felt different in the villages that we passed through after the solstice gathering. Before, we were always welcomed, not as enthusiastically as we were here, but people would seek us out to help heal the sick and repay us with food or things that they had made. The last few months, before we made our camp in the cave, the villages seemed quieter, without the usual bustle in the market squares. People seemed preoccupied with their own lives, less curious about the news we brought, and less generous with their offerings of food.

I wondered if the villagers here would also be less welcoming than before. I did not know what to expect.

It took a long time for Zora to return to our wagon and when she did, the jug in her hand was still empty.

"Zora," I said, "where is the water for washing?"

She looked down at the empty jug in her hand.

"Oh," she said, a blush rising to her cheeks. "I forgot to bring it."

"I'll go bring some," Adela said, grabbing the jug from Zora's hand. "There is probably some warm water now that the fires have been lit. I'll be right back."

She ran off with Blackie following at her heels.

"Zora," I said, "it's not like you to forget what you went for!"

"I know," she said, with a little giggle, "I guess I was distracted".

"What distracted you," I asked, "or *who*! Was it that man from the North?"

Zora's blush deepened. "Yes, it was Maxim," she said.

"You like him a lot, don't you?" I asked.

"Yes," Zora said, "I do".

"I can see he likes you," I said. "Whenever he sees you coming he leaves the other men and comes to be with you".

"I feel like we have known each other forever," Zora said. "It is so easy to talk to him, and when we are not together I think about him all the time".

"I've been thinking a lot about Goran," I said, quietly. "I had hoped he would have come by now."

"You will see him tonight," Zora said.

"I am afraid that my father's brother will try to catch me again and keep me here," I told her.

"So you won't come to the feast?" she asked, looking surprised, "You always enjoy such festivities, the music, dancing and delicious food".

"Maybe there won't be as much feasting as before," I said. "Have you noticed a change in the villages that we visited after the gathering?"

"Maxim says that people are afraid. Those men who killed Palé and Niku and others like them have been raiding the villages and taking crops and provisions," she said.

"Who are they and where do they come from?" I asked her.

"The are a tribe from far to the northeast. They have a great leader who wants to control more and more land, get more and more power. He has sent his armies far and wide with the command to take over the villages and collect a tax of food and money from the people," she replied.

"And if the people don't want pay?" I asked.

"The village is burnt and the people who don't manage to run away are killed or captured and either ransomed for gold or taken back to the land of the ruler to work as slaves," she said.

"What is a "slave'?" I asked.

"A slave is someone without freedom," she replied, "someone who must do whatever he is told, without payment or choice."

"That's awful!" I said, not being able to imagine such a thing. "I would run away!"

"If the slave's master chooses he can have him beaten or even killed. If a slave is caught running away, the punishment is death. That's what Maxim told me," Zora said.

"I wouldn't be caught!" I said, thinking about outwitting the man who had caught me once before. "Can I wear your brown dress tonight?"

"My brown dress?" Zora said, looking puzzled. "You usually prefer red!"

"That's why I want to wear your brown dress," I explained, "so that man will not recognize me! I'll tie up my hair and wear a kerchief and I'll blend in with the villagers".

Zora laughed, "You think you will blend in with the villagers?" she said.

"Why not?" I was annoyed at her laughter.

"The way you toss your head," she said, "the bounce in your walk".

"I'll wear those tight shoes I still have," I said, "so I'll hobble like and old lady!"

"This I have to see!" said Zora, still smiling. "You can wear my brown dress if you want. I will see what remains in the chest that belonged to my mother. I think I remember a golden one. You want to look like a wren tonight. I want to look like a peacock!"

Chapter 71

My Meeting With Goran

The sun set early and the air was chill. I felt very strange with my long hair tied up under a kerchief and wearing the drab brown dress. I recognized the red skirt that Adela wore as one I had once worn and loved. I was happy to see how she liked it, showing it off with a twirl.

"I love this skirt!" she said, spinning round and round. The skirt opened around her like a flower, showing the thick woollen stockings and her muslin drawers beneath.

When Zora emerged from the wagon, I hardly recognized her. She smiled when she saw me staring.

"What is it?" she said.

"You look so beautiful!" I told her. Her long dark hair framed her face in a stunning contrast with the rich, bright colour of her dress.

"You don't think it's too much?" she asked, smoothing down the richly embroidered golden fabric.

"No," I replied, "The dress just brings out your beauty. I always thought about you as being really smart but sort of plain. But tonight I see I was wrong. You are really smart and really beautiful!"

"It's because she's happy," Adela piped in, with wisdom beyond her years. "But *you* look really funny!" she said to me.

"Thanks!" I said, laughing. "I hope I never really look like this!"

The three of us set out for the village. I followed behind Zora and Adela, watching the spangles on their clothes reflecting the light of the full moon.

I was beginning to have doubts. What if the man recognized me, even with my disguise? Or what if Goran saw me like this and thought I'd really changed. He hadn't come out to the camp to see me. Maybe it would have been better to wear my favourite dress and let my hair flow free, as usual. I thought about going back to the wagon to change, but then I would have to go to the village alone, and that could be dangerous. I had made my decision. Now I was stuck with it.

I had trouble keeping up with the others in my tight shoes. When we reached the village square I took a seat on a bench to rest my feet and see if I could spot Goran anywhere.

Many people were coming and going, sharing out the meat from the spit and the cabbage from the huge earthenware pots on the coals. I thought I saw that girl, my cousin Yagoda, but was straining to see in the dim light. I was about to get up and go closer to the fire when I felt a hand on my arm.

"Milada, is that you?" I familiar voice spoke close to my ear.

"Goran! It's so good to see you!" I said, throwing myself into his arms.

He was much taller than I remembered. We used to embrace shoulder to shoulder but now my head rested on his wide chest. I felt the strong muscles of his arms, muscles that were not there last year when we parted.

I looked up into his face. His eyes were the same merry brown but a thick brown moustache covered his lip.

I ran my finger over it, "Where'd you get this little brown mouse?" I asked, trying to look serious.

"Look who's talking about a little brown mouse!" he said. "What happened to *you*?"

"I'm hiding from that man!" I said. "Don't worry, I'm still the same girl who likes bright colours and wild hair."

"I've missed that girl," he said, looking down into my eyes.

"Oh, Goran," I said, "and I've missed you! A lot more than I thought I would!"

"You sit here and hide," he said, "and I will get us some food and we can catch up on all our news."

I was sorry when he moved away. It felt so good to be in his arms. Why hadn't I realized before that I loved him?

Soon he was back with two plates piled high with delicious morsels.

"So, how do I look?" he asked with a cheeky grim, obviously pleased with himself.

"Well, except for the brown mouse," I said, "you look just fine!"

"I feel good," he said. "I have found my way here in the village."

I was surprised at his words. I thought that he would be anxious to hear about our travels, but here he was saying how good it was in this village.

"But isn't it boring to stay in one place all the time?" I asked, hoping he would say 'yes'".

"I have not been bored at all," he said. "It was difficult at first to learn the blacksmith's trade. I could hardly pick up the hammer! But little by little I got stronger and learned the right way to handle the tools."

"You are working for that man," I asked, "the one who locked me in the storeroom".

"Dunia's father isn't as bad as he seems, once you get to know him," he said. "And I have big news for you".

He turned to face me and took both of my hands in his. "Your father is back!"

I pulled my hands away and jumped up, the plate of food clattered from my lap.

"Let me go!" I said, "I have no interest in these people. The gypsies are my family! No one can keep me here."

"Wait, Milada," he said, catching me by the waist.

I struggled to get free but his arms were too strong. Holding me tight with his right arm his left hand came up to stroke my head.

"This is no good," he muttered and pulled off the silly kerchief. He untied my hair and stroked it as he would to calm down an animal.

"Milada," he murmured, "it's all right."

"Oh, Goran!" I said turning to rest my head on his strong shoulder, "I've missed you so. So many times I wanted to share my thoughts with you, or a funny thing that happened during the day".

"I've missed you, too," he said, "especially at the beginning".

"And then you forgot about me?" I teased, looking up into his eyes.

"It's not that I forgot you," he looked down at me seriously. "How could I ever forget you? It's just that you had made your choice and I had to get on with my life."

"Maybe I made the wrong choice," I said, trying to read the look in his eyes. It was if a flash of pain passed through him.

"Milada," he said, holding me closer.

"Goran, I love you," I whispered.

He held me tight.

"Milada," why didn't you tell me before," he murmured.

I felt so good, so safe in his embrace. I told him how I felt; now surely he would come with us. I wanted to stay like this forever but a voice interrupted our private moment.

"Goran! Is that you?"

I looked over my shoulder to see Radha standing there, smiling.

Goran's arms dropped and he stepped away from me.

"Tanya!" he said, "Well look at you!"

"I am called 'Radha' now," she said. "Since Dragan and I were wed!"

"You and Dragan married?" he said, giving her a hug.

"Yes, didn't Milada tell you?" she asked, looking at me.

Goran shook his head.

"It was at the Summer Solstice gathering," she said. "Come and say 'hello' to Iovan and the others."

"Iovan?" he asked.

"My husband!" she replied.

"I'll come in a moment," he said, "I have something to say to Milada".

"Don't be too long," she said with a smile, "we've all missed you".

Radha walked toward the fire. Her once light step was slowed by the weight of the child within.

Goran turned to look at me, his eyes cold. "So now you love me," he said, "Now that your precious Dragan is wed."

"Is that what you think?" I said. "I have always loved you".

"That is not what you said last year when I was ready to go against my better judgment to stay with the gypsies to be with you," he said.

"You can come now!" I said. "We can be together."

"It is too late, Milada," he said firmly, "much too late".

"What do you mean?" I said, but before he could answer Yagoda called out to him,

"Goran! Where have you been? We've been looking for you every where."

Our eyes met.

"Goran is that Milada?" she asked, as if I wasn't there.

Before waiting for an answer she ran off.

"I have to go," I said. "She will tell her father!"

"Wait, Milada. Many things have changed. I have to tell you something," he said, grasping my wrist tightly.

"Let me go! That hurts!" I yelled. "You are just as bad as they are!"

"Calm down, Milada. I won't hurt you and I won't let anyone else hurt you," he said. "Please, just sit down for a moment and listen."

That moment I saw the old Goran, the loving concern in his eyes. I sat down on the bench, with my head in my hands, my now free hair falling around my face. Goran gently stroked my back.

"When you left, I was very sad," he said. "I had lost my best friend, and the girl I loved. I thought the two of us had a special bond since we were not of the band. I could see you thought you loved Dragan. I hoped that you would realize that you could never be together."

"I do now," I said softly.

"Now it is too late," he said.

"You don't love me now?" I asked.

"I'll always love you," he said.

"So it's not too late," I said, hopefully looking into his eyes.

"You told me that you could never love me," he said, "so I decided to make my life here. Dunia was very good to me. She prepared special food. She kept my clothes clean and always had a kind word for me when I returned from the forge."

"Dunia?" I whispered.

"And she does look like you," he continued. "I thought if I can't be with Milada, at least I could be with someone like her".

"You can be with me now," I said, taking his hand in mine.

"It is not that easy," he said.

"Goran," a voice called out.

"Dunia and I are going to be married," he said, just as Dunia and Yagoda approached the bench where we sat.

I dropped Goran's hand when I saw Dunia's rounded belly. She was not as far along as Radha but it was obvious that Dunia was carrying a child, Goran's child.

Chapter 72

Two Men at My Wagon

In that moment, all my hopes and dreams were shattered. I knew that even if Goran loved me he would not leave Dunia and the child. I could not stay there a moment longer. I got up and ran as fast as I could back toward the comfort of my wagon. The old shoes pinched my feet as I ran. As soon as I was out of the village with it's hard cobblestones I kicked them off and ran the rest of the way with my bare feet slapping on the cold, hard earth.

I climbed into my wagon and pulled off the awful brown dress. Maybe if I had looked more beautiful, more grown up, more womanly, Goran would have said he would come away with me.

But in my heart I knew that the clothes I wore made no difference. Goran had grown into a man of honour. He would not leave his responsibilities. It was my own stupidity to think that Dragan and I could be wed that led to this moment of misery. It was no one's fault but my own.

The picture lied! The Lovers was chosen. But the lover was not mine. It was Dunia and Goran who would be together, not Goran and I.

Instead of dancing by the fire, or lying in Goran's arms, that night I was alone in the wagon, crying myself to sleep, without even Blackie for company and consolation.

I awoke the next morning to find Adela curled in the quilt, still wearing the red skirt. Blackie was asleep at the foot of her bed, keeping her bare feet warm. Zora's bed was empty.

I got up quietly so I wouldn't wake Adela. I pulled on my warm woollen socks, a thick shirt and a brightly coloured, quilted patchwork skirt. As I wrapped myself in a warm shawl a loud sneeze exploded from my nose! Adela stirred but did not wake up. I turned up the flame on the small fire we kept burning in a brazier to keep the wagon warm and brewed a cup of herbal tea to stave off the cold that tickled my nose.

Cupping the tea in my hands to keep them warm I stepped out of the wagon. I saw two men sitting there as if they were waiting for me.

"Good morning, Milada. Why did you run off like that last night! You missed all the dancing. That's not like you at all."

"Goran, it's you," I said. He looked even more different in the daylight. "I was not in the mood for dancing."

I looked at the man that was with Goran, afraid that he was Dunia's father, come to take me to their house.

The man looked at me. He looked like the girl's father but he was slighter of build. His eyes were kind. I saw a tear in one of them.

"Milada," Goran said, "come down and meet your father".

I felt all the air rush out of me. My heart was pounding. I reached out to steady myself on the doorframe, then sat down on the wagon's bench.

The man took a step toward me. I expected to feel afraid, but I didn't; yet I could not speak.

"Milada," he said, "I can't believe it's really you".

He took another step and then another, approaching me as if I were a shy forest deer. Tears now ran freely from his eyes. Goran hoped up beside me on the bench and put his arm around me.

"Don't be afraid, Milada," he said. "Milan won't hurt you or try to make you stay. I've told him all about you and he just wanted to see you."

I took Goran's hand and felt stronger.

"You are my father?" I asked the man.

"Yes," he said, "I am."

"Why did you leave me," the words popped out before I could think what to say.

"I am so sorry, Milada," he said. "When your mother passed away my heart broke and I lost my reason. I loved your mother very much," he continued, "everybody did. My brother had wanted to marry her, but she chose me even though I was the younger of the two of us. If my parents had lived, they would have insisted that he be wed first".

"What happened to your parents?" I asked, curious for the first time about my birth family.

"They both perished in the sickness that came to the village when my brother and I were very young; the sickness that your gypsies helped us survive. I can remember one beautiful lady. She impressed me, even at my young age with her knowledge and her beauty. I even remember her name."

"What was it?" I asked.

"Miriana," he replied. "Is she still among you?"

"She left us last summer," I said.

"Mother Miriana is gone?" Goran asked. "I always liked the old thing, even if she didn't always approve of me!"

"She thought you were fine," I said.

"How did she die?" Goran asked. "She couldn't have been all that old."

"She decided that it was time and just died," I said. "The gypsies say 'she died of death'".

"I think that the gypsies are very wise," said Milan, my father.

"Who took care of you and your brother?" I asked. "Did you live with the gypsies?"

"The gypsies came in time to save my Grandparents. My brother and I went to live with them, in the house where you lived and where Goran lives now," he said.

"So my Grandma and Grandpa were your Grandparents?" I asked.

"Yes," he replied, "they were very old, too old to care for a child like you".

"Why didn't you leave her with your brother?" Goran asked. "After all, he and his wife had Dunia who is not much older than Milada".

"My brother and I had never spoken after I married Anna, Milada's mother. I was afraid he would mistreat the child out of anger and resentment for me," he said.

"My mother was called 'Anna'?" I asked.

"Yes," my father replied, "that's why they called you Anna. But I think 'Milada' suits you better".

"Do I look like my mother?" I asked, sensing the return of my curiosity. The shock of meeting my father was passing. He seemed like a very nice man.

"You have her beautiful, wild hair," he said, "but your features resemble my mother".

"So do Dunia's," Goran said. "That's why you are so alike".

At the mention of Dunia I felt my body becoming tense.

"Milada is much prettier that Dunia," my father said, further endearing himself to me. "Sorry, Goran. I know you and she will wed, but just look at this girl!"

"Are you all right with your father, Milada?" Goran asked, patting my hand.

I looked at my father then back at Goran. "Yes," I said, "I think I am".

"Then I will leave you," he said, "I have work to do".

He hopped off the wagon and disappeared down the forest path.

"Shall I make you a cup of herbal tea?" I asked my father.

"Yes," he replied, "I would like that".

Chapter 73

A Traveller's Tale

When I offered him the mug of steaming tea I saw that our hands were the same shape. We both had large, square palms and long, thin fingers. My father followed my glance.

"They are alike," he said, placing the mug on the wagon's bench and taking my hand in his. He opened my palm and traced the lines with his finger.

"Did the gypsies teach you how to see the future from the lines in your palm?" he asked.

"I was told that the lines have significance," I said. "This is the life line". I ran my finger along the line from the base of my thumb up and around beneath my index finger.

"You have a long one," my father said. "May it be happy"?

"Has yours been happy?" I asked.

"Some of it has been," he replied. "The years of my childhood, before my parents died; some of the time with my Grandparents. I knew they loved me and were doing their best to raise us, but I missed my mother's comforting embrace."

"The happiest times were those I spent with your mother," he said. "I have never been really happy since she left."

"How did she die?" I asked, seeing the sadness in his eyes.

"She died giving life to you," he said, looking down at his hands. "It was a difficult birth. After you were born she did not stop bleeding. Soon she was gone."

"Wasn't she given Shepherds' Purse or Ladies Mantle to stop the flow of blood?" I asked.

"The village's midwife had perished years before during the great disease. She did not pass down her skills to another," he said, sadly.

"She died giving life to me," I said with a sigh. "I'm so sorry."

"It was not up to you, or anyone," my father said, squeezing my hand. "I realize that now. But at the time, I think I did blame you. I was angry and sad and hurt. I just had to get away from everyone and everything."

"Where did you go?" I asked.

"I don't remember those first months. After we buried Anna, I asked my grandmother to look after the baby; you," he said looking into my eyes and giving me a hint of a smile. "I got on my horse and rode as fast as I could where ever the road took me, stopping each night at a tavern and drinking ale or mead until I passed into a deep sleep".

"The first place I remember was a town by the sea. I met a kind man at the tavern. He took me to his home and helped me to see that I had to face the fact that my beloved wife was gone. He too had lost his wife and his children as well when his village was attacked. He was not there to protect them, or die with them. He told me he nearly took his own life because of his feeling of sadness and guilt."

"Hearing his story and seeing that he had found a way to go on gave me courage. I thought of the child I had left behind and vowed to return and care for her, to be a good father," he said.

"So, did you return to the village?" I asked.

"It took me four years to make my way back. During that time I became a merchant, travelling from towns to villages, buying from one place and selling at another. I liked going from place to place, meeting different people and seeing different things," he said.

I thought to myself, maybe that's why I always liked moving around instead of staying at home in the village.

"When I finally found my way back home, my grandmother had died. I asked about the child and was told that you had gone to live with the healing gypsies. Every night my grandfather put a candle in the window. He said it was to welcome you and guide you home. But you never came," he continued.

"I waited for one turn of the moon but then needed to travel along to get to the coast before winter set in. I thought about looking for the gypsy band, but I had no idea which way to go. I left it to fate to bring us together."

"And fate has finally done so," I said, "What is it like on the coast of the sea?"

"The air smells different there," he said. "Water stretching out as far as you can see, always moving, always changing."

"I would like to see it someday," I said.

"I'm sure you will," he said. "Are you happy travelling with the gypsies? You know you are welcome to stay in the village."

"Will you stay here?" I asked him.

"I have more places to see," he said. "Maybe when I am an old man I will settle back here, but for now I like the life of a merchant. I have good friends in many villages. They have grown to depend on me for news and supplies."

"You never married again?" I wondered aloud.

"I never met a woman that compared with your mother," he said.

"What was she like?" I asked.

"She was very beautiful. She had long, shining hair and brown eyes that sparkled when she laughed, which was often. She could sing like a bird and dance like a gypsy. Some of the people in the village, especially some of the other girls, thought she was too free and easy. She had no patience with housework. She would do her chores as fast as she could and then be out and about, chatting in the square or running errands for the old ones".

There was a faraway look in the father's eyes. He looked happy remembering, yet at the same time, sad at his loss.

"She loved animals and they loved her," he continued. "She always had a dog or two following her around".

As if on cue, Blackie loped up the path and put his front paws up on the wagon's bench, asking for a pat on the head.

We both smiled and caressed his curly black fur. Then my father sighed, "I will never find another like my Anna," he said. "Now, instead of being so sad at loosing her I am grateful for the years we had together. And the beautiful child that we brought into the world".

I was glad to see him smile. Now there was no trace of sadness there, instead his eyes were full of love.

"I have something for you," he said, taking a small leather pouch from his pocket.

"Every year since the first time I returned to the village I have saved one gold coin from the proceeds of my trading for my child, for you. I thought that when the time would come I would use the gold to build you a house in the village, as is our custom. But meeting you, I know that you do not want to stay here, not now, anyway. So take this gold and use it to help you make the life you want for yourself."

He opened the pouch and counted nine golden coins into my hand.

I did not know what to say. I had heard about gold coins and their great value but I had never seen one, let alone held one in my hand. They sparked in the sunlight.

I looked up at my father, the coins heavy in my hand. I didn't know what to say.

My father took my hand, and with his, guided the coins back into the pouch.

"Tell no one of this," he said. "Some people would do you harm to get their hands on so much gold. Keep it safe and use it only when you need to. It is unusual for a woman to have so much gold, so it should be safe, as long as you keep it secret."

I held the pouch close to my heart and wrapped my other arm around my father.

"I don't know how to thank you!" I said. "Thank you for these coins and thank you for telling me about yourself and about my mother. I think I understand myself better, now that I have met you".

"Oh, my child, how different life might have been," he said, hugging me tightly. "I'm so happy that we finally met".

Chapter 74

My First Birth

Adela appeared, running and out of breath.

"There you are, you naughty dog!" she said, hugging Blackie.

"Who is this?" my father asked.

"This is my friend, Adela," I replied. "Adela, this is my father".

Adela's large eyes grew even wider.

"I didn't know you had one!" she said.

"I never met him before this day," I said.

"Hello Adela," my father said, reaching out his hand to help Adela climb up beside us on the bench. Blackie hopped up, too, and rested his head on Adela's lap.

"Any friend of my lovely daughter's is a friend of mine," he said.

Suddenly, there was the sound of someone with heavy footsteps running down the path, crashing through the bushes. We all turned to see who it was.

Goran appeared through the trees. He stood in front of the wagon, his hands resting on his bent knees, trying to catch his breath so he could speak. His face was red and he looked very upset.

"What is it Goran? I asked. "What is the matter?"

"It's Dunia," he managed to say, his heart pounding in his chest. "The baby is coming!"

"But it is not her time for some weeks," I said.

"Yes, that is what the women say. But she is in great pain and her waters have broken," he replied. "Is there someone here who can help her? The women of the village can help when a child is born in its time, but they do not know what to do to help Dunia now."

"Adela," I said, "do you know where Zora is?"

"I saw her this morning going out of the camp with the boy from the Band of the North. They had a big basket with them. They probably went for a picnic."

"You don't have time to look for them," Goran said. "Can someone else help? Can you help us, Milada?"

"I have helped with birthing," I said, "I will come and do whatever I can".

I went into the wagon to get some dried herbs that I knew could help a woman in childbirth. I reached for a pouch of mugwort. My hand mistakenly took hold of the pouch with the little statue that I found in the cave. I started to put it down, but then changed my mind and slipped it into my pocket. I found the herbs I needed and hurried out of the wagon. My father and Adela were waiting.

"Goran, run back to be with Dunia and tell her that we are coming," my father said.

"Shall I come to?" Adela asked. "Maybe I can be of help."

"Yes, come with us, Adela. "We may need some help and it's good for you to begin to learn what to do when a baby comes."

We hurried back to the village as fast as our legs would carry us. For a moment I felt fear in the pit of my stomach as I approached the house, remembering how my uncle had imprisoned me there and Yagoda's cruel words. I wondered if Dunia would accept help from me. But I knew I had to offer. It was up to her to choose to accept my help or not.

I heard Dunia's screams before Yagoda, looking very pale, opened the door.

"Oh, it's you," she said, standing aside to let us in.

"Hello, Yagoda," I said, ignoring her rudeness. "Where is Dunia?"

"Over there," she said, indicating the low divan next to the fire.

"Please boil some water so we can infuse these herbs," I told Yagoda.

" Here, Adela," I said, handing her a pouch of dried herbs. "When the boiled water has cooled a little, pour it over the leaves. Make enough for four cups."

"Yes, Milada," Adela said, taking the pouch as I went to join Goran at Dunia's side.

"Hello, Dunia," I said, gently taking her hand. Her contraction had passed and she lay quiet, catching her breath.

Milada," she said, "you are back."

"Lucky for us that the gypsies are here now," Goran said. "They will know what to do".

"So why didn't they come? Why send Milada?" Dunia asked, turning her face to the wall.

I felt a strong hand on my shoulder. My father stood at my side.

"Milada knows what to do," he said. "Rest now while you can and be thankful for her help."

"When was the baby expected?" I asked.

"Not for another turn of the moon," Goran replied.

"And when did the pains start?"

"About an hour ago," he said, "when I brought your father to the camp."

Dunia screamed again in pain. "Get this out of me. I want to die!" she yelled.

I called Adela over, "Bring me a cloth soaked in cool water, please."

She quickly did as she was told. I lay the cool cloth on Dunia's brow, resting my hand for a moment on her forehead.

"Don't say such things, Dunia," I said softly, when the pain had passed. "The child will hear you. Welcome this child, yours and Goran's child, with love".

"But it hurts so much," Dunia moaned.

Adela brought over a mug of the warm herbal tea.

"Have a sip of this," I told Dunia, "It will help you to relax. Try to flow with the spasms in your body rather than fight them. Giving birth is a natural process, let it happen".

Dunia drank the tea. She turned and looked up at me, her eyes searching mine.

"You are doing this for Goran," she said, "I know you love him".

I felt like a knife had plunged into my heart. Yes, I did love him. Like a brother or like a husband, I couldn't say which, but right now, my focus was on helping Dunia and the baby to survive. I put all other thoughts aside.

"I am here because Goran asked me to help you," I said, gently. "If you would like me to go, I will."

"No, Milada," Goran said. "You must help us".

He turned to Dunia and said roughly "Be quiet now, Milada is here to help. We need her."

Dunia opened her mouth to speak but before she could another contraction came. I saw her eyes glaze over with fear. Without realizing what I was doing, I felt my hand closing over the pouch in my pocket. It was as if the little statue was calling me.

I took the statue out of the pouch and pressed it into Dunia's hand.

"Hold this," I told her, "and keep breathing."

Dunia took the little statue and held it tightly. Her breathing became more regular and, although I could see that she was still in pain, the look of terror had left her eyes.

Adela had brought another cool rag for Dunia's head. As I changed it, I looked deeply into Dunia's eyes and with all my heart wished her and the baby a safe delivery.

She opened her eyes and looked back at me. At first she looked confused, but then relaxed and smiled. Soon another pain came. One followed the other with less and less time in between.

I rested my hand on Dunia's abdomen and could feel that the baby was ready to be born. I helped her sit on a low stool, with her feet flat on the floor and the straw-filled mattress from the bed leaning on the wall to cushion her back.

"Let mother earth call the baby to herself," I told Dunia. "Push with you feet on the earth, breath and let the baby come".

I took the statue from her hand and placed it on the table. "Put your hands on your knees and when the pain starts again, push!"

Dunia followed my instructions. Soon I could see the baby's head. A few more breaths and the baby wriggled out. I caught the small child in my hands as Dunia collapsed back into the softness of the mattress.

I gently held the baby, a little girl. She was small, but perfectly formed. I gently wiped the moisture from the baby's nose and passed her over to Dunia.

"Hold her close to your breast," I told her, "and tell her how much you love her".

"Is she alright?" Dunia asked as she reached out her arms to take the baby.

"She looks beautiful," I said as the baby let out its first tentative cry.

Adela and I cleaned up the afterbirth, wrapping the placenta in a clean rag and placing it close to Dunia. I had learned from Mother Miriana that it was better for the child not to cut the cord too soon, to ease its transition from it's warm, wet cocoon into the air-breathing world.

Soon Dunia was asleep and the small child cooed on her breast. Goran looked exhausted and relieved.

Dunia's mother, who quietly stood by, came over and thanked me. Yagoda just glared, without saying a word.

I washed my hands and then placed the little statue back in its pouch in my pocket. Adela and I gathered up the herbs.

I left some dried angelica root with Dunia's mother with instructions to give Dunia the herbal infusion for the next few days and was ready to be on my way.

Goran took my hand and said, "Milada, I don't know how to thank you. Let me walk you back to your wagon."

"No, Goran," I said. "Your place is here with Dunia and your child. Be here when she awakens. I will return later to see how they are doing."

I saw my father smile at my words. I felt that he was proud of me. It was a good feeling.

Chapter 75

A Family Dinner

The sun had set by the time Adela and I returned to our wagon.

"I didn't realize that it was so late," I said, as I unpacked the herbs and placed the pouch with the little statue back on its shelf.

It had been a long day and I felt very, very tired. I lay on my bed, regretting that I had promised to return to check on Dunia and the baby. I would just rest for a while, I thought to myself.

But, even though I was so tired, sleep would not come. I kept thinking about my father and the stories he had told me. For the first time I really felt a part of something. Goran had been right about the way the gypsies saw us, I know that they loved me, but I would never truly be one of them. I wondered if I should stay in the village, now that I had found my father. But what would be the point if he were travelling all the time? I couldn't live with Dunia and Goran! No, my life was here with my friends, my family of choice, the gypsies.

"Milada," I heard Adela's voice calling me from the doorway. "Are you going back to check on the baby? It's getting late."

It felt as if I had just lain down but I could see that the full moon was already high in the sky. I took a deep breath, stood up and smoothed down my clothes.

"Yes," I told her. "Do you want to come with me?"

"If you don't need me," she said, "I'd rather stay here with the gypsies. The villagers had given us many tasty things to eat! And the music has already started."

I could hear the musicians playing in the distance. It was a happy tune. I would rather have stayed there by the fire, warmed by it's flames, the good food, the music and the comfort of my familiar friends, but Dunia's baby was so small and vulnerable I felt I needed to at least check and see that they were comfortable and safe.

"I'll go alone," I told Adela. "I won't stay to long. I'll see you later by the fire."

I made my way back to my grandfather's house. He was really my *great-grandfather*, I thought as I walked. What a strange path my life had taken to bring me back here. When I reached the house, there was a candle burning in the window. I was sure that my father had left it there for me. I smiled as I knocked on the heavy door.

After a moment, Yagoda opened it.

"Oh, you are back," she said. "I wasn't sure you would come again. My father is home now".

I would not let Yagoda's bad temper spoil this moment. Even the thought of her father didn't scare me, since I knew that *my* own father was there to protect me.

"Good evening, Yagoda," I said. "How are Dunia and the baby?"

"See for yourself," she said, turning on her heel and letting the door swing behind her so I had to reach out to keep it from hitting me in the face. I took a deep breath and followed her into the dim room.

The family sat around the heavy oaken table, all except for Dunia who was where I left her on the cushions beside the fireplace. When my father saw me he came over to me and wrapped me in his arms.

"Milada, my girl, welcome," he said. "Come and join us for supper".

I looked up at my father and smiled.

"Thank you," I said, "let me check on Dunia and the baby and then I will join you. I haven't eaten at all today."

Dunia's mother smiled at me and rose to bring another wooden plate and spoon.

"You are welcome, Milada," she said. "Thank you for your help today".

I approached Dunia and saw that she was looking at the baby.

"Isn't she beautiful?" she asked.

"Yes, she is," I replied. "What will you call her?"

"It is the custom to call the first born girl after the father's mother," she said.

"I don't want to call her after my mother," Goran said, without rising from his place at the table. "She had a hard life, and a short one. I want better for our girl."

"You can call her 'Milada' since Milada helped her get born," said Yagoda with a sneer, knowing how her sister would react to the suggestion.

"What about calling her after your mother?" I said quickly before anyone had time to react to Yagoda's words.

"Gahla," said Dunia, looking at her daughter. "Do you like that name?"

The tiny baby girl opened her eyes and looked at Dunia as if to say yes.

"We'll call her Gahla then, after your, mother, if that is all right with you, dear," she added in Goran's direction.

"'Gahla' it is!" He exclaimed, smiling widely at his mother-in-law. "Let's drink a toast to Gahla!"

By the tone of his voice and the way he poured the clear liquid into his beaker, letting it splash onto the table top, I could see that it not the first toast of the day by far.

The men raised their beakers as Goran said, "To my daughter, Gahla, my father-in-law who has taught me his trade, to my mother-in-law who feeds me and to Dunia who will soon be my wife!" They all downed their liquor in one long sip.

My father refilled the beakers. "Would you like one, Milada?" he asked.

"Yes, a small one, please, to toast the health and happiness of this family," I said, "and to celebrate meeting you!"

He passed me over a beaker of the plum brandy, so famous in these parts.

"This toast is for Milada," he said, "I am so happy to have met you at last. Thank you for you help today and may you be happy always!"

We drank. I had a sip, while the men drained their beakers once again. The drink opened my appetite. I devoured the savoury stew that was placed in front of me.

All this time, the girls' father had not spoken a word. I avoided looking at him in case it brought back the fear in the pit of my stomach. Before we finished eating he pushed his empty plate away.

"I'm going to the tavern," he said. "This place smells like a baby. It is not place for a man. Goran, are you coming?"

I looked at Goran and then at Dunia, sitting alone with her child. Goran also looked at Dunia, and then at me, with an odd expression.

"Well," he growled at Goran, "are you coming with me or staying with the women?"

"I'm coming," Goran said, putting on his cloak and following the man out the door.

Chapter 76

Tunes By The Fireplace

As the door slammed shut I looked at my father.

"He still isn't speaking to me, much," he said, "but I don't mind. Do you think it would disturb Dunia and the baby if we had some music?"

Dunia said, without a moment's hesitation, "Oh, Uncle, please play for us".

Even Yagoda looked pleased at the suggestion. The girls' mother silently cleared the table while my father went to the corner of the room and returned with his instrument.

I had seen one like it at the Summer Gatherings but no one in our band played one. It was a fat instrument shaped like a pear, with a long neck with a bend in it. It had five strings that stretched from a bridge below the sound hole to tuning pegs at the top of its neck.

My father sat on a chair next to the fire, near Dunia and the baby. We gathered around him as he closed his eyes and began to play a mournful tune. I felt tears come to my eyes even though a moment before I had felt happy.

The piece ended. My father looked around him and saw all the tearful faces.

"That's enough of that!" he said, and struck up a much happier song. This one had us all tapping our feet. Before I knew what I was doing, I began to dance around the small room. I saw Yagoda, swaying back and forth and went over and stretched my arms out to her, inviting her to join me in the dance.

As if there were never bad feelings between us, we danced together in the firelight's glow, finally collapsing in laughter when the delightful tune came to its end.

"It's a good thing that your father didn't come home," the girls' mother muttered.

"That man never did learn to have fun," my father replied, "It's a shame. All he thinks about is his work. He doesn't see what a beautiful family he has here."

"He is a good man," the woman said. "He keeps food on the table, and wood on the fire."

"Does he make you happy?" he asked.

"I told you," she replied, "we are provided for."

"Where did you learn to play that instrument?" I asked my father, wanting to change the subject.

"I learned to play the barbat in the port city," he replied. "It's mournful tones matched my feelings. I only could play the sad songs at the start."

"I'm glad you can play the happy ones now, too!" I said. "Would you mind excusing us for a moment. I need to check Dunia."

"I will step outside," he said, "but not as far as the tavern!"

I sat beside Dunia. She said to me in a low voice, "I think I am bleeding."

"That is the way it should be," I told her. "You will bleed for a few weeks. The colour of the blood will change with time and then it will stop all together and your regular moontime will begin again."

"What is 'moontime'?" she asked.

"It is the days when a woman bleeds each month," I replied.

"I thought I had hurt myself," she said, "when I saw blood from time to time".

"Didn't you ask your mother?" I said.

"She told me that it was a part of growing up, but not that it would happen every month. It didn't happen for a while," she said.

"When you have a child growing within you, the monthly bleeding stops. That blood is used to cushion and nurture the baby. Now that the baby has been born, the blood will come out," I explained. "Has the baby suckled?"

"Yes", she said, "and then she slept".

"That's good. Now, let me cut the her cord, since she is comfortable with you."

I asked the woman for her sharpest knife, then held the blade in the fire as I had seen Mother Miriana do.

"Will it hurt?" she asked, with fear in her eyes.

"No, not at all," I said. "It will not hurt you or the child."

When the blade had cooled I gently pulled the cord taut, sliced it with one stroke and tied it off near the baby's belly.

"The little bit that is left will fall off in a week or so," I said. "You rest as much as you can because little Gahla will cry for food often throughout the day and the night. If you feel that there is not enough milk in your breasts, ask Yagoda to pick you some nettles, they are coming into season now. Make some tea with the leaves and it will help you make more milk. You stay quite and nurture yourself and your child."

I made Dunia comfortable and then said goodnight to Yagoda and her mother.

"I had fun dancing with you tonight, Milada," Yagoda said at the door.

"Yagoda, don't let your parent's heaviness weigh down your life. Help Dunia with her child and keep the fire of love in your heart. Someday you will be free."

She smiled sadly as she closed the door behind me.

My father sat on the low wall in front of the house that I remembered as being so high when I lived here with my Grandma.

"Goodnight, father," I said as I headed back to the gypsy camp. He was lost in his own thoughts and said nothing.

Chapter 77

The Impending Danger

I visited Dunia and the baby every day. One morning when I arrived another girl was in the house with her.

"Hello, Milada," she said. I was surprised that she knew my name. "You don't remember me".

I smiled at the pleasant looking girl. "I'm afraid I don't," I replied.

"I'm Janka. You helped my brother when he was very ill," she said.

"Yes," I said, remembering her now, "the boy with the earache. How is your brother?"

"He's back to his old, naughty self!" she said with a smile. "I was so impressed at how much you knew and how quickly my brother's pain went away with the treatment."

"Mother Miriana taught me many useful things," I said.

"Dunia told me how you helped birth her beautiful baby," she said. "The women of the village help each other when a baby comes, but none of them would know what to do if something goes wrong".

Dunia said, "Maybe Milada will stay here with us so we will have someone to help when we are ill or when a baby comes."

Janka looked at me hopefully. "I am myself expecting a child," she said, resting her hand on her still flat belly and blushing a little.

"I cannot stay here in the village," I said. "There is still much for me to learn with the gypsies."

"Can you teach us so we can help ourselves?" Janka asked.

"I can teach you some things, yes," I replied, "if you would like to learn."

"Oh, yes!" Janka exclaimed. "I would very much like to learn how to take good care of my own children and help other people, if I can."

"I don't know how long we will stay here," I said, "but while I am here I'd be happy to tell you some things that can be of help".

So, each morning over the next weeks Janka appeared at my wagon soon after the sun had risen. I showed her and Adela many of the things that I had learned from Mother Miriana. Sometimes Zora would be around to contribute her knowledge but most of the time she was keeping company with her young man.

There was a glow about her that I had never seen before. Instead of her usual sombre coloured clothing she wore lovely bright skirts. I guessed that them came out of the big wooden trunk and had once been worn by her mother, like the beautiful dress she had given me. I hoped that she wouldn't ask for it back!

We stayed near the village until the new moon. Then the Baron announced it was time to move on. On our last morning, I walked into the village with a big basket of herbs for Janka.

"Hang these herbs in a dark place," I said. "Now you know what they can be used for and how to find them yourself when this stock runs out".

"Thank you so much, Milada!" she said. "I look forward to seeing you again and learning more."

"It was a pleasure to share my knowledge with you," I told her. "I wish you and your baby well!"

I continued to my old house to find Dunia sitting in the sun on the low wall, singing gently to baby Gahla. I thought how well she looked and how motherhood suited her.

"Good morning, Dunia!" I called.

She looked up at me, startled to be caught in such an intimate moment.

"Hello, Milada," she said. "What brings you here so early?"

"I've come to say goodbye," I said. "We are moving on this afternoon."

"So you are really leaving then?" she said.

I wondered at her words. There was never any serious consideration of my staying.

"…and leaving Goran to me?" she added.

Goran. After that first day when I realized that he had made a life for himself in the village I hadn't thought about him in that way. In the excitement of meeting my father and then Gahla's birth I'd forgotten about my feelings for Goran! The realization took me by surprise. The young man Goran had become bore little resemblance to the imp of a boy that I had come to love as a brother.

"Goran belongs here," I said, "with you and the baby. I wish you every happiness."

"Do you mean that?" she said.

"Truly," I replied, placing my hand on her shoulder. "Is my father inside?"

"No, he went to the market square to do some business there," she said.

"I will go and find him. Please tell everyone I bid them goodbye and wish them well."

"I will do that," Dunia said.

I smiled at her and turned to go.

"Milada," I heard her say as I walked away, "thank you".

I did not turn back. I smiled to myself and kept on walking, looking forward to seeing the man who was my father, but also sad at the thought that we would soon be parted again.

I found him sitting on a bench on the sunny side of the square, in earnest conversation with three other men. When they saw me, they stopped talking, but not before I caught a few of the words they were saying.. "dangerous," "killing," "fire"...

My father's serious look was replaced by a smile when he turned to see what the men were looking at and saw me standing there.

"Milada, my girl', he said, "what brings you to the village square this lovely morning?"

I've come to find you," I said, "to say goodbye".

His smile faded. "Is the gypsy band moving on?" he asked.

"Yes," I replied, "the Baron has decided it's time to go."

"What did I tell you?" said one of the men. "They know something is going to happen."

"Do not speak in front of the girl," said another of the men.

"No," said my father. "She is old enough to understand. Milada, come sit here with us."

I sat beside him on the stone bench, warmed by the bright morning sunshine.

"On such a day," he said, "it is hard to imagine that anything is amiss; that we may be in great danger."

"What danger?" I asked.

"There are people from a distant land who have come seeking the bounty of this place," my father said. "I have seen the bloody result of their visits on my travels."

"What do they do?" I asked, thinking of what happened to the men while we were staying in the cave that winter.

"They ride into a village with many men," he said. "They demand food and money and if they do not receive what they desire they kill the people, take what they find of value and burn the rest."

"But why?" I asked, "why do such a thing?"

"Greed," one man replied. "These fields are rich. There are many people in their land, too many to feed, so they spread out and take the lands of others."

"What can we do to stop them?" I wondered aloud.

"That is what we are talking about," my father said. "Maybe together we will be strong enough to fight them off. But many people will loose their lives."

"If the villages give them food and money will they go away?" I asked, sad at the thought of people fighting and dying.

"Maybe they will," said my father, "maybe they will leave us in peace for a while but they may return at any time."

"I say we fight them and take care of them once and for all," one of the men said.

"So the gypsies are running away," said another. "That means that the enemy is close. Will you leave as well, Milan, or will you stay and fight for your village."

"I do not think that fighting is the answer," my father replied. "We are not strong enough on our own. This time we must pay the tribute and go along with them. I will visit the closest towns and spread the word of what is happening in this region. Only by working together will we have a chance to expel them for good."

"Father, would you like to come and meet the Baron?" I asked. "Men from our band were slain. Maybe he has information about these people that will help you make your plans."

"That is a good idea, my child," he said. "Let's go now, if the band will be departing soon."

He bade farewell to the other men. "We'll speak this evening," he said to them as we left for the gypsy camp.

Chapter 78

On The Wing

We hurried back to the camp to catch the Baron before he left. He always rode ahead of the rest of us. I had never given it a thought before now. Maybe it was to make sure the road was safe.

We entered the clearing where the main campfire had been. Most of the wagons were already hitched up. Zora had been making preparations in our wagon since early that morning. I saw Iovan helping Radha climb the steep steps to their wagon.

"Iovan," I called, "Has the Baron left?"

He made sure that Radha was safe in their wagon then turned to me a said, "Not yet. But he will be off soon".

"We must speak with him," I said, "before he goes".

Iovan hopped down from the wagon, looking from the man to me, then back at the man.

"This is my father," I said. "Father, this is my friend, Iovan, the Baron's son".

The men bowed formally, then Iovan let out a laugh. "I thought you looked familiar!" he told my father. "I can see something of Milada in you. Have you come to take her from us?"

"Milada is free to stay in the village if she chooses," my father replied," but I think she feels more at home here with your band."

"Yes, Iovan," I said. "I am staying with the band, though it was unexpected pleasure to find my father after all these years."

"What do you want with the Baron?" he asked.

"Please catch him before he goes and I will tell you," said my father.

"Join Radha in my wagon," he said. "I will bring my father and come".

Radha lay on the divan, nestled in many soft, thick cushions.

"Hello, my friend," she said. "I heard you speak of your father."

"Yes, Radha," I said. "Here he is!"

My father knelt on one knee and gently took Radha's hand and kissed it. Radha smiled at his gesture.

"I am pleased to meet you," he said.

"And I you," she replied. "Do sit down".

She indicated the divan on the opposite side of the wagon.

"If Adela were around I'd ask her to make us some tea," she said.

"That seems to be her main job," I said.

"She told me that you taught her and a girl from the village many useful things," Radha said. "It is good that you are sharing your knowledge with others".

"I feel privileged to have been taught these things," I said. "I am happy to pass them on".

"Some people would want to keep the knowledge to themselves," my father said. "On my travels I have met many men with healing skills. People pay them money to be healed. They do not give away their secrets."

I was shocked by his words.

"They take money to help people?" I said, "How can they? Would they stand by and watch someone suffer or even die if they didn't have money to pay them? They must be bad people."

"It is their choice how to use their knowledge, Milada," Radha said.

"That may be, but I don't think it is right," I said.

"Milada, you are a very generous girl," my father said, "but you are also young and have not yet experienced the hard ways of the word."

Before I could ask him what he meant, I heard footsteps coming up the wagon's steps.

Iovan and the Baron entered. My father stood up out of respect as Iovan introduced them.

"My son told me that you wished a word with me," the Baron said.

"Yes, my Lord," replied my father.

"Sit down and tell me what it is," the Baron said, settling himself on a wide wooden chair.

"May I speak freely here?" my father asked, "among the ladies?"

"Milada may stay if she wishes," the Baron said, "She is trusted as one of us. It is important for Radha and Iovan to know what you have to say as they take part in the decisions that affect the band."

"I, along with the people of the village, am concerned about the recent invasions from the East. Villages are being attacked, people held for ransom," my father explained.

"I have heard as much," the Baron replied.

"We cannot fight them alone," said my father. "I am a merchant, travelling form town to town. I have heard many stories over the past few months. It seems that the invaders are getting close to this region now. We must unite and fight in order to survive."

"Our band does not fight," the Baron said. "We hold knowledge of the healing arts and need to preserve it. We will do what we can to help if people are hurt but we cannot and will not fight."

"I respect your stance," my father said. "I do not like the idea of fighting, but if our homes, our families, our lives are threatened what else can we do? You can move your homes and families out of harm's way, but we cannot."

"How can we help you"? the Baron asked.

"You can let us know if you see the enemy or hear anything of their whereabouts," he said. "At least if we have some warning we may be able to avoid the worst."

"We travel as do you," the Baron said, "how will we get word to you?"

"One of the men in the village keeps pigeons," my father said. "He has trained them to fly back to his home from where ever they are taken. I am taking some with me. You may take some, as well. If you see or hear about the enemy, tie a message on the bird's leg and release it. It will fly back to the village."

"I will make a circle, like this," the Baron said, tracing the shape on the palm of his hand. "The centre of the circle is your village. I will mark the location, north, south, east or west, and the distance from the village."

"If the mark is here," he said, pointing to a spot at the base of his little finger, "it means the danger will approach from the northwest, but still a ways off."

"If the mark is here," he said, pointing to a spot just above the centre of his palm, "the danger comes from the north and is very close".

"That is clear, my Lord," my father replied.

"Now I must take my leave," the Baron said. "It is a long journey to the secret lake, the place that Radha is destined to bring her child into this world. Her time is nearly come, so we must depart."

"Iovan, go with Milada's father and get the birds," he continued, "and then we will be off."

"Thank you, my Lord," my father said as the three men left the wagon.

Radha fell back on the cushions. She looked tired.

"Are you alright?" I asked. "Would you like some water?"

"Yes, please, Milada. There is a jug over there on the shelf," she said.

When I went to get the water jug I saw Radha's crystal sphere on the shelf beside it.

"May I look at your stone?" I asked.

"Yes," she replied. "Bring it over here."

I poured us each a beaker of water, replaced the jug and gently brought the crystal over to Radha. I took a cushion from the free divan and put it on the floor near her.

"What can you see?" I asked.

She held the stone, silently breathing for a few moments. Then she began in a soft voice, deeper that her usual tone.

"I see you, Milada, but you look different, older," she began. "You are sitting on the edge of a wooden chair in front of a blue painted table. You are writing something.

"I don't know how to write," I said. There was no response. Maybe someday I would learn to write…

"What am I writing?" I asked.

"You are writing our story. It is preserved through you," she said, "though you are not using a quill or a brush."

"In front of you there is a box. It is open. Your fingers are tapping a rhythm on the open box. You are writing words of light."

"What does that mean," I asked.

Radha shook her head, and opened her eyes as if coming out of a dream.

"I don't know," she said. "I have not seen anything like that before. We will just have to wait and see."

Radha gasped.

"What is the matter?" I asked, "Are you all right?"

"It was the baby," she said, rubbing her very extended belly. "I can feel him turning".

"Is he going to be born now?" I asked with concern, knowing that the band would be moving soon. I didn't think they would stay even if Radha's baby were on its way.

"No," she said, "I do not think he is ready yet. He will wait for us to get to the sacred lake."

"I thought the Baron said we were going to the "secret" lake," I said.

"Maybe it's a secret that it is sacred," Radha said, with a twinkle in her eye that I remembered from the happy days we shared the wagon.

Impulsively, I threw my arms around her. "I love you Radha!" I said.

"And I love you, Milada".

Soon we heard the sound of many cooing birds. I went out to see Iovan and my father returning with a huge woven basket carried between them on a long pole. Iovan secured the basket of pigeons to the back of his wagon.

"Milada, come a moment," my father said to me.

He raised his hand to help me down from the high step of the wagon and drew me a little way off from the others.

"I am sad to bid you farewell, my child," he said, "but I am also very happy that we finally met and had some time together."

"Yes," I said, "I am happy and sad, too".

He drew me close to him in a warm embrace.

"You and I are both gypsies in our own ways. I do not know when our paths will cross again. If you need me, you can wait for me at this village or leave a message for me with Dunia. I will try to come every year," he said. "But if your travels take you far away, know I love you and I send you my blessings. Keep those gold coins safe, and secret, and you shall not want for food or shelter".

I had no words to express how I felt at that moment; such love and gratitude toward this man and such sorrow at the thought that he might be lost now that I had found him. I hugged him tighter and felt that he understood my unspoken feelings.

After a moment, he released me and took a step back. He looked into my face. I saw a tear in the corner of his eye.

"Go well, my child," he said. He took my right hand in his, lifted it to his lips and kissed it gently. "And know I will always hold you in my heart".

Then he turned and strode down the path away from our camp, away from me. Forever?

I could hear the sound of horses' hooves moving on the dusty ground. It was time to go.

PART 4

THE LAST QUARTER

Chapter 79

On The Road

I ran back to my wagon to find Zora and Adela sitting on the high seat and manoeuvring the wagon into its place in the line.

"There you are," Zora said. "I thought that maybe you decided to stay in your village."

"No," I said, climbing up to join them on the seat, "I am happy travelling with the gypsy band".

"Goran seems happy in the village," Zora said. "It was good of you to help with Dunia's baby and to teach the village girls how to help the others."

"I'm surprised at how little they know!" I replied. "If I had not chanced to come and live with you, I would also not know what to do when people are ill or when a child is born".

"It was your fate to come to us," Zora said.

"And mine, too," said Adela.

"Yes," said Zora, "and yours, too!"

Once we reached the tree-lined road we travelled in silence, each lost in our own thoughts. The road was rutted with the spring run off and I wondered how Radha was faring. She was cocooned in nest of many soft cushions, but the wagons jarred as they clattered down the bumpy lane.

We ate our lunch while we rode, not taking time to stop. By nightfall we still had not reached the lake. I heard the sound of beating hoofs. Soon, Iovan appeared. He was riding down the line of wagons to tell us that we would stop here for the night and continue at first light.

"Do not unpack," he said. "Unhitch your horse and let her graze with the others. We will not light a fire tonight. Stay in your wagon and have an early night. We still have a long way to travel to reach the secret lake by nightfall tomorrow."

When I climbed down the wagon's steps I noticed that my moon blood had started to flow. This was the first time for that to happen while we were still on the road.

"Zora," I said, "My moon blood has started."

"Yes" she replied, "mine has as well. Tomorrow night we will sleep in the moon tent, but for now we will continue our normal ways."

We made a small fire and brewed some tea to warm us. We ate the last of our bread and cheese and had a good night's sleep, before being awakened early the next morning by the sound of people readying their wagons to move on.

We travelled all that day. It was not a comfortable ride. We did not stop for our mid-day meal, nor did we have any food left to nibble on the long day's journey.

So we were very happy when the lake appeared on our left side and the word came that we had finally arrived. The wagons grouped in a large clearing on the shore of a vast lake. I had never seen so much water! Maybe this was what the sea was like, I thought.

Zora unhitched Kizi and we all set off to find the kitchen wagon and help to prepare our long awaited meal. I saw that the moon tent was being constructed and looked forward to the few days of rest and reflection that this time offered.

We passed Radha and Iovan's wagon, near to the central fire. Iovan was sitting on the high seat with his head in his hands.

"Is Radha alright?" I asked, concerned.

"She is sleeping now," he replied, "but it was a hard journey for her. The child would not let her rest while the wagon moved."

"I'll pass by later to say hello, if she is awake" I said. "Shall I bring you a plate of food or will you come?"

"I am too tired to eat right now," Iovan said. "Maybe I will come later."

I could sense that he was worried and wondered why. I had never seen him like this. The journey had been hard, but so had many journeys in the past. Radha was a strong girl and the gypsies never had any problems bringing their children into the world.

I joined the other women at the long table that was already set up next to the roaring fire. It would have to die down before we could grill the sausages that the villagers had pressed on us before we left. I was helping prepare the dried wheat that would go into a stew that would sustain us for a few days when Zora came up behind me.

"Come, Milada," she said, "it is our moon time and the tent has been erected. Let the others do that now."

I enjoyed preparing food, but was happy to go to the moon tent with Zora and sink into the soft cushions with the other young women. In a while Adela appeared at the entrance to the tent carrying a large tray of food for us.

I ate and then fell into a deep sleep, forgetting my intention to see Radha that evening. Before the first light I felt someone tapping on my shoulder.

"Milada, wake up," the voice said.

It was a man's voice. What was a man doing in the moon tent? Drowsily, I opened my eyes and saw my father standing there.

"Milada, you must come with me, now," he said with urgency in his voice.

I looked around, to see all the other women fast asleep. No one noticed him coming in.

"What is it? What are you doing here"? I whispered, not wishing to wake the others.

"A baby is coming and the mother needs your help," he said.

"I rose as quietly as I could and wrapped the warm shawl I was using as a blanket around my shoulders. I followed my father past the glowing embers of the fire and down a narrow path that ran along the edge of the lake. Ahead of us was a low wall that looked like the one at my grandfather's house.

We passed into the yard and then entered the house without knocking. The room was very familiar. A woman lay on a low bed next to the fire.

"Here she is," my father said. "Please help her."

I as approached the woman she seemed to be asleep. Her long hair obscured her face. A newborn baby wriggled at her side. I gently brushed the hair from her forehead. Her eyes were open, staring up into the ceiling. I could see that there was no life in her. I closed her eyes and looked back at my father, who had dissolved in tears.

"My Anna has left me, what will I do?" he repeated over and over, his face in his hands. I picked up the baby and looked down into its tiny face. As I gazed into her eyes, her face seemed to age and I realized that I was looking at my own face. I felt another tapping on my shoulder.

"Father?" I said.

"Milada, wake up!" It was Zora.

"Is it morning?" I asked, still confused by my dream.

"Yes, Radha's child is coming," Zora said, "and she is asking for you".

I rose from my cushion, and once again wrapped the shawl around my shoulders, wondering if this was yet another dream.

Chapter 80

The Child of the Stars

I stepped out of the tent into the chilly morning air. Zora lead me to a great willow tree, with feathery branches overhanging the placid lake, its water pink in the reflected light of dawn.

A low wall separated the tree from the lakeside path, and there, leaning against piles of pillows and swaddled in a thick down quilt lay Radha, surrounded by the other women. The men waited on the other side of the wall.

"Radha," Zora said, gently touching her friend's shoulder, "Milada is here".

Radha opened her eyes. They were unfocused, as if she were waking from a deep sleep. There were lines of pain between her eyebrows that I had never seen before.

"Milada," she said softly, as her eyes fixed themselves on mine. "Come and hold my hand."

I sat down beside her. "Are you in pain?" I asked.

"I feel very strange," she replied. "I've watched many births, both animal and human, I thought I knew what to expect."

Just then her body twisted into the air, wracked with a strong convulsion. It happened so fast I took me by surprise. I moved away as her shoulder came up towards my face. Then it was over. She lay back on the cushions, with tears of pain in her eyes, panting.

When she could speak again, she said, "I don't know what this means. They told me this child would be special; a new star child coming to this earth for the first time. Milada, I am afraid".

I took her in my arms. "Dear Radha," I said. "I don't know what is happening, but you will be all right. Keep breathing and relax between the pains."

"How many times I've said that to women giving birth," she said.

I rubbed her back, the spot between her shoulder blades to help her to relax.

"Shall I bring you some raspberry leaf tea?" I asked.

"I've been drinking so much of it these past months," she replied. "It helps us at this time. But don't you go. Ask one of the others to bring it."

As she finished the sentence, once again her body went into a spasm. I moved closer to Zora, who knelt beside me.

When Radha settled down again I whispered to Zora, "Have you ever seen anything like this?"

"No, never," Zora replied.

"What did she mean "a new star child"?" I asked.

"You know that our people have come from the stars," Zora whispered while I stroked Radha's warm hand.

"Yes, I've heard that said," I replied.

"Every so often a new soul comes in," Zora said, "to bring new knowledge to our tribe. Radha and Iovan were selected to bring this child into the world. It is not an easy task."

Radha opened her eyes. "Help me to sit up," she said.

"Are you ready to mount the birthing stool?" Annika asked.

"Where is the sun?" Radha asked.

"It is just above the horizon of the hills," Annika replied.

"Yes," said Radha, "the child should come with the first rays of the sun.

"Why is she giving birth here, outdoor in the morning chill?" I asked Zora.

"It is the will of the child. The first of our tribe arrived by this lake. It is sacred to us," she replied.

"We have never been here before, have we?" I asked.

"No," said Zora, rising to help settle Radha on the birthing stool. Annika supported her on the other side and the other women gathered around and began to sing a haunting chant that I had never heard before.

I dared not ask what it was, and how they all knew it. On the other side of the wall the men also began to chant. There was a rustle in the willow branches. Iovan pushed them aside the way I'd often see him push his hair off his forehead. For a moment I felt a pang of the love I'd carried for him for so long. I knew I loved him still, but my love had changed its form to encompass both him and Radha as a couple.

He knelt behind Radha, supporting her back and whispering into her ear. I saw her body shake again, her belly rippling like a giant snake. Her eyes were closed and she rocked back and forth, as if soothed by Iovan's words.

Although the sun was rising, the day seemed to be getting darker instead of becoming more bright. It seemed as if a shadow was touching the edge of the sun. The day was growing cooler instead of warming up. The birds had stopped their singing.

"What is happening?" I asked Zora.

"It is a sign from the heavens of the importance of this birth," she said.

Iovan added, stroking Radha's long hair, "The moon is joining the sun to usher in this child of the stars."

It became so dark that the stars themselves could be seen sparking though the wispy leaves of the willow.

Radha looked up and smiled at the sight.

"Stars in the daytime," she said, "stars to welcome their little boy."

Her contractions continued throughout the dark of the artificial night. Above us I could see a bright band shining around the edge of the moon's shadow. Slowly the sun emerged, shining brightly like a jewelled ring in the sky. The birds started up their chorus as if joining the gypsies' mysterious chant.

The sun rose higher and higher and yet the child did not come. As the morning chill finally wore off, beads of perspiration appeared on Radha's forehead.

She bore down, trying to push the child out as each new contraction came. Her small body used all its strength, but maybe that was not enough. I could see that she was tired and in pain, but she did not cry out. She released her breath in a deep sigh as she pushed.

A breeze moved the low hanging branches and for a brief moment Radha was bathed in light. As though in a dream, I saw, instead of my friend, the little statue grown to human size, baring down to give birth.

Silently I rose from my place among the woman. When I came out from under the sheltering branches of the tree I ran as fast as I could back to my wagon. I took the little statue from the shelf and ran back to the lakeside.

Some of the women were looking worried. I heard one woman whisper, "This birth is taking too long. It is not our way."

I made my way back to where Radha sat, slumped on the birthing stool.

"Radha, my friend," I said. "Here, hold this." I placed the small statue in her hand.

"What is this? Oh," she said, her eyes focusing on the little statue, "it's the Mother!"

Another contraction came and then another. Radha held tight to the statue and Iovan held tight to Radha. I heard the Baron's voice from the other side of the wall, adding his deep voice to the strange song. Both the volume and the pace were increasing until with a deep sigh, a child slipped from between Radha's legs.

Lazara, as the eldest, was ready to catch the child, a little boy. Iovan eased Radha back down onto the cushions and Lazara laid the baby on her breast. Instead of lying quietly, the child stretched its legs and arms and rolled its face in the direction of the lake and the sun, now high in the sky.

"We will wash him in water of the sacred lake," Iovan said, "and welcome him to his new world."

Chapter 81

Ransom

We camped by the lake most of that spring, watching the new leaves opening and the animals awaken from their winter's sleep. Radha's child grew quickly. He was never still, moving in his cradle from the first light until dusk. Radha, as was the custom, carried him with her throughout the day, but whereas most babies would sleep almost all the day Satarma, as he was called, never once shut his eyes.

We sat together one day, dangling our feet in the cool water of the lake Satarma squirming in his mother's lap.

"In all my years of raising small creatures," Radha said, "I have never known one as active as this baby!"

"He is so curious about the world around him," I said.

"He's trying to crawl already," Radha laughed. "Look how he is moving his little legs!"

"I think if we threw him in the lake he would swim like a fish," I said, watching the small creature struggling to escape from his mother's lap.

"He probably would," said Radha, "but let's not try that just yet!"

"Will we be leaving soon for the Summer Gathering?" I asked.

"We are a long way from the gathering place," she replied. "I asked Iovan when we would leave. I can't wait to see my mother and introduce her to Satarma and to meet my little sister!"

"What did Iovan tell you?" I asked, thinking how much I looked forward to the gathering, to seeing the Queen and Vasa again. Zora had been inseparable from the young man she met at last summer's gathering. Maybe I would meet someone at this one.

"He told me that the Baron had not said," she replied. "I think he plans to ride ahead to make sure the route is safe for us".

That night at the campfire it was announced that both the Baron and Iovan would leave the next day, taking a small party of men with them. The rest of us were to stay put until they returned with news.

Although this was a beautiful place, I was anxious to get to the gathering of the clans. It was exciting to speak with people from the other bands, to taste foods from different places and hear different music. The days were long now, so I knew that the bands would already be making their way to the high field, and we were still here, and would have to wait even longer while the men checked our route.

Early the next morning we bade farewell to the Baron, Iovan and the others. I thought I saw a look of apprehension in Radha's eyes as she embraced Iovan and wished him well on his journey.

In the days following, the atmosphere in the camp was strange. There was a tension in the air that was not usual among us. We went about our day to day tasks, collecting herbs that now bloomed in profusion and laying them to dry in the shade, netting fish from the many streams that ran into the lake and drying them to serve as our provisions for the winter. The evenings were spent gathered around the fire as usual. The musicians still played, but no one felt like hearing the cheerful dance tunes that we usually enjoyed on the warm summer nights.

The party departed at the moon's first quarter. By the time it was full they still had not returned. There was talk of sending out another party to find the first but no one knew which direction they would take once they reached the main road.

The morning after the full moon I went to find Radha in her wagon. I climbed up the steep steps and called to her.

"Come in, Milada," Radha said when I peeked into the wagon, "I've just made some tea. Come and join me".

Radha took another cup from the high shelf and poured me a cup of hot, fragrant tea. The baby, Satarma, swung in a miniature hammock that Iovan had fashioned out of thin strips of soft leather loosely woven together. Satarma was happier in the hammock that in the cradle because he could see all around him and also had more freedom to move.

Radha saw me watching him.

"The only time that child is still is when he is asleep," she said with a smile and a sigh.

"He is a beautiful baby," I said, trying to lift him from the hammock but then placing him quickly back in it again because he wriggled so much. I was afraid that I would drop him!

"Beautiful and active!" she said. "Always moving, like the stars he came from".

She sighed again and took a sip of her tea.

"I'm worried about the men," she said. "I feel like there is something wrong. They should have returned by now."

Just then we could hear the clattering of hooves. Radha's face lit up.

"It's them!" she said, rushing outside to look.

I followed her and saw Iovan dismounting his old horse, Dobro, and flicking his hair out of his worried eyes.

"What is it?" Radha said as she ran down the steps into his arms. For a moment Iovan did not speak. He held Radha tightly in his embrace.

Slowly he released her and said, "Bring the child and come to the fire. Tell the others. There is news I must share with all of you."

"I'll get the baby," I said. I picked up Satarma and wrapped him tightly in a shawl so he wouldn't wriggle out of my arms. I handed him down to Radha and we walked quickly to the centre of our camp where the others were gathering.

Iovan sat on the table so all could see him and hear his news. One of the men that had gone with him was slumped next to the table, his head in his hands. There was no sign of the other man or of our Baron.

"Friends," Iovan began. "When we set forth from here some days ago we knew not what we would find. There were stories of armies coming from the East and plundering villages. We wanted to make sure it was safe for our band to travel to the Summer Gathering."

There was not a sound in the band. Even the children were silent, sensing that something was not as it should be.

"Two days out on the road we were ambushed by strangers, people not of these parts. They brought us to a village. None of the village's inhabitants remained. Some had been killed, others had managed to escape and find refuge in the forest. We met them on our way back here. They told us that many men had come with fire and iron weapons and demanded the villagers give up all their food and their gold."

"Those who did so at first were spared, but then the men wanted more and more. They wanted to live in the people's houses. The ones who would not leave were killed, their bodies burnt in the village square."

"Zoran tried to fight them," Iovan continued. "He thought he could buy time for the rest of us to escape but he was cut down".

A shudder ran through the band and a sigh at the thought of loosing our friend.

"The three of us were taken to the village and locked in a room. They gave us no food, no water for a day and a night. Their leader saw that we were men of substance and would be worth something to our people. They decide to hold my father. They let the two of us go, making us promise to return before the last quarter of the moon with ten gold coins to pay the ransom for the Baron's freedom."

A gasp rose from the gathered people at the price of the ransom demand.

"We do not have so much gold," one woman said. "If we do not pay?"

"The Baron will die," Iovan said.

My thoughts turned to my dear Layla, remembering how she had been kidnapped and the choice that she had made. Could our band afford to loose our leader, the Baron? Iovan was still young to lead us alone.

"What will we do?" said one of the men.

"My father instructed me to pay the ransom," Iovan said. "He has a plan for us to escape the worst of what these men can do. He told me that he must be freed to carry it out."

At least the Baron will not leave us as Layla did, I thought. I was ready to say that I had gold but Iovan began to speak again.

"I have six gold coins," he said. "They were given to the band over the years by people who were grateful for our help."

"I have two," Lazara said. "Mother Miriana gave them to me before she left us.

"That makes eight," Iovan said. "Let's see what we can find of value and take it to the market. There is a town not to far from here. But we must do it quickly. These men will not wait and two days have already passed with our journey."

There was a hum among the gypsies as they moved towards the wagons to look for items that could be sold for money.

"Iovan," I said, running to his side. "Will you come to my wagon? I would like to speak with you."

"Now, Milada? I have just returned and am very tired. Can I come by later?"

"No," I said, "please come now. It is important."

Together we walked to my wagon and climbed inside. Iovan sat down heavily on the bed. I could see his fatigue and his worry.

"What is it, Milada?" he asked. "What is it that is so important it cannot wait?"

"My father," I began, "is a merchant."

"Yes, I know that," Iovan said, "and a good man".

"He travels from town to town, buying goods in one place and selling them in another," I continued.

"Yes, Milada," he said, "that's what merchants do".

"And he made money doing it," I said.

"Then he is a good merchant." Iovan said. "Milada, I'm tired. What is your point?"

"My father told me not to tell anyone," I said.

"Not tell anyone what?" he asked, impatiently.

"That he gave me some gold coins," I said, taking the pouch out of its hiding place.

"What?" he said.

I took two shining gold coins out of the pouch and handed them to Iovan.

"Here," I said, "Take these."

"Milada," he said, "your father gave these to you, to secure your future. Are you sure you want me to have them? "

"I give them freely," I said, "in gratitude for all the gypsy band has given me. You have fed me, clothed me, passed on amazing knowledge and loved me as one of your own. It is my greatest pleasure to be able to help."

Iovan knelt at my feet, took both my hands in his and planted a kiss on each of my palms.

"Thank you, Milada. Thank you," he said. "Tonight I will rest but tomorrow at dawn I'll be off to bring the Baron back to lead us. Thank you, my friend."

"You are welcome, Iovan," I said. "Don't tell the others where you got the coins. Let this be between us. Say you got them from Radha, from her mother the Queen."

"As you wish, Milada," he said. "May I tell Radha?"

"Yes," I replied. "But let it stay our secret."

Chapter 82

A Decision

Iovan turned to go but before he reached the doorway I remembered something and called to him.

"Iovan," I said, "I know that you are tired but please before you go to bed, send a message to my father."

Iovan stopped, then turned and sat down wearily at my small table.

"Yes, I will, Milada," he said. "That is a good idea".

"Here, you can use this," I said, handing him a small piece of cotton rag. "It should be big enough, but not too heavy for the bird to carry."

"Do you have another piece?" He asked me. "I will send two birds, so that there will be a better chance of the message reaching the village."

I tore of another small square of cloth, then realized that I had no quill or brush.

"What will you write with?" I asked Iovan.

"Come with me," he said. "I'll show you."

I followed him down the path that lead to the centre of our camp. I thought we were going on to the wagon he and Radha shared but he stopped when we reached the fire. I saw him bend down and take a small, half burnt twig from the fire. He blew out the flaming end, and then sat down at the long table.

"Milada," he said, "come and pull the fabric tight so it will remain still while I make the marks".

I did as he asked, happy that I could be of help. First he made a dot to represent the village in the centre of the cloth, using the black coal that remained at the end of the twig. Then he paused.

"We travelled due west from the village to the lake," he said. "Then my father and I doubled back and headed north. So the enemy is northwest of the village, fairly close by."

He made another mark on the cloth a bit above and to the left of the central dot. I let go of the cloth and he rolled in up so that it was very small. He then repeated the process on the second rag.

"I will ask Radha to tie these to the birds' legs," he said. "She is always so good with animals, so gentle."

I could see the love he had for Radha reflected in his eyes as he said these words. I wished that someday someone would love me like that.

"Good night, Milada," he said, taking my hand and kissing it once again. "And thank you again," he whispered.

The next morning he was off before breakfast, riding with the other men, back the way they had come. By nightfall they had returned, the Baron with them. Word spread quickly around the camp and we all gathered by the fire, wanting to celebrate the Baron's release. But when we saw the Baron he did not seem to be himself. I had never seen him look tired but this night he looked exhausted. He walked slowly, back and forth near the fire, in deep conversation with Iovan and some of the others. His back was bent as if he carried a great weight on his shoulders and his boots that usually shone with polish were scuffed and dusty.

I heard Radha's child, Satarma wailing. I knew it was Satarma because none of the other gypsy babies cried like that. They cooed and gurgled, but they did not wail. Only Satarma. Sometimes the whole band was set on edge with his cries. Radha was very patient with him, as she was with all the small creatures that she tended, but sometimes even she was puzzled by Satarma's restlessness.

I found Zora, Annika and some of the other women sitting by the fire, speaking quietly together.

"Come and join us, Milada," Annika said.

"Do you know what's going on?" I asked.

"I think the Baron will tell us all later," Zora said. "But the feeling is that we will travel further west, around the lake."

"But if we don't head back toward the east," I said, "we will not be in time for the Summer Gathering".

"That's why it is such a big decision," Zora said.

It's all right for her, I thought. She met a young man at the gathering last year and he decided to travel with our band, with her. She spent most of her time in his wagon now, leaving me alone with Adela. I liked Adela, but she was very young. I felt more like her teacher than like a friend. I missed the days with Tanya, chatting and giggling well into the night, with Zora telling us to be quiet so she could get some sleep. I hoped to meet someone at the gathering. And now I would have to wait another year.

I liked the boys in our band, but they were more like brothers. We all grew up together, and although I could see that one or two of them liked me, by the way they looked at me, offered me food and flowers, I couldn't see loving any of them the way that Radha loved Iovan.

"Milada," Zora said, patting my hand, "where are you? You are lost again".

"What are you thinking about," Annika asked.

"Oh, nothing," I said, "Just that I'll be disappointed if we don't go to the Gathering. We won't get to see Madam Eleeza's new baby or catch up on the news or restock our herbs from the other bands."

"It would be a shame," Zora said. "Maxim will be sad not to see his family and friends."

"I don't think that he misses them much," Annika said with a giggle. "It seems that his eyes are only on you".

"I think we would have married at the gathering," Zora said. "It doesn't really matter, though. We can have a celebration next year."

The usual babble of voices around the fire suddenly went silent. We looked over and saw that the Baron was standing at the head of the long table, ready to speak.

We all drew closer to hear his words.

"My friends," he began, "first of all, thank you for sending the gold to release me from my kidnappers. I think, though, that they only let me go so that they could capture me, or some other of our band and demand more gold. I am sorry to have to tell you what we saw on our journey. Villages have been attacked and people are very fearful. The invaders from the east are very well armed. They sweep through a village taking everything of value. Anyone who tries to resist them is killed."

"We must not go that way," he continued. "We will travel west. We will leave in the morning and keep going as long as we can to put distance between the soldiers and ourselves. It is not safe for us to go to the Summer Gathering in the highland this year."

I thought of how lucky we were that we could take our homes to safety with us, unlike people who lived in the villages. I hoped that Goran and the others would be all right. At least they had a little warning that the enemy was nearby, that is if the birds arrived safely.

After a quiet meal the gypsies dispersed to prepare for the long journey ahead. I couldn't remember the band ever having travelled so far west before. The Baron said that we would stay near the lake, so we would have plenty of water to drink and fish to eat. But, although I was a little excited about travelling somewhere new and different, my heart was heavy at the thought of what might happen in the village and of the special young man that I might have met at the gathering.

Chapter 83

A Portable Stream

We set off the next morning at first light, following a narrow road in a westerly direction that skirted the lake. Each night we camped only long enough to rest ourselves and the horses and then moved on. My moontime came and went, without the pleasure of spending time in the special tent with the other women.

We pressed on, following the dusty track, past Midsummer's day. Finally word came that we would stop for a while when the road turned from west to north. It was necessary to restock our provisions with fish to smoke and fruit and herbs to dry for our winter provisions.

The Baron selected a spot where a small river ran into the lake. By this time, Zora had moved all of her things into Maxim's wagon. Adela and I were happy at the prospect of staying put for a while and having time to enjoy the long days of summer, exploring the woods and collecting the bounty of nature to contribute to the winter food stock of the band.

We rose with the sun and headed into the woods with empty baskets to see what we could find. Wild greens like lovage and rue would add flavour to our winter stews. Wild raspberries and the tiny mountain strawberries provided our breakfast. One day, on our way back to the camp, I came across Radha and her baby, sitting quietly by the side of the small, babbling river.

Satarma was surprising still. At first I though he was sleeping, but then I noticed that he was laying on his back, watching the way the light played in the branches of the trees above.

"Hello, Radha," I said softly, not wanting to disturb the baby and shatter the peace of the moment. I sat down on the bank beside her while Adela continue her search for the wild strawberries that grew in profusion beside the river.

"Good morning, Milada," Radha said. "Isn't it beautiful here? It's hard to imagine that there is anything other than peace in our world on a morning like this."

"Yes," I whispered, "We are lucky to be here, living as we do off the bounty of the land".

"Why are you whispering?" she whispered back to me.

"Satarma," I said, looking over toward the baby.

"He isn't sleeping," Radha said.

"I know, but he is quiet!" I said.

Radha laughed. "Is it that unusual for him to be quiet?" she said.

"Yes!" I replied, "Yes, it is!"

"I guess you are right," Radha said with a sigh. "The sound of the stream seems to calm him. It's nice for me to be able to rest. This has been a difficult journey."

"I've never known one of the gypsy babies to cry like he does," I said.

"The Baron and Lazara say that is because he is new to our world and feels heavy in his body. While at our home in the stars we do not have bodies like we do here. We think of something and it comes to pass. We don't have to *do* anything," Radha explained.

"But the rest of you seem happy," I said. "The other babies are born easily and are contented".

"We have lived many times on this earth and have learned how to handle the heaviness. Sometimes, though, I still remember what it is like to be free of the heaviness of a physical body. But now, only in my dreams can I fly," she said.

Radha had a far away look in her eyes. I saw a sadness there that I had never noticed before. Although her face was young and unlined, for a moment her eyes looked ancient, as if she had witnessed hundreds of years going by.

"Look what I found!" Adela said, plopping down next to us, her radiant smile lifting our pensive mood.

"What did you find, little one?" Radha asked.

"Lots and lots of berries!" Adela said, holding out her full basket for us to see.

"Have some," she said. "There are lots more".

We spend a pleasant, peaceful morning there by the river, enjoying the warm air, the sweet berries and each other's company.

We spent most of the long summers days at this lovely spot but when the days began to draw in it was time to move along once again. The Baron decided that we would continue our course around the lake, taking us further away from the villages that we knew and the enemy that we did not want to meet.

The leaves of the trees turned from their summer green to the blazing reds and golds of autumn. Radha's child was growing fast, already trying his stout little legs, making his way from bench to bench around the campfire.

One day in the early fall, during our moontime, I was relaxing in the tent with Annika and Radha. Zora was absent. She was expecting a child of her own. The calm was shattered by the sound of Satarma wailing. This was the first moontime that Radha had left him with one of the elder women. The plan was to bring him to her to feed from her breast several times each day. The previous day had gone smoothly, but today there was trouble.

"I should go to him," Radha said, with a small sigh.

"Maybe he is hungry," Annika said.

"He shouldn't be hungry again so soon," Radha said. "I'll wait a while and if see if he stops."

But the cries did not stop. They seemed to get louder and more strident still.

"I'm coming, little one," Radha said, rising from the soft cushions.

Soon she has returned with her crying child. Adela followed her, carrying a bucket of water and a small pot.

Radha sat down on the cushions and placed the wriggling baby beside her. She put her hand on Satarma's belly and motioned Adela to set down the bucket of water.

Adela set the bucket down next to Radha and left the tent. Then Radha scooped up some water in the pot and poured back into the bucket. She repeated the rhythmic movement over and over again. Soon the baby lay still, lulled by the sound of the water. It was having the same effect on all of us.

After a while, Radha stopped. I moved closer to her, whispering in her ear.

"How did you know that would soothe Satarma?" I asked her.

"I noticed that he was always calm when we sat by a stream," she whispered back, "so I learned how to make my own, portable stream."

"It made us all relax," I said.

"Yes," she replied, "I'm ready for a nap".

We spent the rest of the day dozing on our cushions, watching the light change as the sun followed its course across the sky. When Adela came with our evening meal she brought the now calm Satarma back into the camp with her so that Radha could have a good night's sleep.

When our moontime had passed the band moved on again. We travelled on for another turn of the moon, scarcely stopping until we reached a sheltered spot on the north side of the lake. There was a hill just above the road. The Baron instructed that a hidden shelter be built there. The men of the band would take turns standing as lookouts to warn us if anyone approached. We had a good stock of food to last us though the winter, and I felt secure in this place and happy that we would be staying put, like the bears in their snug dens, through the cold of winter.

Chapter 84

Dangers on the Road

The winter passed without incident. Satarma seemed to grow bigger each day. He could walk if he held on to someone's hand for support and seemed to be trying to talk, making all sorts of sounds then looking puzzled and sometimes even angry when we couldn't answer him. He was still active, but not as restless as before. Radha told me that every evening she would sooth him to sleep with the sound of water.

Radha looked like her old self again, smiling and relaxed. Zora was glowing, blossoming with Maxim's love and their child growing inside of her.

As the first warm days of spring arrived my thoughts turned once again to the Summer Gathering. The Baron had said that we could get there from the north, not by going our usual route. A scouting party would travel ahead to make sure the route was safe. We stayed put in our winter camp until the time when day and night were of equal length and the first leaves were beginning to appear on the naked branches. Then the word came that we would be on the move once again. I felt disappointed that we would not pass through my village. I longed to meet with my father again, but my excitement about the Summer Gathering was mounting.

We moved along slowly, travelling for a day and then camping for a night or two. The fields were full of fresh new plants and we were busy collecting the young shoots and roots for our own use and also to supply the other bands that we would soon meet at the gathering. Everyone was excited at the thought of being re-united with friends and family and hearing the news of their travels.

When the days had become long and warm we took a road that led us away from the lake. We had camped along its shores for a year, travelling slowly almost back to the point from which we began. We were preparing our evening meal under a huge oak tree when the day's advance party returned from scouting the road ahead.

Here come the men," Adela said to me as we stood side by side chopping fresh herbs to enhance the stew boiling in the large iron cauldron.

She waved at them as they rode past. Usually they would stop and greet us, and have a sample of whatever was cooking, but this evening they didn't even seem to see us, let alone wave or stop their horses' brisk pace.

"Something is the matter," I said, putting down my knife and wiping my damp fingers on my apron.

"You finish up here," I told Adela, "while I go and find out."

"Come back and tell me, will you please," Adela said, looking concerned.

"Yes, of course I will," I said and ran off in the direction the men rode, toward the Baron's wagon.

The Baron and Iovan stood outside the wagon, speaking with the men, their voices too low for me to hear. Iovan saw me and called me over.

"Come over, Milada," he said, "you should hear this news".

"Do you think it's safe to continue?" I heard the Baron ask Leon, one of the scouts.

"We saw no living person," he said.

"What did you see?" I asked, forgetting myself, shocked by his words and sombre expression.

The Baron looked down at me and placed his hand on my shoulder.

"We will speak with all the band this evening, Milada," the Baron said, "and share the news.

"I think we should send a bird," Iovan said, "to Milada's village".

"What has happened?" I asked.

"Go and get me two pieces of cloth," said Iovan, "like the ones you gave me for messages before and I will explain while I prepare the messages".

I ran to my wagon and returned shortly with two small pieces of cotton rag.

"Here, Iovan," I said, panting from running so fast.

We climbed into his wagon. I could hear the birds cooing in their woven cage at the rear of the wagon.

"What did the men see?" I asked when I caught my breath.

"They saw villages," Iovan replied, "villages that had been burnt to the ground".

"Oh, no!" I said, shocked at his words.

"They saw bodies of people, some with their throats slashed, others charred from the fires," he continued sadly.

"And their animals?" I asked.

"There was no sign of any living thing," he said. "The enemy must have taken all the livestock to feed themselves".

Iovan lit a twig from the small oil lamp that always burned in the wagon. Charring the end, he was ready to make the diagram to send to my village.

"Hold the cloth tightly," he told me.

I held the cloth while he marked out the position of the burnt villages in relation to my home village. He drew small flames at the points where the villages once stood.

"Do you think that they will understand this?" he asked me.

"It looks like fire," I said. "I think they will."

"I wonder if my father will be in the village," I continued.

"Do you miss him," Iovan asked.

"I don't miss him as a father," I said, "since I never really knew him in that role, but I really liked him as a person. I like that he told me about my mother and our family. But I still feel more connected to the gypsy band. Travelling with you has made me who I am."

"You were who you are before you joined us," Iovan said. "I remember that active little girl, always asking questions."

"Yes, but I think I would be very different if I had stayed in the village," I said.

"I'm sure you would be," Iovan said, "in some ways. But in other ways, your intelligence, your kindness, you would still be Milada".

No, I wouldn't!" I said, enjoying this easy banter with Iovan after so long, "I'd be 'Anna'!"

Iovan looked at me and smiled. He planted a kiss on my forehead.

"I do love you, little one," he said. "For a moment you made me forget about the sadness that lies on the road ahead. Let's go and get the birds and then see what my father has decided."

I followed Iovan to the rear of the wagon and watched him take a bird out of the cage, fasten the note to its leg with a bit of thin leather and then release it into the sky. It circled once and then was off, flying due south. Iovan then took a second bird and attached the other note. This bird, too, rose high into the sky and then was off in the same direction as the first.

"How do they know which way is home?" I asked Iovan as we walked together back to the central fire.

"I think they feel the pull of energy lines of the earth," he said.

"What are energy lines?" I asked.

"You know how lodestones are attracted to one another?" he said.

"Yes".

"Do you know that if you rub a lodestone on a piece of metal and then float the metal in a cup of water the side that you rubbed will move to the north?" he asked.

"No," I replied, "I've seen Leon looking in a cup of water before deciding which way to ride, but I didn't know why," I said.

"I'm surprised you didn't ask him," Iovan laughed.

"I thought about it, but he seems so serious and in such a hurry to set off that I never did," I told him.

"Well, now you know," he said.

"Tomorrow I will ask Zora if I can borrow her lodestones. I have an iron shaving I found somewhere and was saving, I don't know why…I will try rubbing it and see what happens," I said.

"If you put an iron shaving in a cup of water," Iovan said, "It will sink to the bottom. You need to put it on something that will float."

"How about a thick leaf or a small twig?" I asked.

"Try it," he said. "If your iron shaving is small enough then it should work".

We had reached the centre of our camp. I could smell the fragrant stew bubbling over the fire.

People had gathered around the Baron. By now, they knew that something had happened and were waiting for him to share the news and let us know if we would proceed to the gathering or not. The stew would have to wait.

The Baron rose and everyone was quiet, waiting for him to speak.

"My friends," he began, "today I have received news from Leon and Stefan of the road ahead."

A murmur ran through our band.

"About a half a day's ride from here they found several villages that had been destroyed," the Baron continued, "there was no sign of life, no living person, no animals."

"What will we do?" Adela, who had sidled up beside me, quietly asked.

The Baron spoke again, "We will stay at this camp and watch the road for a few days. If there is no sign of the enemy, we will make our way toward the gathering. Otherwise, we will return to the safety of the lake."

Everyone began to speak at once. What if we missed the gathering for yet another year? We would just have to wait and see. Hopefully, we would be able to go on.

Chapter 85

A Reunion

The next three days passed slowly. We continued our preparations as though we were going to the gathering while waiting for word from the scouts to let us know if it would be safe.

Finally, one morning at breakfast the Baron announced that we would continue. A great cheer went up among the gypsies. We had all been longing to go to the gathering and catch up with our friends.

Adela ran to me and took both my hands. We spun around together, giggling with excitement.

"I'm so happy that we are going!" Adela said as we twirled around. "I have missed Madam Eleeza so much. I can't wait to see her child. She must be walking by now."

"She is almost two years old," I said. "She must have been born just after the gathering."

"Are you talking about my little sister?" Radha said, joining us in our circle dance.

"That we are," said Adela. "Maybe little Satarma will be walking by then, too".

"He probably will be," Radha said with a sigh, "then I'll *never* get any rest!"

"I'll help you take care of him," Adela said.

"You already are a big help," said Radha, "and so are you, Milada. I don't know what I would do without the two of you."

"Where is Satarma now?" I asked Radha.

"Iovan took him for a ride on old Dobro," she replied. "I think we will be leaving as soon as they return, so let's get our wagons ready."

Within the hour we were on the road. We travelled until the sun was high, stopping briefly to eat a picnic lunch of bread and cheese while the horses rested. When the sun hung low in the western sky the road took a turn to the north. As we rounded the curve we were met with an awful sight.

The road had gone through a village, but what once had been a bustling little town was now nothing more than charred stone and ashes. What had been green fields lined with tall trees was nothing now but scorched earth.

Where once we would have stopped and had a feast with the villagers, sharing their bounty and offering our help in case someone was ill, we rode by without pausing.

"Do you think that anyone is there?" I said, thinking aloud.

I looked at Adela and saw that there were tears in her eyes. I remembered what had happened to her village, to her family. I lay my hand on hers. I could think of no words to say.

At nightfall we stopped in the shelter of a deep forest. Iovan rode down the line of wagons informing us that we would stay only one night and go on with the first light of morning. There was no central fire that night. We gathered in small groups and ate our evening meal, still excited about the Summer Gathering but sobered by what we had seen.

As dawn broke the next morning we were ready to move on. Once again we travelled all of the day with only small breaks so we could stretch our legs and the horses could rest theirs.

The sun set but we kept on. The moon was high in the sky when I heard a cheer from the wagons ahead of us in the line.

"I think we are here!" Adela said.

She and I let out a cheer of our own that was soon echoed by our friends in the wagons behind us.

In the dark of night I hadn't recognized the familiar field where we had camped two summers before.

Kizi knew just where to lead our wagon so it would be in its place with the others of the Band of the West. I hopped down and unhitched her. She nuzzled me and then slowly walked away to join the other horses at the hay pile.

I was very tired after two days on the road, but I was also very excited.

Adela had jumped down from the wagon, her hair freshly brushed and tied with a bright green ribbon.

"Come on!" she said, pulling on my hand, "Let's go to the fire and say 'hello" to everybody.

There was no thought of sleeping. People were coming from all the wagons, some carrying food, others flagons of wine or musical instruments all going to the central fire. I followed the sound of merry music, half dancing, half running hand in hand with Adela.

By the time we reached the roaring fire Radha, Iovan and their child had already joined Madam Eleeza and Vasa at a long table. A little girl with bright red hair sat on Radha's lap. Satarma fingered the girl's hair, fascinated, but didn't pull it.

Adela dropped my hand and ran to Madam Eleeza, who stood up and opened her arms to receive the happy child.

For a moment they just stood, holding each other. I saw tears moistening Adela's cheeks.

Madam Eleeza took her seat and beckoned Adela to sit beside her. She placed her arm protectively around her thin shoulder.

"I have missed you, my little one," she said. Then she saw me. "Milada! You have blossomed! Come sit with us. Girls, this is my daughter."

The child's big green eyes looked up at me through long dark lashes. There was something very familiar about her. Yes, the auburn hair was like her mother's and like Radha's, even though theirs was a warm brown rather than this child's flaming red. Her completion was darker, more like Vasa's, as were her eyelashes. It wasn't so much her features that were familiar as something in her expression.

As I bent down to stroke her downy cheek, she smiled at me and reached out and grasped the amber necklace that I always wore.

"Do you like my beads? I asked her. "A special friend gave them to me".

She let go of the beads and giggled.

"Layla," I thought I heard her say. I looked at Radha, but before I could utter another word Iovan approached the table with a huge platter of roasted meat seasoned with garlic and herbs. Its fragrance made my mouth water.

"I wasn't sure we would make it," he said, "but here we are!"

We all smiled at his words.

"Now it's time to enjoy each other's company," he said, "and partake of this wonderful food. Then, after we eat, we will dance until the sun comes up, we will dance the sun back into our souls."

Chapter 86

The Circle Dance

After I ate my fill of the delicious meal I wandered over to where the musicians were. I smiled at Bora as he played and he smiled back. He was no longer the child that I knew, but a strong young man. Yet when I watched him play I could see the boy he was, still very much present in his smiling eyes.

The tune that they played was unfamiliar to me, but soon the music took me. I closed my eyes and began to sway in time with the beat. Someone gently took my right hand and said, "Come".

Without opening my eyes I allowed myself to be lead into the dance. Someone took my other hand. I opened my eyes and I found myself part of a great circle of people all moving around the fire as one. I looked to my right, to see who it was that had called me to the dance.

First I saw the hand that held mine so gently, yet firmly. It was dark, with long tapering fingers. My eyes followed up his arm. The sleeves of his linen shirt were rolled up to the elbows exposing strong, tanned forearms.

His shoulders were broad and his long brown hair just brushed the top of them. He turned to look at me and my eyes finally met his. They were dark brown, set deep into his smiling face. He said nothing. I wouldn't have heard him over the sound of the music playing anyway. He just kept smiling as we circled round and round, sharing this time of joy together.

He was not of our band and I didn't remember ever seeing him before. Maybe I had, but it was two years since the last gathering. I saw how much Bora had changed, and Goran; maybe I knew him as a boy and didn't recognize the man he had become. I looked forward to finding out more about him.

The music stopped, but before I could catch my breath and introduce myself he had disappeared into the crowd of people. When the musicians began again, I joined the dance, keeping my eyes open in case he returned.

Iovan was right, the music played and we danced until the sun came up, but I didn't see the young man with the brown eyes again that night.

I returned to my wagon for a much needed rest. Adela was fast asleep in her bed with Blackie snoring by her side. I closed the curtains to keep out the morning light and quickly fell into a deep sleep.

It seemed like only a minute had passed when I felt someone's hand on my shoulder.

"Good morning," Adela whispered, "or should I say 'good afternoon'!"

The sun was shining through the curtains on the west side of he wagon. I realized that it was late in the day.

"I've brought you some tea," she said, holding a cup full of warm fragrant liquid.

"Thank you, Adela," I said.

"Isn't Madam Eleeza's girl beautiful," Adela said.

"I've never seen such red hair!" I replied. "I feel like I've seen her before, but that's impossible".

"Radha asked me to bring you to Madam Eleeza's wagon before the sun goes down," Adela said.

"We still have some time, I think," I replied, wanting to wash off the dust of our long journey. "Would you like to come with me for a dip in the stream?"

"What a good idea" she said and the two of us were soon enjoying the cool, babbling water.

"I liked that dance we did in a circle last night," Adela said as we sat side-by-side drying our hair in the sunlight.

"I have seen dances like that in some of the villages that we visit," I told her, "but never by our own fire".

"I think the Band of the South brought the music with them," Adela said. "I remember something like it from my village."

"Do you ever think about going back?" I asked her.

"Sometimes I do," she said. "I miss the sea, its non-stop rhythm and colours that change from one moment to the next."

"I cannot imagine what it would be like," I said wishing I could see the sea for myself. "Is it like the lake?"

"No," Adela said, "It's much bigger and has a kind of power and movement that the lake does not possess."

We sat in silence for a while, both lost in our own thoughts.

Then Adela said, "Who was the young man next to you in the circle dance? He kept smiling at you!"

"I don't know," I told her, feeling my cheeks growing warm.

"Do you like him?" she asked.

"I liked his smile and the feel of his hand," I said, "but after that dance he disappeared."

"You'll see him again," she said, with a smile.

"I hope so!" I replied, meaning it.

"We had better get going," Adela said, as I noted the lengthening shadows.

We stopped at our wagon to tidy ourselves and put on fresh clothes to greet the Queen. Then we went to find Madam Eleeza.

As we approached her wagon I had to smile. Fixed beneath all the windows were wooden boxes full of bright red flowers. When we got closer I saw that each large flower was comprised of many, many small flowers. I reached up and touched one of the dark green leaves. It felt fuzzy. Vasa's face appeared in the window above me.

"Greetings, Milada!" he said, "do you like the flowers?"

"Hello Mr. Vasa!" I replied. "Yes, they are beautiful; so cheerful looking."

"I will give you some to grow," he said. "Come on up, the Ladies await you."

Adela and I climbed the high steps into the wagon. It felt good to be back within this golden cocoon.

"Milada, Adela, come!" Madam Eleeza beckoned us to the divan where she sat with Radha and the two small children sitting quietly holding each other's hands.

Madam Eleeza opened her arms to me. I ran to her and let myself be lost in her embrace.

"It's so good to see you again," I said, "and to meet your beautiful little girl".

I looked down at the child and she smiled up at me in a way that felt so familiar.

"She seems to have a calming effect on Satarma," I said, looking at the two of them sitting side by side.

"Yes, she does," Radha said, with a big smile.

"She seems so familiar to me," I said as we settled ourselves on the soft cushions.

"That's because you know her," Radha said, with a twinkle in her eye.

"I met her last night," I said. "I would like to get to know her, but I don't know her yet!"

"Look deeply into her eyes," Radha said.

I started to ask why, but Radha continued.

"Do not speak," she said softly. "Let your mind be still. Just look."

I looked over at the smiling child. She looked back at me and fixed my eyes with hers. I knew I knew her, but how could that be? I tried to quiet my mind, but questions kept coming - *Why am I doing this? I feel silly? I can't know this child...*

The child reached out and gently touched the amber beads that hung, as always, around my neck. She looked up into my eyes.

"Layla" I whispered. The child smiled. "Layla..."

The girl's smile widened and for a moment her face changed into the one that I knew and loved so well. I blinked my eyes and the little red haired girl was back, but for moment, a miniature Layla sat on the divan in Madam Eleeza's wagon.

Chapter 87

Layla Remembered

"Layla?" I said looking first at Madam Eleeza and then at Radha. They both were smiling.

"That is what we call her," Madam Eleeza said.

"But how can it be? Are you related to her, that she carries such a strong resemblance?" I asked, even though I could see that she really didn't look like Layla.

"Maybe we are, but she doesn't look like Layla," Madam Eleeza said, "She *is* Layla".

"How do you know that?" I asked, feeling the truth of her words and wanting to believe them but not understanding how such a thing could be.

"She recognized those amber beads," Radha said.

"It's true that she seemed to" I said, "but any child might have been attracted to their bright colour."

"I know," said Radha, "wait a minute, I'll be right back".

She rose from the divan and looked over to where Satarma sat.

"He will be fine here," her mother said, noting the look of concern on Radha's face.

She was back in a moment, but did not enter the wagon.

"Milada, come out here a moment," she said.

I joined her on the bench of the wagon. She had something in her hand.

"Remember this?" she asked, showing me the crystal sphere that Layla had entrusted me to give her all those years ago.

"Yes" I said, gently touching the stone. "That was Layla's".

"Do you remember what she told you?" Radha asked.

How could I forget her words, words that had given me so much hope that she hadn't really died?

"Yes, I remember." I said softly, remembering only too well Layla's kind ways.

"What did she tell you to tell me?" Radha prompted.

"She said to ask you to keep it for her," I replied.

"And I have," she said.

"This one is mine," she said, taking a pouch out of her apron pocket. "My mother also has a crystal sphere. Let's see if Layla will claim her own stone."

She put the crystal back in its pouch and we entered the wagon together. Radha whispered something in her mother's ear.

"Over there, in the small drawer under the window," Madam Eleeza said.

Radha took a small pouch out of the drawer, then opened the curtain to let in more of the late afternoon's light.

She brought a low stool, covered it with a white cloth from the table and placed it in front of the children.

She gently laid each stone on the top of its pouch in a row on the stool, first her own then the one that had belonged to Layla and finally the one from Madam Eleeza's drawer. Both children looked fascinated by the rainbows of light that danced in the crystals.

"Layla," Radha said, "which is your stone?"

Without a moment's hesitation, the girl reached out and touched the one in the middle.

"Would you like it back?" Madam Eleeza said.

The child smiled and nodded her head.

Radha placed the stone in the girl's upturned palms. For an instant, once again I saw Layla's features on her small face.

I lifted the beads off my neck and held them out toward the child.

"These are your beads," I said, now without a doubt that this child was indeed the girl I had come to love so dearly.

But the child would not take them. She shook her head.

"For Milada," she said. "Remember Layla."

I placed the beads back on my neck as little Layla put the crystal back on its pouch. She came beside me where I knelt on the rug and opened her little arms. I hugged her tightly and felt like I had as a child in Layla's arms, safe and comforted. Then we sat together on the divan. It felt odd that I was so big and she so small!

"How can this be?" I asked Radha.

"This is how we remember," she said. "We are born again within the band, and we remember who we are and what we knew before".

"Is that how Bora knew how to play the viol?" I asked, "and you all know which herbs to use when someone is ill?"

"Yes," she replied. "In each life we have new experiences and add new things to our knowledge, but we bring much in with us from the start."

"Except Satarma," Madam Eleeza said.

"That's why he can be a little difficult," Radha sighed. "But he will bring us much new knowledge from our home in the stars."

For a moment I thought of Goran. He said that we would never understand the gypsies or be a real part of their band. In a way he was right. But at least now I was learning about why this was so. Adela and I were not a part of this lineage, yet we had been given a great opportunity to live with these people and learn some of their wisdom.

By now the sun had set and twilight's glow had dimmed to darkness. I felt overwhelmed by these revelations and felt I needed to have a rest before the evening's festivities continued.

I excused myself and headed back to the wagon, leaving the others chatting cheerfully on the divan.

Lost in my own thoughts, I was startled when Vasa came up from behind me with a basket of the bright red flowers still on their thick stems.

"Milada," he said, "I promised you these".

"Thank you, Mr. Vasa," I said, startled.

"I hope I didn't scare you," he said.

"I was just thinking," I told him.

"About Layla and remembering?" he asked.

"Yes," I said. "I mean, it's a strange thing. She's your daughter, yet she is someone else."

"Each child is him or herself," Vasa said. "We as parents provide the physical body, but the actual person is very individual".

"Don't you find it strange that everyone already knows your little girl?" I asked, trying to understand what I had just experienced. "I felt I was back with Layla when I hugged her."

"It is strange that she is known," he said, "but everyone said that Layla was a lovely person."

"Yes," I said, "she was the best!"

"So is it not a wonderful gift to have her back?" he asked.

"Yes," I guess it is," I replied. "It's just so strange."

"It's strange to us," he said, "but it isn't strange to them. It's useful to remember things and not have to learn them all again!"

"Why can't *we* remember?" I asked.

"Maybe we do remember but if the people around us don't then it's easy to forget," he said.

"So, because it's expected for the gypsies to remember, they do?" I asked.

"Maybe that is how it works!" he laughed.

I smiled. Vasa reminded me of my father, with his light and happy manner.

"About these flowers," he said, handing me the basket.

"They are beautiful," I said, 'thank you".

"They are more that just beautiful," he said. "Some travellers from the land beyond the southern sea taught me that placing the leaves of this plant on a serious wound will help it heal when nothing else can."

I caressed one of the velvety leaves.

"Put these stalks in water" Vasa explained." Soon there will be small roots growing. Then just stick them in some soil. They like warmth and sunlight, so bring your boxes inside in the cold months. If you want more, just break off a stalk and start again."

"Thank you so much," I told him, "I'll remember."

"Until you die?" he asked with a grin.

"And beyond!" I replied.

Chapter 88

Brok

I brought the flowers back to my wagon and placed the leafy stalks in a little water as Vasa had said. Then I hurried back to the fire, anxious to see if the boy I had met the night before was there.

Actually, I can't say that I met him, at all! We did not speak, I did not know his name but I looked forward to finding him and learning all about him.

The music was already playing when I reached the central fire. Crowds of people sat in groups, eating and chatting. I scanned the crowd for the young man. I didn't even know which band he was with!

I felt a hand on my shoulder. When I turned I saw Iovan standing beside me with a smile.

"Good evening, Milada!" he said, "Who are you looking for?"

"Hello, Iovan!" I said, "no one in particular."

He smiled and I thought I saw him wink!

"I heard you met my sister," he said.

"I met Radha's sister," I corrected.

"But Layla is *my* sister, too," he said, "or at least she *was*!"

"Did you all know one another before?" I asked.

"Most of us did," he replied.

"So your parents become you children?" I asked.

"Sometimes that is the case," he said.

"It's strange," I said.

"Not to us," he replied. "It's just the way it is."

"Are all the bands here now?" I asked, changing the subject to one I felt more comfortable with.

"The Band of the East did not arrive," he said. I saw a shadow pass across his eyes. "We will celebrate the feast of the longest day tomorrow. I hope that they will come in time."

"Maybe it was too dangerous to come," I said, "like it was for us last summer."

"Maybe that is the case," he agreed. "It is better to avoid trouble than to go looking for it."

Just then I spotted the young man from the dance. He was sitting close to the fire with a group of other young people who were not familiar to me. I caught his eye and saw him looking at me and then looking at Iovan. I quickly looked away.

Iovan followed my glace to the group by the fire.

"Have you met them yet?" he asked, "They are from the Band of the South".

"I saw some of them last night," I said.

"They brought us the dance in a circle," he said, his eyes sparkling. "You looked like you were enjoying it".

"You know I love to dance," I said, smiling in spite of myself.

"Go and introduce yourself," he said. "I will find Radha and the child and return in a while.

Iovan headed in the direction of his wagon. I smoothed my skirt, ran my fingers through my shining, clean hair and went over to the group of young people by the fire.

"Hello," I said, taking a seat on the long wooden bench. "I am Milada, from the Band of the West."

"Hello," said one girl with a thick plait of hair hanging over one shoulder. "I remember you from another gathering. You are not one of the gypsies. You merely travel with them."

"I've lived with them since I was very young," I said, feeling anger and annoyance at her words. "I feel like one of them".

"Well, maybe," she said.

"Hello Milada," said the boy who drew me to the dance before the girl could start up again. "My name is Brok. Did you like the dance?"

"Yes, very much," I said.

"I think she liked dancing with *you*," said one of the boys, jabbing Brok with his elbow.

"We all danced together," I said, "in the circle. But I *did* like holding your hand".

Did I say that! I hoped that I just thought it but I heard the others say "oooooh" and saw the boys jab Brok again with their elbows. I felt a blush rise to my cheeks and was pleased to see that Brok's cheeks were growing pink as well.

"Have you eaten?" he said.

"Not yet," I replied.

"Let's go get something to eat and find somewhere quiet to sit," he said. He stood up and then held out his hand to me. I took it once again and we went together to the long table laden with tasty things to eat. We settled down on a blanket at the edge of the clearing beneath a sheltering plane tree.

"Don't mind my sister," Brok said. "She can be a pain sometimes".

"It's all right," I said. "She is right, I am not one of the gypsies, but theirs is the only life I've known."

"I remember you from before," he said. "That's why I asked you to dance. I was hoping to meet you again last summer but your band did not come."

"I was really looking forward to coming last summer," I told him, "but our Baron said it was much to dangerous."

"Times are changing," Brok said. "I have never seen villages burnt to the ground, people slain and crops crushed and uprooted before now".

"Let's not speak of such things," I said, "We are here to celebrate summer, to see old friends and to make new ones."

"I'd like to be your new friend," Brok said.

I felt myself blushing again at his words. He put his empty plate on the ground, took mine and placed it on top then grabbed my hand and said, "Let's go dance."

We joined the others whirling around the fire. The musicians played familiar tunes and also some new ones that sounded strange to my ears. We repeated the circle dance from the night before, this time the tempo kept rising and rising until we were nearly running around the fire. When the music stopped I collapsed into Brok's arms, laughing and trying to catch my breath.

"That was fun!" I said, when I could speak.

He kept his arms around me. With one strong hand he lifted my chin so I looked up into his eyes.

"*You* are fun," he said and planted a gentle kiss on my lips.

I could hear the fire crackling, the music playing and voices chatting and laughing, but it all seemed to come to me through a fog. I could make out the colour of the flames and the bright clothes of the revellers, but it felt as if the world was spinning around Brok and me.

The only thing that I could see clearly was Brok's face, his eyes smiling down at mine. Without thinking, I rose up high on my toes and kissed him back. I don't know how long we stood there, close to the fire, looking into each other's eyes and exploring each other's lips.

"It's hot here by the fire," Brok said, breaking the magic silence, "let's take a walk by the stream".

Hand in hand we walked down the path past the wagons. I heard the water splashing over the rocks.

"I like to be by the water," I said. "All last year we camped beside the lake".

Brok put his finger on my lips.

"Shush," he whispered, "let's listen to the sound of the night."

We continued down the path in silence. I wanted to ask Brok many questions, where he's been, what he did in the band, why he remembered me.

"Brok," I whispered

"Shush," he repeated, this time instead of putting this finger, he put his own lips on mine.

Chapter 89

Running

We embraced in the shadows, kissing in the moonlit silence. The magic was shattered by the sound of someone running down the path.

"Milada! Milada! Where are you?"

"Adela" I said, pulling away from Brok's arms, "Adela, what is it?"

"Milada!" she said, out of breath from running. "You must come now, we are leaving."

"Leaving?" Brok said.

"Yes," said Adela, "now!"

"But we never leave a camp at night," I said.

"Milada, you must come now," she said, grabbing my hand and pulling it as hard as her slender arms could.

"And you, too," she said to Brok. "Your people have already started to leave."

"Come on," said Brok as he sprinted up the path.

Adela and I followed as fast as we could.

"What's happened?" I asked as we ran.

"The invaders," she said. "The invaders are coming".

I reached my wagon and saw Bora hitching up my horse.

"Milada, where were you?" he asked. "We are ready to go".

Before I had a chance to answer, Bora had finished the job and was already heading down the path to his own wagon.

"Come on, Milada," he yelled. "There is no time to loose."

I gathered the few things that were drying on the branch hanging over my wagon then climbed up the steps and clicked to Kizi. She seemed confused at being hitched up in the middle of the night. Where did Brok go? And where was Adela?

The wagons fell into a line and moved through the clearing. The huge central fire, where we had been dancing moments ago, had been put out and the place was covered over with soil so that not a trace remained.

Where was Adela? I could not go looking for her. She must know that I would be in our wagon. I saw the wagons going their separate directions as they left the clearing. Would it be a year before I saw Brok again?

Adela must be in another wagon. Maybe she went with Zora, who was expecting her child any day now. I could not wait. I took my place in the line and continued along the road, retracing the route from where we had just arrived.

I should have felt tired, but I didn't. There were so many thoughts in my mind. Layla's return as Madam Eleeza's child, Brok's strong arms and soft lips, Adela's disappearance. We followed the road all night and well into the next day until the signal finally came down the line of wagons that we would stop to rest the horses and ourselves.

Here it was, the longest day of the year. Instead of enjoying a feast we were running for our lives. I unhitched my horse. She wandered off to join the others where they grazed in the sun.

I ran up the line of wagons, looking for Adela. First I went to Zora's wagon.

"Zora," I called, "Zora, is Adela with you?"

Before I could climb up the wagon's steps Maxim poked his head out of the doorway.

"Shush, Milada, they are sleeping," he whispered.

"Who? Zora and Adela?" I asked softly.

"Zora and the baby!" he said.

"The baby! When did it come?"

"Last night," he replied. "Lazara came with us just in case the baby arrived. It was a good thing that she did."

"Did you stop the wagon?" I asked, remembering Radha's difficult delivery.

"No," Maxim said, "Zora rested on many cushions to soften the road. And the little one seemed anxious to join us. He came very easily."

"Zora had little boy! He will be a good companion for Satarma," I said, "if he can keep up with him!"

Maxim laughed, then slapped his hand over his mouth, not to wake Zora or the baby sleeping inside.

"He'll be alright, I'm sure!" he whispered with a smile.

"Adela is not with you?" I asked, remembering why I had come.

"No," he said, "I haven't seen her since yesterday afternoon".

"She came to tell me we had to leave," I said, "but then she disappeared. I don't know who she went with."

"Once we make camp you'll find each other," he said, putting a reassuring hand on my shoulder.

"You're right," I said. "Do you know when we will stop?"

"I'm not sure," he said. "I think we will start up again soon and then make camp when night falls."

"This is the longest day of the year," I said, "we have a long way yet to go before nightfall".

"I think I hear the signal to start again," he said.

I looked over to see people leading their horses back to the wagons.

"Give Zora my love, and the baby, too," I said.

I wonder if we will know this baby, I thought as I left to find my horse and hitch her up again to continue our long day's ride. I was ready for a rest, but there was no one else to guide my wagon.

I ate some fruit as we bumped long the rutted track. It felt very lonely on the wagon's high seat with no one for company. Where was Blackie? He was missing, too. In the excitement of the night before I didn't even think about him. I tied the reins to the side of the seat. The horse would follow the wagon in front. I wouldn't be long; I just needed to see if Blackie was asleep in the back.

I pushed open the curtain and had a good look around the wagon. Not only was Blackie nowhere to be seen but I also realized that Adela's things were gone. What could that mean?

I went back to my seat, watching the dust rising from the road at each hoof beat. Adela was gone; moved to another wagon? Whose? All my dear friends had left. Tanya to her new life as Radha, wife and mother; Goran to the village, to make shoes for horses and iron pots for cooking as a husband to Dunia; and now little Adela whom I had come to love like a little sister was gone.

I felt a tear trickle down my cheek. And Brok. I had hardly met him and now we were travelling down separate roads, away from each other. The trickle of tears became a flood, unstoppable as the ocean tide that I had heard of but never seen.

Chapter 90

The Longest Day

Finally, the longest day of the year came to an end. I think I must have dozed on and off throughout the long day, my memories mixing with my dreams. Had I really sat in Madam Eleeza's opulent wagon gazing at the eyes of my dear Layla once again? Was it only yesterday that I felt myself enveloped in Brok's warm embrace? Or was it all a dream? Maybe this journey was a dream and soon I would wake up and enjoy the Midsummer's feast.

I heard the sound of hoof beats approaching and soon Iovan came into view.

"Milada," he said, "we will be stopping soon to camp for the night."

"It has been a long day!" I said, wearily.

"That it has!" he said with a sigh.

"Will we stay long at our new camp?" I asked.

"I think not," he replied. "We must return to the lake where we will be safe".

He rode on, passing the message down the line of wagons.

We gathered around a small fire and ate some of the dishes that had been prepared for the feast. In the fire's glow I saw Zora nursing her new son. Radha sat beside her with Satarma asleep, his head resting on her lap. I went over to join them and meet the newest member of the gypsy band.

I quietly sat down next to Zora, smiled at her and placed a gentle kiss on her cheek.

"He's beautiful," I said, looking down at the tiny baby contentedly suckling.

"Isn't he just!" Zora whispered. "He looks like his father".

"His father has a lot more hair!" I whispered, looking across the fire where Maxim's long hair glowed in its golden light. "And you look beautiful, too!"

"What a shame we had to move camp," Radha said, leaning over Zora and looking into my eyes. "I saw the way you were dancing with that boy from the band of the South. I thought maybe you had found your partner."

I couldn't help the tears that flowed down my cheeks. I could not speak for the sadness in my heart. Radha gently slid her son's head onto a cushion on the floor and came to sit beside me.

"Oh, Milada," she said, "I was only teasing you. I didn't mean to make you cry."

"I'm sorry," I said, letting myself fall into to her warm and comforting arms.

"You know everything happens for a reason," she whispered into my hair. "We might not understand it today, but after time passes, when we look back, we can see clearly how the twists and turn in our lives lead us to a place of peace and happiness, if we can accept them for what they are."

"Even running away and missing the celebration?" I asked in disbelief.

"Everything," she whispered.

I was too tired to argue. I let myself rest in her arms until her peaceful presence soothed me and I felt a little better.

"Have you seen Adela?" I asked. "All her things are gone from our wagon."

"She returned to my mother's wagon," Radha said.

"What?" I exclaimed. "Why didn't she tell me?"

"I guess there wasn't time," Radha said.

"She had time to pack her things," I said, feeling angry and hurt.

"Don't be angry, Milada," Radha said as of she read my mind. "Adela loves you. She told me that you taught her so much."

"So why did she leave?" I demanded.

"Madam Eleeza asked her to return," she replied.

To that, there was nothing I could say.

"Wait here a moment," Radha said.

She rose quietly and went off in the direction of her wagon. Soon she was back with something in her hands.

"I think my mother knew you would miss Adela," she said. "She gave me these for you".

Radha placed a packet on my lap. I untied the leather thong that held the heavy fabric covering in place and gasped when I saw what was inside.

"Radha!" I exclaimed, "These are wonderful! I can't believe it!"

Inside the packet was another set of the beautiful cards.

"She made them for you last year," Radha said, "but since we didn't make it to the gathering you had to wait a long time for them".

"That was so kind of her," I said. "How can I ever thank her?"

"Using them wisely to help others will be all the thanks she needs," Radha said, thoughtfully.

We sat by the fire a little longer and then one by one people drifted back to their wagons to catch a few hours of sleep before we moved off again at dawn.

It was lonely waking up all alone in my wagon. I made a small fire and brewed my morning tea; something that Adela had done for me since she had joined our band. I expected Blackie to come and put a dirty paw on my lap, his way of saying "good morning," but he must have gone with Adela.

I opened the packet of cards and looked at them one by one. They were so beautiful. While I was looking at them the call to move was sounded. I quickly gathered them into a pile to wrap them into their protective packet. One card fell to the floor. When I bent to pick it up I saw that it was The Lovers.

I tried not to think of Brok as I returned it to the pile and tied the leather thong.

Soon we were on the dusty road again, riding away from the rising sun. We did not stop for a midday meal. We did not stop to rest the horses. We kept on at a steady pace until the afternoon sun shone in my face. I pulled the brim of my straw hat low over my eyes and trusted that Kizi would follow the wagon in front of us.

I let my eyelids fall shut as we continued down the rutted road; the squeaks of the wagon and hypnotic rhythm of my horse's hooves eased my mind into a half sleep. The wagon rolled over a stone and I was jolted awake to the smell of something burning. I opened my eyes and could see smoke rising from beyond the trees in front of the line of wagons.

The signal to stop was passed down the line and I reined Kizi in just in time not to collide with the wagon in front of mine.

I hoped down and ran to Bora's wagon.

"Do you know why we are stopping?" I asked him.

He pointed ahead at the rising smoke.

"Someone needs to see what is happening ahead," he said. "It may not be safe to go on."

"It's not safe to go back," I said, a shiver of fear rising in my spine. "If it isn't safe to go forward what will we do?"

"We will wait and see," Bora said. "Until we know what the situation is ahead we do not need to worry."

"But, what if…"

"Milada, stop. Right now we are safe. Do not use your precious energy on 'what if's'. When we have more information we will know what we must do. I'm sure the Baron and Iovan are riding ahead to see," he said.

"I guess you are right," I said.

"Why don't you lie down for a while and get some rest," Bora said. "That's what I am going to do."

I returned to my wagon and settled down on my bed, sinking into its softness and enjoying the stillness of the summer afternoon. I realized that at this moment, right now, I was happy. Thoughts drifted back into my mind, the long bumpy road, missing the festival, losing Adela and Brok, not knowing if it is safe to go on. But all of that is in the past or in the future. Right now, in this moment, I was happy, resting on my soft bed, in the shelter of my wagon, with the breath of warm air caressing my skin.

Chapter 91

The Village of the Wounded

When the call came to move on the sun hung low in the sky. We continued through the dense woods then came to a clearing where a village had stood. Now little remained but smouldering ruins that once were people's homes.

We made camp upwind in the shade of a grove of oak trees that was spared the flames. Just as I unhitched my horse, Radha called out to me.

"Milada, come quickly," she called, "there are some people here who need help. Now!"

I patted Kizi, threw the halter into the wagon and ran after Radha toward what was left of the village.

I tried not to look at charred corpses of people and animals that lined the cobbled streets of the village. I could not help stopping at the sight of a small child lying in a doorway. Her delicate body was curled up. She looked like she was asleep. Maybe she is hurt, I thought. But when I reached down to touch her, her skin was cold.

"Milada, hurry!" Radha called.

I left the child there and followed Radha, hoping that we were not too late to help anyone who might still be alive.

We passed through the ruins of the village square. Here some buildings still stood, but the doors had been broken down and the contents of the homes and shops looted or destroyed.

I turned a corner and saw Radha and others of our band gathered around the doorway of one of the few buildings that was still intact.

"We have come to help you," a voice said. "Let us come in".

I caught up with Radha, out of breath.

"Are they afraid to let us in?" I asked.

"I'm not surprised, after what they have been through," she replied as we moved closer to the locked door.

The others parted to let Radha approach the door. Without a word, she placed both of her hands on the heavy wooden door. Then she leaned forward and placed her forehead on the door. I heard a low humming sound and realized that it was Radha.

After a moment, she backed away from the door and said quietly, "Open the door. We are here to help you".

We all waited in silence. After a moment the door opened a crack. A woman gazed out at us, her eyes terrified. We all remained silent. Radha took a step forward and extended her arms toward the woman, the palms of her hands facing outwards as if making an offering.

The woman looked at Radha and then at the rest of us, waiting in silence. Without a word, she opened the door wider, turned and went inside.

Radha followed her and we followed Radha into the dark room. When my eyes grew accustomed to the light they were met by a sad sight. The stone walls were lined with injured people; some were conscious, some were not. A few of the village women helped as best they could, gently holding cups of water to the parched lips of the injured.

I didn't know where to start. I looked at Radha. She was already kneeling by a child, whispering comforting words. The other gypsy women were spreading out, each connecting with one of the people on the ground. I heard a low moan coming from a blanket in the corner, a little way off from the others. I approached it and saw that there was a young man in a very bad state.

His long hair was matted with dirt and dried blood. He moaned softly, his eyes closed. I reached out and touch his forehead. It was burning. I knew that I must get his fever down.

I touched the man's hot hand and said softly, "Take courage, my friend. I will do what I can to help you".

I cannot say if he understood or even heard my words. I rose and asked one of the village women where I could get some water. She indicated a barrel by the door. It was not the cleanest water, but it would have to do for now. I saw that Annika was stoking the fire in the already hot room and figured that she must be boiling water to purify it and brew the teas that would help these people recover, if it was not too late.

I tore off a piece of my skirt and soaked it in the water barrel. At least the water was cool. I returned to the moaning man and placed the cool rag on his forehead. Immediately, his moaning stopped and he let out a deep sigh, without opening his eyes.

I found a bowl that was not in use and filled it with water. With another strip torn from my skirt, I gently sponged the dirt and blood off the young man's face. Once done, I could see that the wounds on his head were not deep or serious. But the rag on his forehead was now very hot again. I replaced with a fresh one and was ready to see if I could help someone else when Radha called me over.

"Milada," she said, "go to my wagon and bring me the bags of herbs. You know where they are kept."

"Yes, Radha," I said. "Anything else?"

"Bring rags for bandages and some pots to boil water," she said. "And look in on Zora to make sure she is alright with Satarma. He's not used to being away from me for so long."

I ran back to our camp as fast as I could. The men were preparing a meal since most of the women were busy in the village. I saw Zora with her baby and Satarma playing by the fire.

"Are you alright?" I asked. "Radha was concerned about Satarma".

"We are fine," she said. "I wish I could help you in the village".

"You need to keep your strength for your child now. Everyone understands that," I said.

"Yes, I know. If you need anything, let me know," she said.

"I will," I said as I hurried to Radha and Iovan's wagon.

I climbed up the high step and found Iovan inside, packing up bundles of herbs and strips of cloth.

"Hello, Milada," he said. "Have you come for these?"

"Yes," I said. "How did you know?"

"I heard Radha's voice in my head," he said, "Take them and hurry back. How many people are there? We will bring some food to you when it is ready".

I realized that I was hungry but there was no time to eat now. "Besides us there are about six women who are well and a dozen or so who are injured."

"We will make some broth for those who are poorly," he said. "Go now and do what you can to help".

The bag of herbs was large but not heavy. I took two pots from the cooking wagon and hurried back to the village in the twilight.

Chapter 92

Survivors

I tapped on the door. The woman opened it and silently took the pots from my hand. I found Radha sitting beside a small boy, not much older than Satarma. I watched as she set his broken arm using a splint made from a broken chair leg.

"Did you bring the rags?" she said without looking up from her work.

"Yes," I replied, "here they are".

She took a long strip and wrapped it around the boy's fragile arm. When she finished she kissed his forehead and stood up.

"We need to make some chamomile flower tea to help them sleep and ease their pain," she said.

I was going to make the tea myself but then heard groans coming from the young man in the corner. Radha noticed my concern.

Radha said, "I will brew the tea. Go to him".

Although the man looked a bit better since I cleaned his face, I could see that he was in pain. I replaced the water soaked rag with a fresh one. Once again the moaning stopped. Gingerly, I lifted the blanket that covered him. His chest and arms, like his head had been, were covered with a mixture of dried blood and earth. I gently opened his shirt. Although there were some bruises, there was no major wound. I felt his arms. They seemed all right, not broken or cut.

I pulled the blanket further down. The left leg of his trousers was a dirty tan brown colour. The right one was a bright red. Blood.

I looked around for Radha or Lazara but they were both busy helping others. I found a sharp knife by the cooking fire and used it to cut through the fabric of the young man's trousers. What I saw made me wretch. The skin was cut in ragged patches right through to the bone. By removing the material I had unknowingly pulled off the dried blood that held the wounds closed. Blood began to flow again. I had no way of knowing how much blood had already been lost. I needed to stop the bleeding and quickly!

I ran to Radha and took some of the strips of cloth. I placed them on the man's wounds and pushed as hard as I could. I tied one piece high on his thigh and pulled it tight to slow the blood that flowed into his leg. I was relieved to see that the bleeding was slowing down. Soon it stopped. I sat back on my heels and took a deep breath.

The young man opened his eyes and looked straight into mine. For a brief moment, in spite of the smell of blood and death all around me I felt a spark of joy. His eyes were green, like the soft new growth at the tips of the pines branches. I knew that he must be in great pain, but in his eyes all I could see was gratitude and peace.

"Good work, my child". I hadn't noticed Lazara standing behind me. "That is a very serious wound. Run back to the camp and get some cabbage leaves. Warm them and put them on his leg. It will help prevent worsening disease."

The man's eyes were closed. Did I imagine seeing them open? I heeded Lazara's words and ran to get the leaves. Supper was ready and I helped carry food back to the village though by this time I had gone beyond hunger. I knew I had to help that young man back to life.

I placed the leaves on a cloth above a pot of hot water to warm while I gently removed the bandage from the young man's leg. I replaced the cloth with the warm cabbage leaves then loosed the band at the top of his leg, watching carefully that the blood did not begin to gush again. Yet again I changed the cool rag on his forehead. He seemed calmer now and although his brow was still very hot it was not burning as before. I lay my hand gently on top of the rag and whispered. "You will be well, my friend. Sleep now and dream yourself better".

Without opening his eyes, the young man sighed and seemed to relax. Was he dead? I placed my hand on his chest and could feel the faint beating of his heart. He was asleep.

I stood up and looked around the room. It seemed as if we had all finished the first round of our care. Most of the injured people were sleeping. One or two who where not so badly hurt were speaking in low voices, asking about their families or trying to piece together what had happened. There was one person covered in a blanket. As I watched, Bora and Iovan lifted it gently and brought it outside. One of the injured had not survived. I hoped that we had arrived in time to save the others.

I sat at the table beside the hearth with the other women.

"What went on here," Radha asked the woman who had let us in the house.

"It all happened so fast," she said. "One minute we are going about our business on a day like any other and the next minute our world is destroyed."

"They came from the east," a younger woman said. "I was in the field, harvesting the wheat with my sister."

"Were you two alone?" Radha asked.

"My brothers were conscripted into the army," she said, "as were all the young men of the village."

Looking around, I saw that there were only women at the table. The injured were also women and children, all except for the young man in the corner.

"I heard them before I saw them," she said.

"Heard who?" Radha asked.

"The horsemen," she replied. "There were hundred's of them. My sister and I lay down in the field out of sight. They rode right by us. It was a good thing that I heard them first!"

I thought of the time I was lost in the field of millet and knew how one could become invisible in a field awaiting harvest.

"We stayed in the field for many hours," the girl continued.

"We could hear people screaming," a second girl said. She must be the sister, I thought.

"Then we smelled the fires," the first girl said.

"I wanted to go and help our people," the younger girl said.

"But I told her that we needed to keep ourselves safe. We couldn't help if we were hurt, too," said her sister.

"And you were right," said the younger girl, looking at her sister with love and gratitude. "If we had returned we probably would have been killed or taken as prisoners," at these words she broke down and sobbed, "like Maria and Agata and Shona and the others."

The older girl embraced her sister.

"Shh, Elena, shh, crying will not bring our world back.

"I don't want to live without them," she said. "What will we do?"

"I do not know yet," replied the elder girl, "but we have the gift of our life. We will find a way."

"But our people are gone. Our village is gone. Our world is gone," she cried.

"This is a big world," she said, "we will find our way."

"You can come with us," Radha said. "Travel with us until you find a place to your liking."

"No, thank you," replied the young woman. "Our family land is here. We will stay on our land and rebuild our lives as we can."

I wondered at her words. How she could want to stay in a place that had been totally destroyed. Why not move on and start a life somewhere else?

Those who could, ate quietly. The day's events weighed heavy on us all. I thought about what the girls had said.

As usual, my curiosity got the best of me and I broke the silence with a question.

"If all the men had been conscripted to the army, who is that young man in the corner?" I asked.

The woman who opened the door spat on the floor.

"He is one of them," the elder sister whispered. "She," she indicated the older woman, 'thought we should just let him die, but I saw he was so young and took pity on him. My sister and I brought him here".

"Let him die like a dog!" the older woman spat. "I don't want him here".

"Peace, mother," said the girl. "If our brother lay wounded somewhere wouldn't you want some kind person to help him?"

The woman was silent.

"There is nothing more we can do here tonight," Radha said.

"I will stay and watch over the wounded," Lazara said. "You all go and get some rest."

I went to the corner and saw that the young man was still sleeping. I changed the rag one last time and whispered, "Good night. I will see you in the morning".

We collected the food baskets and made our way back to our camp through the burnt out village.

"What do you think happened here?" I asked Radha.

"When he brought the food, Iovan told me that it was probably a raiding party, not the main force."

"What's that?" I asked.

"Part of the army goes to different villages to get food for the rest," she said.

"Can't they just ask for it?" I said, "Why burn everything and kill the people?"

"In war people do things that they would not do otherwise," Radha said. "I can't say I understand it. War is not our way. We find a safe place and wait."

"And if nowhere is safe?" I asked.

"If there is a peaceful place in your heart you can create a safe place," she replied as we arrived back at our camp.

I fell into my bed exhausted. In my dreams villages burnt and people screamed. I woke up more tired that when I went to bed but was anxious to get up and see how the young man was doing.

I had a quick breakfast, grabbed some cabbage leaves then returned to the devastated village. When I arrived at the house some of there others were already there, brewing tea and ladling out broth to those who were strong enough to drink it.

I looked over to the corner. The young man was there, but moving fitfully. I touched his brow and once again it was burning.

I felt Lazara standing beside me.

"He is not doing well," she said, looking down at the boy.

I pulled down the blanket, removed the discoloured cabbage leaves and saw that the wounds on his leg were festering.

"I think it may have to be removed," Lazara said, "to save his life."

"Removed?" I asked, puzzled. "You mean cut off his leg?"

She nodded gravely.

"There must be something else we can try," I said.

"There's nothing else that I know," Lazara replied.

I cleaned the wounds and placed new cabbage leaves on them. A thought played around in my head, an idea or a memory.

I left the young man and wandered around the room looking at the other people there. The child with the broken arm was looking much better this morning. He was sitting up, drinking broth and asking for bread. He would recover. Some of the others sat staring into space, not physically hurt but in deep shock.

"Milada," Radha called.

I went over to her. "Yes, Radha," I said.

"We have used all the chamomile," she said. "Do you have some in your wagon?

"Yes," I said, "I have a bag full".

Will you please bring me some more and also some honey?"

"Yes, of course," I said and hurried back to our camp.

Chapter 93

Tomas

I thought as I walked. I felt like there was something I could do to save the young man's leg. But if Lazara said she didn't know anything else to try why did I think I knew something. I put it out of my mind as I looked around the blackened village. Our men were busy burying the bodies of the dead.

I pushed the curtain of my wagon open. My eyes fell on the bright red flower cuttings that Vasa had given me to plant. That's it! I thought. Vasa told me that this plant's leaves could heal wounds that no other can.

I cut off several of the biggest leaves and hopped down from the wagon. I got as far as the central fire then remembered I had come for chamomile. I ran back to my wagon and grabbed the muslin bag of dried chamomile flowers. Radha had also asked for something else. What was it? What was happening to my memory! I heard the sound of a bee buzzing in the warm morning air. 'Oh yes', I thought, 'that was it. Honey!'

The honey was kept in a large barrel in the kitchen wagon. I needed to find a container to put some in. There were some small tin buckets hanging from the ceiling that we used to collect berries. I reached up and took one from its hook and scooped up some honey, using my fingers to remove the excess from the edge of the bucket. I licked my fingers, enjoying the sweetness of the honey, the gift of the bees.

With the bucket of honey I had run out of hands. I stuffed the leaves into my blouse. Their furry surface ticked my skin, but I didn't want to have to come back again for them.

I returned to the house in the village and gave Radha the chamomile and the honey. She had water ready and soon a pot of chamomile tea gave a much more pleasant fragrance to the stuffy room.

I returned to the corner. The young man laid there, his eyes open. I saw him before he saw me. There was a look of fear in his green eyes.

"Good morning," I said softly.

"Are you my angel?" he said.

"What?"

"Last night," he said, "I thought I saw an angel looking down at me".

"I am not an angel," I said. "But I was here last night".

"Then you are she," he said, before his eyelids fell.

I sat beside him and took the fuzzy leaves from my blouse.

The boy's eyes half opened and I thought I saw a smile cross his lips.

Gently, I removed the cabbage leaves and replaced them with the leaves of the red flowers.

I reached out to collect the discarded cabbage leaves and felt the young man's hand on top of mine.

"Thank you, my angel," he said. And then he was asleep once more.

I left him to rest, confident that the fuzzy leaves would help his wounds. I joined Annika, Radha and the sisters from the wheat field. We searched the village for anything that could be used to help the survivors.

"Are you sure that you want to stay here?" Radha asked the girls, "There are so few people left."

"Maybe the horsemen will return," Annika added.

"There is nothing left here for them to take," said the elder sister. "I think more people survived and are hiding in the woods. Just this morning our cousin Maria returned with her flock of goats. She was in the high pasture when the raiders came. Others were there as well."

"And our brothers will return one day," the younger sister said. "What if we are not here when they come back? They won't know where to find us."

By the end of the day we found enough household goods to make the buildings that still stood at the far side of the village square habitable. Some of the injured were well enough now to be moved out of the cramped condition of the first house.

Radha and I helped the remaining ones to settle more comfortable on cushions filled with lamb's wool that we had collected.

The young man in the corner smiled as we approached him. He was very pale, but looked much better than he had that morning.

"Hello, my angel," he said, his green eyes smiling. "Your leaves are magic!"

"Not magic," I said, smiling, "knowledge".

"What leaves?" Radha said, "cabbage?"

"I tried the cabbage leaves but they did not help enough," I told her. "Do you remember those lovely red flowers in your mother's window boxes?"

"Yes," Radha said, "I had never seen them before."

"Vasa told me that their leaves could heal wounds that nothing else could. He gave me some shoots to plant and I used some of the leaves on this man."

Radha lifted one of the leaves and looked at the wounds.

"These are very deep," she said. "But they seem to be closing".

"I think his fever is less, too," I said.

I felt shy to feel his forehead with the boy looking up at me. As if he sensed my awkwardness he said, "We have not really met, my angel. I am Tomas. And you are?"

"I am called Milada," I said, "and this is my dear friend, Radha".

"I would bow if I could stand," the boy said gallantly, "or tip my hat if I knew where it went. But as it is, all I can do is say how very glad I am to meet you".

"And thank you for giving me back my life," he added softly, letting his eyes fall to his wounded leg.

Radha excused herself to check on the child with the broken arm.

"I hear that you are not of this village," I said to Tomas.

"No," he said quietly, "I am not".

"Are you one of the invaders?" I asked.

"I rode with them because I had no choice," he said.

I kept silent, weighing his words and he continued his story.

"They came to my village as they came to this one, looting and burning all in their path. I was at home with my parents and my sister when three men pushed open our door".

He paused, gathering energy to continue his tale.

"One of the men held a flaming torch. Another grabbed my sister. My parents were too shocked to move. We had no idea what was happening."

"The third man yelled at me. "You will come with us!" he shouted".

I could see that the story was tiring the young man.

"Don't talk now," I said.

"I would like to tell you," he said. "Might I have some water, then I will continue.

I brought a beaker of fresh water and held it to his lips. Then he continued with his story.

"I tried to protest but the man grabbed my arms and I couldn't move. "Take whatever you find," he shouted to the others. Our eyes met and for a moment, his eyes seemed to soften. "Leave the girl alone" he said. "We have enough of them, it's strong arms that we need now".

"As if to make up for his moment of pity he roughly pushed me out of the house. He shoved me onto a wagon and tied my legs to its slats. He went back into the house and the three men returned laden with all our provisions."

"Shall I torch the house?" the man with fire asked.

"Leave it," the leader said. We might need supplies again. Let the ladies bring in the harvest for us".

"Rest a while, Tomas," I said. "Later you will tell me more". I had so many questions to ask him, but I knew he needed to sleep. "I will bring you some broth. I think you are strong enough now to take some," I added.

He nodded at me then closed his eyes. I took my time to bring the broth to let him have some rest. When I returned, his eyes were open. I held the bowl of warm broth to his lips and he took a few sips.

"That's enough for now," he said, letting his head fall back onto the straw mattress.

"Rest now," I said.

"So I was taken," he continued, as if in a dream, "and made to ride into villages like mine looking for food."

"I did as I was told," he said, "up to a point. I took food from the villagers, but I did not harm them."

I saw a tear running down his cheek and without thinking, I took his hand in mine.

"I couldn't stop what they were doing," he said so softly that I had to put my ear close to his lips to hear his words.

"I was afraid that if I tried to stop them they would kill me and I would never be able to return to my family".

"I'm sure you did the best you could," I said. We sat in silence, his hand in mine.

"I have always wanted to see the sea."

"What?" I asked, wondering if he was dreaming.

Tomas opened his eyes.

"The sea," he repeated. "My grandfather was a merchant. Before he died, he told me many stories of his travels. My favourites were the stories of the cities by the sea."

"When I thought that I would die, my biggest regret is that I would never see the sea," he said, with a faraway look in his eye.

"You are alive," I said, "with any luck your leg will mend. Won't you go back to your village to live?"

"I will go back," he said, "to make sure my family is safe. But then I will follow in the footsteps of my grandfather and make my way to the sea."

"I, too, have a wish to see the sea," I said softly as I felt Radha's hand on my shoulder.

"Come, Milada," she said, "the Baron has called a meeting at our camp. Tomas will be all right here for a while.

I could see that he had drifted back to sleep. I would come back later with some fresh leaves to dress his wounds.

Chapter 94

Time to Go

Most of the others were already assembled around the fire. The sun was low in the sky and the smell of the evening meal made me realize how hungry I was. But before we could eat, the Baron wished to speak to us.

"Friends," he began, with Iovan and Radha beside him. "These are very troubled times. In order to survive we must move back to our refuge of safety and stay there for as long as there is danger."

"Tomorrow we will leave this place and keep riding until we are on the far side of the great lake, beyond the reach of the invaders. Eat well tonight, prepare food to take in your wagons because we will not stop to make camp until we reach safety."

There were murmurs in the group. We all knew that it must be this way but we dreaded the long journey ahead. I ate in silence and thought about the coming days; long lonely days in the wagon without even a puppy for company. Then I thought of Tomas. Maybe he could come with us. He was not able to take care of himself yet. And maybe some of the villagers would not want to help him since he came with the invaders. They might not understand that it was not his fault.

I went to find Radha and Iovan to ask them if Tomas could accompany us on our journey. I found them by them fire, sitting with Lazara and the other elders. They greeted me warmly and I sat down beside Radha. Satarma sat on her lap, playfully pulling at her curls.

"May I ask you something," I said.

"Of course you may, Milada," Iovan said.

"It's about that young man, Tomas," I began.

"He has very serious wounds in his leg," Lazara said.

"He isn't able to care for himself at all yet. And some of the villagers might harm him since he came with the invaders," I explained.

"Is he one of them?" Iovan asked.

"He was taken from his village and forced to fight with them," I said. "I know he is not like them."

"How do you know that?" Iovan asked. "Do you think he would tell you if he were an enemy?"

"I can see it in his eyes," I said, feeling annoyed that Iovan would think I'd been duped.

"She is right, my love" Radha said, laying her hand on Iovan's arm. "He is not of their tribe, his features and accent are from nearby, not like the invaders' at all."

I smiled at Radha for taking my part.

"What I want to know is, can Tomas come with us tomorrow?" I asked.

"Yes, of course he can," Iovan said.

I smiled and thought of how I would nurse Tomas back to health.

"He can stay in my wagon. I am alone now that Adela has left," I said.

"That would not be good," Lazara said.

"Why not?" I said without thinking, without due respect for an elder.

"Tomas seemed better today but he is far from well. The journey could easily kill him," she said.

I had to admit that she was right. She had far more experience than I did in treating wounds and even with Vasa's leaves I could see that Tomas was not out of danger. Maybe it was my own selfishness that wanted to bring him with us.

"But will he be all right if we leave him here?" I asked.

"I cannot say," Lazara replied. "He needs care from someone who knows the healing arts."

"But the Baron said that we must leave," I said, feeling desperate, "tomorrow!"

"What the Baron decrees, we do," Lazara said.

"Milada," Radha said gently, "this has been a very long day. Go to your wagon and rest. In stillness you will find an answer."

"Good night," I said and slowly walked back to my wagon.

My horse grazed nearby. I was surprised that she was not with the other horses. I hugged her neck.

"Ah, Kizi," I said, feeling the softness of her mane, "I have you for company, at least."

She nuzzled me and I patted the velvety tip of her nose.

"Shall we go for a ride?" I asked the horse. It had been a long time since I had climbed on her back.

I stood on the first step of the wagon. She understood what I wanted and came beside me so I could mount her. I held on to her neck as she cantered away from the village through the forest and then out into the open fields. The other horses were there, standing in a row facing the rising moon. I slid off of her back and she took her place with the others.

I lay down in the field, letting the moonlight wash over me. Its light was so bright that I could almost see colours in the darkness. The horse's shadows stretched out like giants behind them.

I breathed deeply the night air, still warm from the summer's day. I let my mind drift and my thoughts rise to the distant stars. The sun's light reflecting off the full moon meant that I could not see the familiar constellations, but I knew they were there, watching us here below.

A lone cloud drifted across the face of the moon and for a moment the stars appeared to wink at me. A breeze rustled the ripe heads of wheat rippling like the current of a stream. It seemed to speak, to say a word, to bring me a message. What I heard it say was "Stay…. stay."

Stay? What, stay here? Stay in a burnt out village rather than travel on with my friends, with the people who I know as my family? Stay? With Tomas, the young man with the green eyes, who calls me "his angel"?

But we wouldn't stay. We would go to the sea. We would visit his family and mine. When these troubled times had passed could join the gypsies at the Solstice Gathering. Stay? Maybe that is the answer.

I felt Kizi nuzzling my face. I must have fallen asleep; the moon was now high overhead. The other horses had drifted away, back to camp or deeper into the forest.

I walked beside my horse, back to the wagon. 'Stay' I thought as I took off my dirty clothes. 'Stay' I thought as I looked at the red flower cuttings on my little table. 'Stay' I thought as I lay down on my soft bed and drifted off into deep slumber.

Chapter 95

Parting of Our Ways

I awoke at the first light of dawn. I washed my face and put on clean clothes; an embroidered blouse and bright red skirt. I reached up to the shelf and put my hand on the pouch with the little figurine. Gently I took her out and traced her rounded shape gently with my finger. Then I put her back in the pouch and slipped it into my pocket. Kizi greeted me with a whinny as I jumped down from the wagon and ran to find Radha.

I approached the wagon she shared with her family. I could not tell if she was awake yet. I stood beneath her window.

"Radha!" I whispered, loudly. "Radha, are you up?"

I saw the curtain flicker and Radha's sleepy face peering out.

"Milada, is that you?" she whispered back.

"Yes," I said, "I need to talk to you!"

"Now?"

"Yes!"

"I'm coming" she whispered, "I don't want to wake Satarma!"

In a moment Radha tiptoed down the wagon's steps. I took her hand and we moved away from the wagon where we could speak without waking the others. Standing there with her hand in mine I began to have doubts about my decision. I felt tears welling up in my eyes and the smile leaving my lips.

"Milada," Radha said, "what is it? What's the matter?"

"Oh Radha!" I said, falling into her arms. "I love you like a sister, I love you all".

"And we love you, too, Milada," she said. "That's nothing to cry about!"

"I thought I had decided," I said, "but now I'm not sure."

"What are you talking about," Radha said. I realized that I was not making any sense.

"Last night," I began, "in the stillness, I thought I heard a message".

"What was the message?" Radha asked.

"Stay."

"Stay?"

"Stay," I said. "Stay here. With Tomas."

"Stay and take care of Tomas?" she asked. "Would you do that for him?"

"He needs me," I said. "I feel I could help him, that I could give him back his life".

"Leaving us would be a great sacrifice," she said, "are you sure it is what you want?"

"How can I be sure?" I asked. "It feels right. He wants to see the sea. So do I. When he gets well we can see the world together. We can find you on your travels".

"And if he does not get better?" Radha asked.

"Then I will make another decision," I said, my words surprising myself. Suddenly it felt right. How could I know what would come? All I knew is that today, this morning, now, I knew I had to stay.

"You can keep the wagon and your horse," Radha said. "That way you can leave the village as soon as Tomas is well enough to travel.

"Thank you, my friend," I said. "I will go to him now".

Radha and I embraced. As we hugged I felt the hardness of the little figurine in my pocket. I reached it at took out the pouch.

"Here," I told Radha. "Take this".

I placed the ancient pouch in her hand.

"The Mother?" she said. "You will leave her here?"

"She belongs to all women," I said. "You will have many opportunities to call on for her support".

"Thank you, Milada," she said, gathering me into her arms once again, "on behalf of us all".

I could not bring myself to say goodbye. I ran back to my wagon, hitched up Kizi and guided her into the remains of the village. I left the wagon on the far side of the square and made my way to the house where Tomas lay.

Inside it was still dark. I went quietly to the corner where he lay sleeping and sat beside him, my hand lightly resting on his.

"Milada?" he said, looking up at me when he awoke.

"I am here," I said, offering him water to drink.

"My angel," he said, looking deeply into my eyes. I felt something move inside of me, like a release, a flood of love.

In the distance the sound of horses' hooves could be heard.

"What's that noise?" someone said.

"Maybe the invaders have returned," said another.

"No," said a third, "I can hear wagons. It's the gypsies. The old woman told me they are leaving today."

Tomas took my hand.

"Have you come to say 'goodbye'?" he asked, his face falling and the light going out of his beautiful eyes.

"In a way I have," I told him.

I stood up and went to the doorway. I opened the door and watched the gypsy wagons passing. Some of the band waved when they saw me, others threw me kisses. Some just smiled. Then the last wagon turned the corner and was gone, leaving me in a cloud of dust, gilded by the rising sun.

The beginning...

Fasoula, Cyprus April 20, 2008 - full moon

Thanks and acknowledgements:

I would like to thank my father for teaching me to love nature and my mother for teaching me to love words. The story would not have come about without my friend Diana Allan who introduced me to the star children and Sally in Glastonbury who, through her contact with "Old Chinese", introduced me to Milada.

Thanks to my teachers, Susan Cole for her knowledge of the esoteric Tarot; Konstantin Pavlidis for working with the four elements and showing me that there are truly only 3 teachers: nature, your body and direct knowing; Layne Redmond, author of the ground-breaking book "When The Drummers Were Women," who reintroduced frame drumming to the women of Cyprus and showed me how to access the balancing power of rhythm through the tambourine, and especially to my dear partner Dr. Igor with whom I came to understand the energetic nature of the human body (and everything else) and that two people don't necessary have to speak the same language to build a beautiful relationship.

Thanks to my beautiful lady friends for their support and inspiration, particularly Maria Stavrou, Hatzy Joyce, Barbara Jones and Barbara Davies for reading the manuscript and suggesting improvements and to Suzanna Buxton, a "true Romany" for her insights.

Two of Mother Miriana's stories are based on traditional folktales; the story of the wastrel lad and the bird in the hand. Some of the information on herbal remedies comes from the work of Juliette be Bairacli Levy.